KEVIN BROOKS

2 Palmer Street, Frome, Somerset BA11 1DS

This edition 2006

First published in Great Britain in 2005
The Chicken House
2 Palmer Street
Frome, Somerset, BA11 1DS
United Kingdom
www.doublecluck.com

Cover design by Radio
Designed and typeset by Dorchester Typesetting Group Ltd
Printed in the UK by CPI Bookmarque, Croydon, CR0 4TD

5 7 9 10 8 6 4

British Library Cataloguing in Publication data available.

ISBN 978-1-904442-61-5 PB

chapter one

It's hard to imagine life before Candy. Sometimes I sit here for hours, staring into the past, trying to remember what it was like, but I never seem to get very far. I just can't see myself without her. About the best I can manage is the last half-hour before we met, the last few moments of my pre-Candy existence, when I was still just a boy ... just a boy on a train, a boy with a lump, a boy in a starry black hat.

I was innocent then.

Just a boy.

On a train.

With a lump.

And a hat.

That was all the world I needed to know.

It was Thursday, February 6, about five o'clock in the afternoon, and the London-bound train was almost empty. The trains passing by on the opposite track were packed to the roof with steamed-up commuters heading back home after a hard day's work, but the only other passengers travelling with me were a couple of shift workers, a drunk guy in a suit, and a gaggle of good-time girls setting off early for a night on the town. I couldn't actually *see* the girls – they were sitting somewhere behind me – but I could hear them giggling and laughing and screeching at each other, letting everyone know how much they were enjoying themselves. It was hard *not* to listen to them; harder still when they started their full-volume whispering –

You shoulda seen it, Jen – like THIS ...

No!

I nearly DIED, girl ...

Heeeeee!!

When the girls had got on the train – at the stop after mine – I'd slouched down low in my seat and turned my head to the window. I was pretty sure they couldn't see me – they were right at the back of the carriage, and I was somewhere in the middle – but I didn't want to take any chances. You know how it is – there's six of them and only one of you ... and they're all dolled up, flashing themselves about, and they've had a few drinks ... and you're wearing a brand-new hat, which you're not quite sure about, so you're already feeling a bit self-conscious ... and you know what'll happen if they see you ... they'll *say* something, or *do* something – just for a laugh – and you'll start getting embarrassed, and that'll encourage them to say something else, and then you'll get even *more* embarrassed ...

Well, anyway, that's what I'd done when the girls had got on the train. I'd slumped down low in my seat and kept out of sight, resting my head against the window and watching the world pass by.

And I was still watching it now.

There wasn't much to see in the greying light – trackside towerblocks and low-rise estates, packing factories, parks, city lights winking in the distance – and after a while I found myself staring at nothing and listening to the rattle and hum of the carriage, the rhythm of the tracks – *ducka-dah-dum, DACKa-dah-dum, ducka-dah-dum, DACKa-dah-dum* ... making up songs in my head.

I was always doing that back then – making up songs, playing tunes in my head, dreaming the music ...

It used to keep me going.

It used to mean something.

One day, hopefully, it'll mean something again.

As the train approached Liverpool Street station, I carried on staring through the window and listening to the sounds of the carriage. The announcer was reminding us not to leave our personal belongings on the train, the girls were laughing at his Asian accent, and the other passengers were standing up, getting their bags, getting ready to leave. We were trundling along through an old brick tunnel lined with wires and cables and trackside waste. There were dark little caves in the tunnel wall, small shadowed arches, like tunnels within tunnels. In some of these caves I could see statues – strange crumbling figures entombed in brick, their weather-worn faces fringed with purple weeds – and as the train rattled past, I wondered idly what they were – ancient decorations? relics? railway gods? – and what they were doing there. I mean, why put statues in a *tunnel*?

I was still thinking about it when the train slowed to a crawl, the darkness lifted, and we hissed to a halt in the sterile light of the station platform.

Psshhhh ...

Dunk.

Aaaahhh ...

I let the other passengers off first. As the girls pushed and shoved and cackled their way through the door and headed off along the platform, their high-heeled shrieks echoing coldly around the station, I sneaked a quick look at them through the window. I was surprised to see how young they were. From the way they'd been talking I'd imagined them to be in their late teens or early twenties, but most of them were only about fifteen or sixteen – and that confused me for a minute. They were about the same age as me ... but somehow they didn't *feel* the same age, and I wasn't sure how or why. I didn't feel older than them, but I didn't feel younger either.

I just felt different.

For a moment or two, I wondered where they were going, and what they were going to do, and what they'd find at the end of their night – love, sex, happiness, oblivion, a drunken slap in the face?

Then I picked up my carrier bag, adjusted my hat, and got off the train.

The concourse was crowded with hordes of commuters, everyone rushing and racing and fighting for trains. There were thousands of them, pouring in from the streets and the tube station in a never-ending tide of dark suits and briefcases and hurry-up faces, like some kind of manic migration. The noise was incredible – a swirling cacophony of shuffling feet and crowded voices, tannoy announcements, railway shouts, hissing trains, squealing wheels, the metallic clacking of the indicator board – all of it merging together to form a vast blind noise that whirled and swarmed and rose up into the glass-domed roof like the sound of a million birds.

I moved across the concourse as quickly as I could –

dodging from side to side, struggling against the tide – and made my way down to the tube station. More struggling. More harried faces. More cacophony. I kept going – through the ticket barriers, along the corridor, over the bridge, down the steps – and then, with a last-second sprint and a heart-stopping leap, I was just another face on a Circle Line train, heading back into the darkness.

Breathing hard, I leaned against the door and wiped the cold sweat from my face and looked up at the tube map on the wall: Liverpool Street, Moorgate, Barbican, Farringdon, King's Cross.

Four stops.

Not long to go, now.

Not long for the boy.

Whenever I go to London I always feel embarrassed if I have to look at an A-Z map. I know it's stupid. I know there's no *reason* to feel embarrassed. It's only a *map*, for God's sake. If you don't know where you're going, you take a map, don't you? What's wrong with that? It's a perfectly sensible thing to do.

I *know* that.

It's just ... I don't know. It's just a matter of *cool*, I suppose. London is cool. Londoners are cool. You don't want them thinking you're some kind of village idiot, do you?

I mean, come *on* ...

Yeah, I know – it's pathetic. But pathetic's not so bad, is it? I mean, there are worse things in the world than being pathetic.

Anyway, that's why I was carrying my A-Z wrapped up in a Tesco carrier bag and hidden away in my pocket, and that's why, when I came out of King's Cross tube station, out into the cold city night, I didn't know where I was. I knew where I was *supposed* to be, and I knew where I was supposed to be going, but I hadn't come out where I'd expected to come out, and I'd lost all sense of direction. The place I was going to was in Pentonville Road, and I knew where that was because I'd looked it up earlier in the A-Z. But I only knew where it was in relation to Euston Road, which runs alongside the front of the station, and I hadn't come out at the front of the station, I'd come out somewhere else, a side exit or something. And all I could see, everywhere I looked, was chaos: cars, buses, taxis, speeding bikes, flashing lights, roadworks, cranes, building sites, pelican crossings, bollards, junctions, more commuters, street people, mad people, blank-faced hippies with long dirty hair and scabs on their faces ...

None of *that* was in the A-Z.

And I didn't want to get it out of my pocket, anyway. There were far too many people around, and I was feeling pretty uncool as it was – standing there like a slack-jawed yokel, blinking at the lights and the noise. I wouldn't have looked more out of place if I'd been dressed in a dirty old vest and dungarees, with a blade of dry grass sticking out of my mouth ... and a little white pig at my feet ... a little white piggy on a tattered rope leash ...

Shaking the image from my head, I stepped back and leaned against a wall for a minute to get my bearings. Taking my time, breathing in the rubbery stink of buses, the choke of exhaust fumes ... looking around, thinking about things, looking around some more ... looking looking looking ... thinking thinking thinking ... until, finally, it dawned on me what I had to do. It was so simple I felt like an idiot for not thinking of it before. To find out where I was, all I had to do was head for the main station building – which I could see looming up in the black sky behind me – and start from there.

So that's what I did.

Up the street, around a corner, and there I was – on a broad paved area, dotted with telephone boxes and newspaper stands, right outside the station. Right next to Euston Road.

Piece of cake.

Now all I had to do was follow Euston Road ...

But ... which way?

This way?

Or that way?

Left or right?

I closed my eyes, trying to picture the A-Z. I could see it, I could see all the roads, but the map was upside down in my head. The page was the wrong way round. The station was on the wrong side of the road. *All right,* I said to myself, *if the road's upside down on the map, all you have to do is go the other way. If you're on* this *side of the road, which is the* other *side on the map, then instead of going right, you have to go left.*

I started moving off to the left, then paused, remembering something – the map was *supposed* to be upside down. When I'd looked at the A-Z before leaving home, I'd turned it upside down so the page *was* the right way round. The map in my head was right all along. I didn't want to go right, I wanted to go left.

So I turned around, bumping into a crazy old woman pushing a shopping trolley full of rags – 'Yageddabadda geddaahh!' – and moved off back the way I'd come.

But I hadn't taken more than half a dozen steps when I stopped again, reconsidering the map. Had I *really* turned it around? Maybe not. Maybe I was right in the first place?

I half-turned, thought about it again, turned back, and

was just about to get going for the final time, when a voice called out from behind me.

'You want to make your mind up.'

It was a girl's voice – sweet and clear, like a shining jewel in the gutter. It wasn't particularly loud – she wasn't shouting or yelling – but somehow the sound of it managed to cut through the chaos and pinpoint my mind like the diamond-tipped blade of a knife. I turned around, taking in a sea of blurred faces, and there she was – standing in the doorway of Boots, leaning against the wall, smiling at me. It was the kind of smile that rips a hole in your heart – lips, teeth, sparkling eyes ...

God, she could smile.

I didn't do anything. I *couldn't* do anything. All I could do was stand there looking at her. Looking at everything. Her face, her lips, her cheeks, her dark almond eyes. Her neck, her legs, the shape of her body. Her pale white skin. The gleam of her chestnut hair, tied in a ponytail ...

God ... her skin.

She was wearing a tight little skirt and a loose crop top, revealing a flash of bare skin that turned me to stone. Then there was the lipstick, the mascara, the bracelets on her wrist, the leather bands on her upper arm, the silver cross around her neck, the black leather boots ...

I didn't know what to do.

What was I supposed to do?

I tried to smile, but my mouth was bone dry, my lips stuck together at the corners. I probably looked like a mental patient. I wiped my mouth and looked at her again, trying to think of something to say, but my head was empty. She cocked her head and glanced to one side, then smiled and looked back at me again.

'Nice hat,' she said.

Without thinking, I put my hand to my head and touched my hat. It was a new one – a black beanie with a ring of gold stars round the edge. I really liked it. The thing about hats, though – sometimes they can give out the wrong signals. People think you're trying to be special – wearing a hat, showing off, trying to be something you're not. I don't know ... maybe it's just me, maybe I'm paranoid or something. I mean, I know it doesn't matter – it's only a *hat,* for God's sake. And, besides, who *cares* what other people think?

Not me, obviously.

Anyway, I didn't put my hand to my head because I thought the girl was being malicious or anything, I did it out of habit. I knew she wasn't being malicious. It was just a compliment, that's all.

She liked my hat.

I *knew* that.

So ... what did I say?

'Uh ... yeah.'

That's what I said.

Uh ... yeah.

Stunning, eh?

Highly impressive.

Cool as hell.

And now the girl was going. She'd folded up a small carrier bag in her hand, adjusted her handbag, pushed herself away from the wall, and now she was walking off – just like that. She was going. A sway of her hips, a quick smile over her shoulder ... then she turned her head and melted back into the chaos.

No, I thought.

Hold on ...

No ...

But I was too late.

She'd gone.

Shit.

I stood there for a while, staring after her, replaying the scene in my head. *It happened,* I told myself. *You didn't imagine it. It happened. She was there ... and now she's gone. She was there ...*

And now she's gone.

So forget it.

It was nothing – OK? She probably wasn't even talking to you anyway. She was probably talking to a friend of hers, someone standing behind you ... yeah, that's probably it.

No wonder she's gone.

Think about it.

She's having a chat with someone, she sees this kid in a dumb black hat and a triple-x hood ... she sees him standing there, gawping at her, his mouth hanging open, his tongue hanging out, dribbling like a moron ...

What do you think she's going to do?

Ask him for a dance?

I shook my head and got moving, trying not to think about it, trying not to think about *her* – the way she'd stood there looking at me, the way she'd cocked her head and smiled, the way her skin rippled lightly around her midriff, like the gently-lapping surface of a pale white sea ...

God's sake, Joe ...

Don't even *think* about it.

I was caught up in a crowd of pedestrians now, getting carried along with the flow. I didn't really know where I was going. I started to turn around, to get out of the crowd, but there were too many people moving in the same direction, and someone was swearing at me for getting in the way, and then someone else shoved me in the back, so I decided they were probably going my way anyway and I might as well just go with the flow.

We crossed a busy road, waited on a traffic island, then crossed again to the other side. As the crowd began to split up, moving off in different directions, I stepped to one side and got behind a pillar box and started looking around again to see where the tide had taken me. I could see a junction, another traffic island, another junction, a few burger places, a bank, a couple of cafés, a bureau de change, all sorts of grimy little shops – and there, stretching out in front of me, was Pentonville Road. Just what I wanted. All I had to do now was cross the junction and keep on going for about another half-mile, and I'd be there. Ten minutes at the most. My appointment wasn't until 6.30. It was quarter to six now. I had some time to spare. And I hadn't eaten since lunchtime.

There was a McDonald's across the road.

I could nip in there, get something to eat, sit down for a few minutes ...

Sit by the window.

Watch the streets.

Watch the station.

Yeah, I could do that ... I mean, it wouldn't be like I was looking for anyone in *particular*, would it? I wouldn't be sitting there wringing my hands and leering at the streets like some sappy little kid with hormone trouble ...

No, I'd just be sitting there, eating a burger, gazing coolly through the window, just passing the time ...

Nothing wrong with that.

It was fairly busy inside. Most of the tables were already

taken and there were queues of customers shuffling around in front of the counter – bunches of kids, older couples, some hard-looking black guys in hoods and chains. I joined the back of the queue and started scanning the menu boards. I don't know why I bothered, really. I can never understand them – large meals, extra meals, extra-large meals, two somethings for 99p, regular this and regular that ... it's way too complicated for me. I always get the same thing, anyway – a quarter-pounder-with-cheese meal and a black coffee.

The queue shuffled forward.

The woman in front of me was thinking about joining the queue to our left. I could see her weighing it up, trying to work out which queue was moving the fastest. She hesitated, changed her mind, then decided to go for it. As she stepped to one side, I stepped up, but then she changed her mind again and squeezed back in front of me.

I moved back to give her some room, then started digging around in my pocket, looking for some money. Dad had given me £20 that morning, and I still had most of it left.

'Make sure you get yourself something to eat,' he'd told me. 'And get a taxi back from the station if it's late.'

He'd given me the look then, the look that says – *I'm not going to lecture you about what sort of food to eat or what to spend my money on, because you're old enough to act responsibly now ... and I'd like to think I can trust you ... but just watch it – OK?*

His face flashed into my mind for a moment – long and grey and serious – and I wondered, as I've often wondered before, why he always appeared so distant to me ... so detached, so remote. It sometimes felt as if he wasn't my father at all, just a tall grey man called Doctor Beck who lived in the same house as me and told me what to do.

I pulled a £5 note from my pocket. It was folded up into a tight little square and, as I yanked it out, the edge got caught in the lining of my pocket and a handful of coins came flying out. I made a grab for them with my other hand, but they were already clattering to the floor – *chink-chink-chink* – and rolling like mad all over the place. Everyone looked around, of course – looking at the floor, watching the coins, watching them roll. God, they rolled a long way. A few people started stamping on them, or bending down to pick them up, but most of the others couldn't care less. After a quick look to check out the dumb kid throwing his money around, they just shook their heads and got back to their business.

I could still feel my face turning red, though.

I knew I was expected to do something, but I didn't *want* to do anything. I didn't want to go scrabbling around on my hands and knees looking for 10p pieces. I didn't want people *looking* at me. But then, if I *didn't* start picking them up, if I just stood there and left them on the floor, everyone would think I was a spoilt little brat, some fancy-pants rich kid with too much money for his own good. I could imagine them thinking – *look at him, who does he think he is, standing there throwing his money away ...*

I didn't know what to do.

I wished I'd never come in here.

Eventually, I decided on a compromise. I'd pick up the coins I could see, then have a quick look round, like I was looking for the rest of them, then I'd shrug my shoulders and casually stroll back to the queue. Maybe I could even try smiling a bit ... you know, one of those self-mocking smiles that says – *sheesh, I dunno, what am I like, eh? what an idiot ...*

I was just starting to practise the look when a young

woman came up and handed me a £1 coin.

'Thanks,' I said.

She smiled and pointed across the room. 'There's another one over there – it went under that table.'

'Right,' I said, looking anxiously at the black guys sitting at the table – shaved heads, hammered eyes, skull-caps. One of them turned his head and gave me a look that froze my blood. 'Uh ... yeah, thanks,' I told the woman. 'I'll probably get it later.'

She shrugged and went back to the queue. I looked down at the floor. I could feel the black guys watching me, and I could feel my face getting hotter and hotter, and I could feel the sweat seeping out from under my hat – and then someone tapped me on the shoulder and said, 'You want me to get it for you?'

I was too flustered to recognise the voice at first. It was just another voice, just another Good Samaritan sticking their nose in, making things worse. I sighed to myself and turned around, getting ready to say thanks-but-no-thanks, but when I saw who it was, the words disappeared from my head.

Everything disappeared.

It was the girl, of course. The girl from the station. The girl with the smile and the skin and the eyes ...

'They're not as bad as they look,' she said.

I tried to say *who?*, but my mouth had gone numb. All I could do was pout my lips and look stupid.

The girl smiled. 'Those guys at the table ... they're not as scary as they look. They won't mind you getting your quid back.'

'Oh,' I said.

She looked at me.

I could feel myself drowning in her eyes.

Her head shook with a little laugh, then she turned away and walked across to the table where the black guys were sitting. They looked up as she approached, and she raised her hand and said something to one of them. He shrugged his shoulders and showed his palms, then smiled and said something back. She laughed, touched his arm, then bent down and picked up the £1 coin from under the table. As she stooped down, her skirt rode up, and the guys at the table leaned across to get a better look. One of them closed his eyes and shook his head, as if it was just too much to take.

The girl straightened up, nodded at the black guys, then turned around and came back to me.

'There you go,' she said, passing me the coin.

'Thanks,' I told her. 'You didn't have to ...'

'No problem.'

'I was just ... I was going to ...'

She touched my arm and looked behind me. 'You're next.'

'What?'

She nodded at the counter. 'You're next. They're waiting for you.'

I looked around. I was standing at the counter. Somehow I'd managed to get to the front of the queue. A lanky kid with a floppy fringe was standing behind the till, looking expectantly at me.

'Help you?' he said.

'Yeah ... sorry. I'd like, uh ... I'll have ... um ...' I was looking up at the menu board again, not seeing anything, just looking for the sake of looking, because I didn't know where else to look, and I needed time to think, to find the courage to say what I wanted to say. I must have stood there for a thousand years, looking up at that menu board, staring blindly at the senseless blur of pictures and words, my heart ticking away like a frantic clock, pumping blood and oxygen into my muscles, my cells, my nerves ... heightening my senses. It was a really weird feeling. My mind was racing, but I couldn't think. I could see everything, every dot and every movement, but none of it made any sense. The silence inside me was deafening.

In the end, I took a deep breath, swallowed hard, emptied my mind, and turned to the girl.

'Would you like something to eat?' I asked her.

She smiled. 'I thought you'd never ask.'

We found a table by the window, cleared off all the rubbish, and sat down. I'd got myself the usual, and the girl had gone for a chocolate doughnut with an extra-large Coke and tons of ice. I watched her now as she put the drink on the table and lowered her mouth to the straw.

'Are you sure that's all you want?' I asked.

She nodded, sucking hard on the straw, drinking with the breathless concentration of a child. I unwrapped my burger and started to eat. I wasn't really hungry any more, but I was glad to have something to do with my hands. Nervous hands are hard to disguise when they're idle. I chewed and swallowed, wiped some relish from my lips, glanced at my watch ...

'Meeting someone?' the girl asked.

'Not really,' I said.

'Sorry?'

I coughed, choking on a bit of lettuce, realising the stupidity of my answer. *Not really*, I'd said, *not really* ... How can you *not really* be meeting someone?

God ...

'You all right?' the girl said.

'Yeah ... I've got a – *huh-uhh* – excuse me. I've got a

doctor's appointment.'

'You've got a what?'

'You asked if I was meeting someone ...'

'Yeah?'

'I've got a doctor's appointment.'

'Oh, right – I thought you meant that's why you were coughing.'

'No ... that was just ... I was just coughing.'

'Right,' she nodded, smiling to herself. 'That's that sorted out then.'

'Yeah ...'

She went back to her Coke for a while, and I picked a few crumbs from my burger and fiddled around with the napkin, folding it and twisting it and wiping my fingers with it, all the time listening to the sweet little slurps from across the table. Then we both looked up and started speaking at the same time.

'Where are you—?'

'I don't usually—'

'Sorry,' I said. 'After you.'

She smiled. 'I was just going to ask where you're going. I didn't know there were any doctors around here.'

'Pentonville Road,' I told her. 'It's a private place ...'

She raised her eyebrows, as if to say – *private, eh? well, well, well* – but she didn't say anything, just nodded quietly and bit into her doughnut.

'My dad's a doctor,' I explained. 'He knows other doctors, you know, friends of his ...'

'Right,' she said through a mouthful of doughnut.

'It's quite handy sometimes ...'

'It must be. What's the matter with you?'

I pulled up my sleeve and showed her the lump on my wrist.

'Ugh!' she said. 'What's *that*?'

'It's nothing really ... just a lump. It's called a ganglion.'

She laughed, spitting out bits of chocolate. 'A gangly *what*?'

'Ganglion – it's like a ... like a muscle thing ...' I was trying to remember what Dad had told me about the lump. He'd explained it all to me, drawing little pictures and everything, but I hadn't really been listening. 'It's something to do with the fluid from your muscle,' I told the girl. 'It kind of leaks out and forms this lump—'

'Why?'

'Why what?'

'Why does it leak out?'

'I don't know.'

She'd finished her doughnut now and was digging out lumps of ice from her Coke, popping them into her mouth and sucking them.

'Can't your dad fix it?' she said. 'You said he was a doctor ...'

'He's not that sort of a doctor.'

'What sort is he then?'

I blushed, as I always do when this question comes up. 'He's a ... uh ... he's a gynaecologist.'

She didn't laugh, or smirk, or make any jokes. She just crunched an ice cube and looked at me. 'A gynaecologist?'

'Yeah ... this other doctor, the one I'm going to see, he's a specialist—'

'A lump specialist?'

'Right,' I said, smiling.

Her face changed when I smiled. I wouldn't have thought it possible, but it was almost as if a layer of skin had sloughed away, revealing another face, an even prettier face, hiding beneath a mask. 'That's the first time I've seen you smile,' she said, looking into my eyes. 'You ought to do it more often. It looks really nice.'

My head crumpled under the strain of the compliment, and I had to look down at the table. My skin was so hot I could hear it sizzling.

'Sorry,' she said quietly. 'I didn't mean to embarrass you. I'm not coming on to you or anything, I was just saying, you know ... you've got a nice smile. That's all. It's the truth.' She paused. 'You want me to say you're ugly?'

I looked up, cracking an ugly smile.

'That's better,' she said. 'My name's Candy, by the way.'

'Joe,' I told her. 'Joe Beck.'

She nodded. 'Thanks for the doughnut, Lumpy Joe.'

'You're welcome.'

We looked at each other, grinning like idiots, then my nerves got the better of me again and I buried my head in my coffee cup.

Candy laughed.

'What?' I said.

'You.'

'What?'

'Nothing ...'

She was still chuckling as she reached into a little black handbag and took out a packet of cigarettes. She tapped one out and lit it with a disposable lighter.

My surprise must have showed on my face.

'Sorry,' she said, reaching for the packet. 'Did you want one?'

'No ... no, thanks. I don't smoke.' I looked anxiously round the room. 'Are you sure you're allowed to smoke in here?'

She didn't say anything, just shrugged, blowing out smoke and tapping ash into the doughnut wrapper. She looked around, casting her eyes over the black guys, then out of the window, up and down the street, over at the station, then she took another drag on her cigarette and looked back at me. Her eyes smiled and she nodded at my hat. 'Do you wear that all the time?'

'Not always ...'

'It's nice.'

'Thanks.'

'Why don't you take it off?'

'What?'

'Take it off ... I want to see if the rest of your hair is as messy as the bits I can see.'

For some reason, I started feeling uncomfortable again. 'Well ...' I said, 'you know, I have to get going soon ... I'm late already.'

She just looked at me.

I sighed and took off my hat.

Her eyes widened at the sight of my hair. 'Wow! How do you *get* it like that? How do you get it so messy?'

'It's not easy ... it takes years of careful cultivation.'

She laughed.

'I'm not joking,' I said. 'The trick with messy hair is making it look messy without it looking like it's *supposed* to look messy.'

'You've done a pretty good job of it.'

'Thanks very much.'

'You're welcome.'

This time I didn't look away. I just grinned and pushed my burger to one side. It was cold now. Cold and forgotten. I didn't care. Who needs a cold burger when you're talking to a pretty girl? And I *was* talking to her, I realised. I wasn't just sitting there mumbling and looking embarrassed, I was actually *talking* to her. Not only that, but I was starting to enjoy it, too. Which was really surprising, because I *never* felt good talking to girls. I always felt nervy and shaky, unsure of myself ... especially with girls that I liked. And I liked Candy. I liked her a lot. I liked the way she looked – her face, her eyes, her lips, her legs, her skin – and I liked the way she smelled – of soap and talcum powder. Everything about her excited me. She made me feel fresh. She made me hot. She made me cold. She fired me up and turned my body inside out. And usually that would have messed me up so much I wouldn't have been able to feel anything, but this time I could feel it. God, I could feel it. And it felt good, like a rush of pure adrenalin ...

Of course, that's not to say I *wasn't* feeling nervy and shaky and unsure of myself, because I was. To tell you the truth, I was scared to death – scared and wary and unable to think of one good reason why this stunning girl was sitting here talking to me. Why wasn't she talking to someone else? Someone older than me, or smarter than me, or taller or cooler ...?

Why pick on me?

What did I have to offer?

I didn't waste *too* much time thinking about it, though.

I mean – who cares?

She was leaning on the table now, resting her chin in her hand, smoking her cigarette and gazing idly around the room. The tip of the cigarette was rimmed with crimson lipstick. Her eyes shone darkly, moist with black shadow and mascara, and although they looked unbelievably good, there was something slightly unsettling about them. I couldn't work it out at first, but after a while I realised what it was – it was her pupils. They were really small, like tiny black holes, shrunken and empty. Like pinpricks of darkness.

'What's that on your fingers?' she said suddenly.

'What?'

'Your fingers.'

I looked at my hands. 'Where?'

'There,' she said, touching the fingers of my left hand. I stiffened. Her touch was electric, hot and cold, like nothing I'd ever felt before. 'What's the matter?' she said, still holding my fingers.

'Nothing ...'

'Does it hurt?'

'No ...'

'What is it?'

I looked down again, suddenly realising what she was talking about. 'Oh, that,' I said. 'It's just hardened skin – calluses ... from playing the guitar.'

'You play the guitar?'

I nodded.

She looked at me. 'You any good?'

'I don't know. I'm all right, I suppose ...'

'You get fingers like this from playing the guitar?'

'Yeah, you know, pressing the strings ...'

'What kind of guitar?'

'Bass, mostly.'

'Really? Are you in a band or anything?'

'Well,' I said, starting to feel embarrassed again, 'sort of ...'

'What do you mean – *sort of*?'

'Yeah, I am.'

'What – a real band? You play gigs and stuff?'

'Yeah.'

'Seriously?'

'Well, you know, it's mostly local stuff. Pubs and clubs, school things ...'

I never liked talking about being in a band. It always

made me feel so pretentious, like – *oh yeah, I'm in a band, you know* ... as if being in a band is some kind of awe-somely admirable achievement. I didn't mind *doing* it – I loved being in a band – I just didn't like talking about it. It made me feel uncomfortable – and, just then, I was uncomfortable enough as it was. Candy was still touching my fingertips, brushing them lightly with her nails, which was nice, but it was starting to get a bit *too* nice ...

'Any records?' she asked.

'Not yet.'

'What are you called?'

I hesitated.

'Go on,' she said, 'tell me – I might have heard of you.'

'I doubt it – we're called The Katies.'

'Katies? Like the girl's name?'

'Yeah.'

'Why?'

I gently removed my hand from hers and wiped a drop of sweat from my lip. 'Well, we used to be called Kate's Bored—'

'Bored as in boring?'

'Yeah – it's kind of a skateboard thing.'

She looked puzzled.

'Skateboard,' I said. 'Skateboard – Kate's Bored ...?'

'Oh, right. What's the skateboard got to do with it?'

'We play kind of skateboardy stuff ...'

'Fast and punky?'

'Yeah, that kind of thing.' I had both my hands back now, and was feeling a bit more relaxed. 'We were looking for a name when we first started,' I explained, 'and some-one came up with Kate's Bored. It's pretty stupid, I know, but we couldn't think of anything else.'

'Then you shortened it to The Katies?'

'Not really, it's just what they started calling us.'

'Who?'

I shrugged. 'The kids who come to see us.'

'You've got fans?'

'Not proper ones ... they're just a bunch of friends who follow us around.'

'That's brilliant. It must be great.'

'Yeah, it's pretty good fun. I mean, we don't get paid much or anything ... not yet, anyway. We've got this big gig coming up ...'

I stopped talking then. Candy wasn't listening to me any more. She was sitting upright and staring wide-eyed over my shoulder.

'Are you all right?' I asked her. 'What's the matter?'

She didn't seem to hear me. Her eyes were frozen and her face had gone white.

'Shit,' she said quietly.

'What? What is it?'

'Don't look round,' she whispered, hurriedly lighting another cigarette. 'Don't say anything. Just pretend you know what I'm talking about – OK?'

'What? What are you—?'

'Please,' she hissed, looking over my shoulder again. She was smiling now, but it wasn't the smile I'd got used to. It was a smile of fear.

Her hands were shaking.

Her lips trembled.

Then a shadow fell across the table – and the air turned cold.

chapter two

The big black guy who sat down between us had the emptiest eyes I've ever seen – empty of feeling, empty of heart, empty of everything but himself. He was tall, well over six feet, with a heavy head, close-cropped hair, and a burnt-looking stubble of beard. His face was a death mask.

He didn't so much as look at me, just sat down and stared hard at Candy. His eyes went right through her. She wasn't there any more. She was a ghost. Fluttering eyes, twitching lips ...

'Hey, Iggy—' she started to say.

'What you doing?' he said to her.

His voice was black and hard.

'Nothing,' she smiled. 'I was just—'

'Don't give me *nothing*.'

'No, I didn't mean—'

'Who's the boy?'

Candy flicked her eyes at me, then immediately looked back at Iggy again. She seemed in awe of him, almost bewitched, her face a conflict of hate and fear and adoration. Iggy just sat there, unmoved. He still hadn't acknowledged my presence. It was as if I didn't exist. I was nothing to him – just a piece of furniture, or a stain on the table. Which had suited me fine ... for a second or two. Now it was starting to scare the hell out of me.

'Who's the boy?' he repeated.

'I ... I just met him,' Candy stuttered. 'At the station ...'

'Business?'

She hesitated a moment, nervously licking her lips, then said, 'Yeah ... yeah, of course—'

'Yeah?' said Iggy, his eyes glistening white. 'So what you doing in here?'

'We were just going,' Candy said, trying to sound casual.

'Don't shit me, girl.'

'I'm *not* ... honest, Iggy. He just wanted to get something to eat first. Then after that—'

'He paid yet?'

'Yeah ...'

'How much?'

'The usual.'

'Show me.

Candy stubbed out her cigarette and started digging around in her purse. Iggy carried on staring at her. I didn't know where to look. I didn't know what was going on. All I knew was that it didn't feel good. My heart was thumping and my mouth was dry and my stomach felt sick and bitter. I glanced nervously around the room. Everything seemed normal – people eating, people queuing, no one caring. The streets outside were a little less busy now, the sky a little darker. The evening was almost over. The daypeople had gone; the nightlife was coming down.

'There,' said Candy, showing Iggy a handful of notes.

'See? I wouldn't lie to you, Iggy, you know I wouldn't ...'

He didn't look at the money, didn't even blink, just carried on staring – silent and dark – crushing Candy into a cowering silence. As she sat there, wilting under his eyes, a £10 note fell from her fingers and fluttered down to the table. She didn't seem to notice.

'Pick it up,' Iggy told her.

She picked it up.

'Put it away,' he said.

She folded all the money into her purse, then looked up at Iggy again. He didn't move. He just waited for her to lower her eyes, then nodded once, sucked his teeth, and slowly turned towards me.

I knew it was coming. I'd been waiting for it. And, despite everything, I really thought I was ready for it. But when his eyes finally fixed on mine, and a surge of fear flooded through me, I knew I was wrong. I'd *never* be ready for this. This – the ice-cold void in Iggy's eyes – this was a different world, a world I knew nothing about, a world of violence and pain and darkness. I felt so small, so weak, so stupid.

'What d'you want?' Iggy said to me.

I opened my mouth, but nothing came out.

'Come on, Iggy,' Candy pleaded. 'He's just—'

'Shut up,' he told her, still staring at me. 'I asked you what you want, boy.'

'Nothing,' I said, swallowing hard.

'Nothing?' he said. 'You paying good money for nothing?'

'No ...' I muttered. 'I didn't mean—'

'You paid the girl?'

I wanted to say – *paid her? paid her for what? I haven't paid her for anything* – but she'd already told him I had, and

I could feel her looking at me, begging me not to say anything different.

So I said, 'Uh ... yeah ... yeah, I paid ...'

'You ain't paid her for nothing,' Iggy said, looking at Candy like a butcher looking at meat. 'You ain't doing *nothing* with a piece like that. Not less you got something wrong with you. You got something wrong with you?'

'No.'

'You fishy?'

'I don't know—'

'You don't *know*?'

I looked down at the table.

'Hey,' said Iggy, 'look at me when I'm talking to you. *Look* at me.'

I looked up. He was smiling now, his mouth a blackened cave rimmed with gold-capped teeth.

'Look at her,' he told me.

'What?'

'Look at the bitch.'

I looked at Candy. She was lifeless, moist-eyed, staring blankly at the table.

'You like it?' Iggy said. 'You want it?'

I couldn't answer.

He laughed at me, a cold hissing sound. 'How much?' he said.

'I don't—'

'How much you give her?'

I looked at Candy again.

'Don't look at her,' Iggy said, 'look at me. I asked you how much.'

I shook my head.

'All right,' he said, 'what d'you pay for?'

'She was—'

'She tell you what it is, yeah? You know what you're getting?'

'I was just—'

'What? You was just *what*?'

'All right,' Candy said quietly. 'That's enough.'

Iggy went silent. He carried on staring at me for a moment, sucking thoughtfully on his cheek, then he sniffed hard and turned to Candy.

'You what?' he said, raising an eyebrow.

She could barely look at him now – head down, eyes hidden, hands fiddling nervously with a small piece of card in her lap, rolling it into a tube, unrolling it, twisting it, folding it ...

'I'm sorry,' she whispered. 'I was just talking to him, that's all. I didn't ... we didn't ... he's just a kid. He doesn't know anything.'

Iggy said nothing.

Candy smiled through her tears. 'It won't happen again—'

'Too right,' Iggy said coldly.

'You don't have to—'

'What?'

'Nothing ... I'm sorry. Please don't—'

'Shut up.' He turned to me and cocked his head at the door. 'Out.'

I stared dumbly at him.

'Get out,' he repeated. 'Now.'

I looked at Candy, then back at Iggy again. 'Look,' I tried to explain, 'it wasn't her fault ...'

But he wasn't listening.

His face had hardened and he was starting to get up. I was too shocked to move. All I could do was sit there and watch as he got to his feet and straightened up and ...

God, he was big. He was *enormous*. Big, tall, heavy, wide, hard, rock-solid ... he towered over the table like a steel-black giant.

As he kicked his chair back and started moving towards me, Candy suddenly leaned across and shoved me in the side.

'*No!*' she said desperately, looking at Iggy. 'No, it's all right ... look, he's going. He's going now. You don't have to do anything. See? He's going.' She glanced at me, her eyes pleading for me to go, but she needn't have bothered – I was already halfway to my feet. Candy reached for my chair. I felt her hand brush my thigh, then she quickly moved back to her seat and looked up at Iggy again. Still standing over me, he glared at her, his jaw set tight beneath his skin, and for a moment I thought he was going to kill her. I could see it in his eyes. He was going to kill her, and then me ... I really believed it. Eventually, though – after what seemed like an age – his face began to relax and he slowly sank back into his seat.

'Lucky boy,' he said quietly.

I stepped back from the table and steadied myself against a chair. My legs were shaking and my throat was tight. I could feel the silence all around me – the hush of violence, sucking the air from my lungs. I could hear people looking on, whispering and muttering, but I couldn't see them. All I could see was a narrow black tunnel, with me at one end and a death mask at the other and a pale white ghost floating somewhere in between.

I tore my eyes away from the mask and glanced at the ghost, but she wouldn't look back at me. Her lowered eyes said – *Go, please ... for God's sake, just go.*

I didn't have enough guts to say no, so I just turned around and started to leave.

'Hey,' said Iggy.

I didn't *want* to stop – I wanted to keep going and never come back – but I couldn't help it. It was that kind of voice.

I stopped.

Paused.

Then turned around.

Iggy was leaning back in his chair and staring at me with a piercing chill in his eyes.

'You like a smile?' he said softly.

I didn't know what to say. I didn't even know what he *meant.* I watched curiously as he grinned and raised his hand, then slowly drew his thumbnail across his throat.

'I see you again,' he said, 'you'll be smiling to the bone.'

chapter three

I don't remember much about the train journey home. I remember going to the doctor's and getting a tube back to Liverpool Street, and I vaguely remember waiting on the concourse, then walking along the platform and getting on the train, but after that – my mind's a blank. I can't remember the journey at all. All I can remember is thinking: thinking about Candy, thinking about Iggy, thinking about me ... thinking myself into a hole. Candy ... Iggy ... Candy ... me ... Candy ... Iggy ... Candy ... me ... voices ... faces ... bodies ... eyes ... Candy ... Iggy ... Candy ... me ...

And the next thing I knew, the train was slowing down and pulling into Heystone station.

Not many passengers got off the train. A couple of half-drunk commuters, a beardy old man in a deerstalker hat, a busy-busy woman in clackety shoes ... and that was about it. They didn't hang around – out into the car park, into their cars, and they were gone before the train had left the platform. I waited for it to leave, watching it rattle out of the station, away up the tracks, disappearing into the distant darkness ... until there was nothing left to see. I stood there for a while, staring at nothing, listening to the station clock clacking away its digital seconds – *clack* ... *clack* ... *clack* – then I turned around and went looking for a taxi.

Outside the station, everything was quiet – the streets, the car park, the surrounding fields. Nothing moved, nothing stirred. No cars, no mad people, no flashing lights ...

No girls.

No threats.

No fear.

No chaos.

And no taxis, either.

The rank was empty. Closed for the night.

I didn't really mind. My house isn't far from the station – along Station Road, over the bridge, down Church Lane and into the avenue – and it was a nice clear night, fresh and wintry, just right for walking. So off I went – walking slowly, breathing deeply, trying to sort myself out.

Sometimes, when I'm walking, the sound of my footsteps helps me to think. It's the steady rhythm, I suppose, the metronomic sound of feet on concrete – *tap, tap ... tap, tap ... tap, tap ... tap, tap* – ticking away like a heartbeat, settling your body and freeing your mind to think. It doesn't always work, but I was hoping it would that night, because my mind and my body were still in a state of shock: the scary-snakes were still wriggling around in my belly, making me feel sick; my jaw was aching from gritting my teeth; my heart was tearing itself apart; and, worst of all, an annoying little voice kept whining away in the back of my head, reminding me over and over again what *might* have happened, what *could* have happened, what *nearly* happened. *You were lucky, really*, it kept telling me. *You know that, don't you? You were lucky. It could have been a whole lot worse ...*

I knew it.

I knew a lot of things.

I knew that Candy was a prostitute and Iggy was her pimp. I knew she sold her body, that she spent all day doing things I could only imagine, that she probably wasn't even *called* Candy. I knew she'd been leading me on, playing some kind of game, amusing herself at my expense. Yes, I knew all that. I didn't *want* to know it. I wanted to believe she was just a girl ... just a girl I'd met at the station ... a girl who liked me ...

But I wasn't *that* naive.

No, there was no getting away from it – Candy was a prostitute and Iggy was her pimp. And that should have been it, really. The end of a very short – and very embarrassing – love story: boy meets girl, girl smiles at boy, he buys her a doughnut, she tickles his fingers, he turns to jelly; then pimp meets boy and scares him to death and boy goes home feeling stupid.

The End.

That's the way it should have been.

And that's the way it was – up to a point.

I *was* scared to death.

I *did* feel stupid.

I *was* going home.

But there was something else ... something that wouldn't let go ... something that started with the touch of her fingers.

The touch was still there.

Candy's touch. I could still feel it, impressed in the memory of my skin: hot, cold, electric, eternal, the touch of another. It was exhilarating, tingling, intoxicating. And as I walked the streets, I couldn't stop looking at my fingers, staring at the contours and whorls, searching for the spot where she'd touched me. I kept wanting to feel my skin, to feel the memory from the outside, but I was afraid that touching it might somehow remove the feeling inside ...

And that was just the start of it.

Deep down inside me, buried beneath all the chaos, I could sense a feeling I'd never felt before. I didn't know what it was. I didn't know if it was a good feeling or a bad feeling or something in between ... I wasn't even sure it was a feeling at all. It was just something – an unknown shade, a barely perceptible signal, like a flickering candle on a distant hill. I knew it was there, but most of the time it was too faint to see, and even when I could see it, I couldn't tell if I was seeing it or hearing it or smelling it or feeling it ...

It was too many things all at once: a light in the darkness, a crying voice, the scent of freshly washed skin, some wonderful oblivion ...

It didn't make sense.

And neither did I.

I'd reached the end of the avenue now, but I couldn't remember getting there. And I didn't know why I was standing at the foot of the driveway outside my house, gazing up at the moon. But that's what I was doing. And I must have been doing it for a while, because my hands and face were freezing cold and my neck was as stiff as a board.

God knows what I was looking for.

There was nothing up there for me.

I opened the gate and headed up the gravel driveway.

The house looked quiet – curtains drawn, soft lights, silent and still – but that wasn't unusual. It's an old vicarage, our house – a three-storey grey stone building set back from the street in a walled half-acre of rolling lawns and pine trees and well-tended hedges. It *always* looks quiet.

Too quiet sometimes.

It wasn't so bad when Mum was still living here and Dad was running his surgery from a couple of rooms on the ground floor, but Mum's been gone for a while now, and Dad opened up a smart new office in Chelmsford last year, so now the house feels bleak and empty most of the time.

Not that I *mind* bleak and empty – in fact, I quite like it. Especially when it's shrouded in comfort, which it is. Comfort, safety, warmth, tranquillity ...

Home sweet home.

Dad's car was parked at the top of the driveway. He'd told me earlier that he was going out that night, and I was hoping he'd already gone, but it looked as if I was out of luck.

Not that it really mattered.

I just didn't feel like seeing him, that's all.

I didn't feel like anything.

When I opened the front door, he was standing in the hallway putting on his coat.

'Where the hell have you *been*?' he said, looking at his watch. 'It's nearly ten o'clock.'

'The trains were late,' I told him, shutting the door.

He shook his head. 'I just rang them – they said there weren't any problems.'

'I meant the underground trains,' I lied. 'The tubes were held up.'

'Really?'

'Yeah. There was some kind of problem at King's

Cross—'

'You should have called me.'

'Yeah, I know—'

'I've been trying to ring you. I couldn't get through to your mobile—'

'I forgot to charge it. Sorry.'

He gave me one of his serious looks – a kind of long-faced doctory stare – then nodded his head, seemingly satisfied, and started to fasten his coat. 'Did you get to Dr Hemmings on time?'

'I was a bit late,' I said. 'He didn't mind ...'

Dad nodded, moving closer. 'How did it go? What did he say about the ganglion? Did he remove it?'

I held out my arm and showed Dad my lumpless wrist. No scars, no stitches, just a small red needle mark.

Dad said, 'He aspirated it?'

'Yeah ... sucked it all out with a big fat needle.'

Dad took my wrist and examined it closely, probing gently with his large delicate hands. 'Hmm ...' he said. 'It looks fine. Did it hurt?'

'Not really – he gave me a cortisone shot.'

'Good.' He carefully ran his finger over my wrist. 'Nice and clean. He's done a good job.' Still holding my hand, he looked at me. 'You really should have rung me, Joe. I was starting to get worried. If you're going to be late—'

'Yeah, sorry—'

'That's what your mobile's *for*—'

'Yeah, I know, Dad ... I just didn't realise what time it was.' I took my hand away and started to take off my jacket. 'Are you going out now?' I asked him, changing the subject.

'Just for a while,' he said, looking at his watch.

'Are you seeing Mum again?'

He nodded, fussing awkwardly with his tie.

I hung my jacket on the coat-rack.

'How is she?' I asked.

'She's fine ...' He smiled tightly and reached for the door handle. 'Look, I'd better get going. Gina's upstairs with Mike. If you want anything to eat, there's some cold chicken in the fridge ... and make sure you have some salad with it.' He opened the door and pulled up his collar. 'And don't stay up too late – you've got school tomorrow.'

'OK.'

He nodded again, hesitated for a moment, then went out and shut the door.

I'll tell you what's weird. When your mum and dad get divorced, and your mum moves out, leaving you and your sister with your dad, and your mum never comes to visit you, and then a year later your mum and dad start seeing each other again, going out with each other again, falling in love with each other again, and she *still* never comes to visit you ...

That's weird.

After Dad left, I went upstairs to my bedroom and lay down on the floor. I like lying down on the floor. It's a good place to be. You can close your eyes and feel the movements of the house rippling through your spine. You can listen to the sound of your heart, the sound of your blood, the sound of the machine beneath your skin. You can open your eyes and stare at the ceiling, imagining it's your very own sky. Or you can just lie there, perfectly still, doing absolutely nothing.

I tried them all that night, but none of them seemed to help. The sound of my heart was too unnerving, and the only movements I could feel were those of Gina and Mike from the room above mine.

Gina's my sister and Mike's her boyfriend.

They'd probably heard me come in, so they weren't actually *doing* anything, if you know what I mean. From what I could hear, they were just sitting around, talking quietly, occasionally moving about, tapping their feet to the low-volume groove of their favourite R&B.

God, I hate R&B. That awful wailing, those miserable wobbly voices – it really gets on my nerves. When she was younger, Gina used to listen to R&B *all* the time, really loud, night and day. It used to drive me mad.

How can you listen to that?

I like it.

But it's so depressing ...

It doesn't bother me so much any more. I still don't like it, and I still have a moan now and then, but I've given up trying to change Gina's mind. She *likes* R&B, it makes her happy, and that's all there is to it.

Anyway, I lay there for a while, trying to ignore the muffled music, trying to lose myself in the patterns of my artexed sky, but it wasn't any good. I couldn't relax.

I got up and turned on the TV, setting the volume just loud enough to drown out the music, then I fetched my guitar from the corner of the room and started to pick out some chords. As far as I was aware, I wasn't playing anything in particular, I was just strumming ... just seeing what happened ... mindlessly repeating the same magical chords – G to C, G to C – over and over again ... nice and slow, deep and heavy, open and raw, letting the harmonies find themselves.

After a while, the essence of a song began to appear. Sweet and haunting, a melody steeped in sadness ...

I didn't mean it to be sad. But that's how I felt. And that's what music is all about – sounding how you feel.

I know it sounds kind of pathetic – sitting there feeling sorry for myself, playing the broken-hearted blues as if I'd just lost the love of my life, when in fact all I'd lost was my dignity – but, like I said before, being pathetic's not the worst thing in the world, is it?

One of the best things about music is the way it takes away time. You can sit around for hours, making up songs, playing little tunes, fiddling around with different chords and different variations, and the time just seems to evaporate. It's really weird sometimes. You can pick up your guitar at ten o'clock in the morning, start playing ... and the next thing you know it's four o'clock in the afternoon. And you haven't moved. You haven't eaten. You haven't even been to the lavatory. It's almost as if you've been drugged, and when you finally come to your senses, you can't remember what you've been doing.

But it feels OK.

And that's how it was that night.

Lost in time, lost in the music, lost in another world, I gradually became aware of a voice. It was faint at first, drifting around on the edge of my consciousness, and I couldn't make out what it was saying. As it got closer, though, the voice became clearer: *Joe,* it was saying. *Hey ... Joe?* I thought perhaps it was my imagination, but then I heard it again, more clearly this time, and I slowly realised that I was still in my room, still sitting on the bed, still playing the guitar, and the voice was Gina's.

'Joe?' she said again. 'Are you all right?'

I stopped playing and looked up to see her standing in the doorway with an amused look on her face.

'Who's Candy?' she said.

'What?'

'Candy ... you were singing about someone called Candy.'

For a brief moment I didn't know what she was talking about, but then my fingers brushed the guitar strings, bringing out the chord I was still holding down, and the melody came back to me. The melody, the tune, the words I'd been singing ...

'How long have you been listening?' I asked Gina, slightly embarrassed.

'Not long,' she smiled. 'I knocked on your door but you didn't answer. I was just checking you were all right, that's all.' She came into the room and went over to the window. 'It sounded really nice,' she said. 'The song you were playing ... did you make it up?'

'I was just messing around,' I said, fixing the plectrum in the strings and putting the guitar down. 'What's the time?'

'Half twelve – something like that.' She turned from the window and went back over to the doorway. 'I was just making some tea before Mike goes. Did you want a cup?'

'Is Dad back yet?'

She shook her head. 'He's getting later all the time. He didn't get home until nearly three the other night.'

'Yeah, I know.'

'We'll have to ground him if this carries on.'

I looked at her, recognising the sadness behind her smile. She didn't really get on with Mum that well, and although she'd never said anything about it, I knew she didn't like the idea of Mum and Dad getting back together again. I wasn't too keen on it myself, to be honest, although it didn't bother me as much as it bothered Gina.

'Do you want some tea, then?' she said.

I nodded.

She smiled again. 'Mike's in the kitchen. Why don't you come down and tell us all about Candy?'

'There's nothing to tell. It's just a song ...'

'Yeah?'

I blushed, thinking of Candy – her presence, her body, her face, her voice, her *being* ...

'Come *on*, Joe,' Gina said. 'I'm your sister – you can tell me. We tell each other everything.'

'No, we don't.'

'Well, we ought to,' she grinned.

'You don't tell me *anything*.'

'I *do*.'

'Like what? When was the last time you told me anything?'

'Just now.'

'When?'

'I just told you I was making some tea, didn't I? What more do you want?'

I gave her a look, then got up and went over to the window to close the curtains.

'All right,' she said. 'I'll tell you what – you come down and tell us about Candy, and we'll tell you something about us. Something that no one else knows. How about that?'

'I'm not sure I *want* to know anything about you.'

'Yeah, you do.'

'It's probably pretty boring—'

'You reckon?'

I looked at her. She was nearly twenty-one now, but she

still didn't look any older than me – in fact, she was often mistaken for my younger sister. She had that wide-eyed freshness of a little girl, all clear blue eyes and golden hair and spotlessly smooth skin. It was enough to make you sick sometimes. That night, though, as she stood there smiling at me, dressed in a simple white T-shirt and jeans, there was no mistaking what she was: a beautiful young woman who meant everything to me.

'Go on, then,' I told her. 'You get the tea on and I'll be down in a minute.'

Gina met Mike a couple of years ago when she was visiting the local hospital as part of her nursing course. Mike was working as a porter back then, and I think they just bumped into each other in the corridor or something. A quick hello, a friendly chat, and that was that. They've been inseparable ever since. Gina's mad about him. She thinks he's the best thing that ever happened to her, and I think she's probably right. He's kind, funny, serious, smart – protective but not possessive, friendly but not patronising, cool without trying – in fact, come to think of it, he's almost too good to be true. But he *is* true. Which makes it all the more baffling why Dad doesn't like him.

'It's because he's black,' Gina said once. 'Dad doesn't like me seeing a black guy.'

'Dad's not like that,' I said. 'He might be a bit old-fashioned, a bit stuck in his ways, but he's not like that.'

'No?'

'Of *course* he's not—'

'Well, why else wouldn't he like Mike?'

'I don't know. Maybe it's because he's a hospital porter—'

'What's wrong with *that*? There's nothing wrong with

being a porter, for God's sake.'

'I *know*. I'm not saying there is, but you know what Dad's like—'

'Yeah, he's a *snob*. He thinks that just because Mike has an unskilled job, he's not *respectable* enough for me. God, he's so narrow-minded. I mean, did you see the look on his face the other day when I told him about Mike being a DJ? He couldn't have looked sicker if I'd told him my boyfriend was a murderer.'

Mike used to spend all his spare time DJing in clubs around Essex and London. It meant a lot of late nights in a lot of strange places with a lot of weird people, but he really liked doing it – which was why he didn't mind being a porter. Being a porter was his job; but being a DJ was what he *did*. Dad, of course, couldn't understand it. He couldn't understand how anyone could just have a job instead of a career, how anyone could just want to do something because they really liked doing it.

It was beyond him.

Anyway, about six months ago Mike packed in the porter's job and opened up his own little business in Romford, selling and hiring out DJ equipment – desks, mixers, sound systems, that kind of thing. At first he carried on DJing as well, but after a while he began to realise that he liked the business side almost as much as the DJing itself – and it was less tiring, too. And more lucrative. So now he's pretty much retired as a DJ, and he's doing really well with the business – making a name for himself and piles of money – but it doesn't make any difference to Dad. He still can't stand him. Which, to put it mildly, makes things a little bit awkward now and then.

So when I went down to the kitchen that night, and Gina told me that Mike had asked her to marry him, I didn't know what to say. I was pleased for them, of course, and it was really nice to see the excitement in their faces, but I couldn't help wondering what Dad was going to say.

'Have you told him yet?' I asked Gina.

She shook her head. 'Mike only asked me tonight – look ...' She waggled her finger at me, showing off a small silver ring.

'Very nice,' I said, looking at Mike. 'I take it you had some crackers left over from Christmas?'

'I'll have you know that's a top-quality platinum ring,' Mike said.

'Who told you that?'

'The guy who was selling them in the pub – top-quality, he said, forty-eight carat platinum, very high-class.'

'High-class goods for a high-class guy.'

'That's right.'

He grinned across the table at Gina, making her smile like an idiot, and I found myself looking at him, wondering why I wasn't scared of him in the same way I'd been scared of Iggy. It was an uncomfortable comparison to make, and it made me feel really stupid, because I knew I was only making the comparison because they were both big and black, and that didn't make any sense at all. I wasn't scared of Iggy because he was big and black, I was scared of Iggy because he was scary. Because he was Iggy. Black had nothing to do with it.

'What's up?' Mike asked me.

'Uh?'

'You're looking at me like I've got two heads or something.'

'Sorry,' I said, 'I was miles away.'

'Thinking about Candy?' asked Gina.

'No—'

'Who's this Candy?' asked Mike, leaning his arms on the table, looking interested.

'No one—' I started to say.

'Come on, Joe,' Gina interrupted. 'We made a deal. I told you our secret, now it's your turn.'

'Yeah,' echoed Mike, 'come on, Joe – give it up, dish the dirt, spill the beans, fess up—'

'I thought you were going home?' I said to him.

'There's no rush,' he smiled.

I didn't want to tell them about Candy. I was afraid of making a fool of myself. But I didn't want to keep it inside me, either. I wanted to let it out, to give it some air, to see how it sounded outside my head ... at least some of it, anyway.

And I had made a deal, after all.

So I drank some tea, settled back in the chair, and told them what had happened. I didn't tell them everything, of course. I didn't tell them about the touch of her fingertips, or the intoxicating scent of her skin, and I certainly didn't tell them about the light in the darkness, or the crying voice, or the stuff I could feel deep down inside me ... whatever it was.

Even if I'd wanted to, I couldn't have told them about that.

But I told them everything else.

When I'd finished, no one said anything for a while. Gina just sat there, looking at me with a slightly dazed expression on her face, while Mike kept his head down and stared thoughtfully at the table. I drained the cold tea from my cup and glanced around the kitchen. White walls, stone floor, pots on the wall – everything was shrouded in the worldless silence of the early morning.

'Well ...' said Gina, clearing her throat.

I looked at her, suddenly feeling anxious, wondering what she thought of me. Did she think I was dumb? Naive? Idiotic? Was she embarrassed by my stupidity? *Maybe I shouldn't have said anything after all,* I thought. *Maybe I* should *have kept it all to myself.*

Gina ran her fingers through her hair, glanced at Mike, then looked back at me again, smiling awkwardly.

'I don't know what to say,' she said. 'You must have been ...'

'What?' I said nervously. 'I must have been what?'

'I don't know ... scared, confused ... I mean, if that had been me—'

'You wouldn't have been so stupid.'

'No, I didn't mean *that.* God, Joe – it wasn't *your* fault. How were you supposed to know?'

I shrugged.

Gina leaned towards me. 'She didn't ask you for anything, did she?'

'What do you mean? Ask me for what?'

'Money.'

'No ... she just started talking to me.'

'Well, then ...'

'What?'

'You weren't to know what she was, were you? It's not like she had a tattoo on her head saying *I'm a prostitute ...*'

I grinned.

Gina grinned back. 'She *didn't,* did she?

'Not that I noticed.'

Gina relaxed. She reached out and squeezed my hand, then glanced across the table. 'What do you think, Mike?'

Mike raised his head and looked at me. 'Are you all

right now?' he asked.

'Yeah, I think so.'

He nodded. 'Did you get his name, this black guy?'

'Iggy. She called him Iggy.'

'Iggy?'

'Yeah.'

Mike shook his head. 'It's probably just a street-name. He could be anyone. There're guys like that all over the place – small-time pimps and dealers who run a couple of girls from a flat somewhere ... King's Cross used to be full of them. The whole area was cleaned up a couple of years ago, but there's still a lot going on down there.' He looked at me. 'How old was this girl?'

'I don't know ... seventeen, maybe eighteen. Something like that. It was hard to tell, the way she was dressed and everything ... she could have been younger, I suppose.'

'Was she using?'

'What do you mean?'

'Using ... taking drugs.'

I thought about it, picturing her face, her fresh-white skin, her arms, her lips, her eyes ... her eyes ...

Like tiny black holes.

'I don't know,' I said, wondering if I was lying. 'I don't think so ... I mean, she *seemed* all right.'

'Any track marks on her arms?'

'No.'

'What about Iggy?'

'I didn't look that closely.'

'But he definitely had some kind of hold over her?'

'She was petrified of him.'

Gina said, 'But she was all right with you?'

'Yeah, she was fine before he turned up. She was just ... I don't know ...' I looked at Gina. 'She was really nice.'

'Pretty?'

'Yeah.'

'What kind of pretty?'

'I don't know – what kinds of pretty are there?'

'All kinds,' she smiled. 'Beautiful pretty, sexy pretty, sultry pretty, tarty pretty ... was she tarty?'

'A bit, I suppose ... but not in a nasty way.'

'Tarty but cute?'

'Yeah ... maybe.'

I looked away then, suddenly feeling tired, and also a little bit ashamed of myself. It didn't feel right, talking about Candy as if she was just something to look at – some shiny little bauble or trinket or something. Whatever she was, and whatever she did, she didn't deserve that.

'I'm tired,' I said, stretching my arms and yawning. 'I think I'll be getting off to bed now.'

'Yeah, well,' said Gina, 'you've had a long day.'

'Yeah.'

'You're sure you're all right now? You're not worried about anything ...?'

'What's there to worry about?'

'Nothing, I suppose,' she shrugged. 'I mean, you're not going to see her again, are you?'

'Not unless I want my throat cut.'

'Don't worry about that,' Mike said. 'Most of these guys are all mouth. They don't want any trouble.'

'They won't get any from me,' I said, trying to sound casual, trying to ignore the sudden image in my mind – the image of a darkened cave, glinting with gold, a death-mask grin ...

I stood up.

'Well,' I said, 'I'll leave you to it then.'

Gina stifled a yawn. 'G'night, Joe.'

'Yeah,' said Mike. 'Take it easy.'

Upstairs, I went to the bathroom, cleaned my teeth, then trudged wearily into my bedroom and sat down on the edge of the bed. It was two-thirty in the morning. My body was exhausted and my head felt drained, but my mind was still buzzing with thoughts – *what's Dad going to say about Gina and Mike getting married? what's it going to be like when Gina moves out? what if Mum and Dad get married again and Mum moves back in?*

I was thinking about these things, but I wasn't really *thinking* about them – they were just there, just floating around like dead leaves drifting on the surface of a pond. They didn't really mean anything to me. Below the surface, though, down in the icy black depths, I could see things that meant something. Moving things, living things, formless shapes, darting and flickering in the darkness, stirring up the silt, whirling in the gloom, forming a narrow black tunnel with me at one end and a death mask at the other and a pale white ghost floating somewhere in between ...

'Shit,' I said to myself, shaking my head. 'I'm too tired for this.'

I got up and started getting undressed.

Shirt off ...

You probably won't even remember her in the morning.

Shoes off ...

She'll just be another lost dream.

Socks off ...

You'll meet some girl at the bus stop and forget that Candy ever existed.

Trousers off ...

What's that?

I was checking my pockets before I took my trousers off, just emptying out the loose change and stuff, when my fingers closed on something unfamiliar. You know how it is with the stuff in your pockets, how you pretty much know what's in them, and even if *you* don't know, your fingers do – that's a £1 coin, that's a train ticket, that's a plectrum – and that odd little feeling you get when you put your hand in your pocket and your fingers close on something out of place, something that shouldn't be there?

Well, that's how I felt at that moment. My fingers had closed on something that shouldn't have been there. It felt like a little piece of card, rolled into a tube, and at first I thought it was a train ticket. But it was too small to be a train ticket, and I wouldn't roll a train ticket into a tube anyway.

I pulled it out.

It *was* a tube of card – white card, rolled tightly into a tube, about two inches long, folded in the middle, smudged with damp fingerprints ...

My heart flipped.

I knew what it was.

I could see it in Candy's hands as she fought back the tears and apologised to Iggy. I could see her rolling it, unrolling it, twisting it, folding it ... and then, just a couple of minutes later, I could feel her slipping it into my pocket, her hand brushing my thigh as she leaned across and reached for my chair as Iggy was moving towards me.

I knew what it was.

It was in my hands.

A moist and grubby jewel.

I sat down on the bed and slowly unfolded it, then

carefully unrolled it, revealing the creased remains of a plain white business card. *CANDY*, it said, in neat black script. No other words, no messages, no details, just *CANDY* – with a mobile phone number printed underneath.

chapter four

I almost called her straightaway. I can still see myself sitting there – two-thirty in the morning, half-naked, perched on the edge of the bed, holding my mobile phone in my hand, my finger poised over the buttons, a voice inside me saying – *go on, ring her, just press the buttons, ring her right now ...*

But then I started thinking about it – *what are you going to say? what if she's asleep? what if Iggy answers?* – and that was that. The moment had gone. I tried getting it back, but it was one of those things that needs to be done without hesitation and without any thought, because once you start thinking about it, it's already too late. There's no going back.

I sat there for a little while longer, staring at the phone in my hand, but I knew that I'd missed my chance.

It's all right, I told myself. *You can ring her tomorrow. You'll feel better about everything then, anyway. You'll have had time to think. Or if not tomorrow, there's always the next day, or the next day, or the day after that ...*

There's no hurry, is there?
You've got to get yourself in the right frame of mind ...

It took me just over a week to realise that there *wasn't* a right frame of mind, that even *looking* for a frame of mind was a complete waste of time, and that the only thing to do was what I should have done in the first place – just ring the damn number.

The week went by with a weird sense of timelessness. Days seemed to last for ever, with long stretched-out mornings, interminable afternoons, and never-ending nights. Yet at the same time, when a new day dawned and I looked back at yesterday, it seemed to have passed so rapidly that it was hard to believe it had happened at all. Tomorrows, on the other hand, were centuries away.

I didn't understand it, and I'm not sure I wanted to. I had enough on my mind without trying to work out the vagaries of time. All I really wanted to do was get on with my life without getting too mixed up about Candy.

Not that there was much to get on with.

School ...

The Katies ...

School ...

Dad.

We didn't see a lot of each other. He left for work quite early each morning, and when I got back from school he was usually in his study, writing reports or answering letters, clicking away on his keyboard, frowning at the walls. Sometimes we'd have dinner together, and sometimes Gina was there, but a lot of the time Dad went out in the evenings, and Gina was either working late or out somewhere with Mike, and I had rehearsals with The Katies. So, all in all, there wasn't much family stuff going on.

I saw Gina on the Sunday and we had a quick chat about things. She asked me how I was doing, and I told her I was fine.

'School OK?'

'Yeah.'

'Met any more hookers lately?'

'No.'

'How's the group going?'

'All right. We've got a gig in London in a couple of weeks.'

'Yeah?'

'Supporting Bluntslide.'

'Who?'

'Bluntslide. They're from Manchester. They've just signed a big deal with Polydor. There'll probably be all sorts of people there – music press, agents, record company people ...'

Gina nodded, impressed. 'Maybe I'll come along.'

'Yeah, that'd be good. You could bring Mike.'

'OK, it's a date.'

I looked at her. 'Have you told Dad yet?'

'About me and Mike getting married?'

'Yeah.'

'I was going to tell him today. I thought he was staying at home.'

'He's gone to London with Mum. They're going to see a show or something.'

'I know.'

Neither of us said anything for a while. I didn't know if Gina wanted to talk about it, and I didn't know if I did, either. It was a hard thing to talk about – uncomfortable, messy, complicated.

'Do you think they're serious?' I said eventually.

Gina didn't say anything, just shook her head.

I looked at her. 'Dad seems to be enjoying himself—'

'Do you know what she said once?' Gina said suddenly.

'Who – Mum?'

'Yeah, when they were getting divorced. I heard them talking one night in Dad's study. She said, "It's not us, Charles, it's never been that. It's just the whole marriage thing. Living together, bringing up children, building a home ... it's not for me. It never was. I'm too selfish for that. I just want you, that's all. I don't want to share you with anyone."'

I stared at Gina, seeing bitterness in her eyes. 'She said that?'

'Yeah, like she wanted a divorce from us. Not from Dad, from *us*.'

I didn't know what to say. It seemed an odd thing for Mum to want, especially after all this time, but it kind of made sense, in a way. It would explain why she never visited us, and why she was seeing Dad again, and why she'd left in the first place ...

But explanations don't change anything, do they? They don't make you feel any better. You either like something or you don't, and if you don't like it, then knowing why it happens doesn't make any difference – it's still going to happen, and you're still not going to like it – so what's the point?

Wednesday night was The Katies night. We practised every week in a draughty old warehouse that was owned by the local arts group. They used it mostly for theatre rehearsals and exhibitions and stuff, but to make ends meet they hired it out when it wasn't being used, and it wasn't used all that much, especially in winter. So every Wednesday night – and occasionally at weekends – we'd book ourselves in for three or four hours, set up our gear, and make lots of noise.

That's how I approached it, anyway – a bit of fun, a bit of a bash, and lots of high-speed noise.

The others were a bit more serious. They'd been together for quite a while before I joined the group, and they were all at least a year older than me, and much more ambitious. Before I joined they used to play some really heavy stuff, all gothy and dark and gruesome, but then they started hanging around the skateboard park where I used to hang out with my friends, and they started hearing the stuff that we were listening to – which was still pretty heavy, but not *heavy*-heavy, and not so pretentious either. And then ... I can't really remember exactly what happened. I think I just got talking to them one day. I didn't really know them, but I knew who they were from school, and I knew they played in a group, so when I heard them raving about the bass line on a New Found Glory track that someone was playing, saying that *that* was the sound they were looking for, I just happened to mention that I had a bass, and I could probably play like that ... and things just progressed from there.

We practised a lot, wrote some decent songs, started getting a few gigs, made a couple of demo tapes, and now things were really starting to move – better gigs, more money, a bit of record company interest here and there. I wasn't sure how I felt about it, but the others were really keen.

When I turned up for the practice that night, everyone was going on about this gig we'd got lined up, the one in London I'd told Gina about. They were discussing what to wear, what to play, what to do if we got offered a deal. *Very* serious. I listened for a while, not really joining in, then I just kind of drifted away and started messing about on the guitar.

It gets a bit boring playing bass all the time, and it's nice to strap on a guitar now and then, especially when you can play it *really* loud – the crackle of the pick-ups when you plug it in, the expectant hum of the amp when you crank up the volume, the incredible buzz of power when you slam out the chords ...

'Hey!' yelled Jason, the singer. 'Hey! *HEY!*'

I stopped playing and looked at him. 'What?'

'We're trying to *talk* here.'

'Sorry ... I'll turn it down.'

Chris – whose guitar I was playing – gave me a dirty look, then he turned back to Jason and Ronny – the drummer – and they all got back to their big-time yapping. The whole thing struck me as a bit ridiculous – telling me to turn it down, like they were my bloody parents or something. I mean, if all they wanted to do was talk, why bother hiring the warehouse at all? Why not book a table in a nice quiet restaurant somewhere?

I turned the volume down, then went over and sat cross-legged in front of the amp and carried on playing. I'd been working at home on the song I'd started the night I met Candy, and I began playing it now. It sounded a lot better on an electric guitar than it did on my old acoustic, and when I put some echo and fuzz on it, and got a bit of feedback going, it sounded *really* good. It was a bit slower than the kind of stuff we usually played, slower and more melodic, but it still had a nice spiky edge to it. As I played, I could hear the vocal line in my head, giving it another dimension, and an off-beat guitar line wailing away in the background, and the rock-steady thump of drums and bass ...

'What's that?' someone said.

I stopped playing again and looked up to see Jason standing in front of me. He looked the perfect loser – baggy jeans, baggy jacket, baggy hair – but I knew for a fact that the jacket alone had set him back £300. That's how it was with us, though – we were the kind of skateboard rebels who had enough money to *really* look like shit.

'Is that one of yours?' Jason said.

'What – the song?'

'Yeah – the *song*. What's it called?'

'I don't know ... nothing really ... *Candy*, maybe ...'

'Play it again,' he said, nodding at the guitar in my hands. 'Turn it up a bit. It sounded pretty good. Maybe we could do something with it.'

After that, we spent the rest of the night working on my song. It was really strange, hearing it *become* something. I'd written plenty of songs before, but Jason and Chris wrote all the stuff for The Katies, and they'd always been a bit funny about listening to anyone else's songs, so I tended to keep mine to myself. I'd *suggested* ideas for songs now and then, and I usually wrote my own bass lines, but I'd never worked with the group on a song that was *mine* before, so it was a whole new experience for me. At first, it felt immensely satisfying – it was *my* song, I'd written it, and now it was turning into something *real*. It was growing, evolving, and – best of all – it was starting to sound fantastic. But as we kept working on it – adding bits here, changing bits there – the satisfaction began to fade and another feeling took over. I couldn't work it out at first. It was an empty kind of feeling ... the sort of feeling you get when you've lost something, or something's been stolen from you ... that nagging sense of *loss.*

Yeah, that's what it was.

I felt as if I'd lost something.

I'd lost my song.

It wasn't *mine* any more.

Its *feelings* weren't mine.

It was still a pretty good song, though. It was the kind of song that sticks in your head for days on end, with a chorus you can't stop humming, and I suppose that was some kind of compensation. On the other hand, because it was a good song, and because I couldn't stop humming it all the time, and because I hadn't been smart enough to change the title, so it was still called *Candy* ... because of all that, I found myself walking around for the next couple of days with a chorus of Candys echoing around in my head.

Which wasn't the best way to get on with my life without getting too mixed up about her. Not that I ever really thought I could. But it was worth a try.

I finally called her on Friday. I'd been thinking about it all week – trying to decide when to do it, where to do it, what to say, how to sound – but the more I thought about it, the more daunting it became. *What if I say something stupid? What if she doesn't remember me? What if she doesn't want to talk to me? What if ... what if ... what if ...?* In the end, I realised that if I didn't just do it, I'd never do it at all.

So what I did was, on Friday morning, I set a trap to catch myself unawares. It wasn't much of a trap, and I didn't really think it'd work, but I couldn't see how I'd be any worse off if it didn't – so what did I have to lose?

The plan was to leave my mobile behind when I went to school in the morning, just leave it lying around in my bedroom somewhere and forget all about it. Forget about phones, forget about Candy, forget about ringing her. Forget about everything. Then later on, after school, some time in the evening, when I wasn't thinking about anything, when I was just hanging around with nothing to do, I'd suddenly come across the phone and ring the number before my brain had a chance to stop me.

As I said, I didn't really think it'd work. I mean, when you're trying *not* to think about something, it can easily become the only thing you *can* think about. And when you're trying to forget your mobile phone, it can easily become the only thing you can remember. You can't *stop* seeing it, in your head, all day ... just lying there, exactly where you left it. And you *know* that later on, after school, some time in the evening, you *won't* be hanging around with nothing to do, not thinking about anything, and you *won't* suddenly come across the phone and ring the number before your brain has a chance to stop you.

So you *are* worse off than you were before.

So you *have* got something to lose.

Unless, of course, you double-double-cross yourself by jumping into a phone box on the way home and punching in the number before you realise what you're doing.

The phone hissed emptily for a second or two, and I wondered if I'd dialled the wrong number, but then the line kicked in with an electric crackle and it started ringing. The familiar tone buzzed through my head – *dee-dee ... dee-dee ... dee-dee* ... the sound of waiting, of hoping, of not-knowing – and I could feel my heart thumping hard in my chest, my throat tightening, my fingers tingling ... and then the line clicked and the ringing stopped and Candy's voice came on.

'Yeah?'

She sounded harsh and hurried, hard and abrupt, her voice a bit slurred. Not quite what I was expecting. But at least it wasn't Iggy.

'Hello?' I said. 'Is that Candy?'

'Yeah ... hold on.' The phone got muffled, covered by a hand, and I could hear low voices mumbling in the background. Female voices ... a shout ... a laugh ... then the line opened up again and Candy came back on. 'Yeah ... hello?'

'Candy?' I said. 'It's Joe ...'

'Who?'

'Joe ... Joe Beck.'

'*Bet?*'

'No, Beck ... B-E-C-K. Joe Beck. We met last week ... Thursday ... I saw you at the station—'

'Where?'

'King's Cross—'

'When?'

'Thursday,' I said, my heart sinking fast. 'Last Thursday ...' I looked down at the credit display on the phone, staring blankly at the numbers, wondering if it was worth putting any more money in. She obviously didn't remember me. Why bother prolonging things? Why not just say goodbye and hang up?

But then her voice piped up – 'Joe!' – and she suddenly sounded fresh and excited. 'Joe from McDonald's?'

'Yeah ...'

'God – why didn't you *say*? Lumpy Joe, right? The guy who dropped all his money?'

'Yeah ...'

'Joe the Hat.'

I laughed.

'Christ,' she said, 'you took your time, didn't you? Why didn't you *ring* me?'

'I just did.'

'It's been over a *week*.'

'Yeah, I know ... I'm sorry ... I didn't know ...'

'I wanted to talk to you.'

A warm glow ballooned in my chest. She wanted to talk to me ... she wanted to talk to *me*! The pips went and I stuck some more coins in.

'Joe?' Candy said. 'Are you still there?'

'Yeah ... I was just ...'

'Are you all right?'

'Yeah ... great.'

'How's the lump?'

'It's gone now. The doctor sucked it out—'

'He *what*?'

'With a needle ... he sucked out all the goo with a needle. It's fine now.'

'You're not lumpy any more?'

'No.'

'Well, that's good. How's the group going? The Katies. You made it big yet?'

'Not quite.'

She sniffed, and I heard her lighting a cigarette.

I said, 'How are you doing? Is everything OK?'

'Yeah,' she said breezily, 'you know ... same old stuff. Anyway, it's really good to talk to you, Joe. I've been waiting for you to call.'

'Really?'

'Yeah, really.' She cleared her throat. 'Look, about what happened ... with Iggy and everything ...'

I waited for her to go on.

'Joe?'

'Yeah?'

'Sorry, I thought you'd gone. I just wanted to say sorry, you know? About Iggy ... he didn't mean anything. He just gets a bit funny sometimes. He gets a bit carried away.'

'Right,' I said hesitantly.

'All that stuff he was saying ...? He was just messing around.'

'Messing around?'

'He's got a weird sense of humour.'

'Yeah?'

'I know it's hard to believe ...'

She was right about that.

'I just wanted to apologise,' she said. 'I feel really bad about it.'

'It's OK,' I found myself saying. 'Don't worry about it.'

'You sure?'

'Yeah ... no problem. As long as he's not really going to cut my throat ...'

She laughed, but it wasn't a very reassuring laugh. It sounded kind of forced.

'Who is he, anyway?' I said.

'Who – Iggy?'

'Yeah.'

'He's just ... well, he's no one, really.' I heard her sucking in smoke. 'He's just a friend of a friend ... you know ... just someone I know. Anyway, listen, I'm really sorry he gave you a hard time. If there's anything I can do to make it up to you ...'

'Sorry?'

She laughed again, but more naturally this time. 'I don't mean like that ... I just meant if you wanted to go somewhere, you know, have a drink or something.'

'Oh, right ... yeah ... yeah, that'd be nice.'

'You don't *have* to—'

'No ... I'd really like to.'

'I could buy you a doughnut.'

'Yeah ...'

'Great ... OK, where do you want to go?'

'I don't know ... where do you live?'

'Anywhere in London's fine with me. Is that all right with you?'

'Yeah ... how about the zoo?'

'The zoo?'

I could have kicked myself. It was such a stupid thing to say, and I had no idea why I'd said it. I mean – the zoo? *What's the* matter *with you?* I asked myself. *She asks you out for a drink ... and you tell her you want to go to the* zoo?

'London Zoo?' Candy said.

'Yeah, but—'

'That'd be great. I'd *love* to go to the zoo. I haven't been there for ages.'

'Really?'

'Yeah ... the only thing is –'

Here we go, I thought.

'– I'm a bit kind of limited for time.'

'Oh ... well, that's OK. We don't have to stay long—'

'No, I mean date-wise. I'm a bit busy at the moment ... the only day I can get away is Tuesday.'

'This Tuesday?'

'Yeah – is that going to be all right?'

'You mean the Tuesday coming ... after this weekend ... in a few days' time?'

'Yes, Joe ... the Tuesday after the Monday after the Sunday—'

'Yeah, all right. I was just making sure ...'

'You sure?'

'Yeah.'

'So?'

'What?'

She laughed. 'Can you make it on Tuesday or not?'

'Yeah,' I said, without even thinking about it. 'Yeah, Tuesday's fine. Where shall I meet you?'

'Outside the main gates?'

'OK – what time?'

'Not too early ...'

'Twelve?'

'Sounds good.'

'Twelve o'clock, Tuesday morning, outside London Zoo.'

'The main gates.'

'Right – the main gates. Do you want my mobile number just in case—'

'Hold on.'

The phone got muffled again. This time I could hear doors slamming in the background, raised voices, heavy footsteps ...

'Candy?' I said. 'Candy—'

'Joe,' she whispered quickly. 'I've got to go—'

'What's happening?'

'Nothing ... I'll tell you later.' Her voice was scarcely audible now. 'See you on Tuesday – OK? Make sure you're there.'

'Yeah, but—'

The line went dead.

I stayed in the phone box for a while, trying to unscramble my thoughts ... replaying the conversation in my head, going over and over what Candy had said, what she'd meant, what it all meant to me and how it made me feel ...

That was the hardest thing to understand.

How did I feel?

She'd lied to me – I was pretty sure of that. She'd lied to me. She was hiding things from me. And I had no way of knowing who she really was. Was she the harsh-sounding Candy who'd answered the phone, the one with the slur in her voice? Or was she the one with the bubbly laugh, the one who'd called me Joe the Hat? *Maybe she's both?* I thought. *Maybe she has a split personality? Maybe she's a schizophrenic prostitute with a serious drug problem and a psychopathic monster for a pimp ...?*

Yeah, I told myself, *maybe she is ... but she's still incredibly pretty, isn't she? She still has the brightest smile and the darkest eyes and that wonderful scent of freshly washed skin ... and everything about her still turns your body inside out ... and she's still going to the zoo with you on Tuesday ...*

BANG! BANG! BANG!

The sudden knocking on the phone box window scared the life out of me. When I'd finished jumping out of my skin, I peered through the window and saw a shrunken old lady leaning on a stick, squinting at me.

'You all right?' she screeched. 'You sick or something?'

I opened the door. 'Sorry?'

'I thought you was dying in there,' she said, clicking her teeth. 'You finished now? Only I got some calls to make.'

I stepped out and held the door open for her.

And then I went home.

chapter five

Sometimes a day is just right: the weather, the world, the way everything feels – your body, your clothes, your presence of mind ... sometimes it all fits together in just the right way, the way it's supposed to be.

Tuesday was one of those days.

It started off frosty and cold, with a misty white haze in the air, but as the morning cleared and the sun came out, the winter mist burned away and the skies shone down with the bright-blue promise of spring. It was still too early for any real warmth in the air, but the flood of fresh light was enough to breathe life into everything.

Birds were singing.

People were smiling.

The air felt vibrant and fresh.

It was a fine day for going to the zoo.

I caught the ten-thirty train, which got me to Liverpool Street at just gone eleven, then I took a tube to Camden Town and walked the rest of the way from there. The streets were busy, but not too busy, and my heart was racing, but not too fast. Fast enough to put a smile on my face and a bounce in my step, but not fast enough to make me feel sick. That kind of fast.

Good fast.

Exciting.

Thrilling.

Energising.

Part of the excitement, I suppose, came from knowing that I should have been at school. It was a childish kind of excitement, a forbidden thrill, and as I walked the down-trodden streets of Camden, then up through Parkway and into the splendour of Regent's Park, I knew in the back of my mind that I'd probably pay for it later. I hadn't had a lot of time to think things through, so all I'd done that morning was wait for Dad to leave for work and then plead with Gina to cover for me. I didn't tell her the truth, of course. I mean, we're pretty close, and she's very understanding, but I'm not sure she would have understood why I was going to the zoo with Candy. So I made up a story about some equipment problems with Friday's gig in London.

'It's really important,' I told her. 'If we don't get it sorted out today, the whole thing's going to be called off.'

'I can't give you a lift into London, if that's what you mean,' she said. 'I have to go to work in a minute. I'm late already.'

'No, it's not that. I just need you to ring up school for me and tell them I'm sick.'

She looked at me. 'You want me to *lie* for you?'

'Yeah – if you wouldn't mind.'

She laughed. 'And what's going to happen when Dad finds out?'

'He won't—'

'Yes, he will – he always finds out. He's like Columbo.'

'What – you mean squinty and out-of-date?'

'You know what I mean.'

'OK,' I said. 'If he does find out, I'll just tell him I lied to you. I'll tell him I pretended to be ill and conned you into ringing up school—'

She shook her head. 'I'm supposed to be a *nurse*, Joe. I'm supposed to *know* whether people are sick or not. And if they *are* sick, I'm supposed to look after them—'

'You *would* be looking after me.'

'No, I wouldn't. I just told you, I have to go to work. I can't stay at home all day looking after you—'

'Yeah, but that's the whole point. You don't *have* to stay home and look after me.'

'Why not?'

'Because I'm *not* ill, am I? And I won't be here anyway – I'll be in London.'

Gina stared at me for a moment, trying to make sense of what I'd just said, and wondering if it was worth arguing about. Then she glanced at the clock and let out a sigh. 'All right,' she said, reaching for the phone. 'But you owe me big-time for this – OK? And when Dad finds out ...'

When Dad finds out ...

Yeah, she was right – he *would* find out. He always did. Then I'd get into trouble, and Gina would have to lie for me again, and Dad would get all huffy and puffy for a couple of weeks, lecturing me all the time, going on and on about careers and responsibility and trust and God-knows-what-else ...

But that was for another day.

It wasn't for now.

Now was just now. Just walking the sun-drenched streets, looking around at the regal white houses and the lush green spread of the park, and the calming waters of the canal, and the little stone bridges, and the barges, and the ducks, and the distant sounds of the zoo, drifting in the air, the faint cries of the birds, the monkeys, the sea-lions ...

Animal sounds.

The way they mixed weirdly with the sounds of the city reminded me of long-forgotten family outings, when I was just a kid, and Gina used to hold my hand and lead me round the zoo, pointing out the animals and telling me what they were, while Mum and Dad strolled along behind us, arm in arm, lost in their own little world ...

'Joe!'

I looked up at the sound of Candy's voice and realised I was approaching the main entrance of the zoo. There were quite a few people milling around – groups of tourists, schoolkids, coach parties – but I couldn't see Candy anywhere. I looked around, scanning the entrance area, craning my neck to see through the crowds, and then I heard her voice again – 'Here ... I'm over here ...' – and I turned to the left, but I still couldn't see her. All I could see was a nice young girl in jeans and a turquoise jumper, leaning against the wall, waving at someone behind me. I looked around to see who she was waving at, expecting to see her family, her mum and dad, or maybe her friend from school ... and then Candy's voice cut through the air again.

'Joe ... for chrissake. What are you doing? It's *me*.'

When I turned round again, the girl in the turquoise jumper was walking towards me, smiling that smile, and I couldn't believe I'd mistaken her for someone else. She was Candy all over – the face, the smile, the walk, the body ... the lingering looks from everyone around her.

'What are you doing?' she said, coming up to me. 'Are you trying to avoid me or something?'

'Sorry,' I said, 'I didn't recognise you. You look different.'

She stopped in front of me, striking a pose – chin out, head back, hands in her back pockets. 'D'you like it?'

The jeans were tight, and so was the jumper – tight and short, drawing my eyes to her midriff, just like before. Her hair was pinned back with clips and baubles, and tied at the back in a ponytail. Although she was still wearing make-up, it wasn't as obvious as it was before. Her face seemed younger and fresher. But no less stunning.

'Very nice,' I said, tearing my eyes away.

'Thanks ... you look pretty good yourself.'

I didn't know what to say to that, so I just stood there, looking stupid. Candy smiled brightly at me for a moment, then she took her hands from her pockets and moved towards me, and before I knew it she'd stepped up and kissed me on the cheek.

It was only a peck ... a friendly little kiss ...

A brush of her lips ...

Barely a touch ...

And it wasn't as if I'd never been kissed before. I was no Romeo, by any stretch of the imagination, but I'd had my moments. I'd been round the block once or twice ... well, maybe not *all* the way round, but far enough to know what's what, if you know what I mean.

This, though ...

This simple kiss.

This was something else.

God ... it felt so good. I thought I was going to *explode*. Something inside me seemed to rise up into the sky, up into the blue, rising higher and higher until the air was so thin I could hardly breathe, and I thought for a moment I was dying.

'You ready then?' Candy said.

'Uh?'

She laughed and patted my arm. 'Come on. If we get going now we might catch the feeding times.'

Once we'd gone through the turnstiles and moved away from the entrance, the zoo wasn't as busy as it had seemed from outside. Although it was a bit smaller than I remembered – with less open spaces and a lot more buildings – it was still a pretty big place, and its myriad pathways and tunnels were enough to spread out the coach parties of schoolkids and tourists, leaving us plenty of room to wander around and take our time. Not that Candy was doing much wandering. As soon as we'd gone through the gates, her face had lit up and she'd started scampering around, flitting from cage to cage, jabbering away like an over-excited child –

'Hey, Joe, look at this ... God, look at the size of that lion! It's e*nor*mous ... have they got any hippos? Where's the hippos? What's that? Looks like some kind of monkey ... where's the sign that tells you what it is? They used to have signs ...'

I hadn't expected her to get so excited, so it was a bit of a surprise at first – in fact, it was a *lot* of a surprise. I suppose I'd assumed she'd be really cool about everything – strolling around, calm as you like, chatting quietly to me, casting occasional curious glances at the animals ...

I don't know why I'd thought that.

It was a pretty stupid assumption to make.

But, even so, it *was* kind of odd that she wasn't chatting away to me. Every time I tried to talk to her, she'd listen for a second and then suddenly shoot off in another direction to look at some more animals, or she'd start jabbering again –

'... I came here once on a school trip and we had to fill in all these forms with questions about the animals, like where they lived and what they ate and everything, and everyone just copied it all down from the information signs on the cages ... where's the penguins? Have they still got penguins? What's that over there ...?'

It was unsettling, and also a bit disappointing. I didn't just want her to be with me, I wanted her to *be* with me. I wanted us to walk together, talk together, be together ... I wanted to be part of her excitement, not just a spectator. Not that I *minded* being a spectator. I mean, although I felt a bit detached from her excitement, there was still something exhilarating about it, something that gave me a strange little kick, as if it *was* me she was getting excited about, even though I knew that it wasn't.

And that was OK.

It wasn't perfect, but I could live with it.

So after a while, that's what I did. I gave up trying to make conversation and just wandered along behind her, watching her every move. At first I tried to be subtle about it – disguising my glances, pretending to look elsewhere – but, as far as I could tell, she wasn't aware of my attention, so in the end I stopped trying to be subtle and just watched her quite openly instead. I knew in my heart that I shouldn't be doing it, and my conscience kept nagging away at me – *you ought to be ashamed of yourself, watching her without her knowing, ogling her like some kind of sicko* – but I just couldn't help it. My eyes had a life of their own, zapping back and forth between her face, her body, her legs, her breasts ... and my thoughts were running wild – *where does she come from? what does she do? is she really a prostitute? what does that mean? how old is she? sixteen? seventeen? fifteen? fourteen? does it matter ...?*

Did it matter?

I couldn't convince myself that it didn't.

And I knew I had to talk to her. No matter how much I wanted to ignore all the questions and just enjoy the thrill of being with her, I knew it wasn't enough. I couldn't spend all day just gawping at her, for God's sake. She was a person, not a photograph in a magazine. She was real.

We were heading towards the penguin pool now. I was walking along on my own, struggling with my guilty thoughts, when I looked up and saw Candy waiting for me at the end of the pathway. She was leaning against a sign-post, smoking a cigarette, studying me closely. I got the feeling she knew exactly what I was thinking.

'Hey,' she said, as I approached. 'It's good, isn't it?'

'What?'

'The *zoo*.'

'Oh, yeah ...'

She rubbed her arms and pulled down her sleeves.

I said, 'Aren't you cold without a coat?'

'Never feel the cold,' she said. 'I've got hot blood.'

Her skin looked cold to me – pale and white and prick-led with goose-bumps – but I didn't say anything.

'Do you want to get a coffee or something?' she said. 'There's a little café over there.'

'OK.'

She dropped her cigarette to the ground and stepped on it, then looped her arm through mine and started leading me up the path. 'I'll buy you that doughnut I promised you,' she said, leaning against me. 'And then you can tell me all about yourself.'

Now *I* was the one with goose-bumps.

It wasn't much of a café, just a medium-sized room with a

dozen or so tables and a serving counter at the front. It was empty and quiet, though, and it had a pretty nice view, and I didn't really care what it was like anyway. They didn't have any doughnuts, so we got ourselves two Jungle Platters and two mugs of coffee, and Candy insisted on paying.

'My treat,' she said.

'But you paid for us to get in—'

'Don't worry about it,' she said, pushing my money away and pulling a wad of notes from her purse. 'See? I'm loaded.'

As we took our trays to a window table, my mind drifted back to the time in McDonald's when she'd shown Iggy a handful of notes and said – *See? I wouldn't lie to you, Iggy, you know I wouldn't* ... and he'd just sat there staring at her – staring his stare – and she'd shrunk back into her seat, cowering in silence ...

I looked at her now – putting her tray on the table, sorting out the cutlery, her face flushed bright with the warmth of the café – and it was hard to imagine that Iggy even existed.

I knew he did, though, and I knew I had to find out about him. But I also knew I had to be careful. If I said the wrong thing, if I got too pushy ... I didn't know what might happen.

'So,' Candy said, tucking into her chips, 'where do you want to start?'

'Start what?'

'I want to know everything about you – where you were born, who you are, what you like doing ... what's the matter?'

'Nothing.'

'Am I being too nosy?'

'No, it's not that—'

'All right,' she said. 'How about if I tell you what I *think* you are, and you tell me if I'm right or wrong? Is that any better?'

'I don't mind ...'

'Right – OK ... let's see. Your dad's a gynaecologist—'

'I already told you that.'

'I *know* – I'm just getting started. It's no good just guessing, is it? You've got to start with the facts and work up from there. Fact number one: your dad's a gynaecologist. Correct?'

'Correct.'

She dipped a forkful of chips into her egg, then paused, the fork in mid-air, looking thoughtfully at me. 'That's got to be hard work,' she said.

'What?'

'Being a gynaecologist ... I mean, you get up in the morning and go to work, and the first thing you do is start poking around inside someone's fanny. That can't be easy ... especially if you've had a few drinks the night before.'

I tried to look composed, as if I wasn't shocked or embarrassed or anything, which I wasn't really, but I somehow felt as if I *ought* to be, and I couldn't keep the feeling from my face.

'What?' she said, looking at me. 'I was only saying—'

'I know ... it's all right. It's nothing.'

I thought for a moment she was going to say something else about Dad, or about gynaecologists in general, or about me getting embarrassed, but she didn't. She just smiled for a second, then popped the eggy chips into her mouth and started talking again. 'OK,' she said. 'Facts number two and number three: you live in Heystone and you're in Year Ten at Heystone High.'

My mouth dropped open in dumb surprise.

'Am I right?' she grinned.

'How do you know that?' I said.

She laughed, wiggling her fingers at her head. 'I'm psychic ... I can fe-e-el your thoughts ... I know everything there is to know ...'

'Did you follow me?'

Her face went still. 'Of course I didn't *follow* you. What do you think I am?'

'So how do you know where I live?'

'Because ...' she said, starting to eat again, '... because ... I used to see you at the skateboard park.'

'What? When?'

'Years ago, when it first opened. You used to hang around there after school, you and your skateboard mates, falling off your boards all the time.'

'How do *you* know?'

'I was there.'

'Where?'

'At the park.'

'I don't get it. What were you doing there?'

'Sneaking around cadging fags most of the time.' She laughed. 'It's no great mystery or anything – I used to live in Heystone, that's all. I went to St Mary's—'

'The convent school?'

'Yeah. I wasn't there for long, though ...'

I looked at her, trying to imagine how she'd look in a St Mary's School uniform – the long blue dress, the stupid little hat, the short white socks – but I couldn't picture it.

'Whereabouts in Heystone did you live?'

'Otley,' she said.

I nodded. Otley's on the posh side of town – or the posh*er* side, to be more exact. Heystone doesn't do poor, it only does varying degrees of rich, and Otley's about as rich as it gets.

'Surprised?' Candy said.

'Well, yeah ... I mean, not about Otley ... just the whole thing. You know, the coincidence.'

'What coincidence?'

'Us ... you and me ... both of us coming from Heystone ...'

'You think that's a coincidence?'

'Well, yeah ...'

She shook her head. 'Why do you think I called out to you at the station?'

'Why?'

'Yeah. D'you think I make a habit of calling out to any old strangers on the street?'

'Well, no ... I suppose not ...'

'I *recognised* you. I just told you that ... I remembered you from the park.' She angled her head and looked at me. 'You haven't changed much, you know. Not that it was *that* long ago – only a couple of years.'

'You recognised me?'

'Yes.'

I didn't know how I felt about that. It was nice, in a way. Nice to be recognised. Nice to know she remembered me. Nice to think I must have had something worth remembering. But I wasn't sure I wanted *nice*. I wasn't sure I wanted to be *recognised* or *remembered*.

I wasn't sure *what* I wanted.

'Are you going to eat that?' Candy said, nodding at my bread.

'Help yourself,' I told her.

As she folded the bread and mopped up the egg yolk from her plate, I gazed out through the café window. The patio outside was deserted. Across the zoo I could see the pathways winding up and down through a landscape of trees and rocks and make-believe animal worlds. Man-made mountains stood glowering in the distance, as pale and grey as poster-painted papier-mâché, and I wondered if the animals knew the mountains weren't real, and if they did know, whether they cared.

'Why do you have to think so much about everything?' Candy said through a mouthful of eggy bread.

I shook my head. I didn't mean to look irritated, but Candy's reaction showed that I did.

'I was only *asking*,' she said sulkily. 'I don't care what you do.'

'Sorry,' I said. 'I was just thinking, that's all.'

She lit a cigarette and breathed out her irritation in a stream of smoke. 'Thinking about what?'

'You.'

It came out before I knew what I was saying, and I think it shocked her a bit. I know it shocked me. She didn't say anything for a while, just looked at me for a moment, then started tidying the table, piling the plates and the cutlery on the tray. When that was done, she sat back, patted her belly, and burped contentedly, like an old man after dinner at his club. Then she took another long drag on her cigarette and looked at me again.

'You've got egg on the side of your mouth,' I told her.

'Where?'

I pointed to the corner of my mouth.

She touched the other side of her mouth. 'Here?'

'No ... the other side.'

'Show me,' she said, sucking the end of a paper napkin and passing it to me. I hesitated a moment, then reached across and touched the napkin to her mouth. Without meaning to, I brushed her cheek with the back of my fingers ... her skin was delicate and smooth. The bones of her face felt small and unknown.

'Thanks,' she said, licking her lips.

I nodded quietly, crumpling the napkin and placing it carefully on the tray. The ball of white tissue paper sat there for a moment, then slowly uncrumpled, revealing an inkblot pattern of lipstick-pink and yellow. I stared at it for a while, looking for hidden meanings in the pattern, but there was nothing there – it was just a smudge of lipstick and egg.

'Joe?' said Candy.

I looked up. Her face was pale and drawn, making her eyes seem even darker than usual.

She said, 'You don't want to know about me.'

'Why not?'

'It's just best if you don't.'

'Best for who?'

'You ... me ... I don't know.'

She seemed tense – fiddling with her cigarette lighter, blinking her eyes, tapping her finger on the table. It was as if she was desperate to go somewhere, or do something, but equally desperate not to.

'It's all right,' I said. 'I don't mind—'

'Sorry,' she interrupted, starting to get up. 'I need to go to the loo.' She picked up her handbag from the table and looked around the café, looking for the lavatory.

'It's over there,' I said, pointing to a doorway across the room.

'Thanks,' she said, walking off quickly. 'I won't be a minute.'

I watched her go, remembering the last time she'd walked away from me, when I'd first seen her at the station. Then she'd walked with a sway of her hips and a quick smile over her shoulder, as if she knew that she was being watched and wanted to make the most of it, but now she was walking without any vanity at all – no swaying hips, no pretence, no frivolity. She was walking with a purpose. Either not knowing, or not caring, that I was watching her.

As she went through the doorway, I wondered briefly if she was running out on me. I imagined her going down the corridor, slipping into the kitchen, then sneaking out the back door and legging it across the zoo ...

Yeah, right, I thought to myself. *She's going to do that, isn't she? She's going to go to all that trouble just to get away from you.*

I sat there for a while, staring through the window, thinking about things, listening to the steamy hiss of tea-urns and the clatter of plates and cutlery, then I got up and went to wait outside.

It was early afternoon now and the temperature was starting to drop. The sun was still shining though, still brightening the sky, and the grounds of the zoo were bathed in a crisp wintry light. The air was crystal clear. I could see for miles. I could see brightly coloured birds, goats on hills, zebras and llamas, capuchin monkeys playing in the tops of trees ...

I looked back inside the café.

Candy was taking a long time.

I wondered what she was doing – washing her hands, fixing her make-up, making a phone call ...? I didn't have a clue. What girls get up to in lavatories is a complete mystery to me. Gina sometimes disappears for hours. I've often been tempted to ask her what she does in there, but it's a tricky subject to talk about. There's always the chance of stumbling into the kind of areas that *shouldn't* embarrass me, but do, and that's the worst kind of embarrassment there is. Because when you feel embarrassed about something that you know you shouldn't feel embarrassed about, you end up in the vicious circle of being embarrassed by your embarrassment ... and that's *really* embarrassing.

I looked over at the café again, willing Candy to appear – *come on ... please ... if you take any longer, I'll have to do something. I'll have to go and ask someone to check the Ladies for me ... that woman behind the counter ... the one in the apron, with the grease-smeared glasses ... I'll have to go up to her and explain what's happened ...*

A door slammed inside the café. I leaned to one side to get a better view. For a second or two, I couldn't see anything ... and then Candy was there, a vision in turquoise, walking through the doorway and adjusting her bag over her shoulder.

I let out a sigh and looked away, doing my best to look casual. Hands in pockets, gazing around, just taking in the view, waiting happily – no worries at all. I was so cool and casual that even when the café door opened I waited a moment before turning around.

'Sorry I took so long,' Candy said.

'That's all right,' I told her, shrugging very slightly, just to let her know that I'd hardly even noticed.

She stopped in front of me, looking down at the ground, and I could sense something different about her. It's hard to describe, but she somehow seemed *looser*. The way she was standing, hanging her head ... the strange little smile on her lips ...

'I was ... uh ...' she mumbled.

'Sorry?'

She raised her head and looked at me, struggling to

focus on my face. 'I'm all right,' she said. 'It's all right ... do you wanna ...?' She wiped her mouth with the back of her hand, then giggled. 'Sorry ...' she said. 'Sorry ... I didn't mean ... do you wanna, you know ...?' She waved her hand, indicating the zoo, then looked back at me again, covering her mouth to stifle a yawn. Her eyes were enormous, like pools of obsidian, but her pupils had shrunk to dim black dots, almost invisible within the darkness.

'Come on,' she said, taking my arm. 'I wanna show you something.'

chapter six

Whatever Candy had taken, it didn't seem to affect her too much ... not outwardly, anyway. I mean, she wasn't stumbling or staggering around, she wasn't singing or shouting or laughing like a lunatic ... she wasn't *doing* anything. She was just walking along quite normally, leading me across to the other side of the zoo, as calm and steady and cool as you like. Apart from her eyes, and a slight flush to her face, it was hard to tell any difference. Her pace was a little slow, perhaps, but at least she wasn't rushing around like a maniac any more. In fact, if anything, she seemed more normal now than she had been before. Her speech was a bit slurred, but it wasn't too bad, just a bit sleepy-sounding, and after the initial bout of mumbling and giggling, she soon settled down and got back to being herself again.

Whatever that was.

I didn't know.

As we walked along the pathways, I didn't know anything – what to think, how to feel, how to react. I mean, when you're with someone you really like, and you haven't known them that long, and they start sneaking off to take drugs ... what the hell are you *supposed* to do? Ignore it? Say something? Run away?

'Loosen up,' Candy said.

'What?'

She jiggled my arm. 'Loosen up ... you're as stiff as a board.'

I tried to relax my arm, but it didn't seem to belong to me any more. Not that I knew what to do with it, anyway. Walking arm in arm was another new experience for me. It wasn't *quite* as perplexing as the drug thing, but it still posed a lot of tough questions – *what should I do with my arm? should I stick my elbow out? should I hold her arm? should I put my hand in my pocket?*

'Where are you taking me?' I asked her, just for something to say.

'Wait and see. It's a surprise.'

We walked on in silence. Candy seemed to be enjoying herself, smiling quietly at everything around us – the passing enclosures, the animals, the signs, the people on the pathways – but there was something about her, some weird sense of detachment, that made me wonder what she was really seeing. It was as if she was living in her own little bubble, all wrapped up and warm inside, and everything outside the bubble was nothing more than a passing curiosity.

'Are you all right?' I asked her.

'Hmm?'

'Are you OK?'

'Fine,' she nodded.

'Do you want to ... uh ... do you want to talk about anything?'

'Like what?'

'I don't know ... anything. Where you live, what you do ... that kind of stuff.'

She smiled. 'That kind of stuff?'

'Yeah.'

She nodded again, and again, then blinked her eyes once or twice, then looked at me and said, 'OK ... yeah ... I can do that kind of stuff. Let's see ...' She looked straight ahead, deep in thought, then started talking. 'Right ... where do I live? OK ... I live about ten minutes' walk from King's Cross station in a nice little third-floor flat in a refurbished Victorian house.' Her voice was flat and expressionless, as if she was reading from a script. 'My flat-mate's called Sophie. She's a dancer in a West End nightclub, which is where we met.' She stopped talking and looked at me. 'How's that?'

'What do you mean?'

'Nothing ...' She smiled. 'I was just wondering what you thought.'

I shook my head.

She tightened her grip on my arm. 'You must have wondered about me ... where I get my money from. What I *do* ...'

'Well ... yeah, I suppose.'

'And?'

'I don't know. I just ... I don't *know* ...'

She didn't say anything for a while, and neither did I. We just carried on walking. I was feeling more comfortable with the arm-in-arm thing now. I was beginning to appreciate that it's actually a pretty good way of walking when one of you knows where you're going and the other one doesn't. You don't need to ask questions or guess which way to go, all you have to do is get used to the other person, and after a while you can sense where they're going through the feel of their body.

We were near the main entrance again now, heading off towards a little tunnel that leads through to the canal-side of the zoo. As we went down into the shade of the tunnel, Candy started talking again, this time in a more natural voice.

'It's just a bit hard to talk about personal things,' she said. 'There's all sorts of family stuff ... you know ... complicated stuff. D'you know what I mean?'

'Yeah.'

She shook her head. 'There was all kinds of crap going on at home ... I couldn't stand it. Then they kicked me out of school, and things just went from bad to worse.' I felt her shoulders shrug. 'So I just left. Got up one morning, called a friend, left a note, and came down here.'

'To London?'

'Yeah ... I knew a girl who had a place in Bethnal Green. I stayed there for a while, then I got myself this dancing job ... and that's about it, really.'

'Dancing?' I said.

'Yeah ... I'm a dancer.'

'Really?'

She stopped walking and turned to face me. 'I just dance, Joe. Nothing else. I don't take my clothes off. I'm just a dancer. No poles, no stripping, just a flashy little top and a micro-skirt. It's nothing – you see more naked flesh on Saturday morning kids' TV.' She shrugged again. 'It's just a job.'

'What about Iggy?'

Her face tensed for a moment, then relaxed again. 'Like I told you,' she said, 'he's just a friend of a friend ... not even that, really. He's just some guy that hangs around.'

She tapped the side of her head. 'He's a bit whacked – too much crack, probably. He lives in his own little world. One minute he thinks he's a pimp, the next he's an undercover cop. It's best to just humour him.'

'Is that what you were doing in McDonald's – humouring him?'

She nodded, looking away. 'He can get a bit funny sometimes ... he's a big guy – you saw him. He doesn't *mean* to be scary ...'

'He doesn't have to.'

She laughed. 'He wouldn't hurt you.'

'No?'

'Well, not much ...'

We looked at each other then – a long, close look. Candy was smiling, but I couldn't work out what kind of smile it was. It seemed real enough, a smile fit for a joke, but jokes – and good lies – are usually based on the truth, and I could see some kind of truth in her eyes. It was a truth that invaded her, like a dark disease, a truth too painful to talk about. And I was beginning to wonder if all I was doing was making it worse.

Candy was still looking at me.

I smiled.

She sighed.

I breathed in deeply, tasting the scent of her breath, and a moment passed between us – a silent agreement to put the truth on hold – and then she took my hand and led me down into Moonlight World.

'It's my favourite place,' Candy said quietly, guiding me down the dimly lit stairs. 'It's always empty and quiet down here, and the air feels nice and cool. Mind the steps.'

I stumbled slightly in the darkness. She tightened her

grip on my hand and pulled me towards her.

'Close your eyes,' she said, 'then open them again. Like this ...' She turned to me with wide-open eyes, looking like a startled owl.

I smiled at her.

'Seriously,' she said. 'It lets more light in.'

'Wouldn't be easier if they just turned up the lights?'

'It's *supposed* to be dark. These are nocturnal animals. If the lights were turned up they'd be asleep all the time.'

The steps led us down into a twilight corridor, and as we started to walk along it, looking in at the glass-fronted enclosures, I could feel the hush of the night seeping into my skin. The silence, the emptiness, the cool of the underground air. It smelled earthy and fresh.

'Nice, isn't it?' Candy whispered.

'Yeah ... it's good.'

'I used to come here on my own sometimes ... I'd stay down here for ages.' Her voice was barely audible. 'It's a good place for sadness ...'

I wasn't sure what she meant. Good for making you sad? Or good for taking the sadness away?

'Look,' she said.

We'd stopped in front of a rainforest scene, a moonlit world of mossy branches and waxy green leaves and strange-looking ferns, all of it misty and dark and dripping with moisture. I moved up closer and peered through the glass, but I couldn't see any animals.

'There,' Candy said, pointing to a corner. 'On that little branch at the back. See?'

I looked closer. A pair of huge yellow eyes was staring curiously at us through the darkness. Behind the eyes I could just make out a small furry animal, no bigger than my hand, sitting quietly on the branch.

'What is it?' I said.

'I don't know ... come on, I'll show you my favourite.'

She took my hand again and led me down to the end of the corridor. Her fingers felt so fine on my skin ... so light and slender, pressing coolly into the palm of my hand ... sending her touch all over me ...

It was more than anything I'd ever felt before.

'Here we are,' she said, stopping in front of another display. 'This is what I wanted to show you.'

I didn't have to search for the animal this time, I could see it straight away. The inside of this enclosure was a lot starker than the other one – just a sandy floor, a stone-coloured background, and a solitary bare-branched tree. Perched uneasily in the tree was a russet-coloured animal with a dopy-looking head and a long thick tail. It was about the size of a small dog, or a big cat, but it didn't look like a dog or a cat – it looked like a small kangaroo. Small front legs, large hind legs, a roundish triangular head ...

'It's a tree kangaroo,' Candy said.

'A *tree* kangaroo?'

She nodded, her eyes glazed with pity. 'It never moves. It just sits there all the time, like it's too scared to go anywhere.'

She was right – it *did* look scared, scared and wobbly, as if it was going to fall off the branch at any moment. I wouldn't have been surprised if it did. It was a kangaroo, for God's sake. Kangaroos aren't designed for climbing trees. And this one seemed to know it. Its face was filled with a sad-eyed bewilderment, a pitiful look that seemed to say – *I* know *I'm a tree kangaroo, and I* know *I'm supposed to climb trees, but I'm just no good at it, and I really don't like it.*

'Poor little sod,' said Candy. 'Stuck in a tree all day ...'

The kangaroo blinked sadly.

Candy sniffed. 'Come on ... let's leave him alone.'

I followed her back down the corridor towards the exit, feeling quietly moved by what I'd just seen. The sadness, the silence, the darkness, the loneliness ... all of it held in a simple little moment. It was just so ...

I don't know.

Just so much.

If nothing else had happened then, if we'd left Moonlight World with only the memory of that sad little moment, it still would have stayed with me for years to come.

But something else *did* happen.

Something that made the moment eternal.

Without so much as a word, Candy led me down to the end of the corridor and into a dark little alcove beside the exit door. I thought she was going to show me something else, another animal or something, but instead she took me by the shoulders and pushed me up against the wall and, before I knew it, we were kissing ourselves to death. Hot kisses, wet kisses, long hard kisses that lasted for ever ... lips and tongues, hands and bodies, everything groaning out of control ...

God ...

It burns me up just thinking about it.

The heat of her mouth, her lips, the rush of her body touching mine, the naked thrill of her skin ...

I don't know how long we stayed there, moaning and sighing against the wall, but if a couple of young kids hadn't come round the corner and surprised us with a sudden shriek of giggles, I'm sure we'd still be there now. Lost in the dark desire, lost in each other ...

As it was, though, the kids brought us back to our senses. We stopped kissing and looked at them for a moment, none of us moving, and then their parents appeared round the corner, and the spell was suddenly broken. The parents didn't know what to do. At first they were wary, a bit suspicious, wondering what we were up to. Then the kids started telling them what we were up to, and their parents got embarrassed, and that got us giggling, which helped to cool things down a bit.

Not a lot, mind you, but enough to let us open the door and walk out into the late afternoon without feeling *too* conspicuous.

'That was fun,' Candy said, still giggling.

My skin was flushed, tingling in the open air, and I felt as if I hadn't breathed for a month. I tried to speak, but all that came out was a throaty sigh.

Candy smiled at me, her dark eyes gleaming. 'Are you all right?

'Uh huh ...'

She grinned again, reaching into her bag for a cigarette. She offered me the pack. 'Sure you don't want one?'

'Nuh uh,' I said.

She stopped to light the cigarette – cupping her hands against the breeze, clicking the lighter, then flicking her head back and blowing out smoke with an irresistible look of delight on her face.

'OK,' she said. 'What's next?'

Next? I thought. *What's next?*

I was just about ready to lie down and die.

'Come on, Joe,' she said, grabbing my hand. 'It's only early yet. There's still a lot to see.' She grinned at me. 'Come *on* ... I'll buy you a Coke – boost your energy levels.'

My legs were still quivering as she dragged me away,

and the ground was an alien surface ten miles beneath me.

Except for one little hiccup, the rest of the day was a nice downhill ride. Candy bought me a Coke – and a bottle of water for herself – and then we just strolled around in the paling light, ambling slowly along the pathways, arm in arm, not really caring where we were going – just walking. The zoo was gradually emptying out, the schoolkids and tourists heading back home, and as the skies began to dim and the afternoon made way for the evening, the atmosphere took on that nice quiet feeling you get at the end of the day – animals slumbering, shops getting ready to close, zookeepers with wheelbarrows preparing for the night.

It felt good to be part of it.

Tired and happy, wandering quietly in a cooling breeze, birds whistling and animals grumbling, growling, shuffling, yawning ...

We were on the far side of the zoo now, the quiet side. All zoos have their far sides: those places furthest away from the restaurants and the souvenir shops where the less popular animals are housed, the animals that are hard to see, or don't do very much – wolves, deer, small brown things that live in burrows, birds that are not quite ostriches. They're lonely places, these quiet sides – the kinds of places where secrets can be shared. Secrets or truths.

Or nothings.

With us, it was nothings.

I told Candy about my parents; she listened. I told her about Gina and Mike; she said she'd like to meet them. I told her about school and exams; and she drifted away, strangely saddened, or maybe just bored. But when I told her about writing songs and playing music and being on stage with The Katies, she perked up again. 'It must be fantastic,' she said, 'doing something you really like.'

'Yeah,' I told her. 'It's pretty good.'

'What's it like on stage, you know, with all those people watching you? Don't you get scared?'

'Not really. I mean, we don't get that many people watching us, and when the lights are down you can't see most of them, anyway. Besides, I'm usually too busy trying to remember the songs to think of anything else.' I looked at her. 'What about you? Do *you* get scared?'

'When?'

'When *you're* on stage – when you're dancing.'

'Oh, right,' she said quickly, lowering her eyes. 'Yeah ... I don't know ... I don't really think about it, I suppose. I just ...' She raised her head and stared emptily into the distance, her face strangely sad again. When she spoke, her voice was cold. 'I just pretend I'm not there. It's the only way ...' She sighed into silence, but only for a moment. With a self-dismissive shake of her head, she turned back to me with her smile restored and said, 'Maybe I could come and see you play some time?'

'Yeah.'

She grinned. 'I could stand at the front and scream your name and throw my knickers at you. What do you reckon? Would you like that?'

'As long as you washed them first.'

She laughed.

'Actually,' I said, reaching into my pocket, 'I just *happen* to have a poster here ...' I unfolded the poster for our London gig and showed it to her. 'It's this Friday,' I said, as she took the poster from me and looked it over. 'I mean, I don't know if you can get there ...'

'The Black Room,' she said, reading the poster.

'It's a club in Hammersmith.'

'Yeah, I know it.' She looked up at me. 'You're playing there?'

'Nine o'clock,' I said. 'This Friday.'

She nodded, smiling. 'I'm impressed.'

'I can put you on the guest list if you want.'

'Access all areas?'

'I don't see why not. Can you make it?'

She chewed her lip, thinking hard. 'I think so ... I'll have to see. It's just a bit ...'

'What?'

'Nothing ... it's all right. It's just a bit complicated, that's all. I might have to sort a few things out ...' Her eyes went back to the poster, and I could see her weighing things up – imagining this, imagining that, balancing out the complications.

'I don't want to get you into any trouble or anything,' I said. 'If you can't come—'

She shut me up with a sudden kiss that was almost painful in its passion. I thought I was going to fall over for a moment, but then she broke off, and I managed to steady myself, and she looked into my eyes and said, 'I'll *be* there – OK?'

'Right ...'

She moved closer, bringing her face up to mine, until I could feel her whispered breath on my lips. 'I'll be there.'

Then her phone rang.

'Shit!' she said angrily, reaching into her bag and pulling out her mobile. She checked the caller ID, swore again, then moved away to one side.

'Sorry,' she said to me. 'I won't be a minute.'

She put the phone to her ear and carried on moving away. I heard her say, 'No – I *told* you ...', then, 'I *know*, but you said ...', and then she was too far away for me to hear anything. I could still see her, though, and although she was standing with her back to me, I could tell she wasn't happy. Her whole body had tensed up, giving her a strangely retracted appearance. The way she was moving – nodding her head and gripping her fists – reminded me of the hunched and withered gestures of an angry old woman.

It wasn't nice to see.

I turned away.

Burying my head in the sand.

When she came back, she didn't tell me what the phone call was about, and I didn't ask. All she said was – 'I'm sorry, Joe, I have to go.'

I just nodded.

She smiled and said, 'Next time ...'

We kissed again, and she whispered things that made me smile, and then we walked through the evening to the end of our day.

And that was it, a day at the zoo. One of the best – and weirdest – days of my life. I'm still living it now, every day, living it out in my mind – following the ups and downs, walking the pathways, re-living the moments of our Moonlight World ...

It's a day that never dies.

chapter seven

'You're wasting your life, Joe,' Dad said sternly. 'You know that, don't you? You're wasting your life. If you carry on like this—'

'Carry on like what?'

'You know what I mean – all this pop music and everything ... you and your Skaties—'

'Katies.'

'What?'

'It's *Katies* – not Skaties.'

'I don't *care* what it is. You've got exams this year. You should be studying—'

'I *am* studying—'

'When?'

'All the time.'

'You weren't studying today, were you? You weren't even at school.'

'Yeah, but—'

'You lied to your teachers, you abused my trust ...'

It was eight-thirty in the evening. I'd been in Dad's

study for the last half-hour. I hadn't meant to get back so late from the zoo, but I'd kind of lost track of the time ... and then the trains had been delayed, and I couldn't ring Dad to let him know because I wasn't supposed to *be* on the train. So when I got back and he called me into his study, I guessed straight away that Gina had told him the truth – or what she thought was the truth – and I knew I was in for some serious talking. And when Dad gets serious, he *really* gets serious.

'... I know it's been tough over the last few years,' he was saying, 'but that's no excuse for wasting your time on things that don't matter—'

'I'm not,' I said.

'No? You could have fooled me. How are you going to get the grades you need if you spend all your time playing at being a pop star?'

'I'm not *playing* at anything. I just enjoy it – it's good fun. And anyway, it's only one evening a week—'

'And weekends.'

'Not every weekend.'

'And days out in London when you should be at school.'

'I've already explained that,' I sighed. 'It was just a one-off thing. It won't happen again—'

'No, it won't,' he said coldly.

'You don't have to—'

'What?'

'Nothing.' I hung my head in shame and stared remorsefully at the floor. I didn't expect Dad to fall for it, but at least it gave me a break from the furious glare of his eyes.

'Why do you have to do it?' he said.

'What?'

'Why do you always have to make things so difficult?'

I raised my head and looked at him. 'Difficult?'

'You know what I mean.'

'Look,' I said, 'I'm sorry – OK? I *know* it was a stupid thing to do, and I *know* I shouldn't have done it ... but it doesn't *mean* anything, Dad – really. It doesn't mean I'm wasting my life—'

'It means you're grounded, Joe.'

'You can't—'

'I can, and I will.'

'No, but listen—'

'No, *you* listen.' He leaned across his desk and gave me the look. 'I'm going away at the end of next week. I'll be gone for six or seven days. Until I get back, you're grounded – do you understand? As of today, you're not to go out at the weekends, or after six in the evening, without my specific permission.'

'But Dad—'

He held up his hand. 'I haven't finished yet – are you listening to me?'

'I just wanted—'

'Are you *listening*?'

'Yes,' I sighed.

'Right – it's half-term when I'm away, but the same rules apply, and I expect you to follow them without any help from Gina. She's got enough on her plate without having to watch over you all the time. I need to know that I can trust you, Joe. I'm giving you the responsibility for your own discipline, and if you don't take it seriously, the only person you'll be letting down is yourself.'

I looked at him, wanting to hate him, but knowing I couldn't. He was my dad. Whatever I felt about him, I couldn't *hate* him. I could hate his stupid reasoning, though, the way he treated me like a kid but expected me to behave like an adult. *Why can't you make your mind up, Dad?* I wanted to say. *Either treat me like a kid or treat me like an adult, but don't keep treating me like something in between.*

'Did you hear what I said?' he asked me.

'Yeah, I heard.'

'Is there a problem?'

I hesitated for a moment, thinking about Friday's gig. I was torn between keeping quiet about it – and sorting out something when the time came – or being honest. It was tempting to keep quiet about it, but getting to London on Friday night without Dad knowing wouldn't be easy. If I was honest, though, if I explained how important the gig was and begged him to let me go, and he said no, then he'd be forewarned, so he'd be on his guard, making it almost impossible to get away without him knowing.

I looked at him, trying to decide how to play it. His face was calmer now. It was still deadly serious, but the fury had faded, and I thought I could detect just a hint of compassion.

Or so I hoped.

'What about Friday?' I asked quietly.

'Friday?'

'You know – the gig ... with the group. The Katies. We're playing in London ... I told you about it, remember?'

'How could I forget?'

'If you'd just let me go to that—'

'I don't think so.'

'It's only one night ...'

He shrugged.

I said, 'But it's really important, Dad. If I don't go, they won't be able to play. I'll be letting everyone down. We've already hired all the equipment and everything, and there's people coming to see us. We've sold tickets—'

'You should have thought about that before, shouldn't you?'

'Come on, Dad ... you're not being fair.'

'Well, now you know how it feels.'

'But you're always telling me about taking responsibility for things. What about my responsibilities to everyone else? The rest of the group, the promoters, the people who've paid—'

'That's different.'

'Why?'

'Because they're not family, they're just ...'

'What? They're just what?'

He shook his head. 'Don't start twisting my words, Joe. You know what I mean.'

'Yeah ...' I said, nodding my head as if I knew what he meant but didn't believe him. Actually, I *didn't* know what he meant, but I could see he was getting a bit flustered about something, and that was all I needed to know. I carried on nodding, trying to look reproachful – which wasn't easy – but, strangely enough, it seemed to work. Dad's face was getting twitchy, and his mouth had lost some of its confidence.

I kept staring at him.

After a moment or two, he cleared his throat and said, 'People are different, that's all I'm saying.'

I didn't reply.

'I don't mean different like *that*,' he said, trying to dig himself out of a hole. 'I just mean that some people *mean* more than others ...' He sighed, realising that he was only making things worse ... and I suddenly understood what I was doing. He was right – I *was* twisting his words. I was making him think that his views offended me. I was forcing him to defend himself when he had nothing to defend. I was manipulating him, basically. Manipulating his fears and his prejudices. I knew it was wrong, and I could feel the guilt stirring inside me ...

But I did my best to ignore it.

Sitting in silence ...

Suffering my false indignation ...

'All right,' Dad said eventually. 'Where is this concert, anyway?'

Yes! I thought.

'Hammersmith,' I said quietly.

'What time does it finish?'

'Not too late ... I'd probably be back by eleven.'

He nodded slowly. 'All right ... I'll think about it.'

'Thanks, Dad.'

'I didn't say you could *go* – I just said I'll think about it. So don't go thinking you've got one over on me, because you haven't – understand?'

'Of course.'

'And,' he continued, 'whatever decision I make, that's it. That's my final answer. I don't want any more arguments – OK?'

'Yeah.'

'I mean it, Joe. I want your word that you'll accept my decision, otherwise I'm not even going to think about it.'

'OK,' I said. 'I promise.'

He gave me a doubtful look.

'Scout's honour,' I said, struggling to find some sincerity. 'Cross my heart and hope to die.'

'It's not a joke.'

'I *know*. I'm serious, Dad – I mean it, honestly. I promise ...'

Another look, this one a tiny bit warmer, then he took a deep breath, stretched his back, and let out a long, drawn-out sigh.

'All right,' he said. 'Go on, then. You'd better get yourself something to eat, and then I think an early night might be in order.'

'OK,' I said, getting up, relieved that it was all over at last.

'And Joe ...?' added Dad.

I looked down at him. He suddenly seemed very old. Tired and grey, his long face ashen and lined, his body framed in the dark formality of an ancient suit ...

He looked as if he'd never been young. Never been anything but old.

'Yes, Dad?' I said.

His eyes fixed sadly on mine for a moment, and I thought he was going to say something, something that would probably embarrass us both ... but after a second or two he blinked the sadness away and said, 'Nothing ... it's nothing. Go on, off you go. I'll see you later.'

'Yeah ... OK. I'm sorry about everything ...'

He nodded silently, staring down at the table.

I stood there for a moment, unsure what to do. Part of me wanted to say something else, to let Dad into my mind, to show him the truth of my feelings; but another part – the cowardly part – just wanted to get out of there. And that part was stronger.

So, with a headful of conflicting emotions, I said goodnight, then turned around and shuffled out.

It's funny how easy it is to believe your own lies. All the time I was in Dad's study, all the time he was lecturing me about responsibility and discipline and wasting my life, all the time I was apologising for skiving off school and spending the day in London ... all that time, and it never even occurred to me that I was lying through my teeth. As far as I was concerned, I *had* gone to London to sort out a problem with the gig. It *didn't* mean anything. I *was* sorry. It *wouldn't* happen again.

I believed it.

It was the only way to live the lie.

But as soon as I was out of Dad's study, the truth suddenly hit me. The real truth – Candy, the zoo, Moonlight World – and I realised that I'd just been lectured and punished for something I hadn't actually done. Admittedly, I'd done something worse and got away with it, but still ...

Still what? said the voice in my head. *You were lucky, really. You know that, don't you? You were lucky. It could have been a whole lot worse ...*

When I went upstairs, I found Gina waiting for me in my bedroom.

'How did it go?' she asked anxiously.

She was sitting on the floor, flicking through the pages of a music magazine, and it looked as if she'd been there a while. A ragged circle of books and CDs and empty coffee cups had formed on the floor around her.

'I hope you're going to clear all that up,' I said, nodding at the mess on the floor.

She gave me a friendly sneer, then got back to the subject. 'Come on – what did Dad have to say?'

'Quite a lot.'

She shook her head. 'I'm sorry, Joe – I had to tell him. He was really worried about you. If I hadn't told him, he would have called the police—'

'It's all right,' I said, sitting on the bed. 'It's not your fault.'

'He would have found out anyway—'

'Yeah, I know – don't worry about it. I shouldn't have got you involved in the first place.' I looked at her. 'What did he say when you told him you'd rung up school for me? Did he go mad at you?'

'Not really. I think he was too pissed off with you to bother about me.' She looked up. 'Are you grounded?'

'Yep.'

'How long?'

'Until he gets back from wherever he's going next week. Where *is* he going, anyway? To the cottage?'

'No, it's a work thing, in Edinburgh – the society's annual conference.' She smiled. 'Gynaecologists galore ...' The smiled faded. 'He's going with Mum, they're making a week of it.'

I nodded absent-mindedly, thinking about the cottage ... Woodland Cottage. I hadn't thought about it for a long time. It's a little holiday place that Dad bought years ago, a rustic wooden bungalow hidden away in a little village on the Suffolk coast. We used to go there quite a lot when Mum was still around. It's a really nice place – right out in the middle of nowhere, quiet and peaceful, surrounded by woods and fields, with a quiet little estuary nearby ...

'Joe?' said Gina.

'Sorry – what?'

'Did you get it sorted out?'

'Get what sorted out?'

'Whatever it was you went to London for – the really important thing about the gig. Remember?'

'Oh, right ... yeah, no problem. It's all ... uhh ...'

'Sorted out?'

'Yeah.' I smiled. 'Everything's ready.'

'You're still doing it?'

'Yeah – why not?'

'I thought you said you were grounded?'

'I'm on parole for the day.'

'That's great. I'm really looking forward to it.'

I looked at her – momentarily speechless. I'd forgotten she was coming.

'What?' she said, frowning at my puzzled look, then realising what it meant. 'Oh, come *on*, Joe ... you *invited* me. Bring Mike along, you said—'

'Yeah, yeah ... I know ...'

'Don't you *want* us to come?'

'Of *course* I do ... it just slipped my mind for a minute, that's all.' I leaned down and ruffled her hair. 'Sorry.'

'Yeah, well ...'

'Don't be such a sulk.'

'I'm not.'

I smiled at her.

She smiled back.

And we were OK again. We carried on talking for a while, not really saying anything, just passing the time, then eventually Gina got up and kissed me goodnight and left me alone with my thoughts.

It was a lot to be left alone with – Dad, lies, Candy, lies, Gina, lies ... so many lies it was hard to keep track of the truth.

I started to clear away the rubbish that Gina had left on the floor.

One thing at a time, I kept telling myself. *Take one thing at a time. There's no point in worrying about Friday until you know for sure that Dad's going to let you go. If he doesn't let you go, then it won't matter what happens when Candy turns up and Gina and Mike are there ... it won't matter how you try to explain things, because you won't be there, and neither will Gina and Mike, so there won't be anything to explain.*

Right?

The thing was, though, I knew in my heart that I *would* be there. It wasn't just wishful thinking, it was a stone-cold fact, as inevitable as night follows day. No matter what Dad said, no matter what he decided, no matter what promises I'd made – I'd be there.

No matter what.

I'd be there, Candy would be there, Gina and Mike would be there ...

It was going to happen.

So, I *could* worry about it.

And I did.

And then, after a while, I stopped worrying, and I started thinking instead. Thinking about Candy, and Gina and Mike, and the gig, and me ...

And, finally, as I got into bed, the thinking turned to something else, and I was alone in the dark with Candy.

chapter eight

The Black Room, Friday night. It was just gone eight o'clock, and things were going from bad to worse. The soundcheck had been a disaster, the dressing room was a toilet, and Jason was out of control. He'd taken some speed to calm his nerves – a monumentally stupid thing to do – and now he was racing around all over the place, all wired up and fried to the eyeballs, sniffing and twitching like a lunatic.

'Where's my fags? Who's got them? Who's got my bloody *cigarettes*? What's this? *Christ!* Who put that in there? What's the time? Where's the song-list? *Jesus!* This is ri*dic*ulous ...'

We'd arrived late, which wasn't the best way to start. There'd been a mix-up with the hire van, so we hadn't left Heystone until nearly six, and then Jason had taken a wrong turn on the way into London, and we'd driven around God-knows-where for ages, trying to find Hammersmith. And then, when we'd finally arrived, there'd been all sorts of problems with the equipment, the worst of which was Bluntslide refusing to lend us their PA. As far as we were concerned, it had all been agreed in advance – as long as their sound engineer ran the show, we could use their PA system. Which was fine with us, seeing as how we didn't have a sound engineer anyway. But when we started setting up our gear for the soundcheck, sorting out the mikes and the sound levels and everything, the guy who managed Bluntslide got all snotty about it.

'That's five grand's worth of brand new equipment there. I'm not having a bunch of kids messing around with that.'

He was a really nasty piece of work – a ratty little guy with razor-sharp shoes and a face to match. I think he thought it was part of his job to argue about things, whether they needed arguing about or not. Either that, or he just enjoyed being a pain in the arse. Anyway, after lots of arguing – and lots of manic screaming from Jason – he eventually changed his mind and grudgingly agreed to let us use their precious PA. But by then it was getting on for eight o'clock, so we didn't have much time for the soundcheck, and Bluntslide's engineer wasn't that interested in helping us out, and Jason kept storming off all the time ...

So, basically, we ended up with a really crappy sound, which was good for Bluntslide – as it'd make them sound better – but really bad for us.

'Even the bloody monitors aren't working properly,' Chris fumed, back in the dressing room. 'I can hardly hear what I'm playing.'

'I can hear what *I'm* playing,' said Ronny, 'but I can't hear anyone else.'

'God!' spat Jason, throwing a beer can against the wall. 'This is *shit*!'

I just sat there, sipping from a can of beer, looking

around the dressing room. It really *was* a toilet. The sinks and cubicles and urinals had been taken out, and a couple of benches and a table put in, but it still looked and smelled like a toilet. The walls were covered in graffiti, bare pipes sagged from the ceiling, and there was just one tiny window at the back, a small square of frosted glass in a mildewed frame.

As Jason and the others carried on drinking and smoking and moaning, I leaned back against the wall and let my mind drift back to the day before, when Dad had called me into his study to give me his decision.

'After careful consideration of the circumstances,' he'd told me in a solemn voice, 'I've decided to let you attend your concert.'

Thanks, Dad, I thought to myself now, looking round the room again, *thanks a lot.* And I started laughing.

Jason stopped ranting and stared at me. 'What's the matter with you?'

'Nothing,' I said, still laughing.

'Come on – what's so funny?'

'This ... us ... everything ...' I waved my hand around the dressing room. 'The Big Time – we've finally made it ...'

Ronny started chuckling along with me, but Jason and Chris didn't get it, or didn't *want* to get it. They just stood there staring at me. Jason kept licking his lips, flicking his tongue in and out like a lizard. His eyes were bulging so much I thought they were going to explode. He looked ridiculous. I couldn't stop laughing. After a while, Jason gave up on me and turned his attention to Ronny. Ronny carried on laughing for a while, but he couldn't keep it up under Jason's glare, and before long his laugh had faded to an embarrassed mumble and he'd lowered his eyes to the floor.

'Idiot,' Jason muttered, turning his back on him. 'God, this place is a shit-hole. What's the time?'

'Eight-thirty,' said Chris.

'Half an hour to go,' said Jason, shaking his head. 'Christ, I need a proper drink.'

'The bar's open,' Chris suggested.

Jason wiped his nose. 'No – let's get out of here. There's a pub across the road. We might as well get pissed – the gig's gonna be shit anyway. Come on ...'

He grabbed his jacket and strode off. Chris tagged along in his wake, leaving me and Ronny behind in the dressing room. I didn't really know Ronny that well. He was always pretty quiet, keeping himself to himself, and he seemed quite happy to stay in the background. I liked him for that, but we'd never got round to talking very much.

'You all right?' I asked him.

'Yeah ...'

'Don't let Jason get to you,' I said.

Ronny shrugged his shoulders. 'Jase is all right, really. He doesn't mean anything. He just gets a bit worked up about things.'

'He wants to lay off the speed,' I said. 'It doesn't agree with him.'

'Not much does.'

I laughed. 'If he carries on flicking his tongue in and out, someone's going to shoot him and turn him into a pair of shoes.'

Ronny grinned quietly.

We sat there for a while, not speaking, just looking around at the grubby walls, the stained ceiling, the empty beer cans scattered around the floor ... and I thought to myself – *if this is the dressing room, imagine what the toilets are like.*

And I started laughing again.

Ronny looked at me.

I shook my head.

He said, 'D'you want to go to the pub?'

'Might as well.'

And off we went.

It was only a short walk across the road, but the sudden shock of the cold night air was enough to set my head spinning. The rush of oxygen, the effect of the beer, the nerves, the adrenalin, the prospect of seeing Candy again ... it all came together at once, filling my head with a raw and dizzying sickness that drained the blood from my legs.

Inside the pub, the atmosphere was hot and sweaty and choked with cigarette smoke. As I followed Ronny across the bar, looking for Jason and Chris, I thought I was going to throw up.

Ronny looked over his shoulder and shouted something at me.

'What?' I shouted back.

He nodded at the jukebox. 'Nine Inch Nails.'

'What?' I yelled.

'Never mind.'

'I CAN'T HEAR YOU!'

'NEVER MIND!'

We found Jason and Chris at a table in the corner. Chris was just drinking Coke, but Jason had what looked like a triple vodka. And from the look on his face, it wasn't his first. Or his second.

Ronny leaned into my ear and said, 'We've only got about fifteen minutes – d'you want me to get you two or three?'

'Two or three what?'

'Whatever ...' He slapped my shoulder. 'Don't worry – I'll get you something.'

He went to the bar.

I sat down and glanced around, looking for Gina and Mike. Gina had said they might go somewhere for a drink first, and this was the nearest pub ... but I couldn't see them anywhere. There was no sign of Candy, either. Not that I expected to see her. Then again, I didn't really know what to expect.

'You fit?' Jason said to me.

I looked at him. His face was deathly white and covered in pale pink blotches. His eyes were all over the place.

'You all right?' I asked him.

'Yeah ... I'm all right,' he slurred. 'How about you? You ready to go ... Joe?'

'I suppose.'

'You suppose?'

'Yeah.'

He laughed and took a long drink, staring wildly at me. I couldn't be bothered with him like that, so I looked away, glancing over at a bunch of black guys standing next to Ronny at the bar. There were about six of them, all mean and hard, and they were giving Ronny some serious looks. He didn't seem to be aware of them. Either that, or he was really good at hiding it. As I was watching, one of them turned his head and looked at me. I held his gaze for a moment, then quickly looked down at the floor. I might have been a bit out of it, but I was sober enough to recognise those eyes. They were the same eyes I'd seen in McDonald's that time, when I'd dropped all my money on the floor – the frozen eyes that had made me sweat. I was sure of it. And I was pretty sure I recognised some of the others now. The hammered eyes, the razored heads, the hoods ... they were the same guys Candy had spoken to when she'd retrieved my £1 coin from under their table.

What did *that* mean?

I was still thinking about it when Ronny came back and sat down next to me. 'There you go,' he said, placing a drink on the table. He looked at Jason. 'Sorry, Jase, did you want—'

'We'd better go,' Jason said, draining his glass. 'Come on, drink up.'

I looked at the glass in front of me – a tall half-pint of clear liquid. I picked it up and sniffed.

'What is it?' I asked Ronny.

'Just *drink* it,' Jason snapped, getting unsteadily to his feet. 'Come on, let's get back and get this done.'

Chris and Ronny got up from the table, and the three of them stood there, looking down at me, waiting for me to finish my drink.

'Are you coming or what?' said Jason.

I raised the glass to my mouth and drank it all down in one, almost gagging on the breathtaking burn of alcohol. Whatever it was, there was a lot of it, and I could already feel the numbing heat seeping into my veins.

'Christ,' muttered Jason, stabbing a glance at his watch. 'Come *on* ... let's *go*.'

'You go on,' I choked. 'I'm just going to the toilet – I'll catch you up in a minute.'

I didn't really need to go to the toilet, I just needed time to be on my own for a while. We'd been buzzing and drinking and arguing ever since we'd left Heystone, and it was all getting a bit too much for me. To tell you the truth, I wasn't really used to it. Not all at once, anyway. I'd had the odd drink before, and it wasn't as if the adrenalin or the friction were anything new, but the non-stop combination of all three, together with the cold and the heat and the noise and the nerves, and the shock of recognising the guys at the bar, and the ever-present clamp that Candy had on my heart ...

It was all too much.

I stumbled into the toilets and threw up in a sink. Coughing, retching, spluttering ... my stomach turning inside out ...

'Christ's sake,' muttered a man at the hand-dryer.

'Sorry,' I said, my head still buried in the sink.

He shook his head in disgust, tutted loudly, then walked out.

I went into a cubicle and locked the door.

Breathe in, I told myself. *Sit down. Breathe deeply. Relax.*

I gazed around the cubicle. The walls were scrawled with graffiti – stupid dirty pictures, stupid dirty words, telephone numbers, dirty messages, threats, taunts, grim little peep-holes stuffed with screwed-up wads of toilet paper ...

Outside, the door swung open, letting in the muffled boom of the jukebox, and I heard the sound of footsteps slouching across the floor. The door slammed shut, the footsteps stopped, and I heard voices – black and hard.

'... he didn't say. Just come here and wait, he said ... ring him if we see her.'

'Why?'

'Dunno ... she's playing around, getting sweet ...'

Feet shuffled, zips unzipped, and I heard the sound of loud peeing and extravagant sighs.

One of them farted.

The other one said, 'You ask me, she's scratching him out for a deal.'

'Yeah?'

'Boys up here, you know? The Westway ...'

'They ain't gonna want her if he finds out. He finds out, she ain't worth *nothing*.'

Then the door opened again and some other people came in – male voices, talking loudly, laughing and swearing, hooting and hollering – and I couldn't hear what the black guys were saying any more. I carried on listening, just in case, but all I could hear was an echoed confusion of voices, shouts, hissing pipes, and the constant roar of the hand-dryer. For all I knew, the black guys weren't even out there any more. *And anyway*, I told myself, *whatever they were talking about, it's not likely to have anything to do with you, is it? Just because you've seen them before, and they're looking for a girl ... I mean, for God's sake ... Candy's not the only girl in the world, is she? What's the* matter *with you?*

I sat there for a while, thinking things over, trying to think reasonably, logically, soberly ... and in the end I decided I was right – I was just being paranoid.

Candy *wasn't* the only girl in the world ...

And I wasn't the only boy.

It just felt that way.

Back in the dressing room, there was just enough time to strap on my bass and run through a tune-up with Jason and Chris, and then we were on. There was no curtain or anything, no dramatic entrance – we just walked out onto the stage and started plugging our guitars in. The house-lights were still on, the DJ was still playing records, and the dance-floor was empty. There were a few bored faces sitting around tables, talking and drinking, and I recognised a couple of kids at the back who'd made the long journey from Heystone to see us, but that was about it. I was hoping there were lots of people still in the bar, and that as soon as we started playing they'd all come rushing out.

But it didn't look too promising.

I was still pretty excited, though. Plugging in, thumping the E-string, cranking up the volume a couple of notches, looking around at the rest of the group. Ronny was cracking his snare drum, adjusting his seat, stomping the bass drum – *domp domp domp*. Chris was checking his pedals, stepping through the buttons – *chunk, sssss, uurr-danggg* – then putting his head down and chopping out some big dirty chords. And Jason ... Jason was looking surprisingly good. Frazzled and weird, and kind of scary, but good. He'd taken his shirt off and slicked back his hair, and with his guitar slung carelessly around his back, and his staring eyes fixed to the floor, he was prowling the stage and muttering to himself like some kind of madman.

I looked at Chris and Ronny, and I knew they were feeling the same as me – that something was about to happen. I don't think any of us knew what it was, but we knew it was there. We could feel it all around us – the charge in the air, the power, the spark ... the thrill of a ticking bomb.

And now it was about to go off.

The DJ was fading out the record, the house-lights were going down, and the stage was dimming to darkness. Just for a moment, the room was silent and black.

Then the DJ said, 'Ladies and gentlemen – The Katies.'

And all at once the stage erupted in a blaze of light, the drums kicked off with a whipcrack beat, and then we all piled in with a deafening blast of guitars.

God, it was good.

It was *incredible*.

I don't know why, or how, but everything just came together – the sound, the energy, the music, the lights ... it all just fused to a gut-wrenching *perfection*. We'd never played so good. We were awesome. We were that good, I almost wished I was out there on the dance-floor myself. The crowd were going mental. I mean, we were killing them, knocking them dead. They couldn't get enough of us. It was unbelievable. The sound was suddenly flawless – raw and loud and clear – and the songs had never sounded better: tight and fast, full of power, fresh, electric, exciting. We were *hot*, and we knew it – me and Ronny thumping out the backbeat, solid as a rock; Chris ripping the hell out of his guitar; Jason singing and dancing and screaming like a god ...

For the first three songs, I just kept my head down and played. It was hot under the lights, and I was soon drenched in sweat. It was flooding out of me, streaming from my skin, and as it poured out I could feel all the sickness and crap I'd been feeling before pouring out with it, until all that was left was the primitive thrill of the music, pumping away inside me. And that didn't *need* any feelings or thoughts. I could sense the crowd without seeing them. I could feel them moving to the music, getting off on it, getting into it. I could hear the applause and the cheering. I was vaguely aware that the crowd was getting bigger all the time, but when I finally looked up, at the end of the third song, I was shocked to see that the club was nearly full. The dance-floor was packed. All the tables were taken. People were coming in from the bar, trying to find somewhere to stand. Even the Bluntslide guys had come out to watch us.

It was amazing.

While Jason introduced the next song, I shielded my

eyes from the lights and scanned the faces in the crowd. It was hard to pick out any details in the darkness, but I was pretty sure that Candy wasn't there. I kept looking though, and when I heard someone call out my name, I thought for a moment I'd found her. At a corner table, at the back, waving a hand ... then I realised it was Gina. She was all dolled up for the night, and I suppose the familiarity of her face confused me for a second ... or maybe I was trying a bit *too* hard to see Candy? I don't know. Anyway, when I realised it wasn't Candy, my heart sank for a second, but then Gina smiled and whooped, and Mike – who was sitting beside her – grinned and raised his fist, and the sinking feeling disappeared.

It was good to see them.

Not as good as seeing Candy ...

But then, you can't have everything, can you?

'You ready, Joe?' Jason said.

I nodded, wiping the sweat from my strings.

Jason lit a cigarette and turned back to the crowd. 'OK,' he said into the microphone. 'This one's called – *Girl on Fire*.'

I hit the opening rockabilly riff, thumping it out hard and fast, and then the drums and guitars came crashing in, and we were off again, tearing the house down.

Half an hour later, when we came to the closing number, the atmosphere inside the club was almost too good to be true. The whole place was jam-packed, a seething mass of noise and sweat and dancing bodies, and no one wanted the show to stop, least of all us. But we didn't have any choice. It was Bluntslide's gig, not ours, and we'd agreed with them on a forty-five-minute set. Anything over that and they'd be seriously pissed off. Mind you, it didn't really matter because we only had enough songs for forty-five minutes, anyway.

Up until then, we'd always played a Lou Reed number to close the set – a song called *Sweet Jane*. It's a bit old-fashioned, but it's got a really nice riff to it, and we play it a lot faster than the original, and we really mash it up at the end ... so it's a pretty good song to finish on.

That night, though, just as we were getting ready to start *Sweet Jane*, Jason called us all over to the drum-kit and suggested we do something different.

'Like what?' said Chris. 'We haven't *got* anything else.'

'Yeah, we have,' Jason said, looking at me. 'Joe's song ... the one we've been working on – *Candy*.'

Chris shook his head. 'No, it's not ready yet ... we've only played it a couple of times—'

'It's *perfect*,' said Jason. 'It'll murder them ... *and* it's ours.' He looked at me again. 'What do you think?'

'I don't know. I suppose ...'

He looked at Ronny. 'You OK with it?'

Ronny nodded.

Chris said, 'I'm not sure, Jase. Let's stick with what we know ...'

But Jason had already made up his mind. He said to me, 'Give Chris the bass, you take the guitar part – OK?'

'Yeah ... all right. What about the words? Can you remember them?'

He grinned at me. 'I don't have to. It's your song – you sing it.' And with that he went back to the microphone, apologised for the delay, and started to introduce the song.

Chris, meanwhile, was giving me a shitty look. I didn't really blame him. It was the last song of a great set, and he wanted to end it doing what he did best – playing the guitar. And now I was stealing his thunder. If I was him, I know I wouldn't have liked it. But Jason was right – *Candy* was a brilliant song to end on. And it *was* one of ours. And I could play the guitar part better than Chris. Not because I was better than him, because I wasn't. Chris was a genius. He could play anything. But *Candy* was a really simple song, and it needed a really simple sound, and Chris was just too *good* to be simple. *Candy* was a blues song – it was made of empty spaces. And, unlike me, Chris was just too good to leave the spaces alone.

'I'm sorry—' I started to tell him.

'It's OK,' he said, unstrapping his guitar and passing it over. He still didn't look too happy about it, but he didn't look *too* sulky, either. I think he knew it was the right thing to do.

With a slight nod of his head, he said, 'Let's make it good.'

I nodded back, gave him my bass, and we both went back to the front of the stage.

Jason introduced me, then stepped aside to let me have the microphone. As I adjusted the mike and strummed a few chords on the guitar, I started feeling really weird. I'd never sung on stage before. I'd never been pushed to the front. I'd never had so many people looking at me. And I didn't know what it was I was feeling. It was like a mixture of fear and some kind of wondrous discovery. A sense of – *this is it, Joe, this is your time and your place, right here, right now.*

I knew I couldn't think about it, though. If I started to think, I'd freeze on the spot. So I just started playing. Quietly at first, just gently stroking the chords, finding the feel and the rhythm ... then gradually I started building things up, strumming more confidently ... and the harmonies rang out across the room, slow and spiky and edgy, and then the bass came in, beefing things up, and the drums, and Jason's guitar started wailing in the background, and I could hear the melody in my head, calling out to be sung, and I raised my head to the microphone ...

And that's when I saw Candy.

She was standing right at the front, just as she said she would. No more than a few metres away from me, looking up, her eyes fixed on mine, her face a picture of pure delight. She was dressed to kill in skin-tight jeans and a short black T-shirt, her arms tied with leather laces, her hair spiked up, her eyes painted black. She looked fantastic.

My breath caught in my throat for a moment, then a wave of energy surged through me, and I opened my mouth and started to sing:

The girl at the station,
the girl with the smile,
the moment's temptation,
to stay for a while ...

Simple words for a simple song. And, somehow, I didn't feel embarrassed singing them. I should have, I suppose, seeing as the girl in question was right there in front of me. But, for some weird reason, I didn't. Maybe it was because I wasn't actually looking at her while I sang. In fact, I wasn't looking at anything. My eyes were closed to the song. The music, the words, the trance-like rhythm, rising through the dark to the echo-sweet swirl of the chorus:

Candy, your eyes
Take me away,
Take me away,
Take me away ...

I don't know what the words mean, if they mean anything. They just came to me the night I first met her, when I was sitting at home, strumming the guitar. They were the words of the moment, and that's all the song was about, really – a moment.

As the chorus finished, I stepped back from the microphone to concentrate on the guitar part that brought us back to the verse again. It was one of my favourite bits of the whole song, a really nice little guitar break. Dead easy to play, but it sounded great.

I glanced down at Candy. She was dancing now. All alone, her eyes closed, dancing for the sheer hell of it, moving like a dream. She looked so alive, like a child lost in time ...

I could have played that song for ever.

It had to come to an end, though, and when it finally did, following a thunderous roar of drums and guitars, the sudden ringing silence seemed to shock everyone. Just for a moment, no one moved, no one made a sound ... and then, all at once, the whole place exploded, with everyone cheering and clapping and calling out for more, and the vibration of their stomping feet echoing through the floor ...

It was breathtaking.

An indescribable feeling.

As Jason said goodnight to the crowd, and we switched off our amps and trooped off the stage, we all had the same dazed look on our faces – a blend of intoxication and pure fatigue. I was exhausted, mentally and physically drained. My ears were ringing, my fingers were bleeding, my clothes were soaked in sweat. I'd never felt better in my life.

I felt so good, I almost forgot about Candy.

I stopped and turned around and stepped back onto the stage. The house-lights were on again, and when some of the still-cheering crowd spotted me, they thought we were coming back for an encore. The cheering got louder – 'more, more, more' – and I started feeling a little bit stupid. I don't know why, but I suddenly felt as if I didn't belong there any more. It was really odd. I'd felt perfectly at home a few minutes ago – standing in the spotlight, singing and playing my heart out – but now the stage felt so alien to me that I was scared to venture too far from the edges.

Until, that is, I saw what was happening.

At first I thought it was just another fight, and I wasn't particularly worried about it. You get them all the time in places like The Black Room – drunken scuffles, a few punches, arguments that get out of hand. They don't usually come to much. This one didn't seem any worse than the rest – raised voices, a bit of pushing and shoving ... I couldn't really see very much as it was all going on at the back of the club, next to the doors, behind a crowd of onlookers. I wasn't that interested anyway. I just wanted to find Candy ... ask her out for a drink or something ... see what she thought of the gig ... maybe introduce her to Gina and Mike. Or maybe not. I didn't know. I just wanted to find her, that's all.

She wasn't down at the front of the stage any more, so I was scanning the crowd, searching the room, looking out for her face ... but so far I wasn't having any luck.

I heard Jason calling out to me from the corridor. 'Joe! Where are you? Come on, there's some record company guys here. They want to talk to us. Joe!'

'Yeah,' I called back. 'I won't be a minute.'

I carried on looking, searching the roomful of faces.

Come on, Candy ... where are *you?*

Just then, the scuffle at the back of the club got louder again, and my eyes were drawn to the noise. A gap had appeared in the crowd now, and I could see some of the people involved. The first person I recognised was one of the black guys I'd seen earlier in the pub. Then – with growing unease – I noticed another, and another ... and another. They were *all* there. Half a dozen of them, standing in a semi-circle with their backs to the door, facing down another black guy. This one had his back to me, so I couldn't see his face ...

But I knew who it was.

It was Mike.

I started moving to the front of the stage.

'Joe!' Jason called after me. 'Come on, man ... what are you *doing*?'

I ignored him, moving faster.

I could see Gina now. She was standing to one side, screaming at someone behind the six black guys. I couldn't see who it was. One of the black guys made a move towards her and Mike stepped up and whacked him in the head. As he went down, two of the others started kicking at Mike, and I jumped off the stage and started pushing my way through the crowd.

It was hard going. Everyone was still buzzing from the show, and people kept grabbing me, telling me how much they'd enjoyed it, asking where we were playing next ...

'Sorry,' I kept saying. 'Excuse me, sorry, sorry ...'

The noise from the doors had quietened now, and I didn't like the sound of it. It was *too* quiet. I squeezed through a gap in the crowd and jumped on a chair to see what was happening ...

And my legs went weak.

What was happening was Iggy.

Backing out of the door, dragging Candy with him, his passionless eyes covering the room like two loaded pistols ... he looked like nothing and everything, all at once. Nothing – no life, no feelings, no fear. And everything – size, strength, the power of violence. He had it all. The rest of his crew were watching his back, guarding his exit, but he didn't need them. He didn't *need* anything.

From the corner of my eye I could see Mike lying prone on the floor, and Gina bending over him with tears in her eyes. The sight of them should have been enough to take my mind off everything else, but when Iggy paused, halfway through the door, and fixed me with his deadly stare, the rest of the world disappeared.

I was alone in the darkness, standing on a chair, and all I could see was the sterile light of Iggy's eyes, searing into mine.

Stilling me.

Draining me.

Shrinking me to impotence.

He still had Candy gripped by the arm. She wasn't struggling at all, she was just standing there, hanging from his hand like a lifeless trophy, waiting to be taken away. Iggy's lips moved – a silent word in her ear – and she languidly turned her head towards me. I caught a brief glimpse of her lightless eyes, a glazed look of recognition, and then she was gone, ghosted away into the night.

chapter nine

By the time I'd got down off the chair and made my way over to the door, there wasn't much left to see. Candy and Iggy were long gone, Iggy's crew had disappeared, and now that the fight was over, most of the onlookers had lost interest and were beginning to drift away. Things seemed strangely *normal*. Apart from the state of Mike's face, and Gina's obvious shock, it was hard to tell there'd been any trouble at all.

Mike wasn't hurt too badly. He'd taken some hefty kicks to his head and his ribs, and his mouth and nose were bleeding a bit, but at least he was back on his feet again. In fact, he was more than back on his feet – he was livid. Standing tall, glaring angrily around the club, trying to work out what had happened.

'Where'd they go?' he spat. 'Where's the big guy? Where's the girl ...?'

Gina was trying to calm him down – holding him, hugging him, fussing with the wounds on his head – but she looked pretty shaky herself. Her hands were trembling, her lips were quivering, and her shocked-white face was streaked with tears.

I didn't know what to do.

I didn't know what I *wanted* to do.

I wanted to rush out into the street and start looking for Candy, but that would mean leaving Gina ... and I didn't want to do that. She was my sister. She was hurt and upset. I wanted to be with *her* ... where I belonged. And besides, I knew in my heart that looking for Candy was a waste of time. Even if I *did* find her, she'd be with Iggy and his crew, and what chance would *I* have against *them*?

So I stayed where I was, my heart beating hard, watching Gina as she hugged the life out of Mike.

After a while, Mike spotted me over her shoulder.

'Hey, Joe,' he grinned. 'Great night out – thanks for inviting us.' He wiped some blood from his mouth.

'Are you all right?' I asked him.

He nodded. 'I'll live.'

Gina let go of him and turned to face me. She was still crying. I went over and put my arms around her.

'Are you OK?' I said.

'Yeah ...' She lowered her voice. 'God, Joe, I thought they were going to *kill* him.'

'What happened?' I said. 'How did it start?'

She sniffed and wiped her nose. 'I don't know ... there was this girl—'

'Christ – what are you *doing*?' a voice interrupted. I looked around to see Jason walking briskly towards us. His face was all twitchy and tight, and his eyes were alight with a curious mixture of anger and excitement. He came over and grabbed me by the arm. 'Come *on*,' he said, pulling me towards the dressing room, 'they wanna see you.'

'Who?' I said, shrugging his hand away.

'The record company guys ...' His face lit up. 'They're really keen, Joe. They wanna talk to us ... *all* of us. Come *on*—'

'I can't—'

'What do you mean, you *can't*? This is big stuff—'

'I have to talk to my sister—'

'Your *sister*?' His face screwed up in disgust. '*Sod* your sister. This is important—'

'So is this.'

He glared at me, his eyes a rage of disbelief, and I thought for a moment he was going to hit me. I know I felt like hitting *him*, and if Gina hadn't stepped forward and put her hand on my arm, I think I probably would have.

'It's all right, Joe,' she said calmly. 'I'd better take Mike home, anyway. We can talk about what happened later ... you go and see your record company people.'

I looked at her ... pale and quiet.

I looked at Jason ... forcing himself to smile, trying to control his anger, his contempt, his impatience.

It wasn't a hard choice to make.

'You'll have to do without me,' I told Jason.

His smile wavered. 'No, you don't understand, they wanna see *you*—'

'Tell them something came up—'

'Christ's *sake*, Beck,' he hissed. 'What's the *matter* with you? You can't just bugger off whenever you feel like it—'

'Look,' I said, 'I'm really sorry – OK? But I *need* to go home with my sister—'

'Why?'

'I just do, that's all.' I turned to Gina. 'Come on, let's go.'

'Are you sure?' she said, slightly puzzled. 'I mean, it's no big deal—'

'Yeah, it is,' I assured her.

She looked at me, her eyes full of questions. 'Is this about—?'

'Not now,' I said.

She gave me another thoughtful look, then nodded slowly, took Mike's arm, and started for the door.

I turned back to Jason. 'I'm sorry,' I said. 'I'll explain everything another time.'

'Yeah?' he said sulkily. 'And who says there'll *be* another time?'

I looked at him for a moment, started to say something, then decided against it. I just couldn't be bothered.

I turned my back on him and walked out.

It rained on the way home, a fine black rain that misted the air and dazzled the night with kaleidoscope lights. As Mike eased the car through the slick city streets and on towards the M25, I stared through the window at the starburst colours spinning in the darkness – the headlights, the streetlights, the bleak neon signs ... all blurred and vacant in the rain.

Blurred and vacant.

Cold as glass.

I couldn't think.

I'd tried ringing Candy on my mobile as soon as I'd got in the car, but the number was dead. No tone, no voice mail, no nothing. I didn't know what that meant. I didn't know what anything meant. I was torn in too many ways. Too many highs, too many lows, too many feelings all at once ... and I couldn't put a voice to a single one of them. I didn't know where to start.

But Gina did.

'I think it's time to talk,' she said, turning around in the passenger seat to face me. 'Is there something we ought to know about what happened tonight?'

'I'm not sure ...' I said.

'Come on, Joe ... all that stuff with what's-his-name, the singer – what was that all about? Why do you need to talk to me so much? Is it something to do with the fight?'

'I think so ...'

'You *think* so?'

'It's hard to explain ... look, I'm not trying to *hide* anything, it's just ... well, I don't know what happened with you and Mike ... and the girl.' I looked hard into Gina's eyes. 'I need to know what happened.'

She looked back at me, thinking hard, then she glanced across at Mike. Without turning his head, he said, 'Tell him.'

She told me.

'It was during the last song,' she said, 'the one you were singing. I was watching you, listening to you ... I couldn't believe how good you were, Joe. It was fantastic. *You* were fantastic. I couldn't take my eyes off you.'

'Yeah,' agreed Mike. 'It was really good.'

'Thanks,' I said.

Gina nodded. 'Anyway, I was watching you, and I was watching the crowd as well. They were really getting into it. Especially the girl at the front ... the one you kept looking at.' She paused, waiting for me to say something. When I didn't, she carried on. 'I thought at first she was just a girl ... you know, just a pretty girl you'd seen in the crowd ... but then I realised I'd seen her earlier—'

'Where?' I asked.

'In the toilets. About five minutes before the last song.' She looked carefully at me, her eyes hesitant, as if she was unsure what to say. 'Is she ... I mean, do you *know* her?'

'What was she doing?'

Gina didn't answer for a moment. She lowered her eyes, then looked up again as Mike flicked her a quick glance. She said to me, 'I went into a cubicle ... I thought it was empty ... but it wasn't. The lock was broken. She was in there ... this girl ... she was crouched on the seat, smoking heroin ...'

'Heroin?'

Gina nodded.

I said, 'Are you sure?'

'Positive. She had a strip of aluminium foil and—'

'She was *smoking* it?'

'Through a plastic straw.'

'I thought you had to inject heroin?'

Mike said, 'You can do what you like with it – smoke it, snort it, pop it ... whatever.'

I don't know why I felt shocked, really. I knew that Candy took drugs, and I'd kind of guessed it was heroin, but I suppose I'd chosen to ignore it, as if it didn't really matter, or it wasn't really *there* ...

But now it *was* there.

In all its dirt-cold reality.

And it was hitting me hard.

'Joe?' said Gina. 'Are you OK?'

I looked up, still plagued with the picture of Candy – crouched in a toilet cubicle, smoking heroin through a plastic straw ...

'Who is she?' Gina asked gently. 'Is it—?'

'What happened then?' I said. 'After you'd seen her?'

Gina hesitated again. Then she said, 'Nothing ... I just apologised and left her to it. She didn't seem to mind. She just sat there, smiling. I found another cubicle, then went back to Mike ... then, five minutes later, that's when I saw her again, dancing in front of you.'

I remembered how Candy looked – dancing alone, her eyes closed, moving like a dream, like a child lost in time ...

I gazed out of the car window. We were heading out of London now, speeding through the orange-lit darkness on the way back to Essex. The rain had stopped and the night was starless and black.

'What about the fight?' I asked Gina. 'How did that happen?'

She took a deep breath, picturing the scene. 'It was near the end of your song. A gang of black guys had been hanging around the door for a while. They seemed as if they were waiting for someone. Mike had noticed them earlier and said they looked like trouble. Then this really big guy came in – big and hard, nasty-looking, scary eyes. One of the guys by the door went up to him and pointed out the girl at the front of the stage. The big guy looked over and nodded his head, then a couple of the guys by the door shoved their way to the front of the stage, grabbed the girl, and started dragging her back to the big guy.' Gina paused and looked at me. 'Didn't you see any of this?'

I shook my head.

'Well,' she continued, 'that's when it happened. I saw the girl getting dragged over to the big guy, and it was obvious she didn't *want* to go, she was really struggling ... and no one else seemed to be doing anything about it ... so I pointed it out to Mike.' She sighed. 'God, I wish I hadn't now. I wish I'd just turned a blind eye like everyone else.'

'No,' said Mike. 'You did the right thing.'

She looked at him. 'What – getting you beaten up?'

She turned to me. 'Mike tried to stop them. He went over and asked the two guys what they were doing, and the next thing I knew he was surrounded by the rest of the gang, getting the crap kicked out of him, and the big guy had taken the girl away.' She glanced at Mike again, reaching out and stroking his hair. 'I'm sorry, Mike – I got you involved for nothing.'

He smiled at her. 'Like I said – you did the right thing.'

Gina smiled back at him, then turned her attention to me. She didn't say anything, she just looked at me, waiting for an explanation.

I thought about lying again, making something up ... but it was all too complicated, and I was too tired to think, and Gina and Mike didn't deserve any more lies.

So I told them all about Candy.

I told them everything – finding her phone number, ringing her up, making a date, going to the zoo, asking her to the gig ...

'You went to the *zoo*?' Gina said incredulously.

'Yeah ...'

She stared at me, her eyes wide open, shaking her head in disbelief. 'Let me get this straight – when you rang her up, you *knew* she was a prostitute, didn't you?'

'Well, yeah ... I suppose ...'

'And this guy who was with her before, the one who threatened to cut your throat – you *knew* he was her pimp?'

'She said he was just someone she knew—'

'What – and you *believed* her?'

'Not really.'

'But you went ahead and made a date with her anyway?'

'Yeah ...'

'And you took her to the zoo?'

'Yeah ...'

'God, Joe ... I don't *believe* it. *Why*? Why would you *do* that?'

'Because ... I don't know ... because I like her, I suppose. She's nice ...'

'*Nice*?'

'Yeah.'

'She's a *prostitute*, for Christ's sake. A heroin addict ...' A sudden flash of fear crossed Gina's face. 'God, *you* haven't taken anything, have you? If she's been trying to get you—'

'No,' I said, shaking my head. 'I haven't taken anything, and she hasn't offered me anything.'

'Honestly?'

'I wasn't even sure what she was taking until you told me.'

'But you knew she was taking *something*?'

'Yeah,' I admitted, looking Gina in the eye, 'but that doesn't make her a monster or anything, does it? I mean, she's just a kid, the same as me. Do you think she *likes* what she's doing?'

'I don't know,' Gina shrugged. 'Have you asked her?'

'Sort of ...'

'And?'

'She lied – she told me she was a dancer.'

'A *dancer*? Oh, right – and this Iggy guy's her choreographer, I suppose?'

'Yeah, all right ... but she's bound to lie, isn't she? She's not going to go round telling everyone she's a prostitute—'

'She probably doesn't have to ...'

'What's *that* supposed to mean?' I said angrily.

'Nothing ... I'm sorry, I shouldn't have said that.'

'God,' I sighed. 'I thought *you'd* understand.'

Gina reached back between the seats and laid her hand on my knee. 'I'm sorry, Joe ... it's just ... well, it's hard. I mean, it's difficult. I'm your sister ...'

'Yeah ...'

'I'm just a bit shocked.'

'Me too.

She smiled gently and squeezed my knee. We looked at each other for a while, renewing our closeness, and my momentary anger began to ease. I don't often lose my temper, and I'm not sure why I did then. I suppose I was just disappointed with Gina – the way she was putting Candy down, making catty remarks, jumping to stupid conclusions ...

I don't know.

Maybe it was too much to expect, but I just wanted someone to understand how I felt.

'Are you OK?' Gina asked me quietly.

I nodded.

We drove on in silence for a while, the three of us lost in our thoughts, just drifting along to the hum of the engine and the hypnotic rush of the road. As I gazed through the rain-snaked window, I found myself wondering at the chain of events that had brought us all together – me, Candy, Gina, Mike, Iggy. How did it happen? Was it fate? Karma? Destiny? Did it mean anything? Or did it just happen, like everything else just happens?

What's the difference? I thought. *However it happened, it still* happened*, didn't it?*

I looked up and saw Mike watching me in the rear-view mirror. I nodded at him.

He nodded back, then cleared his throat and said, 'The big guy at the club ... I take it that was Iggy?'

'Yeah.'

'What about the others?'

'I don't know ... I saw them in the pub across the road earlier on. I think they might have been in McDonald's when I first met Candy.'

He nodded.

I said, 'I heard them talking in the pub ... they were looking out for someone.'

'Candy?'

'I didn't hear any names, but I suppose it must have been.'

Mike nodded again. 'They found her, called Iggy, and he came to get her. How'd they know where she was?'

'I don't know ... I gave her a poster for the gig ... maybe she left it lying around somewhere and Iggy found it.' I looked at Mike's eyes in the mirror. 'What do you think he'll do with her?'

'I don't know. Not much, probably. She works for him. He's not going to do anything that stops her earning ...' He looked at me again. I nodded, letting him know that I knew what he meant. I didn't *really* know, but I assumed he meant that Iggy wouldn't hurt her too much – at least, not where it showed.

'Is there anything we can do to help her?' I asked him.

'Like what?'

'I don't know ... how about calling the police?'

'No point,' he said, shaking his head. 'We don't know where she lives, we don't know where Iggy lives. And even if we did, there's not much the police can do unless she makes a complaint about him, and she won't do that because she needs him. She's an addict and he provides her with drugs. And besides, it's not as if he'll have her locked up or anything. She'll have her own flat, probably ... and there won't be anything to link her with Iggy, anyway – he'll have made sure of that. He knows what'll happen if the police get hold of her – they'll lock her up for a day or two, then let her go, and she'll go straight back to him.'

I didn't want to believe him, but I knew he was right.

'What about her parents?' Gina asked me. 'I mean, do you know where she comes from or anything?'

'Heystone, believe it or not,' I said. 'That's what she told me, anyway. She said she'd had some problems with her mum and dad and she'd left home to live in London. I think she's got a place around King's Cross somewhere.'

'You don't know where?'

'No.'

'Phone number?'

'Nothing – it's dead. Disconnected or something.'

Gina looked concerned now, but I couldn't tell if it was concern for me or concern for Candy. I hoped it was a bit of both.

She turned to Mike. 'Are you sure there's nothing we can do?'

'I could ask around, I suppose,' he said, 'see if anyone knows anything. But I'm not sure it'll make any difference. If she's addicted ...' He shrugged. 'She won't leave him – she *can't*. That's how it works.'

The rest of the journey was quiet. Gina spoke softly to Mike now and then, and occasionally she'd look back at me and ask if I was all right, but apart from that, it was a time for silence. The rain had started again, pattering faintly on the roof of the car, and the sound of it seemed to bring out the tiredness in me. I didn't *want* to be tired, I wanted to think, but my eyes were so heavy ... my mind so dull ... my body so drained ...

I couldn't think.

Couldn't imagine ...

And maybe that was for the best.

Because Candy was somewhere ... doing something ... and no matter how hard I tried to think, no matter how much I imagined ...

There was nothing I could to do to help her.

We got home around midnight. Dad was out, the house was quiet, and the rain was still coming down. Gina took Mike into the kitchen and started seeing to his battered face – cleaning the blood away, disinfecting the wounds, checking his head for unseen damage. I watched them for a while, but then I began to feel as if I was intruding.

I said, 'I think I'll be off to bed.'

'Don't you want any tea or anything?' Gina asked.

'No ... I'm really tired.' I looked at Mike. 'I'm really sorry about everything—'

'Not your fault,' he said kindly. 'Shit happens.'

'Yeah, I suppose ...'

'Hey, try not to worry too much – OK? You can't do anything about it right now ... and she'll probably be all right, anyway.'

'You reckon?'

'Yeah.'

I nodded. I didn't believe him, but I appreciated what he was trying to do.

'Look,' he said, 'I'll do what I can – all right? Like I said, I'll ask around and see what I can find out. If I hear anything, I'll let you know – OK?'

'Yeah, thanks.'

He nodded his head.

I said goodnight and made my way upstairs. In my room, I tried Candy's phone again, but there was still no tone – just an earful of emptiness. I got undressed and turned off the light and lay on the bed, staring into the darkness, trying to sleep. My body was aching with tiredness. My limbs were numb. My sightless eyes were crazed with lights.

I was dying for oblivion.

But it wouldn't come.

I didn't think I'd ever sleep again.

chapter ten

One of the worst things about feeling helpless is the constant intrusion of doubt. Even when you *know* there's nothing you can do about something, even when you're absolutely *sure*, even when you've considered every possibility, over and over again, knowing full well that you're wasting your time ... even then, you *still* can't help feeling that maybe you're wrong.

There must be *something* you can do.

Surely ...

There's *got* to be something ...

That's how it was with me, anyway. I wanted to do something about Candy. I *had* to do something. But what? What *could* I do?

That's all I kept asking myself –

What can I do?

I don't where she is ...

How can I do anything when I don't know where she is?

How can I find her?

What can I do?

There must be something ...

But there wasn't. No matter how hard I tried, I couldn't think of *any*thing. But that didn't stop me thinking, though. Even if I'd wanted to, I *couldn't* have stopped thinking. Thinking, thinking, thinking ... thinking of Candy ... all day Saturday, all day Sunday, sitting in my room, staring through the window, thinking, thinking, thinking ... asking myself the same old questions ... getting no replies ... wondering pointlessly what might have been ...

If only I'd given her my phone number.

If only I'd asked where she lived.

If only she hadn't come to the gig.

If only we could start all over again.

If only ...

I knew I was wasting my time, wishing that things were different, but time was all I had. I was still grounded, and Dad was keeping a close eye on me, so I was stuck in the house all weekend, then back to school on Monday, then straight back home after school, back to my room, back to the window, back to my staring, back to my thinking ...

I kept on trying to ring her, of course. Two or three times every day, I'd key in her number and pray for the phone to ring. I didn't know who – or what – I was praying to, and I didn't really care – I would have worshipped the Devil if he'd answered my prayers. But he didn't.

No one did.

There was no one there.

The days passed, as they do, and life went on.

Tuesday: I bumped into Jason, Chris and Ronny. They were in the year above me, so we didn't often see each other at school, but that Tuesday lunchtime I had a meeting with the careers advisor, and his office was in the building where Jason and the rest of them spent most of their time, and on the way back, as I was passing an empty classroom, I heard Chris's voice calling out to me.

'Joe! Hey, Joe.'

I stopped and looked through the door. All three of them were sitting at a table across the room, eating sandwiches and reading magazines. I hadn't spoken to them since Friday night's gig, so I didn't know what they thought about my unexplained and sudden departure from the club. I knew that Jason would still be pissed off with me, and I could tell by the look on his face that he was, but – at first glance – the rest of them seemed OK. They didn't look *delighted* to see me or anything, but at least they were acknowledging my existence.

Chris beckoned me over, and I went inside and joined them at the table.

'All right?' grinned Ronny.

'Yeah ...'

'What are you doing?' asked Chris.

'Not much.' I looked at Jason. He was pretending to read his magazine. I turned back to the others. 'Sorry about Friday,' I said. 'It was a family thing ... I really had to go—'

'Don't worry about it,' said Chris. 'It would have been better if you were there, but it didn't really matter in the end. They still want us.'

'Who?'

'Dead House – the record company. They're owned by EMI—'

'What – they've offered us a contract?

'Well, not exactly ...' He glanced at Jason, looking for support.

Jason pretended not to notice. He carried on reading his magazine for a moment, then he looked up casually, as if he hadn't been listening, and raised his eyebrows at Chris.

'What?' he said.

'I was just telling Joe about Dead House ...' Chris told him.

'And?'

Chris blinked.

Jason looked at him, then turned to me, trying to look bored. 'Yeah,' he said, 'they want us to do a proper demo for them. They're going to book us into a studio and bring in one of their producers to work with us. They want three tracks – *Girl on Fire*, *Candy*, and something else.'

'That's brilliant,' I said.

'Yeah ...' He shrugged.

'Are they paying for the studio?'

'They're paying for everything – studio, travel, expenses ... they might even buy us some new gear.'

'Fantastic,' I said. 'When do we do it?'

He shrugged again. 'Couple of weeks, maybe – they'll let us know.'

Ronny said, 'Pretty good, eh?'

'Yeah ...' I looked at Jason. He was still trying to appear nonchalant about the whole thing, but I could tell he was really excited. And I could tell he was still really annoyed with me, too.

What I *didn't* know was that it was about to get a lot worse.

'So,' he said to me. 'Are you all right for tomorrow?'

'What's tomorrow?'

'Wednesday,' he sneered. 'The day we practise – remember?'

'Oh, right ... yeah ... well, the thing is ...'

'What?'

'I'm grounded.'

'You're *what*?'

'I'm not allowed out.'

His eyes filled with scorn. 'You're not allowed *out*?'

'It's only for a week—'

'We need to *practise*. We've got to prepare for this demo—'

'Yeah, I know ... I'm sorry, but—'

'Christ!' he spat. 'I don't *believe* it. We're trying to get a deal here, we're *that* close to making it. We *need* to practise – and you're *not allowed out*? What do you think this is? A game? You think we're *playing* at something here?'

I almost said yes, just for the hell of it, just to see what he'd do. But I couldn't be bothered. I couldn't care less, to be honest. Yeah, it was embarrassing – being grounded, treated like a kid. Yeah, it made me feel small and pathetic. And, yeah, Jason was probably right to be angry.

But so what?

What did I care?

To hell with him.

I stood up and walked out.

Wednesday: I should have been thrilled by the record company interest, I *wanted* to be thrilled about it, but I couldn't feel anything. Even if I hadn't been grounded, and even if Jason hadn't ruined the moment by putting me down and bawling me out, I'm still not sure I would have felt anything.

All I could feel was Candy.

Her absence, her mystery, her eyes, her smile ... God, I missed her so much. She was filling my days with pain, and I wasn't sure how much more I could take.

I tried talking to Gina about it. I really *tried*. But it's hard to explain your feelings, especially when they don't make any sense, and that was the problem – they *didn't* make any sense.

I knew it, and Gina knew it.

She said, 'I know how you feel, Joe. I know what it's like to miss someone ... but don't you think you're taking things a bit too far?'

'What do you mean?'

'Well, you know ...'

'What?'

She spoke gently. 'You've only met her twice.'

'Two and a half times,' I corrected her.

'All right – two and a *half* times. But that's still not a lot, is it?'

'It's enough.'

'Come on, Joe ... you hardly *know* her.'

'I know how she makes me feel – what else do I need to know?'

Gina looked at me for a long time. I wasn't sure if she was trying to think of an answer, or if she knew the answer and was trying to decide whether to tell me or not. I was kind of hoping there wasn't an answer at all.

Maybe she read my mind, because after a while she just smiled at me and gave me a hug. 'I don't know, Joe,' she said. 'I don't know what to say. This kind of stuff – it just happens. There's not much you can do about it. All you can do is let it happen. You might not always get what you want, but sometimes that's how it goes.'

Thursday: Jason rang me in the evening. The conversation lasted about thirty seconds.

'Joe?'

'Yeah?'

'It's Jason. I had a call from Dead House. They've booked us into a studio in London on the 8th and 9th of March. That's the week after next – Saturday and Sunday.'

'Right ...'

'We've hired the rehearsal hall for this Saturday and we're trying to get it for an extra couple of nights next week. Are you in or out?'

'Sorry?'

'I need to know if you're going to be there, because if you're not we'll have to get someone else.'

'Yeah,' I said. 'I'll be there.'

'Are you sure? I don't want any more messing around ...'

'I'll be there.'

'You'd better be – this is your last chance.'

And that was it.

End of conversation.

Later on, in my bedroom, I was just sitting around strumming the guitar, hoping to lose myself for an hour or so, when Mike came in. I hadn't seen him since Friday night. His face was still a bit mashed up and bruised, but apart from that he looked fine. He came over to the bed and sat down beside me.

'All right?' he said. 'How's it going?'

'Well, you know ...' I shrugged.

'Gina said you're making a record or something. Is that right?'

'Just a demo tape ...'

'That's pretty good.'

'Yeah.'

He scratched his head and looked around the room. It

felt kind of strange, sitting so close to him. Strange ... but OK. He was a big man, and I could sense his weight, his strength, his power. It felt good. Sort of comforting. The scent of his breath and his skin reminded me of the times when I was a kid, when Dad used to sit with me in my bedroom at night, before I went to sleep ...

'I've been asking around,' Mike said quietly, 'about this Iggy guy.'

'Right,' I said, trying to stay calm.

'I found some people who know him.'

'What people?'

He shook his head. 'You don't want to know ... just people. The kind of people who know things.'

'How did you find them?'

He looked at me for a moment, then said, 'You know I used to work the clubs around London – DJing, raves, that kind of thing?' I nodded. He shrugged. 'Well, it's a shady business ... you meet a lot of shady people. Some of them are shadier than others – d'you know what I mean?'

'Yeah, I think so.'

'Music, clubs, drugs, gangs ...' He scratched his head. 'There's a lot of bad stuff going on out there. It's all about money. Bad stuff, bad people ...'

'What about Iggy?'

Mike looked at me. 'His name's Ignatius – Ignatius Ithacaia. No one seems to know very much about him. Either that, or they're too scared to talk. He's a nasty guy. Very nasty. Very ambitious, too. From what I can gather, he started off as a small-time dealer, then moved on to supplying, and now he's getting involved in just about everything. Girls, guns, protection ...' He paused, wiping his hand across his mouth. 'He's a bad one, Joe ... getting badder by the minute. He's moving up fast.'

'What about Candy?' I said. 'Did you find out anything about her?'

Mike shook his head. 'Iggy's got a lot of places – rooms, flats, houses. He runs a lot of girls. No one knows where he lives. He moves around a lot. Candy could be anywhere.'

I stared despondently at the floor. She could be *anywhere*. She *was* somewhere ... doing something ...

'I don't understand it ...' I muttered.

Mike touched my arm. 'It happens.'

'That's what Gina said, but I still don't understand it. How did she end up with Iggy? How could she get involved with someone like that?'

'Guys like Iggy ... they're clever people. They know how to get what they want. They prey on your weaknesses. They give you what you think you want. They promise you the world, and then – before you know it – you're chained to them. You can't get away.' He looked at me. 'I don't know how Candy was taken in, but I'm pretty sure she wouldn't have known what was happening until it was too late.'

'Is it still too late?'

'I don't know ... I don't think there's anything we can do.'

'There's got to be *some*thing ...'

'It's a shitty world, Joe.' He touched my arm again. 'Sometimes you just have to let things go.'

I looked at him. 'Would *you* let it go if it was Gina?'

That surprised him. He looked back at me for a moment, his eyes awash with confusion, then he lowered his head and just sat there, staring emptily at the floor. I guessed he was imagining how *he* would feel if Gina was lost to a man like Iggy.

'Sorry,' I told him. 'I shouldn't have said that.'

'No,' he said quietly, 'you're right. I wasn't thinking of it like that ...' He raised his head and looked at me. 'I'm sorry. I don't know what to say.'

'If you were me, what would you do?'

His eyes were helpless. 'I don't know, Joe. I really don't know.'

Friday morning, eight o'clock: I was sitting at the kitchen table when Dad came in carrying an overnight bag and a couple of suitcases. He put them by the door, sat down at the breakfast table, and poured himself some coffee. I looked at the bags, then at him. He was dressed for travelling – suit, coat, aftershave, tie, thoughtful face and preoccupied eyes.

'Where are you going?' I asked him.

'Hmm?'

'Where are you going?'

He looked up from the table. 'You *know* where I'm going, Joe – I told you. Edinburgh.' He frowned at me. 'The conference?'

'I thought you were leaving tomorrow?'

'It *starts* tomorrow – that's why I'm going today.' He sighed. 'I *told* you all this. I told you about three times. I *knew* you weren't listening – you've been acting strangely all week. What's the matter with you?'

'Nothing ... I *was* listening. I just got the dates mixed up, that's all.' I looked at the clock. 'Are you driving?' I asked him.

He nodded.

'With Mum?'

'I'm meeting her up there.'

'What time?'

'This evening ...'

'So what time do you have to leave?'

He frowned at me again. 'Why all the sudden interest?'

'No reason ... I was just asking.'

His eyes narrowed. 'Look, you've done really well this week. You haven't asked to go out, and – as far as I know – you haven't tried sneaking out. But you're still grounded, don't forget, and you're still only halfway there, so don't go spoiling things by taking advantage of my absence. You'll only be letting yourself down if you do – you know that, don't you?'

'Yeah,' I said.

'You can lie to me, but you can't lie to your conscience.'

Wanna bet? I thought.

'It's all right, Dad,' I said. 'You can trust me.'

He carried on looking at me for a while, then looked at his watch, hurriedly drained his coffee, and got up from the table. 'Right then,' he said, fetching his suitcases. 'I'd better go. Tell Gina I'll call her midweek, and don't forget to put the bins out on Wednesday. There's plenty of food in the fridge. I've left some money in the drawer. If you need me for anything, you've got my mobile number, and I've put the hotel number in the pad on the hall table.' He started patting his pockets, looking for his car keys. I picked them up off the table and passed them to him. 'Right,' he said. 'Well, I should be back next Saturday.'

'Have a good time,' I said.

He paused for a moment, gave me another long look, then rattled his keys and left.

Half an hour later I was standing on the platform at Heystone station, waiting for the London-bound train.

chapter eleven

I didn't know what I was doing. I hadn't *planned* on going to London to look for Candy. I hadn't been waiting all week for Dad to leave. I hadn't been thinking about it – scheming, plotting, biding my time – I hadn't planned *anything*. Not knowingly, anyway. I suppose the idea must have been there all along, just drifting around inside my head, waiting for me to accept it ... or maybe I *did* know it was there, but was afraid to recognise it, just in case it was all I had and something went wrong and took it away ...

I don't know.

I just didn't know. My actions seemed distant and disconnected, as if my body had a mind of its own. Contradictions made sense: the world was blurred, I was sharp; I was fast, the world was slow ...

It was pretty weird.

But utterly normal, too.

As soon as Dad left, I picked up the phone and called school. My voice remained calm as I explained that I wouldn't be coming in, that I wasn't feeling well, that it wasn't anything serious, and that no – I'm sorry, my father can't come to the phone, he's away on business. Goodbye.

I got my coat.

Left the house.

Got on a train.

Got to London.

Got off the train.

Got on the tube.

Got to King's Cross.

Got off the tube.

Got myself back to where it all started.

Like I said, I didn't know what I was doing – but I knew I was doing it.

Outside the station, the pavements were crowded and the streets were as busy as ever. The chaos roared all around me – cars, buses, taxis, speeding bikes, flashing lights, roadworks, cranes, building sites, pelican crossings, bollards, junctions, commuters, street people, mad people, blank-faced hippies with long dirty hair and scabs on their faces – and I just stood there, immersed in the roar, letting it all wash over me.

I was standing outside Boots, as close to where I'd first met Candy as I could remember. I knew it was irrational. She wasn't going to be there ... not this time. No matter how long I stood there, hoping to hear the sound of her voice, sweet and clear, cutting through the chaos like a diamond-tipped knife ... no matter how many times I looked over at the doorway, hoping to see her standing there, leaning against the wall, smiling at me ... hoping to see those lips, those teeth, those dark almond eyes ...

She wasn't going to be there.

I knew that.

But I had to start somewhere, didn't I? And what better place than the beginning?

So I waited.

And I waited.

And I waited ...

And, after an hour or so, I began seeing things I hadn't noticed before. Hidden things, things within the chaos ... things that took time to see. The guy in the dirty green jacket, for example – going into the station, coming out, looking around, going back in again ... or the beggar with the muddy-grey blanket – cold and sleepy, but never closing his eyes, always watching the streets, looking out for trouble ... and the well-dressed women – waiting for friends, but never waiting too long, and never too pleased to see them ...

It was a world within a world. An underworld. Another world. And simply by being there, I was slowly becoming part of it.

At eleven-thirty, a skinny kid in a stained black coat came scuffling up to me. It was hard to tell how old he was, but he couldn't have been much more than fifteen. His face was thin and his eyes were sunken and glazed.

'Where's the score, John?' he said, looking over his shoulder. He was white, but he talked black.

'What?' I said.

His head snapped around and he leaned towards me, lowering his head and staring up into my eyes. 'What's up? You looking for business?'

'No ...'

'You doing?'

'Nothing – I'm just waiting for someone.'

He licked his lips and smiled. 'Wait somewhere else – OK?' He looked over his shoulder again, then turned back to me, his eyes suddenly cold. 'You still here?'

I didn't move. I said, 'Do you know a girl called Candy?'

He didn't answer, just carried on staring at me.

'How about Iggy?' I said. 'Do you know anyone called Iggy? He's a big black guy—'

'What's the matter with you?' the kid said, suddenly getting agitated. 'This ain't for you. Look at you, all clean and pretty ... shit. You want some of this?' He thrust his face at me, giving me a close-up view of his rotting teeth and his scabbed skin and his dirt-yellow eyes. I almost gagged on the sickly-sweet smell of his breath.

'Nice, eh?' he said coldly, moving back.

I looked at him, trying to hide my distaste, but probably not succeeding. Not that it mattered. I guessed he was trying to warn me off, and that I was *supposed* to feel disgusted, so it didn't really bother me that I did. He didn't care, anyway. His face was hard and blank now, not showing anything, just staring me out, waiting for me to go.

I could have tried again, I suppose – asked him some more questions. But I was fairly sure he wouldn't tell me anything. So, with a parting nod, I turned around and walked away.

Across a busy road, onto a traffic island, across to the other side ... looking around, getting my bearings ... recognising the junction, the traffic island, McDonald's ... remembering the last time I'd been here ... remembering Candy ... her face, her eyes, her lips, her legs, her skin ... rippling lightly around her midriff, like the gently-lapping surface of a pale white sea ...

God's sake, Joe ...

Don't even *think* about it.

I was facing Pentonville Road now. I knew where I was,

but I didn't know where to go. Streets branched off in all directions – big streets, little streets, quiet streets, busy streets – offering me all the options I could ask for – north, south, east, west ... but it didn't make any difference. I still didn't know which way to go. All I knew was that Candy lived 'about ten minutes' walk from King's Cross station in a nice little third-floor flat in a refurbished Victorian house', which wasn't a lot to go on. Without knowing the right direction, ten minutes' walk could take me anywhere. And that's if it *was* ten minutes. It might be five minutes, or fifteen minutes ... or it might be that Candy had made the whole thing up. I mean, for all I knew, she didn't live anywhere *near* King's Cross, she lived miles away, and all I was doing was wandering aimlessly around irrelevant streets, wasting my time ...

Yeah, I told myself, *but you're* not *wandering aimlessly, are you? You're not* wandering *at all. You're just standing aimlessly in the same place, which really* is *a complete waste of time. And, besides – what else are you going to do? Give up? Go home? Forget about it? No, this is the best chance you've got. It's the* only *chance you've got. So, make the most of it. Stop thinking and start walking.*

I spent the rest of the afternoon walking in ever-widening circles around King's Cross. It wasn't much fun, and it wasn't the easiest thing I've ever done, but I couldn't think of a better way of doing it. I'd forgotten to bring the A-Z with me, but even if I *had* brought it, it still would have been hard to trace *perfect* circles around the streets. I constantly found myself getting lost, or walking the same street more than once, or walking in the wrong direction and ending up back where I started ...

But it didn't really matter. As long as I kept going,

covering as much ground as I could, searching as thoroughly as I could ...

That was the main thing.

It *was* pretty depressing, though.

The weather was dull. Leaden skies, grey and low, a lumbering mishmash of nothing. It wasn't hot, it wasn't cold, it wasn't windy, it wasn't calm, it wasn't wet, it wasn't dry ... it wasn't anything. Just dull. And the streets themselves were strangely lifeless, too. I don't know what I was expecting – probably an orgy of sex shops and brothels and rough-looking pubs – but most of the streets weren't too bad. There were *some* sex shops – squat little buildings with blanked-out windows – and there were quite a few rough-looking pubs, and a few dodgy saunas, and some very weird-looking clubs ... but there weren't *hundreds* of them or anything. There weren't hordes of scantily clad women standing around on street corners, or brightly dressed pimps driving around in Cadillacs ... there were just lots of dull streets and lots of dull people ... and only the occasional glimpse of the underworld.

A drugged-up guy with a badly-shaved head, giving me the eye.

A couple of very young girls, sitting in a car with a middle-aged Arab.

Syringes in the gutter.

Stone-faced bruisers in dirty little doorways, checking me out as I passed them by.

I didn't feel threatened, exactly ... but I didn't feel too comfortable, either. I felt small and stupid and out of place. I knew I didn't belong here, and I knew that everyone else knew it too. It made me feel that I mustn't stop walking, that if I stopped walking, something bad would happen.

So I kept walking.

It was tempting to keep my head down, my eyes fixed hard to the ground, but I knew I had to keep looking, no matter what. I had to keep looking for Candy ... or Iggy ... or a nice little third-floor flat in a refurbished Victorian house. The trouble was, I'd know Candy or Iggy if I saw them ... but a refurbished Victorian house?

What the hell did *that* look like?

I had no idea.

So I just carried on walking, carried on looking, carried on going in the hope that something would happen. Otherwise – what? Start all over again? Keep walking in circles for ever? Stop and ask someone?

Yeah, right ... stop and ask someone. 'Excuse me, I'm looking for a prostitute and her pimp ... she's young and pretty and addicted to heroin, and he's big and black and really *scary, and I think they live in a refurbished Victorian house ...'*

Yeah, good idea, Joe.

Good thinking.

Why not ask those policemen over there ...?

Policemen?

There were two of them, just up ahead, in a patrol car parked at the side of the road. They didn't seem to be doing anything – they were just sitting in their car, looking bored and mean – but the sight of them gave me a shock. What if they stopped me and started asking me questions? *What are you doing around here? Where are you going? Why aren't you at school?* I couldn't tell them the truth, could I? And, just at that moment, I couldn't think of any suitable lies ...

So – as casually as possible – I turned around and started walking back the way I'd come.

I don't know what would have happened if I hadn't seen the patrol car. Maybe everything would have turned out OK. Maybe I would have walked around King's Cross for another couple of hours without finding anything, and then maybe I would have gone back home, and then maybe ...

I don't know.

Maybe something else would have happened.

But it didn't ... because I *didn't* walk around King's Cross for another couple of hours without finding anything. Instead, in my eagerness to get away from the patrol car, I found myself hurrying along the backstreets without really thinking where I was going, and it wasn't until I was halfway across a busy main road, waiting for the lights to change, that I came to my senses and realised where I was – I was standing on a traffic island in the middle of Euston Road, directly opposite the main entrance to the station. I was right back where I'd started from.

And that's when I saw Iggy.

He was coming out of the station. Walking tall, in a long black leather coat, with his head held high and his arms swinging confidently and his loaded eyes full of nothing. I could see people avoiding his gaze, getting out of his way, instinctively afraid of his size and his strength and his total lack of feeling. And, although his face was blank, I could see that he loved it.

Without thinking, I shuffled back a few steps and got myself into a position behind some other pedestrians from where I could still see Iggy, but hopefully he couldn't see me. With my heart pumping hard, I watched him – striding across the front of the station, passing the newspaper kiosks, passing Boots, moving with the effortless ease of a man who knows exactly where he's going. And he *was* going. Veering off to the left, heading down behind the station ... heading out of sight ...

I pushed my way to the front of the traffic island, jostling through the bodies and praying for the lights to change. It was the rush hour now, there was too much traffic ... I couldn't cross the road. I looked up in panic. Iggy was disappearing around the corner ... I was losing him ...

Then the beeps sounded and the lights changed and the traffic stopped and I was off, running diagonally across the road, onto the pavement, dodging through the crowds, sprinting to the corner, skidding breathlessly to a halt ... and then, vaguely aware of how stupid I probably looked, I poked my head around the corner and peered down the street. It wasn't too busy – traffic was heavy but the pavements weren't overcrowded – and I spotted Iggy almost immediately. With his size and his height, and his long black coat, he wasn't hard to spot. He was about fifty metres away, walking along the pavement on the right-hand side of the road, swinging his arm, gesturing with his hand, as if he was talking to himself.

My head raced.

I wasn't thinking.

I was set on automatic: *follow him, don't let him see you, follow him, don't let him see you, follow him ...*

I followed him.

I'm not sure how I did it. I'd never followed anyone before. I didn't *know* anything about following people – how close do you get? what if they turn around? what do you do when they go round a corner? – but somehow I managed to keep on his trail without being seen. It probably helped that he didn't know he was being followed. I mean, I didn't have to do anything sneaky. I didn't have to cover my face with a newspaper or pretend to be tying my shoelaces or anything. I just had to follow him: down the back of the station for a few hundred metres, then right into a narrow street lined with warehouses and office blocks, then left, then right again, over a waterway, into a maze of hidden backstreets ...

Things got a little more tricky then. I had to stay close enough to avoid losing sight of him, but I couldn't get *too* close because the streets around here were fairly empty. If he happened to stop and turn around, he was bound to see me. Whether he'd recognise me or not was another matter. Probably not, I thought. But with a man like Iggy, *probably not* wasn't much comfort. So I hung back a bit, watching from the cover of roadside trees, parked cars, pillar boxes, whatever I could find.

Most of the houses around here were three- or four-storey terraced buildings with curtained bay windows and peeling paintwork and rows of hand-written nameplates next to a communal doorbell on the porch wall. Flats and bedsits, I guessed.

Victorian houses?

Maybe ...

They looked vaguely familiar, and I wondered if I'd already been this way when I was trailing around in circles earlier on. Possibly ... probably ... it was hard to tell. The streetlights were on now. Darkness was coming down fast. Things look different in the dark: flatter, colder, more sinister.

Iggy had stopped.

Halfway along a cramped little terrace, shadowed in the sodium glow of a streetlamp, his long black coat reflecting the stark orange light. He wasn't doing anything. Just standing there, outside a tall white house, gazing up at the softly lit windows.

I was about thirty metres away, in a tree-lined street that branched off the terrace at a right-angle. There was a small stretch of park to my left which gave me a perfect view of Iggy and the tall white house. I studied the house. It was the same as all the other houses in the street: terraced, three storeys high, flat-fronted, with stone steps leading up to an unlit porchway. Iggy was climbing the steps now ... pulling out a key ... unlocking the door ... glancing over his shoulder ...

He entered the house.

Now what? I asked myself. *What do you do now? Stay here? Move? Get closer?* How was I supposed to know? I'd never done anything like this before. It was dark. I was cold ... shivering ... sweating ... hungry ... empty ...

Thoughtless.

Just then, a car rolled down the street. Its headlights swept the plane trees, lighting up their paled trunks, the park railings, me. I froze. I saw my shadow looming across the pavement – a hunched black figure with a lengthened head, creeping out from behind the trees ...

Not good, I thought.

The car slowed for a moment ... the engine idling ... and then it moved off again, taking my shadow with it. *You can't stay here,* I told myself, breathing a sigh of relief. *Lurking around in the trees ... you'll get arrested.* I waited until the car had turned the corner at the end of the road, then I moved out from behind the tree and started walking. Down the street, left into the terrace, along the pavement on the park side of the road, keeping in close to the railings. The white house was on the opposite side of the street. As I approached it, I kept my eyes to the ground, not daring to look. I wanted to look ... God, I wanted to look. But if Iggy were to come out now ...

I forced myself not to imagine it.

A few seconds later I came to a wrought-iron gate in the railings. The gate was open, leading into the little park. Before I knew what I was doing, I'd stepped through the gate and was following a little pathway around to the right, pausing at a wooden bench, taking a quick look around, then moving off the pathway and edging my way into a shoulder-high thicket of bushes and shrubs that bordered the park.

I could smell the earth – damp and dark.

Litter.

Leaves.

Sap.

Thorns.

Then I was facing the railings again. Looking through the iron bars at the terrace, the white house ... the windows, the steps, the front door. There was no sign of any movement. I stepped back into the shadows and positioned myself behind a bush, then settled down to wait.

Nothing much happened for a while. The street moved quietly to the early evening sounds of cars and people passing by, but none of them stopped. They were all going somewhere else. Home, probably ... or out for the night ... just cruising around ... looking for fun. No one went into the white house, and no one came out. The curtains stayed shut.

The windows, I noticed, had metal bars on the front. This bothered me for a while – *why does a house need bars on the windows?* – but then I realised that all the other houses had barred windows, too, so I guessed it didn't mean anything. The houses around here had barred windows, that was all. It didn't *mean* anything. But as I crouched there, hiding in the bushes, watching the house, I found myself curiously drawn to these black barred windows. I couldn't stop staring at them. Studying them, concentrating on the regularity of the bars, the black lines, the width of the gaps, the background whiteness of the curtains ... and after a while the lines began forming themselves into a perfectly focused grid, black on white, black on white, black on white ... and I started having really weird thoughts. I imagined the chaos of the last few days distilling itself into clearly defined elements, each embedded in its own neatly outlined rectangle. One, two, three, four, five, six ... six perfect rectangles. And inside the rectangles were symbols ... elements ... nameless shapes of things I didn't understand – shadows, shades, abstractions, forms – flickering colours on a pure white background.

None of it meant anything to me.

It was just there.

And then the front door opened and Iggy came out, and suddenly the bars were just bars again. The curtains were just curtains. And Iggy was leaving the house and walking away up the street.

I gave it a good five minutes before I made a move. I wanted to make sure that Iggy wasn't coming back. I also wanted to give myself time to clear all the crap out of my head. The weird stuff – the bars, the symbols, the elements ... whatever it was. I didn't need it. And, to tell you the truth, it scared me a bit. So I just stayed where I was, breathing in the cold night air, soaking up the woody scent of the bushes, emptying my mind ... until I was fairly sure I was back on Planet Earth again.

Then I stood up ...

And squatted back down again.

How was I going to get in the house?

I couldn't just ring the bell, could I? I didn't know who was in there. I was *hoping* that Candy was in there, but I couldn't be sure. Some of Iggy's crew could be in there. It could be *his* house. It could be empty ...

God.

I wished I knew what I was *doing*.

But I didn't.

And what's the best thing to do when you don't know what to do? Nothing. Just wait. Give it time. See what happens.

So that's what I did.

I waited.

I gave it time.

And, after a while, I saw what happened.

A black woman approached the house. She was big and bulky, dressed in a lumpy beige coat, and she was carrying a full carrier bag in each hand. The bags looked heavy. Sainsbury's bags, full of shopping. She stopped outside the house for a moment and rested the bags on the pavement, then she picked them up again and started struggling up the steps, taking them one at a time.

I moved out of the bushes, ran along the pathway, then slowed to a walk as I passed through the gate and started across the road. The woman was at the top of the steps now. She'd put down the carrier bags and was ringing the bell and leaning towards the intercom. My heart was racing as I approached the house, but I forced myself to smile ... skipping up the steps as the front door swung open and the woman bent down to pick up the bags ...

I stepped up, still smiling, and said, 'Here, let me get those for you.' Before she could say anything, I'd picked up the bags and was holding the door open for her. 'After you,' I said, all bright and breezy. She gave me a funny little look, then shrugged and went inside. I stepped in after her, looking around, taking it all in: the murky corridor, the hall table piled with junk mail, the stained linoleum floor, the steep flight of stairs on my right, the smell of stale air ...

'Where do you want them?' I asked the woman, indicating the bags.

'Just here,' she said.

I put the bags on the floor. She looked at me again, then picked them up and headed off down the corridor, leaving me standing at the foot of the stairs, looking up into the unknown, my insides pounding like a thousand drums.

chapter twelve

The house felt empty as I climbed the stairs. I knew it *wasn't* – I could hear the woman who'd let me in rattling drawers somewhere below, and from somewhere above I could hear the faint sound of a radio playing behind closed doors – but everything still *felt* empty. The dark stairs, the colourless walls, the threadbare carpet beneath my feet ... there was nothing to it. No life, no soul. No comfort. This wasn't a home; it was just a place.

I moved cautiously, pausing after every step, keeping still, looking up, listening hard ... then another step ... another pause ... another step ... another pause. It was slow going, but I didn't want to take any chances. A dim light was shining from the second or third floor, and I could still hear the sound of the radio ...

There were people here.

Somewhere.

I carried on up to the first floor and paused on the landing. A long corridor stretched out to my right. It was similar to the hallway downstairs, only this one had doors

– six doors, three on each side. They were all closed. In the airless silence I could hear cars passing on the street outside. Headlights swept across a curtained window at the end of the corridor, briefly illuminating the scuffed old walls, then the lights passed by and the corridor sank back into its semi-darkness. I breathed in, trying to calm myself. The air up here smelled different to the air downstairs. It smelled almost clean, but not quite – a sort of air-freshenery cleanness. The kind of smell that's supposed to remove the bad smells, but doesn't – it just hides them.

Pots rattled downstairs – the black woman ...

I moved on.

Up the stairs to the second floor ... or was it the *first* floor? I wasn't sure. Does the ground floor count as the first floor? Do houses *have* ground floors?

Does it matter?

No, it didn't. It was just something to think about as I climbed the stairs, something to keep my mind off the grubbiness and the emptiness and the overwhelming stink of fear that pervaded the house and everything in it, including me ...

There was bad stuff going on in here.

Bad stuff, bad people ...

I reached the second-floor landing – another long corridor, another curtained window, another six doors. Same as before. Nothing happening. No life, no joy. I turned away ... and was just about to move on again, when I heard the sound of a door opening. I turned back. Halfway along the hallway, a girl in a white bath robe was coming out of a room. Olive-skinned, barefoot, dark-haired, pretty. She stopped at the sight of me.

I smiled at her.

She didn't smile back. She didn't do anything. Her eyes

were vacant. Her mouth was closed, without expression ... as if it had been closed for ever.

'Excuse me ...' I said.

She just stared at me.

I cleared my throat. 'I was looking for someone ...'

She blinked once, shook her head, then closed the door and walked off down the hallway. I watched her as she opened a door and went into what I guessed was a bathroom. The door closed. Taps started running.

I stood there for a moment, feeling strangely unmoved, then carried on up the stairs.

The third floor was just as dull as the others – dull hallway, dull doors, dull walls, dull window – but it wasn't quite so lifeless. There was a light, for one thing – a pale white light in a cobwebbed paper shade, hanging from the ceiling. And the music was louder, too. The radio music ... it seemed to be coming from the first room on the right.

Music, lights ... it wasn't much, but at least it gave the impression of *some* kind of life.

There were no more stairs now. Nowhere else to go. This was the third floor ... these were third-floor flats. I didn't know if the house was Victorian. It certainly wasn't refurbished, but there wasn't much I could do about that.

I was here now ...

I was here.

I might as well carry on.

I walked down the hallway and stopped outside the room where the music was coming from. It was still muffled, but it sounded pretty good – some kind of Asian hip-hop stuff ... twangy guitars, off-beat drums, nice singing. I listened to it for a while, then took a deep breath, let it out slowly, and knocked on the door.

The girl who answered didn't look well. She had a thin

angular face, pale puffy skin, and yellowed eyes. Her hair was shapeless – short, black, harsh – and her clothes were cheap.

She said nothing, just looked at me through a two-inch gap in the doorway.

'I'm looking for Candy,' I told her.

She didn't answer, just glanced over my shoulder. I turned around to see what she was looking at, but there was nothing there. I turned back to the girl.

'Candy,' I repeated. 'Does she live here?'

'Who're you?' she said. Her voice was quiet, clipped, with a foreign accent. I couldn't tell what it was – Russian, maybe ... East European ...

'My name's Joe,' I told her. 'I'm a friend of Candy's ... we met up a couple of times. Is she here?'

The girl opened the door a little wider. 'Friend?'

I nodded.

'Boyfriend?'

'Well ...' I said, 'I don't know ... not really. I just—'

'Kanagaroo?'

'What?

'Zoo?'

'Oh, yeah ... the *zoo* ... yeah, that's right ... we went to the zoo. Candy showed me the kangaroo. Did she tell you—?'

'There,' the girl said, pointing along the hallway at the last door on the left. 'She hurts.'

'Hurts?'

The girl shrugged. 'You shouldn't come here.'

'Why not?'

She shrugged again, then stepped back and quietly closed the door in my face. I thought about knocking again, or even calling out to her, but there didn't seem much point. She'd told me all I needed to know.

And more.

Imagine: you've spent all day traipsing round London, lost in a maze of chaos, trying to find a hidden illusion; you've been living on hope, ignoring reality, fuelled only by feelings you don't understand. You've been looking for a dream, never truly believing you'd find it, but now – incredibly – you have. It's right there in front of you – just behind that off-white door. It's there ...

She's there.

Behind the door.

Imagine that.

Candy's *in* there ...

All you have to do is raise your hand and knock ...

That's all.

Just raise your hand ...

I couldn't do it. My arm wouldn't move. It was dead, senseless ... unresponsive. It belonged to someone else. For a minute or two, all I could do was stand there in front of the door, staring at the flaking paint, the grimy panels, the ill-fitting lock ... my hands hanging down at my sides ... my head throbbing ... my body burning ... hot ... cold ... inside out ... sick with too many things. Excitement. Fear. Anxiety. Pain. Passion. Hope.

Everything.

Nothing.

'Candy?' I whispered.

Too quiet.

I tried again. 'Candy?'

It was still too quiet, but somehow the sound of my voice brought my arm back to life, and I reached up and knocked on the door.

'Candy?' I called out. 'Are you in there? It's Joe ...'

There was no reply. I put my ear to the door and listened. Nothing at first ... then something ... a faint rustling ... a creak ... a single footstep. Then silence again. I knocked once more.

'Candy ... please ... open the door.'

This time I definitely heard her. Light footsteps, moving slowly towards me, towards the door. I stepped back – I don't know why ... it just seemed the natural thing to do. I stepped back and put my hands in my pockets. Again, I don't know *why* I put my hands in my pockets. I just did.

The door opened ...

And there she was – the imagined face in all its reality: pale, pained, bruised, and beaten. One of her eyes was blackened and her left wrist was swollen and bandaged.

'Candy,' I breathed. 'What happened—?'

'I can't talk to you,' she said weakly. 'You have to go ...'

'I'm not going anywhere. Look at you ... your face ...'

'It's nothing,' she said, brushing at the ugly swelling around her eye. 'I'm all right. Please, Joe ... just go ... leave me alone. You'll only make things worse.'

'I won't.'

'You will ... believe me.'

I shook my head. 'I'm not going anywhere until you talk to me.'

'I *can't* ...'

I didn't reply. I just stood there, staring into her eyes, letting her see my determination. I wasn't leaving. She could shut the door if she wanted to. She could lock it, bolt it, nail it shut ... she could do whatever she liked. But I still wasn't going anywhere.

She looked back at me, nervously chewing her lip.

I said, 'The sooner you let me in, the sooner I'll be gone.'

She closed her eyes for a moment – her face darkened with sadness – then, without looking at me, she stepped back and opened the door.

It wasn't a flat, it was just a room. And it wasn't even much of a room. There was a double bed, a wardrobe, a mirrored dressing table, a few shelves, one or two books ... a cheap CD player on the floor ... clothes and towels piled all over the place. There was a beaded doorway in the far wall that led into a small bathroom, but I couldn't see a kitchen anywhere, nor any kitchen equipment – no food, no fridge, no cooker. No television. No ornaments, no pictures ...

Nothing for living.

It was just somewhere to exist.

I blinked and rubbed my eyes, squinting into the light. The curtains were closed and the room was lit with a dim red glow from a heavy cylindrical lamp on the floor.

'Don't say anything,' Candy said, sitting down gingerly on the bed. 'Please ... just don't say anything.'

The bed was a mess – tangled sheets, scrunched up pillows, a bedside cabinet strewn with all kinds of debris. I went over to the dressing table and sat down on a hard-backed chair. The surface of the dressing table was covered with bottles and tubs and jars and tubes ... bits of foil ... clingfilm ... matches ... cigarette lighters ... packets of painkillers ...

'I couldn't tell you,' Candy said.

I turned around and looked at her. She was sitting cross-legged, leaning slightly to one side, resting her hand on her hip ... as if trying to relieve a pain. Her hair was loose and she was wearing a long white nightgown. The gown looked old – ivory-white, thin and lacy ... thin enough to see that she wasn't wearing anything else. The outline of her body whispered under the cloth.

I lowered my eyes.

She said, 'I *wanted* to tell you ... honestly ...'

'Tell me what?' I said.

'Come *on*, Joe – what do you think? All this ...' She waved her hand around the room. 'What I am ... what I do ...'

I raised my eyes and looked at her. 'Why did he beat you up? Was it because of me?'

She shrugged. 'You ... me ... it doesn't really matter. I know the rules – I've only got myself to blame.' She reached over to the bedside cabinet, wincing slightly, and rummaged through the mess. She found a cigarette and lit it. 'He doesn't usually go this far,' she said, grinning through the cigarette smoke. 'I think he just got carried away.'

'*Carried away?*' I said incredulously. 'Look what he's *done* to you ... how can you let him *do* something like that?'

'*Let* him?' she said, shaking her head. 'God, you really don't get it, do you? You really don't know what it's like.'

'So tell me.'

'Why? What difference will it make?' She flicked cigarette ash into an empty Coke can, then lifted her eyes and looked right into me. 'I'm a whore, Joe. I go with men for money. I give the money to Iggy. He gives me drugs. That's all there is to it.'

'And that's what you want, is it?'

'That's how it is. What I *want* doesn't come into it.'

'What *do* you want?'

She stared at me, her eyes pooled with tears. 'I want you to go. Get out of here. Go home. Don't get involved, Joe ... please ... just go. You can't do anything ...'

She was crying now.

I went over and sat down next to her on the bed. She sniffed and wiped her nose. I took the cigarette from her hand, dropped it in the Coke can, then put my arm around her shoulders.

'Please ...' she snuffled, 'it's not worth it ...'

'Yes, it is,' I said, drawing her close.

She rested her head on my shoulder. I could feel the wetness of her tears on my neck.

'He'll kill you,' she said quietly.

I looked into her eyes and smiled. 'He'll have to catch me first.'

She didn't smile back. She just looked at me for a moment, her tears still flowing, then she breathed out softly and kissed me.

The touch of her body.

The heat of her breath.

Her comfort.

My wonder.

The world in our eyes.

It was more than enough for both of us.

We talked then – both of us lying on our backs, on the bed, staring up at the ceiling ... just talking. It felt OK. Nice and simple. Like two little kids, lying in the grass, staring up at the ever-blue sky ... nothing to worry about ... nothing to fear ...

'Where's Iggy gone?' I asked her.

'Out.'

'Is he coming back?'

'You wouldn't be here if he was. How did you find me, anyway?'

'Very nice, thanks,' I replied.

'I didn't mean that.'

'I know.'

I told her how I'd walked around King's Cross, hoping to find her, how I'd eventually spotted Iggy and followed him, then waited in the park and tricked my way inside by helping the black woman with her bags.

'That's Bamma,' Candy said.

'What?'

'Bamma – the woman with the bags. She's called Bamma. She does the cleaning and shopping and stuff. She's all right. She won't say anything.'

Shadows drifted on the ceiling above me – streetlight shadows, window shadows, the shadowed lines of metal bars – and I remembered all the weird stuff I'd thought about earlier when I was staring at the bars from outside – the chaos, the colours, the nameless shapes ...

I didn't want to think about it.

'How's your wrist?' I asked Candy. 'Is it broken?'

'No, just sprained, I think.' She cautiously flexed her fingers. 'It's all right ...'

'What about the rest of it?'

'Rest of what?'

I sat up and moved my hand towards her hips, where – through the sheerness of her nightgown – I could see her bruised and battered skin. The bruises looked like thunderclouds – blue-black, purple, mustard-yellow.

She flinched away from my hand.

'Sorry,' I said.

'It's all right ... I was just ... it's nothing. It looks a lot worse than it is.'

I sat there in silence for a while, gazing without shame at Candy – her hair adrift on the pillow, the rings in her ears, glinting in the low red light ... her necklace, her neck, her slender fingers gripping a twist of the sheet ...

'You don't have to do this, you know,' I said to her.

'What?'

'Pretend that you're OK, that everything's fine. You don't have to hide things from me.'

'I'm not,' she said quietly 'I'm hiding them from myself. It's the only way ...'

'No, it's not.'

She sighed. 'You don't know what it's like, Joe. You don't understand.'

'I might if you told me.'

She rolled over onto her side and looked up at me. I could feel the intensity in her eyes as she gazed deep inside me, looking for answers. Could she trust me? Did she want to? Was it worth it?

'Promise me something,' she said.

'What?'

'Don't get involved. I'll tell you as much as I can, but only if you promise to keep yourself out of it. I don't want you trying to *do* anything for me – all right?'

I nodded.

She gave me a doubtful look. 'I *mean* it, Joe. You can't get involved.'

'I won't.'

'Promise?'

'Yeah ...'

'Say it.'

'All right – I *promise*. OK?'

Another look, this one touched with a fleeting sadness,

then she took a deep breath, rolled onto her back, and started talking.

This is what she told me:

It all started about four years ago. She'd always been a good-looking girl, the kind of girl that mothers are proud of and fathers feel the need to protect, but when she was about twelve or thirteen she'd suddenly blossomed into the kind of girl that men can't resist, and that's when the trouble began.

'I'm not *bragging* about my looks,' she told me. 'I'm just being honest. I know what I look like. I'm *pretty*. I know it now, and I knew it then.'

At first, it didn't cause her any problems. Why should it? Everyone likes a pretty girl. And she was smart, too. Intelligent, popular, good at sports. She had a more than comfortable home, never wanted for anything, and for the most part she got on reasonably well with her parents. Her father was the managing director of a multinational IT company, so he wasn't at home as much as he might have been, and her mother had a few emotional problems ... but, all in all, things weren't too bad.

But then the jealousy started.

'I didn't even notice it at first,' Candy explained. 'I used to get on all right with all the other girls at school ... I didn't have any real close friends, but there was a gang of us who used to hang around together, and that was OK most of the time. We didn't do all that much ... you know, we'd talk about boys, who we fancied, what we'd do, what we wouldn't ... that kind of thing. It was fine. No problems. Most of it was just talk, anyway. Sometimes we'd all go out to a local club together, and occasionally one of us might get off with someone for an hour or so, but it never changed anything between us. It didn't affect how we were with each other. Do you know what I mean?'

I nodded.

She went on. 'It never ends there, though, does it? It always has to get *serious*. Boys start ringing you up, asking you out. Men start looking at you with different eyes. You start doing things, going to nice places ... and you think it's great. It *is* great. It's exciting. You love it. And because you love it, you want to tell all your friends about it. But when you do, instead of loving it *with* you, they throw it back in your face. They don't like you doing stuff they're not doing. It makes them feel bad. So they call you a liar ... they laugh at you. They reject you. And it's all so *sudden*. One minute they like you ... the next minute they hate you. You're not *with* them any more. You're different. You're trying to be better than them. Or worse. Flashing your tits around, wiggling your bum, begging for it ... you're a slut, a tart, a whore ...'

She paused and lit a cigarette, sucking the smoke deep into her lungs, holding it there, then angrily breathing it out.

'It was horrible, Joe ... the things they said ... the other girls. The way they treated me ... it really *hurt*. I cried myself to sleep almost every night. It's stupid, I know ... I shouldn't have let it bother me, but it did. It still does.'

She lay there quietly for a while, staring at nothing, twisting a knotted tissue in her hands, and then, with a funny little gulp, she started crying again. I put my hand on her shoulder and let her weep. I'm not sure if it helped very much, but after a few minutes she wiped her nose, dried her tears, lit another cigarette, and went on with her story.

'I don't know how it happened,' she told me, 'but everything suddenly changed. No one liked me any more. Everyone started picking on me – the girls at school, the teachers, even my parents ... going on at me all the time, whatever I did ... I couldn't do *anything* right. If I went out with boys, I was a tart; if I didn't, I was frigid. If I worked hard, I was a swot; if I didn't, I was stupid. If I dressed up, I was easy; if I dressed down, I was a tramp. And it just got worse and worse. It got so bad I didn't know who I was any more. I didn't know what I was doing. In the end, I just gave up. I suppose I thought that if everyone hated me, I might as well hate myself, too. So I started doing things to *make* me hate myself – hanging around with the wrong kind of people, drinking myself stupid, staying out all night, sleeping around ...' She took a long drag on her cigarette, then stabbed it out in the ashtray. 'Anyway,' she said, 'it was around then I met Iggy. I'd gone to this club in London with some people I barely knew, and I was whacked out of my head on something, and they'd gone off and left me ... and this creepy old guy was bothering me, trying to get me to go somewhere with him, and then Iggy suddenly appears ... just walks up, cool as you like, and whispers in the creepy guy's ear, and the next thing I know the creepy guy's gone and Iggy's sitting down next to me, asking me if I'm all right. God, he was so *smooth*. Nice clothes, nice manners ... clean and kind and caring.' She rubbed her forehead. 'The thing is, he *was* nice. Charming, polite, funny ... and he didn't try anything, either. Kept his hands to himself, never touched me ... he didn't even try to chat me up. Just talked to me. Asked me all about myself. And he *listened* to me ... that was the thing. I couldn't believe it. No one had listened to me for months. Then, after I'd jabbered away for hours, he gave me a lift back home – drove me all the way back to Heystone in his shiny black BMW, dropped me off at the end of the street and said goodnight.'

She paused then, her eyes lost in thought, drifting back over the memories ... and I just sat there, looking down at her, studying the landscape of her face: the flesh of her lips, her nose, her eyelids, the pretty pink curl of her ears ...

'Excuse me,' she said, getting up off the bed. 'I won't be a minute – just going to the bathroom.'

She walked around the bed, picked up something from the dressing table, then slipped through the beaded doorway into the bathroom. I watched the beads, swinging in her wake, moving to the shape of her passing body, and I remembered the way she'd walked away from me in the café at the zoo – with no vanity, no pretence, no frivolity ... walking with a purpose .... either not knowing, or not caring, that I was watching her.

Just like now.

Getting what she needed.

I guessed it didn't make any difference to her. She was simply getting what she needed, and that's all there was to it. It didn't matter that I didn't understand it. It didn't matter that I didn't *like* it. That's how it was. What I liked or what I wanted didn't come into it. So I just sat there, looking around the room, thinking about things, listening to the secret sounds coming from the bathroom – the creak of taps, the rattle of pipes, the rustle of plastic and foil, the click of a cigarette lighter ...

I got out of bed and went over to the window and pulled back the curtains. They were stiff and cold to the touch. The window was shut. Locked. Barred on the outside. A pattern of blurred marks in the smeared glass showed where Candy had gazed out of the window, resting her nose against the glass.

I wondered what she looked at.

It was fully dark outside.

Streetlights glazed the surface of the road below, and in the distance the lights of the city flickered in their thousands: orange lights, dipping gracefully with the curve of roads; ice-green traffic lights; the circular white glow of roundabouts ... lines of motion, the drop of the sky, lights of lights ...

I could see for miles.

I couldn't see anything.

I looked over at the bathroom, willing Candy to appear – *come on ... please ... if you take any longer, I'll have to do something. I'll have to call out to you ... and you probably won't answer ... and then I'll have to come and find you ... to check that you're OK ... and I'll find you sitting on the toilet smoking smack, all bent over and ugly, with a plastic straw sticking out of your mouth ...*

The toilet flushed. I crossed the room and sat down on the bed. Taps gurgled, pipes roared, the toilet flushed again ... and then the beads in the doorway rattled and swooshed – and there she was, a vision in white, gliding her way around the bed and settling down beside me. She had that look about her again – the way she was sitting, loose and easy, hanging her head ... that strange little smile on her lips ...

'Sorry ...' she said. 'I had to ... you know ...'

'It's all right.'

'I ... uh ...' she mumbled. 'Where was I?'

'Sorry?'

She raised her head and looked at me, her drugged eyes wandering around my face. 'The story ...' she said. 'I was telling you the story ...' She jerked her head and ran her fingers through her hair. 'Christ, it's so *pathetic* ...'

'What is?'

'This ... me ... what happened ... *why* it happened. It's so stupid. It's *nothing*. I mean, I used to be all right ... I was OK. Nothing *bad* happened to start it all off. I didn't get beaten up or raped or abused or anything ... *nothing* happened.' She shook her head. 'All I got was a little bit of jealousy, a little bit of rejection, and a lot of self-pity. It's not much of a reason for ending up like this, is it?'

'A reason's a reason,' I said.

'Yeah, well ...'

Her eyes closed again and her head sank down to her chest. I thought for a moment she'd nodded off, but then she took a deep breath and straightened up and opened her eyes and looked at me.

'What was I saying?' she said.

'You were talking about reasons—'

'No, before that. Before I went to the bathroom.'

'You were telling me about Iggy,' I reminded her. 'When he gave you a lift home ...'

'Yeah, right ... gave me a lift home. That's right. He was *sooo* nice ... when was that?' She shook her head. 'Long time ago ... years ago. I was good then ... I gave him my number ... big mistake ...' She sighed and yawned and lay down on the bed, resting the back of her head in my lap. Despite the growing cold, beads of sweat were glistening on her skin. 'Yeah,' she said, 'good old Iggy. Didn't ring me for a week ... kept me waiting ...' Her head lolled back and she gazed up at me. 'Just like you.' She smiled.

I nodded.

She said, 'Then he rang me ... asked me out ... and that was it. Clubs, compliments, money, clothes ... he gave me everything I wanted. Everything. Told me everything I wanted to hear – I was amazing ... my parents were shit ... they didn't understand me ... I was a *woman* ... I was *special* ...' She shook her head sadly. 'I couldn't get enough of it. I was hooked. He had everything – money, drugs, respect ... it was so *cool*, you know?' Her voice was bitter and hard. 'Doing coke all the time ... feeling good ... a bit of smack now and then to slow things down ... a bit more ... then a bit more ...' She looked at me again. 'You ever tried it?'

'No,' I said.

'Don't ... it's shit. It's like the best thing in the world ... it takes everything away, all the crap ... everything. Nothing matters any more – hot or cold, big or small, good or bad ... you just don't care. You don't give a shit about anything. It's like you're wrapped up inside the warmest blanket imaginable, sleeping like an angel ... all wrapped up in your own little wonderful world ... and then one day you wake up and the blanket's gone, and you feel so cold and empty ... you feel so bad ... you feel so terrible you'll do *anything* to get that feeling back. And I mean anything ... anything at all ... because you don't care, you don't *want* to care. All you want is that wonderful *wonderful* feeling. So when Iggy says the smack's all gone, and he's skint, so he can't get any more ... but he knows this guy, this *friend* of his who fancies me ... and all I've got to do is spend a couple of hours with this guy and we'll have enough money to get what we need ... what *I* need ...' She was speaking in a broken whisper now. 'I mean, it wasn't much to ask, was it? All I had to do was *sleep* with the guy. Iggy didn't mind ... he'd do the same for me. Why should *I* mind? If I loved him ... I loved him, didn't I? And it was good money ... easy money ... and he could probably find something to take my mind off things for a while ...'

She was crying again, but without any tears.

I held her hand.

'There's nothing left after that,' she said quietly. 'The money keeps drying up, you keep doing favours for *friends* ... needing more drugs ... needing more money ... doing more favours ... and after a while you don't know what's happening any more. You don't know what you're doing. You're just doing it, doing what it takes ... living in a shitty little room and working the streets all day and the saunas all night just to keep yourself from going mad ...'

She mouthed a few more silent words, then her lips trembled and she closed her eyes and was quiet. I looked down at her, trying to take it all in – the words, the images, the life ... trying to imagine how it must be ... but I couldn't. I couldn't even get close. It was beyond me. A different world. A world I knew nothing about. A world of violence and pain and darkness. I felt so small, so weak, so stupid ...

What do you want?

I opened my mouth, but nothing came out.

The room could only be silent.

And I knew what it meant – the silence. I knew without knowing. It was a silence that was there to be broken. I could feel it in the air, in the pit of my stomach, in the core of my bones ...

The other world was coming back.

'Candy,' I whispered. 'I think we'd better—'

'Shhh ...' she said, rolling over and putting her finger to my lips. I watched in curious silence as she slipped off the bed and stood in front of me. For a moment I thought she was going to the bathroom again, but then, with her sleepy eyes fixed on mine, she knelt down on the bed and held my hands.

'No,' I started to say, 'I don't think—'

SLAM!

And Candy's eyes were suddenly awake. 'Shit!' she hissed. 'That was the front door.' Her face was white with fear. 'Listen ...' Heavy footsteps were thudding up the stairs. 'Christ, Joe,' she breathed. 'It's Iggy. He's back ... he's coming up here.'

chapter thirteen

'Quick,' gasped Candy, jumping off the bed. 'Get in the bathroom.'

'Maybe it's not Iggy?' I said. 'Maybe it's—'

'It's Iggy. I know what he sounds like.'

'But I thought you said—'

'Just *move*,' she said urgently. 'He'll be here any second.' She took me by the arm and pulled me off the bed and started leading me towards the bathroom. 'Stay in there and keep quiet,' she whispered. 'And whatever happens, don't come out. For my sake. *Whatever* happens ... OK? Now go.' She gave me another shove towards the bathroom.

My legs felt numb as I crossed the room, like lumps of wood with shoes on. I wasn't sure what I was doing. My head was empty – too shocked to feel anything. No fear, not yet. Just killing numbness.

I paused at the beaded doorway, listening to the sound of approaching footsteps – *boom, boom, boom* ... top of the stairs ... *boom, boom, boom* ... along the hallway ...

'Joe!' Candy hissed.

I looked at her – eyes wide, face rigid, teeth bared, hands waving, imploring me to go ... what else could I do? I turned around and stepped through the beads into the bathroom.

It was a small room – off-white, damp, dark. A faint shimmer of street light dappled the glass of a curtainless window set high in the wall, lifting the darkness just enough to show me my surroundings. There wasn't much to see: broken tiles on the wall, a stained sink, a toilet, a bath, a rust-rimmed water heater.

I moved to one side and stood with my back against the wall ... still numb ... but starting to feel it now. The fear. The beating heart, the tightening throat, the rapid breathing ... out of control ... too fast, too strangled, too loud. I could hear Candy outside, scrabbling around, cursing under her breath ... I didn't know what she was doing, but I guessed she was checking around the room to make sure I hadn't left any tell-tale signs. I heard her pause for a moment, and then I heard her skipping across the floor and jumping into bed – and half a second later I heard the sound of the door opening and Iggy's voice booming across the room.

'What you doing?'

'Nothing,' Candy replied, her voice remarkably calm. 'I thought you'd gone over to Karl's?'

A brief silence – the soundless sound of Iggy's eyes sweeping the room – then the door closed and I heard his footsteps crossing the floor.

'Yeah ...' he said. 'You got that number?'

'What number?'

'The guy ... what's the matter with you? What you looking at?'

'Nothing.'

'You out of it?'

'Just a bit ... I was hurting—'

'Don't use it all – you'll need some later. And you ain't getting no more – I told you that.'

'I know.'

'Yeah, well ...'

I heard him move across the room again ... then rummaging sounds, things being thrown on the floor. I guessed he was at Candy's dressing table.

'Shit,' he said, 'look at this mess ... you wanna get yourself cleaned up, girl. You living like a sick pig. Where the hell is it?'

'What?' Candy asked him. 'What are you looking for?'

'I told you – the guy's mobile number ... the guy with the gear ...'

'What gear?'

He didn't answer, just carried on searching through the stuff on the dressing table. I imagined his big hands sweeping the bottles and jars to the floor, his empty eyes searching ... empty of feeling, empty of heart, empty of everything but himself. I could see him. As I stared at the bathroom wall, unable to breathe, I could see him. His heavy head, his close-cropped hair, his death-mask face ...

'You dead, girl?' he said to Candy.

'What ...? I'm not—'

'You gonna lie there all day?'

'I was just—'

'Move yourself ... come *on* – get this shit cleared up. Christ!' An angry fist slammed on the table. 'You *hear* me?'

I heard the sound of Candy getting out of bed. Then silence. Then Iggy's voice again, hard and low – 'Come here.'

Bare feet moved hesitantly across the floor.

Silence.

Iggy sniffed, then spoke again, his voice a polished growl. 'What you waiting for?'

'What d'you want me to do?'

'I just *told* you – clean this shit up.'

'What – now?'

'Just *do* it!'

I heard the sound of things being moved – bottles, jars, bits of paper ...

'I ain't got all day,' Iggy said.

'My wrist hurts—'

'You what?'

'Nothing—'

'You got a problem?'

'No, I was just—'

'Here, give me your hand, let me see.'

'No, it's all right—'

'Gimme your *hand*!'

A frightened silence.

Then, 'Where's it hurt? There?'

Candy yelped.

Iggy laughed.

'Please ... don't,' begged Candy. 'I didn't mean anything—'

As she cried out again, I dug my fingernails into my palm, trying to take my mind off her pain. It didn't work. Her pain was everywhere. I could feel it all around me – in the cold bathroom air, in the sickness of my stomach, in the ache of my bones ... and the worst thing was, I couldn't do anything about it. I couldn't do *anything* ... for Candy's sake. She'd told me to stay where I was – *whatever* happened. For her sake. But I couldn't do that, could I?

How could I do that? How could I stand by and listen to that cold-blooded ugliness next door – the sound of her suffering, her stifled whimpers, his mocking laughter ...

How could I listen to *that*?

I couldn't.

But I couldn't move, either. My back was glued to the wall, my feet nailed down to the floor. I was too scared to move. It sickened me ... *I* sickened me. So frightened, so small, so useless ...

Then my mobile rang.

As the piercing ringtone echoed loudly around the bathroom, amplified by the white-tiled emptiness, I yanked the phone from my pocket and – unbelievably – checked the caller ID. Even as I scanned the display – *GINA* – my mind was already screaming at me – *what are you doing? turn it off, turn it off, TURN IT OFF!!!* I hit the *End* button and the ringtone stopped, but it was far too late. The damage was done. Iggy was already on his way. I could hear his voice – 'What's that?' – and the sound of his footsteps approaching the bathroom – *boom, boom, boom* – and Candy's futile attempts to stop him – 'No, Iggy ... Iggy! It's nothing ...'

There was a brief silence, then – *SLAP!* – and Candy went quiet.

And the footsteps started again.

I still hadn't moved. My body was frozen, my blood turned to ice. Even if I *could* have moved, there was nowhere to go. Nothing I could do. The window was locked and barred on the outside. There was nothing to use as a weapon. There was only one way out – through the beaded doorway ... and Iggy was almost there.

I stopped breathing.

The footsteps slowed.

My eyes fixed on the doorway.

A heavy hand appeared, parting the beads ...

Then a head ...

A skull of black skin.

Eyes of nothing, turning on me.

He smiled, grinning white teeth. 'Well, now ... look at this.'

I forced myself to look him in the eye as he wiped his mouth with the back of his hand and stepped through the beads to stand in front of me – solid as a rock, muscled and scarred, a huge black anvil of a man. My eyes darted down to the cut-throat razor balanced loosely in the palm of his hand. The handle was bone, as white as his eyes; the blade was stained with dry blood. I tried to swallow, but my mouth was too dry.

'This is something,' he said. 'This *is* something.'

The words were directed at me, pushed into my face, but I got the feeling he wasn't really talking to *me* – he was talking to something else. Something he wanted, something he needed, something he took from other people ... something weird.

I didn't want to know what it was.

I inched to one side ... then stopped, the blade of the razor against my cheek.

'Where you going?' said Iggy. 'This is good – right here. You want a bath? Take a shower? Get yourself nice before we start? Hey? You listening, boy?'

I didn't say anything.

He moved his face to within an inch of mine, then slowly ran the edge of the razor down my cheek, over my chin, and onto my throat, resting the blade just below my Adam's apple. I felt no pain, just a cold metallic shiver, so I guessed he hadn't cut me yet. But I was in no doubt he meant to. I could feel him turning the blade in his hand, lightly pricking my skin. I could feel his eyes boring into mine, searching for the fear and the pain.

'See you smile,' he whispered. 'Let's see it ...'

The blade pressed harder, breaking my skin, and I knew it was too late to do anything. The slightest movement from me, and the razor would tear open my throat.

I closed my eyes, hoping for the calmness I'd heard about – the calmness you feel just before you die. It's supposed to anaesthetize you, to make your death a pain-free experience. But I couldn't find it. All I could find inside myself was the snivelling voice of terror – *I don't want to get hurt. I don't want to die. I'll do anything to stay alive ... anything ... anything at all. Just don't kill me ... please. For God's sake, don't kill me ...*

'You ready?' said Iggy, tensing his arm. 'You ready to smile?'

I opened my eyes, not wanting to die in the dark, and just for a moment I saw the light of my death in Iggy's eyes, the black light he lived for – and then his head exploded in a crashing red fury of stars, and all the lights went out.

chapter fourteen

I'm not sure what I thought in that instant – maybe nothing, maybe everything: *am I dead? is this what happens? is this how it ends? with a crash, a heartbeat, a dancing explosion of red and black sparks ...?*

Is this it?

It wasn't, of course.

I knew it wasn't the end. It couldn't be. The end is *not* knowing. The end is senseless. And this wasn't senseless; this was just another world. I could see things, hear things, feel things. I was sentient. In the dim light of the window I could see Iggy's body lying on the bathroom floor. I could see Candy standing over him, breathless and tense, still holding the base of the cylindrical lamp in her hand. I could see the shards of broken red glass, the explosive remains, scattered all over the bathroom – on the floor, in the bath, in the sink ... in the thickening blood on the back of Iggy's head.

I could hear my heart.

And Candy's shallow breaths.

I could feel the fear of death.

Candy looked at me. 'Are you all right? You're bleeding.'

I put my hand to my throat and touched a small nick of pain. It felt sharp and moist. When I looked at my fingers, the thin smear of blood seemed incredibly bright. Like toy blood. Too pink to be real.

I looked down at Iggy. He wasn't moving.

I looked at Candy. Pale and wild.

She said, 'He's still breathing.'

Her voice was strangely remote.

'Are you sure?' I asked her.

She nodded. 'We'd better do something ... before he comes round.'

'Do something?'

She looked at me. 'We're both dead if we don't.'

I looked back at her, wondering what kind of *something* she meant. Tie him up? Run away? Or maybe she was thinking of something more permanent? It was a possibility – I could see it inside her. The way she was looking at him. The long-held hate in her eyes. The way she was standing, gripping the base of the lamp in her fist.

She could kill him, I thought.

If she wanted to.

She could end it right now.

How did that make me feel?

I don't know. I didn't know *how* to know. The truth is, at that moment, *my* feelings meant nothing. They were irrelevant. This was nothing to do with me. I was just a bystander. A spectator. Someone who just happened to be there. This was all about Candy: her life, her death, her choice.

It's up to you, I thought, looking into her eyes. *I can't help you decide. All I can say is – whatever you do, it's OK with me.*

I'm not sure what I thought I was doing – sending unspoken messages, assuming she could read my mind – but it seemed like the right thing to do at the time. And whether it worked or not, I still don't know. But as we carried on looking at each other, breathing in the silence, I saw something fade from Candy's eyes, and I felt as if she'd pulled herself back from a place where she didn't really want to be. The hate and the tension gradually eased from her body, her eyes came slowly back to life, and eventually she blinked and relaxed her shoulders and dropped the base of the lamp on the floor.

'We'd better go,' she said wearily, glancing down at Iggy.

'OK.'

'Find something to tie him up with, and I'll get dressed. All right?'

'Yeah.'

She turned to go, then paused and looked back at me. 'I'm sorry,' she said. 'I shouldn't have—'

'You saved my life,' I said. 'You don't have to be sorry about anything. It was my idea—'

'He would've killed you.'

Just then, Iggy groaned – a low, grunting breath. We both looked down at him. He was still out cold, but his breathing was getting stronger. Candy and I looked at each other for a moment, then we both got moving.

While Candy quickly got dressed and started throwing some stuff into a holdall, I found a roll of Sellotape and began tying up Iggy. Even though he was still unconscious, my hands shook with fear as I knelt down beside him. Up close, his body was enormous. His skin rock-hard. Scarred, patterned, tattooed. His muscles were bigger than my arms. As I unwound the Sellotape and cautiously positioned his arms behind his back, I felt like a vet in a safari park, tending to an anaesthetised beast – ready to jump and run at the slightest sign of life. As quickly as I could, I wound half the roll of Sellotape around his wrists, then I shuffled down and wound the other half around his ankles. It was a lot of tape, and I wound it as tightly as I could, but I didn't think it'd hold him for long when he finally woke up. It was better than nothing, though.

I looked around, found the cut-throat razor, picked it up and closed it and put it in my pocket. I was just standing up as Candy appeared in the doorway. She looked fantastic – hair tied back under a little black hat, jeans, T-shirt, a scruffy old coat.

'OK?' she said, looking at Iggy.

'Yeah – let's go.'

'Just a minute.'

She came over and knelt down beside Iggy and started going through his trouser pockets – first the back pockets, then she pulled him around to get to the ones in the front. As she pushed and pulled at his legs, he started groaning again. His head began to move, too.

'Come on,' I urged Candy. 'He's coming round ...'

'Just a minute ...'

She was digging desperately into his pockets, her face creased in concentration. His body began moving, rolling from side to side. His head turned. Eyes fluttering. Mouth muttering ...

'Gnuhh ... uh ... uh ...'

'Candy!' I hissed. 'Leave it ... come *on*. What are you *doing*?'

She was pulling out the contents of his pockets and stuffing them into her jeans. Cash, keys, credit cards ...

and other things, too. Little packets, plastic bags, bottles of pills ...

I reached down and grabbed her arm. 'That's enough,' I said. 'We have to go – right now.'

'OK,' she said, shoving something else in her pocket, 'I'm coming.'

As she went to stand up, Iggy suddenly flexed his arms and rolled his head to the side. His eyes were still glazed, but the look he gave Candy was enough to stop her in her tracks. She froze, staring back at him.

'Yuh ...' he muttered, his eyes flickering weakly to me. Without meaning to, I stepped back. His arms tensed again, getting stronger, and his eyes refocused on Candy.

'Yuh ... dumbitch ...' he whispered, a pained grin cracking his face. 'Yuh ... yuhshoulda yuh shoulda killed me ...'

Candy's face had ghosted over. The awe had come back. The hate, the fear ... even the adoration. It was all still there. Iggy knew it. Candy knew it. And I knew it, too. There was still a part of her that couldn't resist him. I didn't understand it, and I didn't want to believe it, but it was there, in her face ...

And I wondered then if Iggy was right.

She *should* have killed him.

'Maybe I will,' she said, her voice barely audible.

Iggy laughed, coughed, swallowed his breath. 'Too late ...' he spluttered. 'You had your chance.' Suddenly he opened his mouth and lunged at Candy, as if he was trying to bite her. She flinched away, half stood up, then lost her balance and toppled back against the bathroom wall.

Iggy laughed again and started slithering towards her, his arms and legs wriggling hard against the Sellotape, his body snaking from side to side. Christ – it was *horrifying*. Like something out of a terrible dream. Candy was transfixed ... couldn't move ... couldn't take her eyes off him.

He started humping his back, lurching across the floor, grunting under his breath – 'Come to Daddy ... come to Daddy ...'

I couldn't stand it any more. I stepped up and swung my foot at his head. A juddering pain shot up my leg, and for a moment I thought I'd kicked the wall by mistake, but then I looked down and saw that Iggy had stopped moving, and there was a faint red mark on his cheek, so I guessed I must have hit the target. Not that it made much difference.

He was already starting to move again – straining his arms, his shoulders, his neck ... stretching the bands of tape on his wrists ...

I took Candy's arm and pulled her to her feet. She felt like a puppet in my hands – loose, limp, lifeless.

'Come on,' I said, pulling her towards the doorway. 'Come *on*.'

She started moving, but her eyes were still fixed on Iggy and she was walking in a trance. I put my arm around her waist and dragged her through the doorway.

'Where's your bag?' I said.

'Uh?'

'Candy,' I said firmly. 'Look at me.'

Her head lolled loosely in my direction.

I reached out and balanced her chin in my hand. 'Look at me ... Candy. Come on, snap out of it ... *Candy!*' Her eyes blinked at the sharpness of my voice. 'Where's your bag?' I asked her again.

'Where? she said.

'Your *bag* ... the holdall – where is it?'

She looked at the bed.

I took her hand, walked over to the bed, and picked up

the holdall. She was beginning to move a little less stiffly now. Still holding her hand, I led her over to the door.

'Where are we going?' she said, frowning.

'I'll tell you later. Do you need anything else?'

'What?'

'Do you need—'

A loud crash came from the bathroom.

'Forget it,' I said. 'Let's go.'

I opened the door and ushered her into the hallway. The crashing from the bathroom was getting louder by the second. Crashing, smashing ... then violent shouting – 'Yo, *bitch!* BITCH*BOY!* You running? Hear me? YOU HEAR ME! You better run ... you meats now ... you *my* little meats ...'

I shut the door.

The voice carried on.

I turned around.

Candy was holding a key in her hand.

'Lock it,' she said. 'Lock the door.'

'Are you all right now?' I asked her.

She shook her head. 'Lock him in.'

I took the key and locked the door, then took Candy's hand and walked her quickly down the hallway. She was beginning to look all right again. Not great, but not too bad. Her eyes were fixed to the floor. Her breathing was a little strange. But she seemed to be walking steadily enough. Heading for the stairs, I picked up the pace. Candy responded.

'OK?' I said.

She nodded.

At the end of the hallway, a group of girls were gathered together on the landing, watching us curiously. I recognised the girl in the bathrobe, and the one who'd told me where Candy was. I guessed they'd been alerted by all the noise. As we approached, they stepped aside to let us onto the stairs.

'Candy?' one of them said.

Candy looked up at her. 'Hey, Janine.'

'You OK with this?' Janine asked her, glancing at me.

'Yeah,' Candy smiled. 'He's OK.'

We passed the girls and started down the stairs.

'Good luck,' someone called out.

'She's gonna need it,' another voice added.

All the way down the stairs, I kept expecting to hear the sound of raging footsteps clattering down behind us, or the sound of the front door opening, and Iggy's crew piling up the stairs to meet us ... and I couldn't stop thinking – *is this really happening? is this really me? am I really doing this?*

Doing what? asked a voice in my head. *You don't* know *what you're doing. You don't* know *where you're going. You don't* know *why you're running down the stairs of a dingy old house, with a traumatised girl by your side and a slithering black razor-monster haunting your mind ... you don't* know *anything, do you?*

'No,' I replied out loud, 'I don't.'

'What?' said Candy.

'Nothing,' I said. 'Is there a back way out of here?'

'Yeah, but it's locked. Iggy hides the key.'

We were downstairs now, in the hallway. The lights were on. I could see the woman called Bamma standing in a doorway at the end of the corridor, her impassive figure blocking the background of a dim white kitchen. She wasn't doing anything, just staring at us.

'What about her?' I asked Candy. 'Can she get us out the back?'

'I don't know ...' She glanced at Bamma. 'Maybe ... but if Iggy found out she'd helped us ...' She shook her head. 'Why can't we just go out the front?'

'Because that's where people come in. I don't want to meet anyone else.'

'No one else comes here.'

'Are you sure?'

She nodded.

'OK,' I said, moving towards the front door. 'Let's get out of here.'

chapter fifteen

There wasn't anyone outside the house. I paused on the steps and looked up and down the street, just to make sure, but everything was quiet. Just parked cars, streetlights, empty roads. The cold night air was misted with the smells of the city – traffic fumes, concrete, dust – but it felt good to be outside again.

Out of that house.

Out of that room.

I shut the front door and we scurried down the steps.

The little park across the street looked a lot darker now – the darkness shifting in the rustle of shadows – and I had to squint to see the spot where I'd hidden in the bushes ... the shoulder-high thicket of shrubs ... the smell of the earth ... damp and dark ... litter ... sap ... thorns ...

It seemed like a long time ago.

Just for a moment I thought I could see myself there – crouching down, looking out through the iron bars, watching the house ... the windows, the steps, the front door. *These* steps. *This* front door.

Watching myself.

In the shadows.

'What are you doing?' asked Candy.

'Nothing,' I said.

We left the house behind and hurried away into the night.

There was something between us then, something that hadn't been there before, and wouldn't be there again. I'm not sure what it was, but I think it had something to do with the balance of things. We were both changing, each of us in different ways, and neither of could know what those changes meant, or what they might mean to us in the future. I suppose we were still trying to work out how that made us feel – about ourselves, about each other, about everything.

I don't know ...

It's a difficult thing to think about.

It wasn't simply that we were changing, either, but that the changes themselves kept changing, too. It was like being on a seesaw: one minute I was this, and Candy was that; the next minute *she* was this, and *I* was that.

Up, down.

Down, up.

Scared, calm.

Calm, scared.

In control, out of control ...

It was pretty weird.

But strangely exciting, too – like we were starting all over again.

When Candy hailed a black cab at the end of the street, I went from *up* to *down* in an instant. There I was, Joe the

Hero, Joe the Saviour, Joe the *Man*, and I hadn't even *thought* of getting a taxi. I'd just thought ... well, I hadn't actually thought of anything. We had to hurry, that's all I knew, and hurrying – to me – meant either walking quickly or running. The idea of getting a taxi never even occurred to me. I mean, where was the taxi rank? Where were the rows of Mondeos with *Heystone Cars* written on the side?

Yep, that made me feel *highly* sophisticated.

And then, to make things worse, when the taxi pulled up at the side of the road, I couldn't work out how to open the door. I just stood there, fumbling stupidly with the handle, yanking uselessly at the door ... and suddenly I was the slack-jawed yokel again – the little boy lost, dazed and confused, blinking at the big city lights ...

It was pathetic, I know. I shouldn't have cared about anything except getting away from Iggy as quickly as possible. It was pathetic to even *consider* feeling pathetic. It was like combing your hair just before the end of the world – utterly pointless. But, sometimes, you just can't help yourself, can you? You just can't help feeling what you feel.

'You getting in or what?' the taxi driver said.

I tugged unsuccessfully at the door again, then Candy leaned over and thumbed the latch on the handle. The door swung open and we both clambered in and sat down next to each other.

'Where to?' asked the driver.

'What?' I said.

'Where to?'

I looked at Candy. She looked at me. And then a funny thing happened. As we sat there looking at each other, silently wondering where we were going, I felt the seesaw moving again. Candy started moving down, taking the yokel with her, and as they went down, the balance shifted, and up came Joe the Man again.

'Liverpool Street station,' he told the driver, almost adding, 'and step on it.'

The taxi pulled out into a stream of traffic and we headed off into the bustling chaos of the night.

The further we got from the house, the better it felt, and after a while we both began to relax a little. I think we both knew there was a lot more to come, but just for the moment it was enough to sit back in silence and watch the streets pass by, just breathing and resting and soaking up some reality. We'd both been somewhere else for a while, a place where ordinary things didn't exist, and now was the time to start bringing them home. The ordinary things: other people, time, distance, reason, hunger, thirst, the need to pee ...

I crossed my legs.

I thought about things.

I looked at my watch.

Candy turned to me and whispered, 'What's the time?'

'Six-thirty.'

She nodded. Then whispered, 'Where are we going?'

'Liverpool Street,' I whispered back.

'Why?'

'What?'

'Why are we going to Liverpool Street?'

'Why are you whispering?'

She smiled and whispered. 'I don't know.' Then, speaking in a normal voice, she said, 'Where are we going *after* we get to Liverpool Street?'

'Does it matter?'

'Of course it *matters*—'

'No – to *you,* I mean. Does it matter to you? Is there anywhere you particularly *want* to go?'

'Like where?'

'I don't know ... friends or something ... your parents' place—'

'I'm not going home,' she snapped. 'I'm not ... I *can't* ...'

'All right ... what about friends? Someone you can stay with for a while ...'

'You've just met my friends – back at the house.'

'That's it?'

'Yeah – that's it. What do you expect? You think I go out to dinner parties every night? Dinner parties, wine bars, charity functions—?'

'Yeah, all right. I'm sorry. I was only asking ...'

She turned away and stared out of the window. I looked at her ... in her little black hat and her scruffy old coat – she looked as if she ought to look older, or younger, but she didn't. She just looked different. Different enough to say what I wanted to say? I couldn't tell. I didn't know ... I didn't really know if I wanted to say it or not myself.

'Listen,' I said, 'there's this place ...'

She looked at me. 'What?'

'It's just an idea ...' My voice was shaking. I cleared my throat and started again. 'We've got this place in Suffolk ... my family, I mean. Well, it's my dad's, really ... you know ...'

'Not really.'

'It's a bungalow ... a holiday cottage ... on the Suffolk coast. It's empty at the moment. No one's there. It's right out in the middle of nowhere ...'

'So?'

'Well, I just thought it might be a good place to go. It's safe, for one thing. Iggy'll never find us there. And it's nice and quiet, really peaceful ...' I looked at her to see if she knew what I meant.

'A cottage? she said.

'Yeah ...'

'Just you and me?'

'Yeah ... I mean, there's plenty of room. Three bedrooms. We wouldn't have to—'

'Aren't you supposed to be at school?'

'It's half-term.'

'What about your dad? What will you tell him?'

'He's away for a week. He doesn't have to know.'

She didn't say anything for a while. I could see her thinking about it, picturing things, weighing up the consequences of leaving everything behind – her life, her people, her drugs. It was a struggle for her, I could tell. I had no way of knowing how *much* of a struggle, but if the look in her eyes was anything to go by – it was a bigger struggle than I could even imagine. It was as if there were two separate people inside her head, fighting each other for what they wanted ...

Fighting to the death.

'Is this all right?' the taxi driver said over his shoulder.

I glanced out of the window. We'd stopped on the bend of a busy little street in a crowded maze of office buildings. Everywhere I looked, all I could see was towering walls ... marble and brick ... shimmering sheets of smoked glass windows. I was lost for a moment, completely disorientated, but then I spotted the familiar angles of a rusted metal sculpture, and everything suddenly clicked into place.

Broadgate, I thought. *This is the Broadgate entrance to Liverpool Street station.*

'All right?' the driver asked again.

'Yeah,' I said, glancing at Candy. 'This is fine, thanks.'

The driver said, 'That's eleven-fifty, then.'

I started patting my pockets, looking for some money, but I realised I didn't have any on me. I looked at Candy. She stretched out her leg and dug into her pocket and pulled out a roll of notes. She peeled off a couple of tens and passed them through to the driver.

'Keep the change,' she said.

Without looking at me, she picked up her bag and opened the door and stepped out onto the pavement. The seesaw was moving again. Going up ... going down. I followed her out, almost stumbling on the kerb, and shut the door. The taxi pulled away, leaving the two of us – together on our stupid seesaw – in a streaming tide of pedestrians.

'All right?' I asked Candy.

She nodded, still not looking at me.

I said, 'What do you want to do, then?'

She looked up. 'He'll find us, you know. Wherever we go, he'll find us.'

'How?'

'I don't know – he just will. He always does.'

'Not this time.'

'You wanna bet?'

'50p says you're wrong.'

She smiled. '50p?'

'All right,' I said. 'Make it a quid.'

'You're on.'

She held out her hand. I looked at her for a moment, feeling a wonderful floating sensation all through my body, then I reached out and shook her hand.

My fingers tingled.

It was still there – the touch of her fingertips. It was still there – hot, cold, electric, eternal, intoxicating ...

It still didn't make any sense.

But I was beginning to realise that it didn't *have* to make any sense. Like Gina had said, this kind of stuff – it just happens. There's not much you can do about it, so why bother worrying? Just let it happen. You might not always get what you want, but sometimes that's just how it goes.

'You know I won't pay up if I lose?' Candy said. 'I never do.'

'Me neither. D'you want to get something to eat?'

She smiled. 'I thought you'd never ask.'

We ate at McDonald's, used the station toilets, then just had time to catch the seven-thirty train. It wasn't too crowded – too late for commuters, too early for people going home after a night on the town – and we managed to find an empty table in the smoking compartment. It smelled disgusting, but Candy said she was going to smoke wherever we sat, so I thought it was best to put up with the smell rather than risk drawing attention to ourselves. Candy's black eye was conspicuous enough, and bearing in mind that she'd come out of the toilets with her eyes rolling all over the place, and that her pockets were crammed with the stuff she'd taken from Iggy, the last thing we needed was a bolshy ticket inspector throwing us off the train and calling the police just for the sake of a cigarette.

So, smoking compartment it was.

I wanted to talk about things, but I wasn't sure where to start. There was so much to talk about ... and so much I didn't know – about heroin, addiction, withdrawal ... I didn't even know if Candy *wanted* to stop using heroin. It seemed a pretty simple decision to me – if she stopped taking heroin, she wouldn't need Iggy, and if she didn't need Iggy then she wouldn't have to live the life she was living. What could be simpler than that? But then – what did I know? I'd never been addicted to anything. I didn't have a clue how it felt. Of course, I knew how it felt to *want* something. But wanting something so much you'd give up everything else to get it ...?

That was beyond me.

I knew I had to try to understand it, though – which was why I wanted to talk about it. But, like I said, I didn't know where to start. And, besides, Candy was starting to nod off – her heavy eyes were beginning to close, her shoulders were slumping, her head was resting against the window ...

I waited until she was asleep, then I got out my mobile, turned it back on, and called Gina.

'You're doing *what*?' she said.

'Don't shout—'

'I'm not *shouting*—'

'You could have fooled me.'

'Yeah, well ... what do you expect? I've been worried *sick* about you. I don't know where you are, you don't answer your phone, and when you *do* finally get round to calling me, you tell me you're coming home with this girl and then taking her off to Suffolk. I think that calls for a little bit of shouting, don't you?'

'You sound just like Dad.'

'Christ, Joe ...' she sighed. 'What's got into you? You can't just ...'

'Just what?'

'You can't do it. You can't go to the cottage—'

'Why not?'

'Because it's ridiculous.'

'Why?'

'Well, you hardly *know* this girl, for one thing—'

'Candy.'

'What?'

'You keep calling her *this girl*. Her name's Candy.'

'All right ... Candy. But—'

'And I *do* know her, anyway,' I said, lowering my voice and glancing at Candy's sleeping head. 'I know her better than you think.'

'What's that supposed to mean?'

'She's not a stranger, Gina. She's not just someone I found on the street—'

'Yes, she is.'

'All right ... but you know what I mean. We've been through a lot together. And anyway, I couldn't just leave her where she was, could I? She needs somewhere to stay.'

'And what about this guy she was with, this Iggy? I suppose he's all right with the two of you waltzing off together, is he?'

'Well, I wouldn't say he's *all right* with it ...'

'No? What *would* you say he is, then? A bit miffed? Mildly annoyed?'

'Possibly ...'

'God, Joe – what have you *done*?'

'I don't know. It was just ... I don't know. It's complicated ... I'll tell you all about it later on. Right now, I just want to get home.' I glanced at Candy again. Even in her sleep, her face looked troubled. 'I know it all sounds stupid,' I told Gina quietly, 'and I expect it probably is ... but Candy's completely messed up. I just thought that if I took her to the cottage for a while, she might have a chance of getting off the drugs and getting back to normal again.'

Gina breathed out heavily. 'Have you any idea what that *involves*?'

'No – but it's worth a try, isn't it?'

She sighed again. 'Have you talked to Candy about this?'

'Of course I have.'

'What does she think? Does she think it's a good idea? Is she serious about getting off heroin?'

'Yeah ...'

'Are you sure?'

'Yeah,' I lied, 'absolutely ... she's been meaning to do it for ages, but she hasn't had a chance ... not with Iggy and everything. She just needs some time ...'

I didn't like lying to Gina, and I didn't really know why I was doing it. I hadn't *meant* to – it'd just come out that way. The strange thing was, though, as we carried on talking, and I carried on lying, Gina began to calm down. She still thought the whole idea was ridiculous, but I sensed in her a growing realisation that – however much she tried to dissuade me – I *was* going to the cottage with Candy, so she might as well accept it. She didn't actually *say* it like that ... but she didn't have to – I could tell that's what she was thinking.

'Look,' she said after a while. 'Just come on home and we'll talk about it some more – OK?'

'That's what I'm doing.'

'Yeah ... I know ...'

She changed the subject then, telling me that Jason had called that afternoon, demanding to know where I was, which kind of stumped me for a second. It wasn't that I didn't know what she was talking about – I hadn't *forgotten* about The Katies, the rehearsal that night, the planned recording sessions ... it was just that all that stuff didn't seem to have anything to do with me any more. It belonged to a different life. A different time. A different me.

'What did you tell him?' I asked Gina.

'Nothing,' she said. 'What *could* I tell him? He wanted to know your mobile number – said he'd lost it.'

'Did you give it to him?'

'No ... I might have, if he'd asked me nicely. But the way he was talking to me I felt like telling him to piss off. He's not the nicest person in the world, is he?'

'No,' I agreed.

'Did you want me to give him your number?'

'No, it's all right ... I'll ring him later. Has Dad called yet?'

'No ...'

We carried on talking for a little while longer, then Gina said she had to go and we said our goodbyes and hung up.

I looked at Candy, asleep on the seat beside me, and as the train rattled along, racing through the darkness, I wondered what I thought I was doing – taking her to the cottage, taking over her life, taking things for granted ... I didn't blame Gina for thinking it was ridiculous. It *was* ridiculous. The whole thing was riddled with problems – big problems, little problems, awkward problems ... problems that scared the hell out of me. I didn't know if I could deal with it, and I wasn't even sure I wanted to try.

But *want* didn't come into it.

Nothing came into it.

It was just *there*.

It was going to happen, no matter what. Just like before, when I'd known in my heart that I'd be at The Black Room, no matter what ...

It was *there*.

As inevitable as night follows day.

It could never be anything else.

Candy was still sleeping when the train began slowing for Heystone station. I gave her a gentle nudge.

'Whuh ...?' she said, rubbing her eyes and blearily looking around. 'What's this ... where are we?'

'Heystone,' I said, standing up to get her bag off the luggage rack.

She wiped her mouth and blinked her eyes, looking pained and confused. 'What's going on? What time is it ...?'

'Come on,' I said, offering a hand. 'We're getting off here.'

As the train juddered to a halt – wheels squealing, air hissing, doors opening – I helped Candy out of her seat, then hurried her along the corridor, through the door, and onto the platform.

She was still looking dazed as the doors slammed shut and the train creaked and groaned and began pulling away. I ushered her away from the platform edge and led her across to a bench.

'Sit down a minute,' I said.

She sat down, gazing curiously around the station, like a tired and bewildered child.

'Are you all right?' I asked her.

'Yeah ... I think so.' She was still looking around the station. 'Christ ... this brings back some memories. I haven't been here for years ... it hasn't changed much, has it?'

'No ...'

She fumbled in her pocket for a cigarette. Her hands were shaking as she lit it, but her eyes were beginning to clear. 'What *are* we doing here, anyway?' she said. 'I thought we were going to this cottage.' Her eyes suddenly narrowed. 'Hey, if you're thinking of taking me back to my parents—'

'I'm not.'

'You'd better not be.'

'I'm *not*.'

'Because you're wasting your time if you are—'

'I'm *not*. How many times do I have to *tell* you? I'm *not* taking you back to your parents. I don't even know where they live, do I?'

'Yeah, well ...' she said, puffing moodily on her cigarette. 'What are we doing here, then?'

'We're just going back to my place to pick up a few bits and pieces, then we're coming back here and catching the last train to Lowestoft – OK?'

'Lowestoft?'

'It's the nearest station to the cottage.'

'Why can't we go straight there?'

'I need to pick up the key. And I want to see my sister.'

'Your sister?'

'Gina.'

'She's at your house?'

'Yeah ...'

Candy looked at me. 'I don't have to come in with you, do I?'

'It won't take long.'

'Maybe I'll just stay here ...'

'Why? What's the matter?'

'Nothing ... I just feel a bit funny about ... you know ... meeting other people.'

'It's all right – it's only Gina. You'll like her.'

'How old is she?'

'Twenty.'

'Will she be on her own?'

'Well, her boyfriend might be there – Mike. But he's OK. I've told them all about you. They both know what's what.'

'What do you mean?'

'They know about you and Iggy and everything. They both saw you at The Black Room. Mike was the guy who tried to stop them dragging you away.'

'The big black guy?'

'Yeah.'

'They beat him up ...'

'I know.'

'Is he all right?'

'Yeah ... he's fine. Don't worry about it. It'll be OK.'

She smiled doubtfully. 'You think so?'

'Yeah ... no problem. Everything's cool.'

Her smile brightened. '*Cool?*'

'Yeah,' I grinned, 'cool with a capital K. Just like me.'

'Capital *F*, more like.'

'You think so?'

'Yeah – but you're sweet with it, so I'll forgive you.'

'Thanks very much.'

'You're welcome.'

It would have been nice to have walked back home, but the last train to Lowestoft was due at ten-thirty, and it was already getting on for eight-thirty now, so we didn't have much time. Luckily, there was a taxi waiting at the rank. And this time I didn't have any trouble opening the door.

The taxi dropped us off at the end of the avenue. Candy paid again, and we got out.

'Is this your house?' she said, gazing up the driveway.

'Yeah ...'

'Very nice.'

I opened the gate and we started up the drive.

'What's yours like?' I asked her.

'My what?'

'Your house.'

'You saw it this evening ...'

'No, I mean where you used to live. Your parents' house.'

'Oh, right,' she shrugged. 'Similar to this, I suppose. Not so old ... a bit bigger, maybe ...'

Her voice trailed off, and I guessed she didn't want to talk about it any more, so we walked on in silence. It felt really odd, being back home – back among the rolling lawns and the pine trees and the well-tended hedges ... shrouded in comfort. It felt safe. *It* is *safe*, I thought to myself. *It's peaceful, it's quiet, it's home. It's where you belong. It's where you ought to—*

'I can't stay here,' Candy said.

'What?'

'I can't stay here.'

'I know,' I said. 'We're not going to stay here.'

We were approaching the front door now. I dug the key out of my pocket and guided Candy into the porchway. She was looking really apprehensive, almost timid, like a shy young girl about to meet her boyfriend's parents for the very first time.

'All right?' I asked her.

She nodded.

'Don't worry,' I said. 'We're only going to be about half an hour – OK?'

She nodded again.

I looked at her for a moment – briefly amazed that this beautiful girl was actually *here* ... with *me* ... at *my* house – then I opened the door and we went inside.

chapter sixteen

To tell you the truth, Candy wasn't the only one who felt a bit apprehensive. As I led her along the hallway towards the kitchen, following the sound of Gina's and Mike's voices, I was feeling pretty nervous myself. I really didn't know what to expect. I knew that Gina and Mike would be nice to her, I wasn't worried about that. They were the kind of people who'd be nice to just about anyone I brought home. No, I wasn't worried about that ... I wasn't *worried* about anything, really. I just wanted them to like her, that's all. Especially Gina. I really wanted her to genuinely *like* Candy. It was a selfish thing to hope for, I suppose, and probably a bit immature ...

But what the hell?

If you can't be selfish and immature with your big sister, what's the point in having one?

Anyway, when we reached the kitchen door, I paused for a moment and quietly asked Candy if she was OK.

She nodded.

I said, 'Are you ready?'

She nodded again.

I opened the door and we both walked into the kitchen. Gina and Mike were sitting together at the table, deep in conversation. As we came in, they stopped talking and looked up at us.

'Hey,' I said, nodding at them both. 'This is Candy.'

Gina smiled at her. 'Hello, Candy. I'm Gina and this is Mike.'

'Hi,' Candy replied quietly, nodding her head.

Mike nodded back.

Gina stood up and came over to us. She gave me a quick hug, then shook hands with Candy.

'Nice to meet you,' she said.

'Thanks,' Candy said awkwardly.

Gina stepped back and gave us both a long hard look. 'Christ,' she said. 'The two of you look like you've been through a war.' She reached over and touched the cut on my throat. 'What's this, Joe?'

'Nothing ...'

'It doesn't *look* like nothing.' She turned to Candy. I thought she was going to ask her about my throat, but instead she lifted her hand to Candy's face and gently cradled her chin. Candy stiffened slightly. 'It's all right,' Gina said softly, angling her head to examine the bruises around Candy's eye. 'When did this happen?'

'Couple of days ago,' Candy replied hesitantly.

'Did you get it checked out?'

Candy looked anxiously at me.

'It's all right,' I assured her. 'Gina's a nurse – she can't help asking personal questions.'

'Shut up, Joe,' Gina said, turning her attention to Candy's bandaged wrist. 'What about this?' She took Candy's wrist in her hand, holding it carefully, cautiously flexing the joint. 'Does that hurt?'

'Just a bit ...'

'Who put this dressing on?'

'I did.'

'Pretty good job. It needs changing, though. I don't suppose you've been for an X-ray?'

'No ...'

Gina nodded, then stepped back, looking in Candy's eyes. 'Are you OK? I mean, do you need anything? Food ... something to drink?'

'No ... I'm fine, thanks.'

'When did you last use?'

Candy hesitated again, looking at me.

I looked at Gina.

She said to Candy, 'It's OK, it doesn't matter, I just wanted to know if you're all right, that's all.'

'Yeah ...' Candy said warily. 'I'm OK. I ... uh ... I had some stuff before we got on the train.'

'How much more have you got?'

'Enough for tonight.'

'Then what?'

'I don't know ...'

They looked at each other for a while, and I wondered if Gina was being a bit too pushy, confronting the truth a bit too soon. But then I thought – *maybe that's the best thing to do ... bring it out in the open, confront it, accept it. Maybe that's what* I *should have done?*

'OK,' Gina said, smiling at Candy. 'Do you want to freshen up or anything? Use the bathroom?'

Candy nodded. 'I wouldn't mind.'

'Joe'll show you where it is. If you need anything, my bedroom's on the top floor. Second door on the right. Just take whatever you want. I'll come up in a while and rebandage your wrist – all right?'

'Yeah, thanks,' Candy smiled.

'Joe?' Gina said.

'What?'

'The bathroom ...?'

'Oh, yeah ... right.' I looked at Candy. She was studying Gina with an expression I couldn't quite place – a mixture of confusion, relief, suspicion, and gratitude. 'All right?' I asked her.

She blinked and looked at me. 'Uh huh.'

'OK ... it's this way.'

As I led her upstairs to the bathroom, I felt that the balance had shifted again. There were three of us on the seesaw, now – me, Candy, and Gina. It felt good, in a way ... sort of comforting, like we weren't alone any more, so it wasn't so scary. But there was something else, too ... something about this extra presence that bothered me. I know it sounds childish, but it felt as if someone else was muscling in on our game. It was *our* seesaw, mine and Candy's, and I didn't *want* to share it with anyone else ...

Sounds childish?

It *was* childish.

I knew it even then. *What's the* matter *with you?* I asked myself. *Ten minutes ago you were desperate for Gina to like Candy ... and now – now that you know that she* does *like her – what do you do? You start feeling all niggly about it ...*

'She's nice, isn't she?' said Candy.

'What?'

'Your sister – she's really nice.'

'Yeah ...' I said, feeling ashamed of myself. 'Yeah, she is.'

'It's a shame, really ...'

'What is?'

'I mean, it's a shame we have to go. It would have been

nice to get to know her a bit better.'

'Well, maybe you can. We don't *have* to—'

'No, I told you – I can't stay here.'

'Yeah, I know. But—'

'I *can't* – all right? It wouldn't be fair.'

'Why not?'

'Because ... it just wouldn't.' She looked away from me then, anxious to change the subject. 'Is this the bathroom?'

'Yeah,' I said, opening the door. 'There should be some clean towels in the airing cupboard—'

'Thanks,' she said quickly, stepping inside. 'I'll see you in a minute.'

She shut the door.

I stood there for a moment, wondering why everything had to be so *complicated*, then I went back down to the kitchen.

Gina was standing at the table, packing a holdall with tins of food and clothes and stuff, and Mike was sitting there watching her, sipping black coffee from a big white mug.

'I don't know why I'm doing this,' Gina said, shaking her head. 'That girl needs professional help. She needs rehab, counselling, proper medical advice ... and what am *I* doing? I'm sending her off into the wilderness with my dumb kid brother, for God's sake. I must be mad.'

'She can't afford rehab,' I said, sitting down at the table.

Gina gave me a look. 'I *know* that.'

'She won't go back to her parents, she hasn't got any friends, and she won't stay here because she doesn't want to cause any trouble. Where else *can* she go?'

'I don't know,' Gina said. 'I just don't like it, that's all. I mean, what if something happens? What if Dad finds out?

What if—'

'Nothing's going to happen,' I said. 'And Dad's not going to find out.'

'No? What if he phones up? What if he wants to speak to you?'

'I don't know ... tell him I'm asleep or something.'

'What if he rings at six o'clock? If I tell him you're asleep at six o'clock, he's going to start asking questions—'

'Tell him I'm out.'

'You're supposed to be grounded – remember?'

'Tell him I'm in the bath, then. Tell him anything ... it doesn't matter. He probably won't ring, anyway. He hardly ever does.' I took a deep breath and let it out slowly. 'Listen,' I said, 'I really appreciate what you're doing, and I'm sorry it's all such a mess. I didn't *mean* things to end up like this ... I didn't *mean* anything ...'

Gina sighed. 'How on earth did you *find* her?'

'I just ... I don't know. It's a long story.' I glanced at the clock – it was nearly ten o'clock. 'We'll have to get going soon. We need to catch the last train—'

'You don't have to go tonight,' Gina said. 'Why don't you both stay here? Get some rest. We can talk about things in the morning—'

'No, I think we'd better get going.'

'Why?'

I looked at her, not knowing what to say. I didn't *know* why. It made sense to stay here – it was safe and warm and comfortable, and Gina and Mike would be around, so I wouldn't have to deal with everything myself, and it would probably help Candy to have someone else to talk to ...

But she didn't want that, did she? She didn't *want* to stay here. And I could hardly force her, could I?

'Look,' said Gina, 'if you *really* have to go tonight –

although I still don't see why it's necessary – but if you have to go, at least let us drive you to the cottage.'

'Thanks ... but you don't have to do that. The train's fine.'

'It's no trouble. We don't *mind* driving you—'

'I know you don't mind – I just think it's best if you don't.'

'But why not? It's late, it's cold, the cottage is at least fifteen miles from the station. There won't be any buses this time of night—'

'We'll get a taxi.'

'Don't be *stupid*, Joe. What's the matter with you? We're not going to—'

'Let them get the train,' Mike interrupted. 'They'll be all right.'

A flash of annoyance crossed Gina's face, and I thought for a moment she was going to start yelling at Mike, but then a look passed between them, an intimate exchange of trust, and after a while Gina grudgingly nodded her assent.

Mike said to me, 'I'll drive you to the station. What time's the train?'

'Ten-thirty.'

He glanced at the clock, then turned to Gina. 'You'd better go and see to Candy. We'll have to leave in about ten minutes.'

'What about Joe?' Gina said. 'He needs to know—'

'I'll talk to him.'

Gina nodded. She looked at me, started to say something, then changed her mind and quietly walked out. I watched her go, then turned to Mike. His eyes were fixed on mine, calm and cool and steady.

'Thanks,' I said.

'I'm only giving you a lift.'

'I didn't mean that—'

'I know,' he said, sipping his coffee. He took his time, savouring the taste, then he put the mug down and looked at me again. 'So,' he said, 'did you have a good day?'

'Not bad,' I smiled. 'A bit tiring ...'

He nodded slowly, eyeing the cut on my throat. 'Looks like you had a close shave there.'

'Yeah, you could say that.'

'Do you want to talk about it?'

'Not really ... maybe some other time.'

'OK,' he said, 'that's fair enough.' He took another sip of his coffee. 'Two things, though – two simple questions.'

'I don't think—'

'Listen, Joe,' he said, 'whatever you do with your life is your business, and I'm happy to leave it at that. But if you've done something that might affect Gina or me, that's my business – OK?'

I nodded.

'Right,' he said. 'First question – is Iggy still alive?'

'Yeah.'

'And, second question, does he know who you are?'

'What do you mean?'

'Does he know your *name*?'

'I don't know ... I don't think so ...'

'Well, think about it. It's important. If he knows your name, he can find out where you live.'

I thought about it, trying to remember if he'd ever called me by name. It was hard to think, though ... hard to see through the clouds of fear. 'I'm pretty sure he *doesn't* know it,' I told Mike. 'I've only met him twice, so I don't see how he *could* know ... unless Candy's told him. I'm sure she wouldn't have, though.'

'You need to find out before you go.'

'I'll ask her.'

'OK,' he said, glancing at his watch. 'There's just one more thing before you leave. Gina thinks you ought to know what to expect if Candy is serious about giving up heroin. Personally, I'm not sure that knowing what to expect will make any difference, but I don't suppose it'll do any harm. Do you think she *is* serious?'

'I'm not sure.'

'Has she ever tried giving up before?'

'I don't know.'

'OK. Well, basically, for what it's worth, if she does try packing it in, she's going to feel terrible – I mean, *really* terrible. She'll think she's dying. She'll think she's going mad. She'll be irritable and depressed, sleepless, sick, she'll hurt all over – stomach cramps, muscle pains, diarrhoea, fever – she'll shout at you, she'll hate you, she'll lie to you, she'll probably get violent with you ...' He looked at me. 'Do you think you're ready for all that?'

'I don't know ...'

'But you're willing to give it a try?'

'Yeah, I think so.'

He smiled. 'She must mean a lot to you.'

'Yeah ... she does.'

'OK,' he said, 'but just remember one thing – whatever feelings she has for you, they won't be as strong as the feelings she has for heroin. If you want to help her, you might have to lose her.'

At the time, I didn't know what he meant, but I found out later that he was right. Maybe not in the way he intended, but I don't suppose that matters. He was right, intentionally or not ...

He was right.

Five minutes later we were all in Mike's car, heading for the station. Gina had cleaned up Candy's face and put a fresh bandage on her wrist, and now she was telling us what she'd packed in the bag.

'There's plenty of tinned food, fresh fruit, orange juice, bread ... bandages, aspirin, face cream, toothpaste ... I don't think I've forgotten anything. Did you pick up the key to the cottage, Joe?'

'Yeah.'

'Do you remember where everything is? The fuse box, spare light bulbs, sheets, blankets—'

'Don't worry,' I said, 'we'll be all right. If we need anything, I'll phone you.'

'I put your phone charger in the bag.'

'Thanks.'

We were approaching the station now. Mike glanced at me in the rear-view mirror, flicking his eyes at Candy. I didn't know what he was doing for a moment, then he mouthed the word *name* at me, and I suddenly remembered.

I turned to Candy and said, 'Does Iggy know my name?'

'Your name?'

'Yeah ... I mean, did he ever ask you what I was called?'

'Yeah, he did ... but I lied to him. I said your name was Kevin.'

'Kevin?'

'Yeah,' she smiled. 'Kevin Williams.'

'Why Kevin?'

'I don't know,' she shrugged. 'It was the first thing that came to mind. Maybe it's because you look like a Kevin ...'

'Thanks a lot,' I said. 'So, Iggy thinks I'm Kevin Williams?'

Candy nodded.

I glanced at Mike, then turned back to Candy again. 'Did you tell anyone else my real name?'

'Like who?'

'I don't know ... anyone. What about the girl I spoke to, the one with the black hair? She knew who I was. She knew we'd been to the zoo.'

Candy shook her head. 'I just told her you were a friend. I haven't mentioned your real name to anyone.'

I nodded, trying to remember if *I'd* given my name to the black-haired girl. *I'm a friend of Candy's*, I'd told her. *We met up a couple of times ...*

Was that all I'd said?

I'm a friend of Candy's ...

No, I'd said something else.

My name's Joe.

Shit.

My name's Joe.

I looked up and caught Mike's eye in the mirror again.

'What's up?' he asked.

'Nothing ...'

'Is there a problem?'

'No,' I said. 'No problem.'

'You sure?'

'Yeah.'

I *wasn't* sure, of course ... but I wasn't sure what I wasn't sure about. I couldn't see how the black-haired girl was anything to worry about. I'd given her my first name, that was all. How could that be a problem? She probably wouldn't tell Iggy, anyway. And even if she did ... well, so what? All he'd know was that I was called Joe. How was *that* going to help him find me? *No*, I assured myself, *it's not a problem. It isn't even worth mentioning.*

So I didn't.

But there was something else – something that *did* feel like a problem, and *was* worth mentioning – only I didn't know what it was. It was just a fragment of something, a half-formed thought that had flickered so briefly into my mind that I hadn't had a chance to identify it. All I knew for sure was that it had been there, and now it was gone, and all that was left was a worrying shadow ...

Forget it, I told myself. *If it's important, you'll remember it. If it's not, it doesn't matter.*

So that's what I did.

I forgot it.

The train was approaching the station as Mike pulled up in the car park. I grabbed the bags, Candy opened the door, and we both jumped out of the car.

'Ring us when you get there,' Gina called out through the window.

'OK,' I called back.

'And be careful ... both of you. Take it easy ...'

As we hurried along towards the entrance, I glanced back at the car and waved my hand in acknowledgement. Gina waved back through the window. She was doing her best to look casual, but even from a distance I could see the distress in her face. I could see Mike putting his hand on her shoulder as she started dabbing her eyes, and just for a moment I seriously thought about turning back. She was my sister. She was scared and upset. I wanted to *be* with her ...

But then Candy's voice called out to me.

'Come on, Joe – hurry up. We're going to miss the train ...'

And I couldn't resist it. Despite all the dangers, the

doubts, the fears ... despite everything my rational mind was telling me – and it was telling me a lot – I just couldn't resist it.

I was hooked.

Blind to the rest of the world.

I waved to Gina again, then turned around and followed Candy into the station and onto the waiting train.

chapter seventeen

The cottage lies at the end of a woodland track near a remote little village called Orwold. It's a nice old place – a traditional wood-framed bungalow, with three small bedrooms, a combined main room and kitchen, and a rickety veranda out the front – set in a clearing near the edge of the woods. The surrounding pine trees act as shade in the summer, and during the winter, when a sharp north-easterly wind blows in from the nearby estuary, the trees shield the cottage from the worst of the cold.

Dad bought the cottage about six or seven years ago, which surprised us all at the time. Even Mum didn't know about it. He just came home one day, told us all to get in the car, then drove out to Orwold and proudly showed us the cottage.

'There,' he'd said. 'What do you think of that?'

'What?' Mum had said.

'The cottage. It's ours. I bought it.'

'You *what*?'

'I bought it.'

'You *bought* it?' she'd said incredulously. 'What the hell *for*? What are *we* going to do with a *cottage*?'

After Dad had explained its numerous uses – as a family home for weekends away, a quiet place to work without interruptions, or just somewhere to go to get away from it all – Mum began to calm down, and gradually she came round to his way of thinking. We all did, I think – imagining lazy days in the sun, woodland nights, log fires crackling in winter ...

It never really worked out like that, though. At first we used to go there almost every weekend. Friday night, we'd pack our bags and jump in the car and drive off to Suffolk for a quiet weekend ... and it was fine, for a while. We had our lazy days and our quiet nights – walking in the woods, collecting logs for the fire, or strolling along the estuary and watching the boats in the evening sun ... then we'd all get starving hungry and head back to the cottage for toasted crumpets and big mugs of steaming hot chocolate ...

Yeah, it was OK.

We even spent a whole week there one summer. I was about twelve then, and Gina was seventeen. I remember when she met this boy in the village. I got really upset when she wouldn't let me come with her when she was going out for a walk, and I ended up following her into the woods ... and getting a big surprise when I saw her kissing this boy. And then afterwards, when I asked her who he was, and she realised I'd been spying on her, she threatened to beat me up. But I told her that if she did, I'd tell Mum and Dad what she'd been doing, so instead of getting beaten up I got £5 for promising to keep my mouth shut. I took the money, of course, but for some weird reason I never spent it. In fact, it's still hidden away in my room somewhere, all dirty and creased and faded, like some kind of useless reminder ...

Anyway, I think that was probably the last time we were all at the cottage together. I don't know why, but as the years went by, the weekends away became less and less frequent, until it reached a point when we were hardly going to Orwold at all. Even when we did make the effort, there always seemed to be someone missing. Either Gina couldn't make it, or Mum was working, or Dad was away at a conference somewhere. And, without all four of us, it never felt quite the same. Everything felt false – empty and forced – as if we were trying to revive what used to be there, *trying* to remember the enjoyment, *trying* to have a good time. But it just wasn't there any more. In the end, I think we all realised that it wasn't just pointless trying to find it, it was painful, too.

So we gave up.

By the time Mum and Dad were divorced, the cottage – to me – had faded into the past. It was just somewhere we used to go. A place in my mind. A memory.

But now I was back.

And it was real again.

The village, the woods, the estuary, the cottage ...

Taking us into its sanctuary.

We didn't talk much on the way there. We were both too tired, I think, and maybe a bit too wired, as well. I couldn't get comfortable on the train. My body felt strange, all tight and grainy, as if my flesh was made of sandpaper. My head was cramped and dull with fatigue, and my eyes were heavy and thick.

Candy wasn't doing much better. She'd drugged herself up in the toilet again, but this time it didn't seem to relax her. She kept fidgeting, sniffing, wiping her nose, licking her lips, tapping her fingers on the table. Smoking too much. Coughing too much. Breathing too fast, then too slow, then too fast again ...

I didn't get it.

I didn't *understand* it.

But I was too tired to do anything about it, and Candy was too wired to care. So we both kept our sufferings to ourselves and endured the long journey in fitful silence – half-dozing, half-awake, occasionally muttering half-hearted nothings ...

The time passed neither slowly nor quickly: it just passed.

Forty minutes to Ipswich, across the platform onto the branch line, then a bone-numbing hour-and-a-half grind to Lowestoft, a freezing-cold wait for a taxi, and finally a twenty-minute drive to Orwold.

'Is this it?' Candy asked hopefully as the taxi pulled up at the side of the road by the woods.

'Nearly,' I said. 'Just another few minutes or so.'

But it turned out to be a bit longer than that, because the driver refused to take us down the track into the woods.

'I 'in't going down there, mate. No chance.'

'It's only about half a mile,' I told him.

He shook his head. 'Sorry, mate – this car's my livelihood. I can't afford to wreck it.'

I tried telling him that the track was OK, that he wouldn't have any trouble, but he didn't want to know. So we had to walk through the woods, at one-thirty in the morning, shivering and stumbling and cursing our way through the darkness. It was hard going, and a bit scary at first. I kept worrying that we'd lose sight of the track and wander off into the woods and get lost ... but after a while, as my eyes adjusted to the dark, and we moved on into the heart of the woods without getting lost, I began to feel a lot better.

The moon was almost full, shining down and glazing the woods with a delicate silvery light, and as I breathed in the crystal-clear air, I could feel myself coming alive again. I could *feel* the night's silence, the rustling trees, the smell of the pines, the distant drift of sand and seaweed from the estuary ...

It felt good – pure and fresh and energising.

I almost wished I was on my own.

But I wasn't.

And Candy was still struggling ...

'Joe? *Joe* ... where *are* you?'

'Here ... I'm right next to you.'

'Christ – it's so *dark.*'

I took hold of her hand. 'It's all right, we're nearly there now.'

'Shit,' she muttered. 'I can't see where I'm going.'

'Try closing your eyes,' I suggested, 'then opening them again.' I smiled at her. 'Someone once told me that it lets more light in.'

'Yeah?' she said. 'And you believed them, did you?'

'I'm gullible.'

We carried on down the track, hand in hand, and after a while I started to recognise one or two things – a fallen tree, a curious bend in the path, the shape of the skyline shimmering in the moonlight ...

'It should be just down here,' I said.

'*Should* be?'

'Well, it's been a long time ... hold on – there it is.'

'Where?'

I stopped and pointed straight ahead. 'There ... just to the right of those pines ... the two tall ones ... see?'

Candy squinted into the darkness, shaking her head. 'I can't see *any*thing.'

'That dark shape,' I explained, 'beneath the trees. You can see the roof—'

'It's *all* dark shapes.'

'You'll see it in a minute,' I said, moving off again. 'Come on ... give me your hand.'

And she'd taken my hand, and I'd led her down the final few metres of the track, and now here we were – standing outside the cottage, shadowed in the light of the moon, exhausted and cold and relieved.

'I can see it now,' Candy said, smiling at the cottage.

'Sure?'

'Yeah ... it looks really nice.'

'It could do with a few repairs,' I said, looking it over. 'The veranda needs fixing for a start—'

'Let's just go inside, eh?'

I looked at her.

She said, 'I mean, this is all very nice and everything, but I'm freezing cold and I need a wee.'

'Sorry,' I said. 'I was just having a quick look, that's all. I'll check it out properly tomorrow. It should be all right—'

'Joe?'

'What?'

'Will you please shut up and open the door?'

'Yeah, sorry.'

I got the key out of my pocket and unlocked the door. It was a little stiff – probably warped by the rain – but a couple of good shoves got it open, and then we were looking inside, seeing nothing but a pitch-black darkness.

'Any lights?' asked Candy.

'Just a second.'

I put my hand around the door and flicked the light switch. Nothing happened. I flicked it again. Still nothing.

'What's the matter?' asked Candy.

'It's probably turned off at the mains,' I replied. 'Don't worry, there should be some candles somewhere. Let me have your lighter.'

Candy passed me her cigarette lighter.

I clicked it, testing the flame, then started through the doorway. 'I won't be a minute—'

'I'm right behind you,' she said. 'I'm not staying out here on my own.'

'All right ... but watch your step.'

I moved inside, holding the lighter at arm's length, and began inching my way across the room. Candy stayed close behind me. As we edged further into the darkness, weird shadows began flickering around the walls – shadows of Candy, shadows of me. When I paused for a moment and held up the lighter, the shadows of our figures fused together in a macabre mutation – an ethereal beast with two stooped backs and two large heads and dozens of ghostly limbs ...

I raised my hand to the light and made a shape with my fingers.

'What are you *doing*?' Candy whispered.

'Look,' I said, indicating the shadow I'd made on the wall.

Candy turned her head. 'What's it supposed to be?'

'A duck,' I said, waggling my fingers, opening and closing its beak. 'See? Quack, quack ... quack, quack. That's the beak, there's its head—'

'Just find the candles, Joe.'

I crossed over to the far wall and felt my way along the kitchen counter until I came to the sink. I crouched down, opened the cupboard under the sink, and held the lighter inside. The candles were in a box at the back. I took one out and lit it, passed it to Candy, then grabbed a few more and stood up again, joining Candy in the fluttering light.

'That's better,' she said, placing the candle on the counter. 'Now, where's the bathroom?'

I lit another candle for her and directed her to the bathroom. As she wandered off across the room, I quickly called Gina to let her know we'd arrived, then I set about lighting more candles and positioning them around the cottage. When I'd finished, and the whole place was bathed in the shimmering light of the naked flames, it looked almost spiritual – like the sacred interior of a small wooden chapel, or some kind of godless shrine.

I wasn't sure if it was that, or just the cold, that was making me shiver.

'I'll get the fire going,' I said to Candy as she came out of the bathroom. 'Why don't you make some tea?'

I showed her the gas stove, checked it was still connected, got it going, then left her to it. While she clattered around looking for something to boil the water in, I started making the fire. Everything I needed was there: old newspapers, fire-lighters, kindling, logs.

'How come this place doesn't get vandalised?' Candy asked from across the room.

'It does sometimes,' I said, 'but there isn't much worth stealing, and Dad pays an old couple from the village to keep an eye on things, which helps. Kids still break in now and again, but they don't usually do much damage.' I'd laid the base of the fire now, and was starting to build up the logs. 'We had squatters once,' I told Candy. 'A family of crusties broke in and stayed here for a month. Kids, dogs – the lot. Dad had to call the police to get them out.'

'You ought to rent it out,' she suggested. 'That way you wouldn't have to worry about kids breaking in, plus you'd make some extra cash.'

'Yeah, I suppose ...'

I lit the fire, waited to make sure it was going, then sat back and gazed into the flames. Behind me, I could hear the gas stove hissing, and water boiling, and Candy shuffling around – opening cupboards, looking in drawers, rattling cups and cutlery – and it all sounded so *normal*. She was making some tea. I was sitting in front of the fire. We were talking ...

And that was OK ...

Wasn't it?

Being normal ...

What's wrong with that?

Nothing, I told myself. *Nothing at all* ...

But I wasn't so sure. Firstly, because I knew that things *weren't* normal, and all we were doing by pretending they were was avoiding the inevitable truth. And secondly – and this is the thing that bothered me most – I wasn't so sure I *wanted* us to be normal. I didn't want us to be *abnormal*. I didn't *want* all this chaos and underworld crap ... but that's where we'd come from. The chaos was *part* of us. Part of what we were. And I was afraid if we lost it completely, we might lose part of ourselves ...

I *think* that's what I was thinking, anyway.

I was tired, remember? It was nearly two o'clock in the morning and I was staring dead-eyed into a blazing fire ... entranced by the flames ... not really there ... not really conscious of anything. The thoughts in my head were nothing to do with me. They were just scraps of things – images, words, memories, feelings – floating around without any purpose, like bits of dust in the wind.

'Here's your tea,' Candy said, sitting down beside me and breaking into my trance. She passed me a mug of dreggy black liquid.

'Thanks,' I said.

'There's no milk, I'm afraid, and I couldn't find any sugar.'

I took a sip – it tasted foul.

'Great,' I said.

'Really?'

'Yeah.'

'Liar,' she smiled. 'It's horrible, isn't it?

'Absolutely disgusting.'

We both put our mugs down and stared at the fire. Candy lit a cigarette and smoked it thoughtfully for a while, blowing long streams of smoke into the heat of the flames, then she turned to me and said, 'You know that song you played at The Black Room ... the one you sang at the end?'

'Yeah ...'

'Did you write that?'

'Mostly, yeah ... I mean, we worked it out together—'

'But you wrote it?'

'Yeah.'

'Is it about who I think it's about?'

'I don't know,' I grinned. 'Who do you think it's about?'

'Come on, Joe – don't mess around. It's embarrassing ...'

'What is?'

'You *know* ... if I told you that I thought it was about

me, and it turned out that it *wasn't* ... God, imagine how that'd make me feel.'

'You think it's about *you*?'

She glared at me.

'Yeah, all right,' I admitted, 'I wrote it the night I first met you. I didn't really know you then, so I'm not sure it means very much—'

'It does to *me*. God, when I heard you singing it ... and the *way* you were singing it ... Christ, Joe ... I can't *tell* you what it did to me.'

'You looked good dancing to it.'

'I *felt* good.'

'Me too ...'

Neither of us spoke for a while. We both just sat there, staring into the fire, thinking our thoughts. The room was quiet. The candles burned ... the flame-light flickered ... silent colours played on the walls ... yellow, red, blue, orange ...

'I'm sorry,' Candy said. 'It should have been better than this.'

I looked at her. 'There's plenty of time yet.'

'Yeah ...' she said, lowering her eyes. 'I wanted to say thanks ...'

'What for?'

'The song ... everything. What you've done ... what you're trying to do ... I don't know – just everything, I suppose. I'm sorry. I'm not very good at saying what I mean.'

'You don't have to say anything.'

She looked at me for a moment, her eyes dimmed with sadness, then she reached out and brushed my cheek with her finger. 'You're sitting too close to the fire,' she said. 'Your face is all red ...'

I held her gaze. 'You're changing the subject.'

'I know.'

'We need to talk about things.'

'I know.'

'Look,' I said hesitantly, 'it's up to you what you do. It's your life ... I'm not trying to get you to do anything you don't *want* to do ...' I sighed, wishing I could just say what I meant instead of talking *around* things all the time. I looked at Candy. She was staring into the fire again. I said, 'I can't do this on my own. You have to help me to help you.'

'How?' she asked.

'I don't know ... just *tell* me things. I don't know what you're thinking. I don't know how you feel about anything. I don't know where you *are*.'

'Neither do I,' she said quietly. 'I've never had to think about this before. I've never had to talk to anyone about it.'

'About what?'

'Drugs,' she said slowly, looking at me. 'Heroin ... I don't think about it ... as long as I've got it, there's nothing to think *about*. It's just a requirement, like oxygen. You don't think about breathing, do you? You just do it. It's only when you *can't* do it that you realise you can't do without it. That's why it's so hard to talk about, Joe. I can't imagine *not* doing it, just as you can't imagine not breathing. But I know I have to ... I *have* to stop doing it. There's nothing left for me if I don't.' She was sitting with her knees drawn up to her chest, her arms clamped tightly around her legs, and she was rocking slightly, backwards and forwards, trying not to cry. 'I'm scared, Joe,' she whispered. 'I'm so *scared*. I don't know if I can do it ...'

'It's all right,' I said, moving over to her. 'It'll be all right ...'

'No, it won't,' she said. 'It's going to be really bad—'

'Yeah, but once it's over ... once you're all right again ...'

She was crying now, really bawling. I moved closer and put my arms around her. Her head was buried in her knees and her shoulders were heaving and she was gulping out words in breathless sobs.

'I don't ... dunno ... I don't ...'

'You don't know what?' I asked gently.

'It's like ... it's like ... I dunno ... I c-can't remember ...' She shook her head, then took a deep breath and straightened her back, trying hard to calm herself down. 'God,' she said, wiping her eyes, 'this is so bloody *hard*.' She looked at me. Her lips were quivering and her face was streaked with make-up. When she spoke, her voice was still frail, but not so breathless as before. 'It's not just giving up heroin that scares me,' she explained, 'it's everything else. It's like ... I've been stuck in this place for so long, this place where everything's numbed and dead and you don't have to think about anything or care about anything ... and I can't remember what it feels like to be *outside* this place. I don't know what it's like to be normal any more ... having to *deal* with things, having *feelings* about things, being *myself* again ...' She sighed heavily and looked down at the floor. 'It's a different world, Joe,' she said quietly, 'and it scares me to death.'

After that we just sat there for a while, holding each other in the candle-lit silence. The fire began to burn down, the exhausted logs crackling and hissing in the dying embers, and as the cold night air started creeping into our bones, we held each other closer, sharing the warmth of our bodies. Candy was resting her head on my shoulder, and I could feel her breath whispering faintly on my neck. It was hypnotising – the steady rhythm, the heat, the touch – like a wordless lullaby. Gradually, she began to drift away, and as her breathing became faint with sleep, I closed my eyes and let myself sink down into the darkness.

Some time later, in the small hours of the morning, I woke up to find Candy in the throes of a nightmare. Groaning and whimpering, her body twitching, her eyes and fists closed tightly in pain ...

I nudged her softly. 'Candy ... Candy ... wake up.'

Her head shook from side to side, and she let out a tiny little yelp.

'Wake up,' I repeated, this time taking hold of her hand.

Her eyes jerked open and she stared at me, blinking in confusion at the remains of her dream.

'Whu ...?' she mumbled.

'It's me,' I said, 'Joe ... you were having a nightmare.'

'Joe?' she said.

'Yeah ... are you all right?'

She rubbed her eyes, shook her head, yawned widely, then started rubbing her arms. 'Christ ... it's cold.' Her voice was sleepy. 'What time is it?'

'I don't know,' I said. 'It's still early ...'

'Too cold,' she mumbled. 'Let's go to bed.'

'Bed?' I said stupidly.

She ignored me and started to get up, wobbling slightly on her legs. I reached out to steady her, then got to my feet.

'I'll take the back bedroom,' I muttered, avoiding her eyes. 'You can have the main one.'

'I don't want to sleep on my own,' she said.

I didn't know what to say. I didn't know what to do ... what I *ought* to do ... what I *wanted* to do ... I didn't know anything. All I could do was look at her.

'Just come to bed, Joe,' she said simply.

I still didn't know anything as I blew out the dying candles and followed her into the bedroom. I stood and watched as she got into bed without undressing, and then I clambered in beside her.

You don't have *to know*, I thought to myself. *You don't have to know anything.*

The sheets were cold, the dark of the night ever-silent, and as we lay down together and closed our eyes, everything drained away into nowhere.

We didn't do anything.

We didn't even kiss.

We just fell asleep, fully clothed, holding each other in the darkness.

chapter eighteen

When I opened my eyes, the room was bathed in daylight and Candy was sleeping quietly on my arm. I didn't know what time it was, but it felt quite late. Birds were singing outside the window, the air was cold and fresh, and away in the distance I could hear the faint *chunk-chunk* of someone chopping wood.

I couldn't move my arm.

I looked down at Candy. She was still fast asleep, sucking dreamily on her finger, and her head was still resting heavily on my arm. I lay still for a while, studying her face, her discoloured eye, wondering what she was dreaming about ... and then I set about retrieving my paralysed arm. I didn't want to wake her, so I tried just giving it a gentle tug ... but nothing happened. My arm was completely numb. I tried flexing my fingers ... but still nothing happened. I didn't *have* any fingers. All I had was a lump of dead meat sticking out of my shoulder with some pointy bits stuck on the end.

I lay still again, thinking about it. *Maybe you ought to just wait*, I told myself, *wait for Candy to wake up* ...

But I didn't want to do that.

It might be awkward ...

So I tried again. This time, instead of trying to use my dead arm to move itself, I leaned to one side and used the weight of my body to start dragging the arm from beneath Candy's head. It felt really strange at first, as if I was moving something that didn't belong to me, but gradually, as the arm began to move, and the blood had begun to flow, I started getting some feeling back – a pleasant tingle in my fingertips, a prickling sensation in my arm ... and then something else happened, something *not* so pleasant. As the blood rushed into my arm, a thousand red-hot needles started jabbing into my skin, electrifying my flesh, and I froze in an instant, gritting my teeth against the pain, trying not to scream.

Candy, meanwhile, was still sleeping.

She'd taken her finger out of her mouth now, and was lying there with her lips drawn back against her teeth and her tongue lolling loosely against her gums. It wasn't the most beautiful pose in the world, but there was something strangely appealing about it, and as I waited for my arm to stop zapping, I found myself staring at her face again. I wondered what it was that made it so beautiful – the proportions, the shapes, the textures, the bones beneath the skin ...? Or was it just me? My eyes, my vision, my expectation ...

My thoughts.

After a while, her eyelids began to flicker. I thought she was about to wake up, and I suddenly realised how embarrassing it would be if she opened her eyes and caught me staring at her ... but before I could do anything about it, she breathed out a breath of stale air, chomped her lips, and rolled away from me to lie on her side.

I lifted my senseless arm from the pillow, rubbed some life into it, then slipped out of bed, grabbed some clothes, and padded off to the bathroom for a long hot shower.

About an hour later, I was in the kitchen making some coffee when Candy appeared in the bedroom doorway. She looked terrible. Her eyes were bloodshot, the bandage on her wrist had come loose, and the flimsy T-shirt she was wearing did little to hide the lurid bruising around her midriff. As she shuffled sleepily across the room, all bleary-eyed and bedraggled, I couldn't help thinking of a punch-drunk boxer, struggling to live with the morning after the fight before.

'Morning,' I said breezily. 'Do you want some coffee?'

She ran her hands through her tangled hair and muttered something under her breath.

'Sorry?' I said.

She yawned. 'What time is it?'

'Just gone twelve. Do you want some coffee?'

'What?'

'Coffee,' I said, waggling a cup at her.

'Yeah ... in a minute.'

She stood there for a moment, frowning and mumbling at the floor, then she turned around and shuffled back into the bedroom. I stared after her, wondering what she was doing – getting dressed? getting her make-up? getting back into bed? – but then she came out again, and I knew immediately what she was doing. She was heading straight for the bathroom, not shuffling any more, but walking with a purpose, and she was hiding something behind her back ...

Getting what she needed.

I didn't know what to do about it.

I didn't know what I was *supposed* to do.

Get angry?

Stay calm?

Say something?

Do nothing?

I suppose what I really wanted to do was scream at her, tell her to stop, tell her to *think* about what she was doing ...

But I didn't.

I didn't do anything. I just stood back and watched as she went into the bathroom, closed the door, and locked it. The snap of the lock left me cold. It killed me. Emptied me. That simple little sound said it all – that I was nothing, that she didn't want me, that she didn't need me.

All she needed was heroin.

And I hated it.

I hated its power, its attraction, its control.

I hated the way it took her away ...

From herself.

From me.

From everything.

I *hated* it.

It took some time for the rest of the day to get going. While Candy was busy in the bathroom, I made some toast and drank some coffee ... washed up the cups and plates ... sat around for a while ... made some more coffee ... and then I got up and spent some time just wandering around the cottage.

I don't know if it was because of my mood, but as I looked around the empty rooms, nothing seemed to feel right. There was something missing, but I couldn't work out what it was. It wasn't a physical absence, as far as I could tell – there was nothing actually *missing* from the rooms. It was more of a sensuous thing. Something to do with memories ... memories of me and Gina ... Mum and Dad ... family holidays ... different times ...

That was it, I think.

The memories weren't that old, but for some reason they seemed hard to find. They weren't missing – they were definitely there – they just weren't *here* any more. Even when I came across things that *should* have meant something – a dried-up daisy chain at the back of a drawer, some of Dad's books left on a shelf, forgotten shoes and abandoned clothes – I couldn't seem to *place* them. I recognised them, I knew what they were, but that was all.

I had no sense of *attachment* to anything.

It was kind of sad, really.

I tried not to think about it as I went into the bedroom and unpacked the bag that Gina had prepared for us. I sorted the clothes from the food, put the clothes in the wardrobe and the food in the fridge ... and when that was done, I decided to check the electricity. It turned out that the mains switch *was* turned on after all. The only problem was a dead lightbulb in the front room. I should have known, really. I'd just had a hot shower – I'd been standing there staring at the glowing red light of the power switch for about ten minutes ... of *course* the electricity was on. I just hadn't realised, that's all. My mind had been focused on other things.

Anyway, I changed the lightbulb in the front room, and then I checked all the other bulbs ... and put all the candles away ... and I was just trying to think what else I could do to pass the time, when my mobile rang.

It was Gina.

'Hello?' I said.

'Joe? Is that you?'

'Yeah—'

'I can't hear you ...'

'Hold on ... the reception's no good.' I went outside and sat down in a battered old chair on the veranda. 'Is that better?' I said into the phone. 'Can you hear me now?'

'Yeah, fine,' Gina said. 'So, how's it going? Is everything all right?'

'Yeah, not bad ...'

'How's Candy?'

'She's OK ... we talked about things last night. You know – giving up heroin and stuff. I think she's going to give it a go.'

'I thought you'd already talked about that?'

'Yeah, I know ... I just meant she hasn't changed her mind or anything. She still really wants to do it ...'

'Really?'

'Yeah ...'

'That's great.'

'I know ... it's a bit scary, though.'

'Well, it's bound to be. I mean, it's a really big thing – physically, mentally, emotionally ... everything – it's going to be hell for a while. For both of you, probably. That's why I said to ring us if you need any help. If you can't get hold of me, give Mike a call. He'll be happy to help. Any time, night or day, it doesn't matter ... just pick up the phone – OK?'

'Yeah, thanks.'

'Oh, and by the way, before I forget – Jason called again this morning. He wants you to ring him – says it's urgent.'

'Right ... has Dad been in touch?'

'No, not yet. What do you want me to do if Jason rings again?'

'He won't. Don't worry about it—'

'I'm not. How's the cottage?'

'It's OK. I'm out on the veranda at the moment ... it's really nice.' I was looking around at the woods as I spoke, taking it all in – the winter trees, the brambles, the wide-open skies ...

And it *was* really nice: cold and empty and miles from anywhere.

'Did you sleep all right?' asked Gina.

'What?'

'Did you both sleep all right?'

'Uh ... yeah ...'

'I'm not being nosy ...'

'Yeah, you are.'

She laughed.

'Nothing happened,' I said, 'We're just friends, OK?'

'Yeah? I've heard *that* one before.'

I didn't reply. I didn't know how to. It wasn't simply that I didn't want to talk about Candy and me – although, admittedly, I didn't – but the main thing was, I just didn't know what to say. I didn't *know* what we were. We weren't boyfriend and girlfriend, we weren't lovers ... but then we weren't *just good friends*, either. We were something else. We *had* something else. I just didn't know quite what it was.

'Joe?' said Gina. 'Are you still there?'

'Yeah ...'

'Are you pissed off with me?'

'No ...'

'I didn't mean anything ... I wasn't trying to be funny. I was just being your sister, that's all.'

'I know – it's all right.'

'I *like* Candy. She's a nice girl. And I know you really like her ... I just want you to be careful – OK?'

'Yeah, I will ... I *am*. It's OK – honestly. It's not a problem—'

Just then, the cottage door opened and Candy came out onto the veranda. She was dressed in a thick green jumper and her little black hat, and as she stood there in the morning light, sipping black coffee and smiling at me, nothing else seemed to matter any more. Confusion, sadness, anger, hate ... it all just drifted away in the wind. Everything was all right again. I was all right. Candy was all right. We were all right. Nothing could have been better – the weather, the world, the way that I felt ... my body, my heart, my presence of mind ...

In the skip of a heartbeat, it was all just *right* ...

The way it's supposed to be.

'I have to go,' I told Gina. 'I'll ring you tomorrow, OK?'

'Oh ... OK,' she said, a little surprised by my abruptness. 'Is everything all right?'

'Yeah,' I assured her, glancing at Candy, 'everything's perfect.'

And it was, for a while.

After we'd hung around doing nothing for an hour or so, we put on our coats and locked up the cottage and headed off towards the estuary. As we strolled through the woods, arm in arm, ambling slowly along the pathways, the skies took on a dim grey light that chilled the air with the promise of dusk. It was still only mid-afternoon, but I could already sense the coming night. It was there in the shadows, in the heart of the woods, creeping ever closer, like an unseen beast, stalking the frailty of the day ...

I knew it was coming.

I could feel its dark breath.

But it wasn't here yet.

The cottage isn't far from the estuary, and it wasn't long before the woods began thinning out and the path started winding down through low-lying cliffs towards the narrow shores of sand and mud that run along the waterside. Everything was quiet. The tide was still, the wind had dropped, and the waters of the estuary were high and silver-grey.

We sat on a bench at the edge of the woods and looked out over the estuary. I watched a kingfisher skimming by, its metallic-blue sheen mirrored in the silver surface, and then it was gone, like a flashing star, and the estuary was still and quiet again.

'What's on the other side?' Candy asked me.

'I don't know,' I admitted, gazing across the water at the barren fields and tumbledown barns in the distance. 'Farms, I suppose ...'

'Where's Orwold?'

'Back there,' I said, pointing over my shoulder.

'Is it far?'

'Not really ... a couple of miles.' I looked at her. 'Why do you want to know?'

She squeezed my arm. 'Don't worry, I'm not going to run away. I just need to get a few things, that's all. Is there a shop in the village?'

'Yeah, I think so. We can walk back that way, if you want.'

'OK.'

We were silent again for a while. Candy lit a cigarette and smoked it quietly, and I just sat there, staring at the emptiness. The sun was going down, rimming the horizon with its paling light, and the first faint colours of dusk were beginning to paint the sky. The atmosphere reminded me of our day at the zoo, when it was late afternoon and the schoolkids and tourists were heading back home, and the animals were slumbering, and Candy and me were wandering quietly around the far side of the zoo ...

And I wondered if we were on the far side now. Away from all the people, away from all the chaos ...

Was this our place where secrets could be shared?

I looked at Candy, thinking – *secrets, truths ... or nothing?*

She looked back at me, her eyes adrift in a haunted mist. 'I'll do it today,' she said quietly. 'When we get back ... I'll take a last hit, and then that's it. No more.'

'Are you sure?' I asked her.

'Yeah,' she whispered, wiping away a tear. 'I've had enough, Joe. I don't want to be like this any more.'

By the time we'd made our way up through the woods and along a little road into Orwold, the daylight was dying and the village shops were all closed. Candy was starting to get increasingly grouchy.

'What's this?' she sneered. 'A ghost town? Why's everything shut?'

'It must be gone five,' I said. 'Places close early around here at the weekend. We'll have to go to the petrol station.'

'Great – and how far's *that*?'

'Just down the road.'

It was one of those petrol stations that sells all kinds of stuff – videos, cigarettes, beer, groceries ... whatever you need to keep you going. Candy picked up a shopping basket and started scuttling round the aisles, grabbing things off shelves, and I followed along behind her. She didn't seem to be in the mood for questions, so I didn't bother asking her what she was getting, or why, I just trailed along in her wake, watching curiously as she filled the basket with all kinds of odd little items: chocolate bars, biscuits, sweets, Coke, toilet paper, soluble aspirins, crappy magazines, paperback books, talcum powder ...

At the till, she dumped the basket on the counter, asked for two hundred cigarettes, then paid for the lot with the cash she'd taken from Iggy.

It was fully dark when we got back to the cottage. As soon as we were through the front door, Candy hurried off into the bedroom and almost immediately came rushing back out again, heading towards the bathroom.

'Is this it?' I asked her.

She stopped hesitantly and looked at me.

I said, 'Is this the last time?'

'Yeah ... yeah, it is. Look, I'm sorry ... it's just ... I didn't know we'd be out so long ...' Her eyes darted anxiously at the bathroom. 'I really need it now ...'

'You don't have to go anywhere. I mean, you don't have to hide away from me ... I don't mind—'

'No,' she said quickly, 'it's not nice ... I don't want you to see me. It's nothing, anyway ... it's just ... it's just pathetic.' She shook her head. 'It's just stupid bits of foil and crap ... and I *hate* having to do it ... it's so ugly ...' She looked at me, wiping a sheen of sweat from her brow, and I suddenly realised she was hurting, and all I was doing was prolonging the pain.

'It's all right,' I said, indicating the bathroom. 'Honestly ... I understand. Please, it's OK.'

She tried to smile, but her face was too tense to allow it. All she could manage was a rigid nod, like a tearful child, and then she was off like a shot to the bathroom.

This time, though, she didn't lock the door.

Twenty minutes later we were sitting in front of the fire, drinking tea and talking things through. Candy was a bit dopy, but perfectly lucid, and she seemed quite happy about what she was doing.

'I know it's going to be hard,' she told me, 'but I think I've got my head around it now. It's like I can see myself on the other side ... I can see what I want to be. D'you know what I mean? I can see where I'm going, and I really *want* to get there.' She started emptying her pockets, pulling out all the stuff she'd taken from Iggy and placing it on the floor. 'I'd better get rid of this now,' she explained, 'while I still know what I'm doing.'

I watched the drugs piling up – little packets, plastic bags, bottles of pills. It was strange how harmless it all seemed. It was just stuff – powders and pills – and it was hard to imagine how something so dull could mean so much to anyone.

Candy stood up and showed me her empty pockets. 'All gone,' she said, 'OK?'

I looked at her. 'You don't have to prove anything to me.'

'Yeah, I do. I'm an addict, Joe. We lie and we cheat and we hide things. I can't trust myself to do this – you have to help me.'

'All right,' I said. 'What do you want me to do?'

She nodded at the pile on the floor. 'Get rid of all that first.'

I gathered up all the packets and bags and went to chuck them on the fire.

'Not there!' Candy barked, stopping me just in time. 'Christ ... if you burn that lot we'll both be flying for days. Just flush it all down the toilet.'

I got up and started towards the bathroom.

'Hold on,' said Candy. 'You need to go through my bag as well.'

I stopped and looked at her. 'Your bag?'

'It's in the bedroom. I don't *think* I put any stuff in there, but I wouldn't put it past me.'

I gave her a hesitant look.

'What?' she said.

'Nothing ... it's just ... well, it's your personal stuff, isn't it? I'm not sure—'

'It's only clothes and crap,' she interrupted. 'There's nothing to be embarrassed about. Look, this is serious, Joe. However good my intentions are now, I'm going to get desperate at some point, and when I do I'll probably start searching around for the tiniest scrap of gear. If it's there, I'll find it ... and if I find it, I'll take it. I don't *want* that to happen, but I won't be in a fit state to stop myself. So the only way to make sure I *don't* find anything is to make sure there's nothing for me to find – do you understand?'

'Yeah,' I said, getting up and walking off into the bedroom.

'Check everything,' she called out after me. 'And I mean *everything*.'

I checked everything: her bag, her clothes, her make-up, her handbag, under the bed, under the carpet ... anywhere and everywhere. All I found was some aluminium foil and a couple of plastic straws. I put these in my pocket with the rest of the stuff, then left the bedroom and went into the bathroom, where I flushed all the drugs down the toilet. They didn't all go at first, so I had to keep flushing for a while, but eventually the water cleared and everything was gone.

I was on my way out of the bathroom when I suddenly remembered something Candy had said. *I'm an addict,* she'd told me. *We lie and we cheat and we hide things.*

I looked around the bathroom. It was a perfect place to hide things. It was private, she'd always have an excuse to come in here ... and, what's more, she hadn't suggested I search it.

So I started searching it. Cupboards, shelves, under the carpet ... I didn't really know what I was looking for, but I guessed I'd know if I found it. A couple of minutes later, as I was going through the cabinet over the sink, Candy suddenly appeared in the doorway. She didn't say anything at first, just stood there watching me. It felt a bit weird, but I didn't say anything, I just carried on searching.

'You've got a suspicious mind,' she said, after a while.

'I've hidden things myself once or twice,' I told her. 'I know where to look.'

'Yeah? What kind of things have *you* hidden?'

'Secret things ...'

'Like what?'

'They wouldn't be secret if I told you, would they?'

She nodded in agreement, then continued watching me in silence. As I bent down and looked in the cupboard under the sink, I wondered if she knew I was lying. The truth was, I'd never hidden anything in my life ... not that I could remember anyway. I'd probably put things where they wouldn't be *found* ... but that's not quite the same, is it? That's *amateur* hiding, the kind of hiding that doesn't really matter ...

'Joe?' said Candy, interrupting my thoughts.

'Yeah?'

'Do you want to search *me*?'

I stood up and turned around, and there she was – leaning against the wall, smiling at me. But it was the kind of smile that doesn't mean anything – all lips and teeth and no sparkling eyes ...

'What?' I said.

'I mean, if you don't trust me ...' She raised her arms above her head. 'If you want to do a really *thorough* search ...'

'Don't be stupid ... I don't want to search *you*. I'm just doing what you said. You *told* me not to trust you.' I shook my head. 'Put your arms down.'

She raised a provocative eyebrow. 'Are you sure?'

I didn't say anything. I didn't understand what she was doing. Was she playing games with me – teasing me, tempting me, testing me – or was it something else ... some kind of twisted emotional reaction?

I didn't know.

I didn't really want to think about it.

'I'll go and make some tea,' I said.

As I edged my way past her and went back into the front room, my heart was beating hard. I wished it wasn't. I didn't want to feel anything. I just wanted things to be simple.

When Candy came out of the bathroom and joined me in front of the fire, she looked a bit awkward, as if she knew she'd done something slightly embarrassing and wanted to explain herself, but didn't know how.

'All right?' I asked her as she sat down.

'Yeah ... thanks.' She flicked some imaginary dust from her jeans. 'Look,' she said, 'I didn't mean to—'

'What's in the bag?' I said.

'Sorry?'

I indicated the carrier bag on the table. 'All that stuff you bought at the petrol station. What's it for?'

I think she knew I was changing the subject, steering

her away from the awkwardness, and I think we both knew it was the best thing to do. There was enough awkwardness around as it was – we didn't really need any more. And, besides, avoiding it was also the *easiest* thing to do.

'You mean all the chocolate and stuff?' she said.

'Yeah – and the rest of it.'

'I'm just trying to be practical,' she explained. 'I know what it's like when you start withdrawing – I've been there before. Not like this ... I mean, I've never done it out of choice before, and it's never been for very long, but I know how it feels. Sometimes Iggy used to hold stuff back from me ... if I told him I didn't want to do something, or if I'd pissed him off about something ... he wouldn't give me any smack. He'd just lock me in the room and leave me there until I started climbing up the wall.' She gazed sadly into the fire. 'He always got what he wanted in the end.'

'Couldn't you get the stuff from anywhere else?' I asked.

'I thought about it a couple of times,' she said, 'but it wouldn't have worked. Iggy knows *everyone*. He would have found out. He would have killed whoever sold it to me, and then he would have killed me.'

If she'd told me that a few days ago, I'd probably have thought she was exaggerating. But I knew what Iggy was capable of now – I could still feel his razor cutting into my throat – and I knew she was telling the truth.

'So, anyway,' she went on, 'that's how I know what it's going to be like.' She smiled at me. 'I'm going to eat lots of sugary crap, and I'm going to be sick and sweaty and shitty and mad. In fact, I'm starting to feel it already.'

'Really?'

'Just a bit,' she shrugged. 'It's probably just the fear of

what's coming. A smoke usually lasts me at least two or three hours ...'

'Does smoking it make any difference?' I asked. 'I mean, is it less addictive then using needles or anything?'

'I thought it was when I first started – lots of people do. But it's not. Smoking's just a different way of getting the stuff into your head. Some people think that slamming gets you higher ...' She paused, shaking her head. 'God, will you listen to me? I sound just like a junky. I *hate* talking about drugs. It's so bloody *pissy*.'

'Pissy?'

'Yeah,' she smiled. 'You get all these dealers and junkies rambling on about their *gear* and their *works* and God-knows-what-else ... and it's just so *boring*. It's like listening to a bunch of computer nerds or something.'

'That bad, eh?'

'Yeah,' she grinned, 'only *these* computer nerds are all whacked out of their heads and some of them carry loaded guns.'

I nodded, trying to imagine what it was like – living in this unknown world of drugs and guns and violence – but I still couldn't get there. I couldn't even get close. I could *accept* it. I knew such a world existed, and I wasn't too far away from understanding it – but the idea of *living* in it ...? That was just too much to imagine.

'What are you thinking about?' Candy asked me.

I looked at her. 'Nothing ... I was just ...'

'Thinking?'

'Yeah.'

She looked into the fire again, chewing her lip, staring deeply into her thoughts. After a while she said, 'Why are you doing this, Joe?'

'Doing what?'

'Helping me ... finding me, bringing me out here ...' She looked at me. 'Why are you doing it?'

'Why?' I asked, stuck for words.

'Yeah ... why?'

'I don't know ...' I stammered. 'I just ... I don't know ... does there have to be a reason?'

'I think so.'

As she carried on looking at me, I could feel my mouth making useless little movements, searching for unfound words. *Why* are *you doing this?* I asked myself, but I knew I didn't know. It was a question full of questions. Why do you do *anything*? Why do you like music? Why do you take drugs? Why do you hate yourself? Why do you die? Why do you fall in love?

I didn't have any answers. I didn't *know* why I was doing anything. I was just doing it.

'It's weird, isn't it?' Candy said.

'What?'

'Everything ... I don't know – you and me ... the way things happen ... all this stuff ...' She rubbed the side of her head and sighed. 'I'm sorry ... I don't know what I'm talking about. I'm starting to ramble. Maybe I'd better go and lie down for a bit.'

'How are you feeling now?'

'Not too bad ...' She lowered her head and started picking nervously at her fingernails. 'I might get a bit funny,' she said timidly. 'You know, when it starts ... I might say things I don't mean, things that aren't very nice.' She raised her head and looked at me. 'It won't be me, Joe.'

'I know – it's all right.'

'And don't be afraid to get tough with me. Don't give in – OK? Whatever I say, whatever I ask you to do—'

'Just say no?'

'Yeah,' she smiled. 'Something like that.'

'I'll do my best.'

She looked at me for a moment, and I thought she was going to say something else, but then her smile faded and without another word she started getting to her feet.

'Do you need anything?' I asked her.

'No, thanks. I'm just going to lie down in the bedroom for a while ... I'll leave the door open.'

'OK.'

She started walking off.

'Before you go,' I called after her, 'can I just ask you something?'

'What's that?'

'Your name ...'

She frowned. 'My *name*?'

'Yeah ... I've been wondering about it ever since we met.'

'Wondering what?'

'If Candy's your real name.'

She didn't answer immediately, just gave me a funny look. For a moment I thought she was annoyed with me, but then, to my relief, her eyes lit up in sudden realisation. 'Oh, *right*,' she said, 'I see what you mean. You thought that *Candy* might be a street-name?'

'Yeah, I suppose ...'

She laughed quietly. 'No ... that's one thing I *didn't* have to change. Candy's my real name – well, Candice, actually.'

'Candice?'

She nodded. 'Apparently, it means "pure and virtuous".'

'Really?'

'Yeah.' She smiled. 'What's the matter? You think that's funny?'

'No,' I grinned, 'not at all.'

She stood there smiling at me for a second, tearing a hole in my heart, and then she turned around with a wave of her hand and walked off into the bedroom.

It would be a long time before she smiled like that again.

chapter nineteen

It's hard to relive the rest of the story. I know what *happened* – I can remember every moment. From the first troubled hours of that cold Saturday night, and the endless days that followed, to the deadening silence of the very last second, when everything came to an end ...

I remember it all: every word, every breath, every tick of the clock ... everything that happened is with me for ever.

I can *never* forget it.

But that doesn't mean I can *live* it again. You can't live what's gone, you can only remember it, and memories have no life. They're just pale reminders of a time that's gone – like faded photographs, or a dried-up daisy chain at the back of a drawer. They have no substance. They can't take you back. Nothing can take you back.

Nothing can be the same as it was.

Nothing *is*.

All I can do is tell it.

Saturday night, eight o'clock: I'd stocked up on logs and got the fire going, and now I was just lounging around on the settee, munching biscuits and flipping through Candy's dumb magazines. They weren't that interesting – just lots of photographs of sweating celebrities, celebrities in bad clothes, drunk celebrities ... that kind of thing – but they helped to pass the time.

Candy was still in the bedroom. I'd popped in a couple of times to make sure she was all right, and on both occasions she'd been asleep. The first time I went in, she was curled up like a baby on top of the bed. I thought about covering her up with a blanket or something, but she seemed OK, and I didn't want to wake her, so I just left her as she was. An hour later, when I checked on her again, she was inside the bed with the duvet pulled up over her head. I stayed for a while, just to make sure she was breathing, then I tiptoed out and left her to sleep.

Now I was just waiting.

Passing the time.

Staring at pictures of famous people, emptying my head, listening to the wind in the trees outside, hearing it grow, hearing it howl, hearing it gust down the chimney and rattle the windows ...

It sounded angry.

I wondered where it went when it died.

Eight-thirty: Candy came out of the bedroom and shuffled silently to the bathroom. She was still dressed, but barefoot. I was glad to see her shuffling. Shuffling meant no hurry; no hurry meant no drugs. After a couple of minutes, the bathroom door opened and she came over to the settee and stood beside me. She looked tired and worn out. Her eyes were sleepy and her face was pale, but I was pretty sure she hadn't taken anything. She just looked drained.

'How's it going?' I asked her.

'Not great,' she replied. 'I'm cold ... shivery.' She hugged herself and scratched her arms. 'Itchy.'

'Do you need anything?'

'What do *you* think?' she said miserably.

'Sorry ... I meant did you need a drink or anything?'

'Got any vodka?'

'Uh ... no ... just tea and coffee. Or there's hot chocolate—'

'No alcohol?'

'No ... sorry.'

She sniffed hard and blinked her eyes. 'How about a TV?'

'Yeah, there's a black-and-white portable somewhere. Do you want me to set it up in the bedroom for you?'

'Yeah, I suppose ...' She looked at me. 'Sorry ... I'm feeling crap. I'll take some aspirins and go back to bed.'

'I'll bring the TV in – do you want your magazines?'

She didn't answer, just shrugged and stared at the floor. Her hand was resting on the back of the settee. I gave it a gentle squeeze, but she didn't respond. Her skin felt cold and clammy.

'Go on,' I said. 'Go back to bed.'

She lifted her gaze from the floor, nodded blankly at me, then went back into the bedroom.

Ten-thirty: I was tired and bored and lonely. I wanted to do something, but I didn't know what. I knew there were a few old books around, and I'd seen Dad's chess set earlier on, and I was pretty sure there was a dusty old radio somewhere ... but none of it appealed to me. I didn't want to read. I didn't want to play chess. I didn't want to listen to the radio.

I glanced over at the bedroom door. TV light was flickering in the darkness, and I could hear the sound of a late-night film drifting faintly in the air. I listened hard, trying to guess what it was, but the volume was too low to make sense of anything.

Why don't you join her in there? I asked myself. *She won't mind. You wouldn't have to talk or anything, you could just sit there together, quietly watching the film ...*

I got up and went over to the window.

Outside, the night was still angry. Gusts of rain were peppering the glass like showers of spiteful needles, and the wind was still raging away at the trees, stripping their branches and casting the leaves into the air. The trees didn't look too bothered, though. They'd seen it all before.

I closed the curtain and went back to the settee.

She's probably sleeping, I thought. *The volume she's got the TV on – that's a sleeping volume. It's the kind of volume that says – do not disturb, please leave me alone.*

I lay down on the settee, closed my eyes, and listened to the wind.

Ten forty-five: I was half-asleep when I heard Candy calling my name. I was half-dreaming that I was back in my room, sitting on my bed, playing my guitar ... lost in time, lost in the music, lost in another world ... and I thought for a moment the voice was Gina's. But then I heard it again, more clearly this time, and I got to my feet and headed for the bedroom.

'Joe ...' Candy called out again. 'Joe? Where *are* you?'

'Sorry,' I said, stepping hurriedly through the door, 'I didn't hear you. What's the matter? Are you all right?'

She was scrunched up in bed under a tangled sheet. Her body was drenched in sweat. The portable TV was balanced on the bed beside her, its cold white light flickering silently over her face. Her skin looked puffy and swollen.

'I can't sleep,' she said. 'I'm too hot ... what time is it?'

'About eleven.'

'Shit ... when's this wind going to stop?'

'I don't know.'

'I don't like it – it's too loud. I can't get to sleep.'

She groaned and rolled over onto her side. The sheet came loose, and I saw that she'd changed into her nightgown. It was damp with sweat and rucked up around her legs.

'Can I get you anything?' I asked her.

She moaned into the pillow.

I said, 'Do you want some water? It might cool you down.'

'Wanna sleep,' she muttered. 'I just wanna sleep ...'

I felt pretty useless, just standing there, not knowing what to do. I wanted to make things better, but I didn't know how, and I didn't know how to deal with my ignorance. *What should I do? Should I say anything else? Should I wait for Candy to say anything else? Should I stay ... or should I go?*

After thinking about it for a while, I left the bedroom and went back into the front room. I checked the fire, made sure the cottage was locked up, then grabbed all the cushions off the settee, fetched some blankets from the airing cupboard and went back into the bedroom. Candy had buried her head under the pillow and was moaning quietly. She kept kicking her feet, trying to untangle the knotted sheet, but all she was doing was making it worse.

I tried not to make any noise as I placed the cushions on the floor next to the open door. I wasn't trying to *hide* my presence, I just didn't want to advertise it. I sat down and took off my shoes, then lay down on the cushions, pulled up the blankets, and tried to get comfortable. It took me a while, but I finally got myself into a position that wasn't too lumpy or cold, but still gave me a reasonable view of the bed.

It was a good enough place to be.

I could see Candy.

I could hear the wind in the trees.

I could close my eyes and feel the movements of the night rippling through my spine. I could listen to the sound of my heart, the sound of my blood, the sound of the machine beneath my skin. I could open my eyes and stare at the TV lights strobing on the ceiling, imagining the flashes of a storm-lit sky. Or I could just lie there, perfectly still, doing absolutely nothing.

The night passes slowly when you're awake. I think I dozed off once or twice, but most of the time I just lay there listening to Candy as she tossed and turned and whimpered and cried. She couldn't keep still for a second. She was either too hot or too cold. She was sweating ... then shivering. Sweating ... shivering. Hugging herself. Bashing the pillow. Swearing ... cursing ... shouting ... screaming ... spitting ... coughing ... sniffing ... sobbing ...

Suffering.

It wasn't pretty.

Some time in the early morning, around four o'clock, she groaned and sat up and started getting out of bed. Every little movement seemed to fill her with pain. Her hair was all knotted and her face had aged – she looked like a crazy old woman. As she rolled out of bed and staggered towards the door, clutching her belly, I could hear her muttering under her breath.

'Shit ... Christ ... shit ...'

'Do you need a hand?' I asked quietly.

'Uh?' she grunted, squinting down at me through her bleary eyes. 'What's that ...?'

'It's me ... Joe,' I said, sitting up. 'Do you need any help?'

'I need a shit,' she said blankly.

Her face was drained. There was nothing there – no recognition, no awareness, no self. Her eyes were cold and empty. She stared right through me for a moment or two, then wiped her nose with the back of her hand and stumbled off to the bathroom.

Over the next few hours she was in and out of bed like a yo-yo. She must have gone to the bathroom at least half a dozen times before she finally managed to settle down and drift off into a restless sleep. Dawn was beginning to break by then, and as the grey light of morning crept across the yawning sky, I knew that sleep was beyond me.

I slipped out of the bedroom and made some coffee, then went out onto the veranda and watched the sun rise over the woods.

Sunday morning, nine o'clock: I was in the bedroom, sitting on the edge of the bed, and Candy was crying.

'It hurts, Joe,' she sobbed. 'I'm so cold ... everything hurts. I can't *stand* it ... I *need* something ... please ...'

I gave her some aspirins. She popped them in her mouth, took a drink of water, then suddenly started retching. I didn't know what to do. She was doubled up in pain, clutching her stomach, choking and spluttering, her eyes and nose streaming with moisture ...

All I could do was sit there and watch.

'Oh God ...' she cried, 'oh God, oh God, oh God ...'

This went on for some time – retching, crying, shivering, sobbing – and I did my best to comfort her. I gave her more blankets. I put a bowl by the bed so she wouldn't have to go to the bathroom every time she was sick. I kept her supplied with tissues and water ...

I nursed her, basically.

I'm not sure it helped her that much, but at least it gave me something to do, which was a lot better than sitting around feeling scared to death.

Midday: I was starting to feel the lack of sleep now. My chest was tight, my eyes were sticky, and I kept forgetting stupid little things. I'd fill the kettle, then forget to turn it on ... or I'd open a cupboard, then forget what I was looking for. I kept drinking coffee to wake myself up, but all it did was rattle my brains.

One o'clock: I made some tea and toast and took it into the bedroom. Candy was sitting up in bed smoking a cigarette. Her face was almost white and her eyes looked unnaturally big.

'How are you feeling?' I asked her.

'Great,' she said. 'My skin's on fire, my head's throbbing, my belly hurts ... I can't keep still ... I can't move ...' She sucked on her cigarette and stared at me. 'I feel great.'

'Do you want some toast?'

'No ... I want to feel better.'

'How about some chocolate?'

She didn't answer, just glared at me. I put the tea and

toast on the bedside cabinet, then looked around for the stuff she'd bought from the petrol station. I found the carrier bag on the floor, picked it up, and placed it on the bed. Candy said nothing. Her eyes had hardened and she was staring at me with the nastiness of a vicious child. I didn't know how to deal with it. I *couldn't* deal with it.

'I'm going out for a breath of fresh air,' I told her. 'I'll only be out the front, so if you need me, just shout – OK?'

She still didn't say anything, and as I turned around and left the bedroom I could feel her eyes burning into my back.

Outside, the wind had dropped and the day was bright and cold. I walked across to the edge of the clearing and sat down on the ground beside a bare oak tree. Years ago, the tree had been struck by lightning. Its trunk was scarred and black and its roots jutted up through the leaf litter like the half-buried limbs of giants. I sat back and closed my eyes. The air was thick with the smell of the woods. As I sat there, breathing deeply, I could almost taste the tang of rotting leaves and wind-freshened grass, and I only wished it would clear the stink of confusion out of my head. But I knew it couldn't. There wasn't enough fresh air in the world for that.

I pulled my mobile phone from my pocket, flipped it open, and thumbed the speed-dial number for home. There was no answer. I tried Gina's mobile, but it was switched off. I thought about ringing Mike, but for some reason I didn't feel like talking to him, so – for want of anything better – I called home again and checked the answering machine.

There were two messages – both of them silent. The caller had waited for the beep, kept quiet for a few moments, then hung up.

I didn't like it.

It bothered me.

Forget it, I told myself. *It's probably just Dad, checking up on you.*

No, I thought, *he wouldn't ring without leaving a message.*

All right, then ... how about Jason? It could have been Jason—

No chance. He's already called twice and been blanked. He's too vain to risk it again, isn't he?

So it's a mistake, then ... a wrong number, that's all. Someone rang the wrong number and didn't know what to say ...

Yeah? So how come they called twice?

I didn't know the answer to that.

I stared across at the cottage and wondered what Candy was doing. Was she sleeping? Being sick? Crying? Was she still mad at me? Why did she get mad at me in the first place?

Did it matter?

I didn't know the answer to that one, either.

I looked at the phone in my hand and thought about Jason again. I knew I ought to ring him. I didn't want to, but no matter what I thought of him, he deserved an explanation of some sort, and so did the rest of the group. The recording session was coming up soon, and I'd run off and left them without so much as a word.

That wasn't *right,* was it?

It wasn't *fair* ...

But it wasn't *here,* either. It was somewhere else, and somewhere else didn't matter any more. Somewhere else was nowhere.

I closed the phone and got to my feet and went back into the cottage.

As I opened the door, Candy was just coming out of the

bathroom. She'd combed her hair and was dressed in jeans and a jumper. For a fleeting moment my heart lifted and I thought that everything was going to be OK. She was feeling better ... she'd got over the worst of it ... she was on her way back to normality ...

But then I saw the look on her face, and I knew I was wrong. It wasn't a face of *normality*, it was a face of desperation.

'What are you doing?' I asked her.

'Don't ask,' she said, walking straight past me.

I shut the front door and followed her into the bedroom. It was a mess. All the cupboard drawers had been emptied out and the contents strewn all over the place. The bed had been moved, the mattress turned over ... she'd even searched my bag. Now she was scuttling around the room, grabbing clothes off the floor and shoving them into her bag.

'What are you doing?' I repeated.

'I said – don't ask.'

'I just did.'

'Well don't.'

I watched her as she carried on packing. She looked terrible – everything about her was pained. Her face, her lips, her cheeks, her eyes ... her neck, her legs, the shape of her body ... her pale white skin ...

God ... her skin.

I remembered the first time I'd seen her, the way she'd stood there looking at me, the way she'd cocked her head and smiled, the way her rippling skin had turned me to stone ...

It didn't turn me to stone any more: it just scared me. It was too white, too sweaty, too cold ... like milky plastic left out in the rain.

'You can't do this,' I told her.

'Do what?' she said, zipping up her bag.

'You can't just give *in* to it—'

'No?'

'No.'

'Why not?'

'Because ...'

'Because *what*?' she sneered, turning to face me. 'Come on, Joe ... I wanna know why. Why *can't* I give in to it? Because it'll make me feel better? Because it'll make me feel human again? Because it'll get me out of this shit-hole?' Her voice was icy and cruel. 'Let's hear it, *Joe* ... come on – let's hear your *reasoning*.'

I looked at her, trying to see beyond the sickness. Trying to see Candy.

'You wanna look?' she spat. 'Is that it? You don't want me to go cos you want something to *look* at—'

'You'll die,' I said.

'I'll *what*?'

'If you leave now, you'll go back to Iggy, and one way or another you'll end up dead. If he doesn't kill you, the drugs will. And if the drugs don't do it, your lifestyle will.'

'My *life*style?' she snorted. 'You're worried about my *lifestyle*?'

'I'm worried about *you*.'

'Yeah? What do you know about me? You don't know *anything*. You're just a cute little rich boy looking for thrills. You don't know *shit*.'

'I know you're not leaving.'

She stared at me, her eyes spiked with hatred.

I said, 'You don't want to go back. You pretend you don't care, but you do. You're just scared, that's all.'

She laughed again, cold and hard, but this time it didn't

ring true. She was having to *make* herself sound ugly.

'I've had enough of this,' she said, picking up her bag. 'I'm going ... and don't worry about Iggy. I can get by without him—'

'How?'

She shrugged. 'That's my business.'

'Yeah? What are you going to do for money? How are you going to get your drugs?'

'I don't know ... I'll manage. I don't need much anyway ... just enough to stop hurting. Then I'll sort something out ...'

'Right,' I said.

She glared at me again, then shook her head and started walking towards the door. I stepped in front of her and shut it.

She paused, looking at me. 'Get out of the way.'

I said nothing.

She moved towards me until we were standing face to face, staring into each other's eyes.

'Get out of the way, Joe.'

'I'm not letting you go,' I said.

'You can't stop me.'

'I can try.'

She was doing her best to control herself now, but she wasn't making a very good job of it. Her face was tight, cold with sweat. I could see the nerves twitching under her skin.

She licked her lips. 'Please don't do this. It's not worth it. Just open the door and let me go.'

I couldn't speak any more. I was shaking so much inside that the words just wouldn't come out. Candy was silent, too. Her breaths trembled, sour and stale on my face.

'What do you *want*?' she hissed. 'What do you want me to *do*? You want me to beg? Is that it? You want me to get down on my knees—'

'Don't,' I said.

'Well, get out of the *way* then. For God's sake ... I have to go. I *need* to go. I'm dying here ... you don't understand ...' She moved even closer, pouting her lips and lowering her voice. 'Please, Joe ... please ...?'

I shook my head.

She put her hands on my shoulders and stared into my eyes. For a moment I though she was going to kiss me. I started moving away, but then her grip suddenly tightened and her eyes went cold, and before I knew it she was lurching forward and kneeing me hard in the groin.

The pain exploded in a white-hot roar. The pain ... God! It was *everything*. Ripping through me, emptying my lungs, crashing me down to the floor. I couldn't do anything. I was senseless, a sobbing heap ... groaning, crawling ... I couldn't breathe, couldn't see, couldn't hear ...

Do something.

Breathe.

You have to breathe ...

Suck it down ...

Feel it ...

The floor ...

Eyes ... wet ...

Back ...

The door ...

At your back.

The door ... moving against your back.

Candy.

The fog was beginning to clear, and I dimly realised that I was lying with my back against the door, and that Candy was trying to open it. I looked up at her. She was pulling on the handle, getting her fingers between the door and the frame, trying to widen the gap, trying to squeeze through. Her face was streaming with tears.

I forced myself to sit up and lean my weight against the door.

Candy carried on pulling at it for a while, but it was never going to open now. She had no strength. She was exhausted.

She started screaming – 'No! No! No!' – slapping the back of the door with her hands – 'No! No! No! No! No! ...'

I breathed slowly, focusing on the pain in my belly – calming it, calming myself, keeping my mind off Candy's despair. I couldn't listen to it. It hurt too much. Everything hurt.

She carried on screaming and hitting the door for a while, but gradually she began to tire. The screaming faded to sobbing, the sobbing faded to whimpers, and finally she went quiet. I raised my head and looked at her. She was just standing there, limp and forlorn, staring at nothing.

I reached up and touched her leg.

She didn't respond.

'Candy?' I said.

She looked down at me. Her face was tear-streaked and broken. 'I'm sorry, Joe,' she said weakly. 'I'm so sorry ...'

I held out my hand. She took hold of it and slumped down beside me on the floor. There was blood on her hand from a broken fingernail. I licked my finger and wiped it away.

She looked at me.

I said, 'You hurt yourself.'

She nodded and started to cry. I took her in my arms and closed my eyes and willed the hurting to stop.

The rest of the day was comparatively quiet. I tidied up the bedroom and got Candy back into bed, then I went round the cottage and cleared up the rest of the mess she'd made. It was hard to believe that while I'd been sitting outside, feeling sorry for myself, she'd virtually ransacked the whole place. She'd searched everywhere – the empty bedrooms, the front room, the fridge, even the cooker. The worst of it, though, was the bathroom. She'd just about ripped it apart. I suppose she must have remembered me searching it, and in her confusion she'd taken that to mean there were drugs in there. Or maybe she *had* hidden some drugs in there, but couldn't remember exactly where ...?

Anything was possible ...

As I was beginning to realise.

It was dark by the time I'd finished cleaning up. I grabbed a torch and went outside to get some more logs, then I set the fire and tried to settle down for the night. I was still aching a bit from Candy's low blow, but I'd reached that stage of tiredness when your senses blur and everything starts to feel dull – the light, your body, your mind, your pain ...

I was too tired to hurt.

I lay down on the settee and rang Gina.

The call failed – no reception.

I couldn't be bothered to go outside, so I just closed the phone and lay there, drowning in the silence.

I don't know anything about heroin. I don't know what it is, or how it works, or what it does to your mind and body.

I don't know why it's addictive, and I don't know why you get sick when you stop taking it. What I *do* know, though – what I learned that night – is the hold it has over a body. Or maybe it's the other way round – the hold a body has over heroin? The need .. the desire ... the *demand* ...

The chemistry.

Like I said, I don't understand it, but that night I witnessed its work.

From six o'clock until midnight, Candy's soul screamed in every way possible: her temperature raged from hot to cold; her limbs burned; she sweated slime; her muscles ached; her stomach knotted; her skin itched; her eyes watered; her nose streamed; her head throbbed; she smelled bad; she sneezed so violently I thought she was going to burst something. And all the time, on top of this, there was vomiting and diarrhoea and raging thirst and waking dreams ...

And all because of chemistry.

Her body was holding her to ransom. *Give me what I want or I'll make you sick. I'll hurt you. I'll kill you. I'll drive you insane. GIVE ME WHAT I WANT!*

But she didn't.

Or she couldn't.

It didn't matter which. She stuck it out – her body screaming, hour upon hour, never giving her a moment's rest, until finally she became so exhausted that even the screams couldn't keep her awake, and she fell into a nightmared sleep.

I slept, too. On the floor. Dreaming of kangaroos.

Monday morning, seven o'clock: When I woke up, Candy was sitting on the edge of the bed, smoking a cigarette.

The curtains were open and her gaunt-looking face was framed in the morning light. It was a portrait in grey: her pallid complexion, the clouded skies, the cigarette smoke, the sweat-stained bed ... everything washed-out and dull.

I sat up and stretched the stiffness from my neck.

'Hey,' said Candy, looking around at me.

'Hey, yourself. How's it going?'

'I don't know,' she shrugged. 'About the same, I suppose ... maybe a little bit better.'

'Are you still hurting?'

She nodded. 'Everywhere.'

'When do you think it'll stop?'

'I don't know – the worst of it's usually over in a couple of days, so some time today ... hopefully. I don't think I can go through another night like that.' She stubbed out her cigarette and scratched her head. 'God, I feel so *dirty* ... everything's sticky and scabby ... this bed stinks ...'

'Why don't you go and have a wash?' I suggested. 'I'll change the bed for you – get some fresh sheets and stuff.' I stood up and went over to her. 'Come on, I'll give you a hand.'

I helped her along to the bathroom, then went back and changed the bed. It wasn't pleasant. Fresh sheets, fresh pillows, a fresh duvet. I cleaned up a bit – tissues, chocolate wrappers, magazines – and opened the window to air the room. I was just on my way out to get some fresh water when Candy came back from the bathroom.

She looked as white as a ghost.

'Christ,' I said, hurrying over to her. 'What's the matter?'

'What?'

'Your face ... your skin ...'

'Oh,' she said, touching her cheek. 'Sorry – it's just talcum powder. I can't stand the feel of water on my skin ... it prickles.' She shivered. 'It's horrible. The talc makes me feel a little bit better.'

I helped her back into bed, then tried to get on with the day.

Ten-thirty: There were three more messages on the answering machine at home – two more silent ones, and one from Dad. His message went like this: *Gina, Joe – it's me* (he never calls himself *Dad* when he's talking to us, it's always just *me*, or occasionally *your father*) ... *I'm just ringing to let you know that everything's fine. Listen, don't forget to put the bins out on Wednesday, and if the window cleaner turns up, don't pay him until he's done the conservatory. He missed it the last time. And Joe – where are you? You're supposed to be at home – remember? Look, I'm not checking up on you, and I'm sure there's a perfectly good reason you're not there right now, but I'll want to speak to you about it later on in the week – all right? OK, well I have to go now ... I'll see you both soon – goodbye.*

It was weird hearing his voice – it sounded so *normal*. Talking about bins and window cleaners and conservatory windows ... it all seemed so alien. Which it was, I suppose. It was a voice that belonged to somewhere else.

I tried Gina's mobile, but it was still turned off. I knew she had to switch it off when she was at the hospital, so I wasn't particularly worried, but I hadn't talked to her for a while, and it would have been nice to share a few thoughts.

More than a few, come to that.

Never mind, I thought, *she'll be home tonight. You can ring her then.*

I scrolled through my phonebook and selected Mike's number, but all I got was his voicemail, asking for a message. I didn't leave one – I couldn't think of anything to say.

And that was it.

No one left to call.

I sat on the veranda and watched the clouds.

I was still sitting there half an hour later when I saw someone coming down the pathway. The mere sight of another human being – the movement, the colour, the flesh of a face – sent a surge of adrenalin rushing through my body and a stream of panic into my mind. *Who? How? What do I do? Run? Hide? Shout? What?*

But even before I'd got to my feet, I realised there was nothing to fear. It was just an old man, on his own, walking slowly down the track. No fear, no panic, no worries. The adrenalin settled sickeningly in my stomach, and I started breathing again.

As the old man got closer, I recognised him as Mr Butt – the villager Dad paid to keep an eye on the cottage – and the adrenalin began stirring again. I tried to calm myself down – *there's nothing to worry about ... it's* your *cottage ... you don't need his permission to be here* – but it didn't work. If I'd been on my own, there *wouldn't* have been anything to worry about, but I wasn't on my own, was I? I was with Candy, and she was in bed ...

Which made things difficult.

Mr Butt was about twenty metres away now. I hadn't seen him for a long time, and I wasn't sure he'd recognise me, so I took off my hat and stood up to meet him. I'm not sure *why* I thought that'd help, but I did it anyway.

'Morning, Mr Butt,' I called out. 'It's only me – Joe Beck.'

He paused for a moment, leaning forward and squinting at me, then he raised his hand and ambled up to the veranda. As far as I could tell, he hadn't changed his clothes since the last time I'd seen him – and I still couldn't tell exactly what they were. Some kind of brown jackety thing, a brown outer layer (which might have been a coat), and a shapeless brown hat.

'Who's that?' he said.

'Joe Beck,' I repeated, 'Doctor Beck's son ... Joe. Do you remember me?'

He squinted again. 'Joe ...?'

'Gina's brother ... I used to come here with my mum and dad.'

'Joe Beck?'

'That's right. I'm just staying here for a couple of days. Didn't Dad let you know?'

'Not so's I recall ...' He wiped his nose and peered at me. 'You're young Joe, then?'

'Yeah ... I'll be here for a couple of days. Exams ... I need to get some work done, you know ... for my exams.'

'Aye ... right. Well ...' He looked around. 'You got enough wood?'

'Plenty, thanks.'

'Plenty there.' He nodded at the wood shed. 'Got 'er chopped up after the storm, couple weeks back. S'mostly dry now.'

'Yeah, thanks.'

'Aye, right then ... well ... I'd best get on back.' He looked over his shoulder, but didn't make any move to go. I think he was probably waiting for me to offer him a cup of tea or something. I stayed silent, hoping he'd take the hint. He looked at me again, vaguely nodding his head, and I was sure he was about to leave, but then I heard a voice behind me –

'Joe?'

– and I turned around to see Candy in the doorway. Her hair was tangled, her skin was flushed, and her nightgown was fluttering in the wind.

'What are you—?' she started to say, but then she saw Mr Butt. 'Oh ...' she said, glancing from him to me. 'Sorry ... I didn't—'

'This is Mr Butt,' I said quickly. 'The man from the village—'

'Morning, Gina,' Mr Butt said. 'You're looking fine.'

I turned around and stared at him. He was leaning forward and squinting at Candy, his ruddy face creased with a toothless smile. *He can hardly see,* I realised. *He thinks she's Gina.*

He said to Candy, 'You'll need more'n a summer dress today, young lady. You'll catch your death in that.'

Candy smiled awkwardly and crossed her arms to cover herself up. I wasn't sure if she was embarrassed, or shy, or simply uneasy ... but whatever it was, it was curiously attractive. For a moment or two, I couldn't take my eyes off her. But then I realised she was giving me a look – a stop-staring-at-me-and-get-rid-of-him look – and I turned back to Mr Butt again.

He was still leering at Candy.

'Well, thanks, Mr Butt,' I said, getting his attention. 'It was nice to see you again. Sorry if there was any confusion ... you know ... with the cottage and everything.'

'Aye,' he said.

'We'll probably be gone by the weekend.'

'Aye.'

I nodded at him.

He nodded back.

I waited for him to move.

He stood there nodding to himself for a while, and then – with a parting nod at Candy – he turned around and started ambling back up the pathway. I watched him until I was sure he wasn't coming back, then I turned to Candy. She was still standing with her arms crossed, but she didn't look so shy any more. She just looked freezing cold.

'I think he fancies you,' I said to her.

The faintest trace of a smile warmed her face for a moment, but then the cold and the pain kicked in again, and she hunched her shoulders and rubbed her arms and shuffled back into the cottage.

I stood there for a while, staring after her, picturing her face. *It wasn't much of a smile,* I told myself, *barely a smile at all – but it happened. You didn't imagine it. It happened. It was there ...*

It was there.

Monday afternoon: She was still pretty ill, spending most of the time in bed, but as the day wore on I began to realise that she seemed more settled in her sickness. She wasn't crying so much, for one thing. She had the occasional sob, and at one point she broke down and wept herself into such a state that I almost called for an ambulance, but apart from that she was fairly calm most of the time – just lying in bed, half-asleep, half-watching the TV ... a bit sweaty, a bit cold, a bit achy. She was gradually beginning to talk a bit more, too. She still wasn't saying a lot, but if she was awake when I went in to check on her, she usually managed a few words.

Thanks ...

Yes, please ...

What time is it?

It didn't mean much in itself, but it made me feel pretty

good. In fact, it made me feel fantastic. I knew that I mustn't get *too* carried away, because I guessed we still had a long way to go, but I couldn't help feeling that the worst of it was over. All we had to do now was keep our heads together for a few more days ...

Just a few more days ...

And then ...

And then what? I asked myself. *What are you going to do when this is all over? What's going to happen with Candy? Where's she going to go? And where are* you *going to go? Back to the old life? Back to how it was? Back to Heystone? Back to school? Back to your bedroom, lying on the floor?*

I wished I *couldn't* imagine it, but I could – I could imagine myself somewhere else, thinking back on now, thinking of *here* as somewhere else ...

And it made me want to cry.

Four o'clock: I was sitting in front of the fire, idly burning matches, when I heard Candy's voice from the bedroom doorway.

'There you are,' she said. 'I thought you'd run out on me.'

When I turned round and looked at her, I couldn't help smiling. She'd borrowed one of my jumpers – a scruffy old thing with extra-long sleeves – and she was wearing it over her nightgown, together with a pair of socks that must have been at least four sizes too big.

'What?' she said, looking at me. 'What's the matter?

'Nothing ... I was just admiring your outfit, that's all. It's very nice.'

'You think so?' She waggled the sleeves of the jumper and looked down at her feet. When she lifted her leg, the toe of the sock flopped to the floor. She gave it a quick wiggle, then put her foot down and smiled at me. 'That's tired me out,' she said.

I started to get up, but she waved me back down and came over and joined me at the fire. Her skin was still pale, and she looked really gaunt, but beneath the surface I could see good things – the light in her eyes, the way she moved, a hint of life ...

She groaned a little as she lowered herself to the floor, and I held out a hand to help her. Her fingers were cold – but not *deathly* cold. The touch was coming back. Candy's touch – the unknown shade, the tingle, the feeling inside ...

'All right?' I asked her.

She nodded. 'A lot better, thanks.' She crossed her legs and made herself comfortable. 'I don't think I'm *there* yet ... I mean, I still feel crap, but at least I'm not climbing the walls any more. I just feel as if someone's been beating me up for the last two days.'

'I know what you mean,' I said, rubbing my belly.

She didn't get it for a second, then her eyes widened in realisation. 'Oh God,' she said. 'I hit you, didn't I?'

'Sort of ...'

'Did I hit you? I can't remember ...'

'It was more of a well-placed knee.'

'Oh, no ...' Her eyes glanced between my legs. 'I *didn't*, did I?'

'It doesn't matter—'

'I'm sorry, Joe ... I didn't know what I was doing—'

'I know,' I said. 'It doesn't matter – honestly. Forget it.'

She looked at me, half in sympathy, half in amusement. 'Did it hurt?'

'Nah,' I said, shaking my head. 'I'm tougher than I look.'

'Really?' she smiled.

'Yeah ... there's not many girls get the better of *me* in a fight.'

She laughed quietly. It wasn't much of a sound – just a gentle laugh – but it felt like a song to me. A really good song. The kind of song that makes you feel funny inside.

'Do you think you can manage some toast?' I asked her.

She nodded. 'That'd be nice.'

So I made us some toast, and we talked some more ... and the song just kept on playing. It was good. Even when Candy began to feel tired, and I helped her back into bed, everything still felt OK. She wasn't *sick*-tired any more – just sleepy-tired. Worn out. Talked out. Dreamy.

'Thanks, Joe,' she whispered as I tucked her in.

'You're welcome.'

When she raised her head from the pillow and kissed me, her lips touched mine with the crystal breath of a snowflake.

Everything *was* going to be fine.

I really believed it.

chapter twenty

I don't know exactly what happened in the next hour or so. I know I walked out of the bedroom and quietly shut the door, and I know I wandered around the cottage for a while – feeling good, feeling fine, still believing that everything was going to be OK – but I'm not sure how I ended up at the front-room window, staring out at the moonlit woods, thinking about Candy, thinking about me ... thinking myself into a hole. Candy ... sleeping ... Candy ... me ... Candy's touch ... Candy ... me ... Candy's kiss ... Candy ... me ...

The touch was still there.

The touch of her kiss.

I could still feel it, impressed in the memory of my skin – the cold heat, the crystal breath – and I kept wanting to lick my lips, to taste the snowflake on my tongue, but I was afraid that the heat of my breath would melt it ...

And that wasn't all I was afraid of.

Deep down inside, I was afraid of everything. My thoughts, my doubts, my desires, my lies, my honesty ...

myself. As I stared through the window, my reflection looked back at me, paling in the darkened glass, ghosting my face to another ... another face, another boy ...

Another me.

And I didn't like the look of him. I didn't like what he wanted. But I couldn't stop seeing him ... I couldn't stop *being* him.

It didn't make sense.

I didn't know what he was. He was me ... but he *wasn't* me. His feelings were wrong, and mine were right; but then mine were wrong and his were right ... it was madness. It was too many things to know: lightness, darkness, crying, laughing, hurting, needing, hating, loving ...

Why does it always have to be like this? I thought.

Why does it have to hurt so much?

And then my phone rang.

And I was about to find out the *true* meaning of hurt.

I wanted to think it was Gina calling, but even as I pulled the phone from my pocket, I somehow knew that it wasn't. There was something about the sound of the ringtone ... something cold and empty ...

I checked the display.

17:27, it read, *UNKNOWN CALLER*.

The phone kept ringing.

I checked the reception.

The signal was fine.

The phone kept ringing, cold and empty, demanding an answer.

Just leave it, I told myself. *It's probably just a junk call or a wrong number or something. Ignore it. Let it ring. Turn it off ...*

But I knew I couldn't.

My hand felt heavy as I opened the phone – heavy and slow and unfamiliar. It was as if I was underwater. Steadying my arm, I lifted the phone to my ear.

'Hello?'

The line was silent for a moment – not dead, just hollow and silent. I could tell there was someone there ... I could hear them breathing. And I *knew* – in an instant – I knew what I'd known all along. I knew who it was. I'd heard that silence before – on the answering machine at home, in Candy's room ...

It was the silence of the other world.

Iggy.

'Still smiling, boy?' he said.

I stared at myself in the window – a shrinking face in a void of darkness. I opened my mouth, but nothing came out.

'You *there*?' Iggy said.

'Yeah,' I muttered, 'I'm here.'

'Good,' he sniffed. 'What you doing?'

'Sorry?'

'Don't gimme that *sorry* shit – I said what you *doing*?'

'I don't ... I'm not ... I'm not doing anything ...'

'Yeah?'

'I don't—'

'You got the bitch?'

'What?'

'You *deaf*?'

'No ... I just ... I mean, I don't know what you want ...'

He laughed. 'You don't know what I *want*? Shit – you put me on the floor, man. You put me down and shamed me. You *robbed* me. What d'you *think* I want?'

I didn't reply.

'C'mon, *Joey*,' he sneered, 'think about it. Take an *educated* guess.'

I stayed quiet.

He breathed his silence.

I tried to steady my heart.

'Ah, shit,' he said eventually, 'I ain't got time for this. Listen – you listening?'

'Yeah.'

'OK, I'll say it again. You got the bitch?'

'You mean Candy?'

'Yeah, I mean *Candy* ... you got her? Yes or no?'

'I know where she is.'

'You'd better, for your sake.'

'I'm not going to—'

'You ain't gonna *nothing* – all you're gonna do is gimme the bitch and walk away, and that's it. No shit, no questions. Nothing to pay.'

'What do you mean?'

'What d'you *think* I mean? You took what's mine – I want it back. I'm *getting* it back.'

'I don't think she wants—'

'Don't think – just listen. I'm talking to you. Not her. She's nothing. You hear me? I'm talking to *you*. You gimme the bitch, you walk away.'

'What if I say no?' I heard myself say.

'You ain't *gonna* say no.'

'Why's that?'

'Why?' He laughed. 'You wanna know why? This is why ...' The line went quiet for a moment. I could hear muffled voices in the background, then some kind of movement, a shuffling sound, like something being dragged across the floor ... and then a sobbing voice came on the phone, and my heart went cold.

'Joe ... Joe ... is that you?'

'*Gina,*' I breathed.

Her voice wept down the phone, 'Joe ... thank God ... he's got me ... the bastard took me and *ummmmff—*'

'Gina!' I yelled. 'Are you all right? Where are you? Has he hurt you? Gina ... Gina? ... *GINA!*'

But she'd already gone. I could hear her being dragged away, her gagged voice fading into the background, and the phone being passed around ... and then Iggy's voice came back on the line.

'Nice girl,' he said. 'Very nice.'

'You're dead,' I hissed. 'You're a dead man.'

And I meant it. If he'd been standing beside me then, I would have killed him without even blinking. Killed him, spat on his body, then killed him again.

I could feel his emptiness inside me.

No feeling.

No heart.

Only his death.

I could see it in my windowed eyes. White in the glass, like mirrors ... white in the darkened glass ...

A vision in white.

In me ...

Through me ...

In the woods outside.

White in the dark.

'Joe?'

'Gina?'

'Joe?'

Candy ...?

Behind me. She was standing behind me ... in the middle of the room ... her gowned reflection merging with mine in the window. Her figure ... my face. Gina in my eyes ... Iggy in hers. The devil in the woods. For a moment I could see us all – me, Candy, Gina, Iggy – drawn together in the mirrored glass, like spectres in the dark ...

And I was strangely calmed.

Then Candy spoke and the calmness crashed.

'What's going on?' she said. 'I woke up and heard you shouting ... who's that on the phone? Who are you talking to?'

No one, I suddenly realised. I wasn't talking to anyone. I wasn't listening. I wasn't doing *anything*. Gina was in serious trouble, she *needed* me, and what was I doing? Nothing. Just standing there, lost in myself, staring pathetically at shapes in the window ...

I screwed my eyes shut and screamed at myself in hateful silence – *Christ, what's the* matter *with you ... how* could *you ...?*

Then stopped.

There wasn't time.

All I could hope for – as I cleared the self-disgust from my mind and turned my attention back to the phone – was that I hadn't been lost for too long. That I hadn't missed anything. Because if I had ... and Iggy had hung up ...

I didn't want to think about it.

With hope beating hard in my heart, I gestured at Candy to keep quiet, and pressed the phone to my ear. The line was still open, thank God. I could hear Iggy muttering to someone in the background. He had his hand over the mouthpiece. I blocked my other ear with my finger and listened hard, but I still couldn't make out what he was saying. I thought about turning the phone volume up, but I couldn't remember where the control switch was, and I didn't want to risk pressing the wrong button, so I just kept the phone pressed close to my ear and waited.

After a moment or two, the muttering stopped and a smothered silence filled my ear. I heard a scraping sound, wood on wood, like a chair being moved on floorboards. Then silence again. A muffled laugh. And then the silence opened up as Iggy removed his hand from the mouthpiece, sniffed hard, and spoke into the phone.

'Hey, Killer ... you there?'

'I'm here,' I said.

'You gonna listen now?'

'I'm listening.'

'All right, listen good.' A dull slap echoed down the line, followed immediately by a stifled cry. I felt a knife ripping through my heart. 'Hear that?' Iggy said. 'That's your sister. You threaten me again, and the next time you see her she won't have a face to slap – OK?'

'Please don't—'

'*OK?*'

'Yes ... yes, OK.'

'See, the thing is, Joey, I could lie to you, I could tell you I don't wanna hurt your sister ... but the truth is, I don't give a shit. You know what I'm saying? She's meat to me, same as the rest – meat for money. Money for meat. The only thing stopping me from cutting her up and getting *her* to tell me where you are ... well, like I said, she's a nice piece. It'd be a shame to waste it. I mean, she ain't no Candy, but she's still fresh enough to turn a profit. Course, she'd need some encouragement ...' He paused to let that sink in, then went on. 'You see what I'm saying, Joey? I can't lose ... either way, I can't lose. You want your sister, I get the bitch – you want the bitch, I get your sister. It don't make no odds to me ... but if I was you, I'd give up the bitch. Cos if she stays with you, she'll mess you up, and if she comes back to me ... well, I'll have some fun messing *her* up. But that's just a personal thing, you know? I mean, business-wise, there ain't much in it for me.' He sniffed again. 'So, like I said, you gimme the bitch and walk away, or you say goodbye to your sister. And that's it – that's the deal. No strings. No shit.' He sniffed again. 'You got any questions *now*?'

'How do I know I can trust you?'

'You don't. Anything else?'

I looked across at Candy. She was shivering. Staring at me. Her eyes full of nothing. I turned back to the phone.

'Call me back in ten minutes,' I said quietly.

'What?'

'I need time to think.'

'Shit ... are you for *real*?'

'Just give me ten minutes – please? It won't change anything, will it? Ten minutes, that's all.'

'You got five,' he said angrily, 'five minutes. And when I call back, I want an answer – you want your sister, I want to know where the bitch is. I want an address. I'll ask you once, that's all. One question – one answer. Anything else and your sister's mine.'

After he'd hung up, I couldn't move for a minute. I didn't *want* to move. All I wanted was to be somewhere else – a place where this never happened. I wanted to be the *other* Joe Beck – the Joe Beck who'd never had a lump on his wrist,. never gone to the doctor, never got lost at King's Cross station ...

The Joe Beck who'd never met Candy.

I wanted to be wherever *he* was.

'He's got Gina, hasn't he?' Candy said after a while.

I looked at her. She hadn't moved. She was still standing in the middle of the room, still staring at me. Still shivering.

'Yeah,' I said.

She didn't say anything, just carried on staring at me. There was nothing left in her eyes. No questions, no shock ... not even fear. Just absolute surrender.

I crossed the room and took hold of her. She didn't respond, just hung there, limp and lifeless in my arms.

'Come on,' I said, leading her over to the settee.

She sat on the edge of the settee and stared at the floor. 'God, I'm so sorry,' she said, shaking her head. 'Poor Gina ... if I hadn't—'

'No one's to blame except Iggy,' I told her. 'It's not your fault.'

She carried on staring at the floor, speaking as if she hadn't heard me. 'I knew it – I *knew* he'd do something like this. I shouldn't have let you—'

'Listen to me,' I said firmly. 'We don't have time for this. Iggy's going to call back in a minute. We need to work out what we're going to do.'

She looked at me. 'There's only one thing we *can* do – he wants me back, doesn't he?'

'Yeah, but—'

'And he's got Gina.'

I nodded.

She touched my hand. 'You know what he'll do with her if he doesn't get me?'

I nodded again, trying not to think about it.

'I've been there, Joe,' she said. 'I know what it's like – I can live with it. Gina can't.'

'He'll kill you.'

'No, he won't – he's not stupid. He might smack me about a bit, but as long as I'm making him money, he won't kill me.'

'You're not going back to him,' I said. 'You can't ...

there has to be another way. There has to be something else we can do ...'

'He'll know if we're setting him up, Joe. He *always* knows. That's why he's still alive. You don't mess with Iggy and come out on top – believe me. You do what he says ... or you lose.'

I knew she was right, but I couldn't accept what it meant. I couldn't let her go back to him ... I'd never be able to live with myself. But if I *didn't* let her go ... and Iggy took Gina ...

No, that was unthinkable. Impossible. The world couldn't allow it. Not Gina ... not ever.

Never, never, never ...

Never.

I looked at Candy again, looking at nothing. She was a ghost. I was a ghost. The only existence we had between us was the mobile phone in my hand.

I looked down at it.

It rang.

I flipped it open and put it to my ear.

Silence.

Then, 'Where is she?'

'Woodland Cottage,' I said.

'Where the hell's that?'

I told him.

He didn't ask for any directions, just took down the address, read it back to me, then started talking.

'You're both there, right?'

'Yeah.'

'Anyone else?'

'No.'

'Neighbours?'

'No.'

'This track – the one through the woods – it's driveable?'

'Yeah.'

'Right, listen – I'll be there in two hours. This is what you do – you don't go out, you don't ring anyone, you don't do nothing. When I get there, I wanna see the lights turned on and the curtains open. I wanna see you and the bitch at the window. You stand there, right? Just stand there. You got that?'

'What about Gina?'

'You want her in pieces?'

'What?'

'You keep asking me questions and I'll bring her back to you in plastic bags. You *got* that?'

'Yeah ...'

'Sure?'

'I've got it.'

'All right – what do I see when I get there?'

'What do you—?'

'What do I *see*!'

'The lights,' I said rapidly, 'you see the lights turned on and the curtains open, and you see me standing at the window ...'

'With the bitch.'

'Right.'

'Say it.'

'What?'

'*Say it.*'

'With the bitch,' I forced myself to say. 'I'm standing at the window with the bitch.'

'Yeah,' he sniffed, 'that's right.' He paused for a moment, then said, 'She there now? She listening?'

'No.'

He laughed, knowing I was lying, then suddenly his voice went cold. 'Two hours,' he said. 'Make the most of it.'

The line went dead.

I breathed out slowly and closed the phone and sat there staring into space. The fire had gone out. The room was cold. I could feel Candy's stillness beside me. She hadn't moved. She was still staring at the floor.

'I'm sorry,' I said quietly, 'he made me say it.'

'I know,' she said, without looking up. 'It's all right. When do you think he'll get here?'

'I don't know ... it depends where he's coming from. He said he'd be here in two hours, but if he's in London, I think it'll take longer.' I glanced at the clock. It was five to six. I knew it didn't matter, but I had to say something. 'I don't think he'll get here until nine at the earliest—'

The phone rang again, cutting me off.

I stared at it.

Too shocked to think ...

It's Iggy.

Too scared to hope ...

It's Gina.

I snatched up the phone and read the display: *17:56*, it said, *MIKE*.

I fumbled it open. 'Mike!' I gasped. 'Where are you? Mike?'

'Hey, Joe – is Gina there?'

'What?'

'Gina ... is she with you?'

Oh, God, I thought, *he doesn't know.*

'Joe? Can you hear me? I'm trying to find Gina ... I was supposed to meet her at four, but she never showed up.

She's not at home, and her phone's switched off. I thought she might have gone to see you ... Joe? Can you hear me?'

'Yeah, I can hear you ...'

'Have you heard from her? Has she called you?'

Tell him, I thought. *You've got to tell him.*

'Joe ... for God's sake – what's the matter with you?'

'Gina's in trouble,' I said.

'What? What trouble? What do you mean? Where is she?'

'Iggy's got her.'

'*What?*'

'He just called me ... about five minutes ago. He's got Gina. I spoke to her. I think she's all right—'

'I don't understand,' Mike said.

'He took her ... he's holding her somewhere. He wants Candy back—'

'Iggy?'

'Yeah.'

'Iggy's got Gina?'

'Yeah ...'

'No.'

'He's bringing her to the cottage—'

'No.'

His voice was bleak. Dead. Broken. I didn't know what else to say to him. What could I say? *Help me?* Don't *help me? Don't worry, it'll be all right. Just don't do anything stupid ...?*

'Tell me what happened,' he said, his voice suddenly calm. 'Tell me exactly what happened.'

I explained everything as quickly as possible – the phone call, the threat, the deal, the instructions – and as I talked, I could tell by Mike's silence what he was thinking. I could hear his thoughts echoed in mine: *there's no* deal ... *there never was – no one's walking away from anything ... not you, not Gina, not Candy. No one. Once Iggy gets there, you're all dead and buried.*

He didn't have to tell me. I knew what I'd done. I'd *done* it. I'd told Iggy where we were. I'd given up our only bargaining tool. He didn't *need* anything else. He didn't need us. Not any more. We were expendable.

I *knew* that.

And Mike knew it, too.

But I think we both realised there was no point in talking about it. It was done. Talking wouldn't change anything. All it would do was make things real, and that was too much to bear.

'All right,' Mike said, after I'd told him everything. 'What time was it when Iggy hung up?'

'Five to six.'

'OK ... I'm leaving now. I'm in Heystone, at your place, so I should get to the cottage before Iggy. Don't do anything till I get there. Just lock the doors and wait. If he rings again, just do whatever he says, but let me know. Have you got my number?'

'Yeah.'

'Good.'

'He won't come alone, Mike.'

'I know.'

'What are we going to do?'

'Whatever it takes.'

The next couple of hours could have been anything – a couple of days, a couple of seconds, a couple of years ... it was impossible to tell. The passage of time seemed to melt. If I was thinking of Mike, waiting for him to arrive, every minute felt like an hour, but when my mind turned to Iggy, and I found myself waiting for *him*, the world started spinning like crazy.

Too slow ...

Too fast ...

Too slow ...

Too fast ...

It made me feel sick.

Or maybe that was just the fear?

Because, believe me, I was scared. I was *more* than scared – I was scared of dying, and that's almost indescribable. It's like coming face to face with all your deepest fears, all at once – only ten times worse. It reaches inside you and crushes your heart. It kills you. It screams. It makes you small. It makes you nothing ...

It makes you sick and selfish and incapable.

Just like heroin, I suppose.

Just like Candy.

Too fast ...

Too slow ...

Too fast ...

Too slow ...

She hadn't moved since I'd told her that Mike was coming. She was just sitting there like a zombie, staring at the floor, not saying anything. I couldn't tell what she was thinking ... or even if she was thinking at all. I couldn't imagine how she felt. I just couldn't imagine it. I sat beside her for a while, sharing her silence, then I got up and went to the bathroom.

It was a strange thing to think, but I guessed if I *was* going to die, I might as well die with an empty bladder.

When I came back from the bathroom, Candy still hadn't moved.

I sat down and put my hand on her shoulder.

She looked at me. 'It's not going to work, you know.'

'What isn't?'

'Whatever Mike thinks he can do – it won't work. He'll just get himself killed. You too, probably. It's stupid.'

'Maybe,' I said, 'but there's no harm in listening to him, is there? We can decide what to do when he gets here.'

'And what if Iggy gets here first? We don't *know* that he's starting from London, do we? He could be coming from anywhere. For all we know, he could arrive any minute.'

'Well, if he does, it won't matter what Mike thinks, will it?'

'No ... I suppose not.'

She went back to staring at the floor again.

And I went back to wondering about her.

Does she *think she's going to die?*

Is she as scared of it as I am?

Or does she really believe she's going back to her old life?

And if she does ... God, how scary must that *be?*

Back to Iggy.

Back to the drugs.

Back to the prostitution.

Maybe she'd prefer to die ...?

Maybe that's what she wants?

Maybe—?

'Don't worry,' she said.

I looked at her. 'What?'

'Don't worry about Gina – she'll be all right. Iggy won't do anything to her. If he was going to hurt her, he wouldn't have called you. He would have just done it. He's not stupid – he knows the easiest way to get what he wants. This is the easiest way. Hurting Gina would just mean trouble. He doesn't want any trouble.'

'No?'

'Not that kind. That kind of trouble's more trouble than it's worth.'

She giggled then, which shocked me, and then it struck me how much she was jabbering ... and I guessed she was going a little bit crazy. Not *mad* crazy, just scared crazy – the kind of craziness that protects your mind from facing the truth. I didn't like it – it was unnerving, and kind of sad – but I could see how it served a purpose, so I didn't say anything. I just let her jabber away.

'And another thing,' she said, 'another thing ...' She frowned at me. 'What was I saying?'

'That Iggy wouldn't hurt Gina ...'

'Oh, yeah ... because of the phone. That's how he must have got your mobile number – from Gina's phone. He didn't have to *make* her tell him – all he had to do was take her phone and look through the phonebook. You see? He didn't *have* to hurt her.'

'Right,' I said, playing along.

She frowned again. 'What I don't understand is how he found Gina in the first place.' She looked at me. 'What do you think?'

I think I should have listened to myself before we got on the train, I thought. *I think I should have had faith in that half-formed worrying shadow ...*

'I think he probably went back to The Black Room,' I said. 'That's the only link he had between me and you.'

Her eyes brightened. 'Of *course* ... God, I'd forgotten all about that.'

'Me too.'

'But would The Black Room have had a contact number for you?'

'No, but they would have had one for Jason. He's been ringing me at home, leaving urgent messages ... but I thought it was about the group so I never called back.'

'Who's Jason?'

'The singer in The Katies.'

'You think Iggy rang him?'

'Probably.'

'And Jason wanted to let you know?'

I nodded. 'He probably gave Iggy my home number. There were a couple of silent messages on the answering machine. Maybe he told him where I lived, too.'

'Iggy could have found that out from the telephone number. He knows people ... he knows people who can do that ... I don't know who they are ... I don't know ... he knows ...' Her voice trailed off and she put her hand to her head and breathed out heavily. Her eyes were suddenly dull.

The craziness had evaporated.

The room was ice cold.

'God, Joe,' she whispered. 'I'm so scared ... what are we going to *do*?'

I looked at the clock.

It was seven-thirty.

I didn't know what we were going to do.

I still don't know if there was anything else I could have done. I've thought about it over and over again – thinking, thinking, thinking ... staring out of the window ... lying on the floor ... staring into the past ... trying to convince myself that I was right, that there *wasn't* anything else I could have done – and most of the time I come to the same conclusion.

You had no options.

You had *to tell Iggy where you were.*
You couldn't hide.
You couldn't run away.
You couldn't call the police.
You couldn't do *anything.*
All you could do was wait.
And hope.
And I think I'm right ... most of the time.
I'm almost convinced.
But it still doesn't make me feel any better.

As the minutes passed, and the time melted around from seven-thirty to eight, we carried on waiting and hoping. Candy slipped back into a state of mind that was somewhere between crazy and zombie, and I tried to keep my hopes up by behaving as normally as possible. I got the fire going, washed some dishes, tidied up, and then I started packing.

It sounds ridiculous, I know. And at the time, I don't think I knew why I was doing it. But I suppose I thought – in the back of my mind – that if I *didn't* start packing, I was giving in. *Not* packing up meant we weren't going anywhere. We weren't leaving. *Not* packing up meant no future.

So I went into the bedroom and started packing.

After I'd gathered up all my clothes and stuffed them into my bag, I turned my attention to Candy's stuff. Her clothes were still strewn all over the place – jeans, vests, jumpers, all sorts. I wasn't quite sure whether to pack them away myself, or leave them to her. I couldn't make up my mind, and the more I thought about it, the more it bothered me. I knew it *shouldn't* bother me, that there were far more important things to worry about, but I just couldn't help it. It was really weird.

I was still standing there, undecided, when Candy appeared in the doorway and asked me what I was doing.

'Packing,' I told her. 'I was just wondering what to do with all your stuff.'

'Packing?'

'Yeah.'

She didn't say anything, just blinked in confusion, then looked at the floor. I thought at first she simply didn't know what to say, but then I realised there was more to it than that.

I was packing.

Packing meant leaving.

Leaving meant a future.

And Candy didn't want to know about the future. It was all right for *me* to look to the future and hope for the best, because I had a best to hope for. If *I* got out of this mess in one piece, I'd probably end up OK. But the best that Candy could hope for was a return to the life she'd led before ...

So why bother hoping at all?

I should have realised, I suppose.

I should have given it a bit more thought ...

But I didn't.

And now I felt bad.

'It doesn't matter,' I said, trying to sound casual, 'I was just—'

'I'll do it,' she said.

'What?'

'I'll sort out my clothes and pack my bag. I need to get dressed anyway.'

Her eyes were glazed, her voice emotionless ... and as she stood there, staring blankly, my mind went back to our day at the zoo, to the day that never dies, when we were alone together in our Moonlight World, sharing the sadness of the tree kangaroo. I could feel again the hush of the darkness, the silence, the emptiness, the cool of the underground air ... and I could see that face, that sad-eyed bewilderment, that pitiful fear ...

All of it held in a simple little moment.

It was just so ...

I don't know.

Just so much.

chapter twenty-one

I heard the car coming from a long way off. It was one of those nights when the air is perfectly still and the stars shine brightly and the world seems cold and silent. The kind of night when you can hear for miles. I was waiting at the open window, my breath turning white in the misty air, and I could hear everything: the darkness, the emptiness, the rush of my heart. When the first faint sounds of the car pricked the air, I heard it in every part of my body. The low hum, the rolling tyres, the faint crunch of rubber on damp earth ...

It was moving slowly. Carefully.

I leaned out of the window and peered into the dark.

'Is it Iggy?' asked Candy, coming up behind me.

'I don't know yet – I can't see anything.'

She'd dressed and showered and washed her hair, and as she stood there beside me, with her hand on my shoulder, I could smell the scent of her skin – the scent of fresh soap and talcum powder. It was just as good as it ever was. And I couldn't understand how that could be.

'There,' she said suddenly, pointing into the distance. 'I think I saw lights ... headlights ... over there, through the trees.'

'Where?'

'They've gone now.'

'How many?' I asked her.

'I don't know ... it was just a flash.'

'It's got to be Mike,' I muttered. 'It's only eight-twenty ... it *has* to be Mike.' I squinted through the darkness, searching for the headlights. If there was only one car, it was probably Mike; more than one, and it was definitely Iggy.

I closed my eyes for a second, squeezing them shut, then opened them again. The mist seemed to be thickening now, and as I gazed out into the darkness, trying to make out the lane, my mind seemed to be thickening, too. I kept seeing things that weren't there: mossy branches, waxy green leaves, strange-looking ferns ... all of them misty and dark and dripping with moisture. *Memories,* I told myself, *they're just sense-memories. Hopes. Denials ...*

Whatever they were, they disappeared as a beam of headlights lit up the woods at the far end of the lane.

'Turn on the lights,' I said to Candy.

'Why?'

'Iggy's instructions. Open all the curtains and turn on the lights, then come back and wait here with me.'

The headlights were coming down the lane now. Moving slowly, dipping up and down with the contours of the lane, the harsh white lights greying the passing trees. As far as I could tell, there was only one car.

'Do you think it's Iggy?' Candy asked.

'I don't know ... I don't think so, but we'd better do as he said – just in case. And it'll make things easier for Mike if the lights are on, anyway. He'll have a better view of the cottage.'

While Candy went around turning on lights and opening the curtains, I stayed at the window, my eyes fixed on the approaching car. As it drew closer, the purr of the engine filled the night, robbing the woods of their silence. I could see the exhaust fumes mingling with the mist, and I could see the dark gleam of metal ... but I still couldn't see the driver. The lights were too bright. All I could see was a vague silhouette in a starburst reflection of glass.

It was a man's silhouette.

He was big.

He was dark.

He was turning the car into the clearing outside the cottage.

As the twin beam of the headlights swept around the trees, Candy came up beside me and looked through the window.

'Is it him?' she said.

'I don't know ...'

The car stopped. It was about twenty metres away from the cottage, angled towards us. The headlights were still on. The engine was idling. The driver was faceless and still.

I suddenly realised how cold I was. Cold, useless, scared to death. What if it *was* Iggy? I had no idea what I was going to do. I hadn't even thought about it. I couldn't. I was just hoping ...

'Look,' said Candy, touching my arm.

I watched as the driver leaned forward in his seat, and then the headlights went out, and I couldn't see anything. The sudden darkness was blinding. My eyes burned with the dazzling white after-image of the headlights, but beyond that I couldn't see *anything*. I could feel Candy's hand gripping my arm, and I could hear the sound of the engine being turned off ... and the car door opening ... slamming shut ... and then footsteps moving across the clearing ...

Moving towards us.

Getting louder.

Getting closer.

Taking shape ...

The darkness was lifting. My eyes were re-adjusting to the starlight glow. I could see ...

A shape.

A figure.

A moonlit face.

'Mike?' I said hopefully.

His eyes shone coldly as he stepped into the light of the window. He was dressed in only a T-shirt and jeans, but if the icy air was bothering him, he didn't show it. He didn't show anything. He just looked around, checking things out, then turned to me and spoke quietly.

'You all right?' he said.

'Yeah.'

'You alone?'

I nodded.

He stared hard at me for a couple of moments, making sure I was telling the truth, then he looked at Candy, nodded his head, and disappeared towards the front door. As I hurried across the room to let him in, I looked at the clock. It was eight thirty-five.

The world was spinning like crazy.

'Have you heard anything?' Mike asked as he came through the door. 'Has Iggy called?'

'No.'

'OK, first things first – we need to get the car out of sight.'

'You can park it round the back of the cottage.'

'Good.' He gazed cautiously around the room, taking it all in, then – satisfied with what he'd seen – he leaned down and put his hand on my shoulder. 'Don't worry,' he said, looking me in the eye. 'It's going to be all right. Trust me – Gina's going to be fine.' He glanced over at Candy, then turned back to me again and lowered his voice. 'How's she doing? Is she still using heroin?'

'No,' I told him. 'Not since Saturday.'

He gave my shoulder a quick squeeze, then straightened up and went over to Candy at the window.

'Can you drive?' he asked her.

'Can I *what*?'

'Drive,' he repeated. 'Can you drive?'

'Well ... yeah,' she said hesitantly.

'Here,' said Mike, passing her a bunch of keys. 'Move the car round the back of the cottage so it can't be seen from the lane. If you see anyone coming, hit the horn and get back in here – OK?'

Candy nodded, but didn't move.

'We don't have much time,' Mike told her.

She looked at him. 'What are you going to do when Iggy gets here?'

'I'm going to put things right.'

'How?'

'That depends on him.'

'You're making a big mistake.'

'Yeah?'

'Iggy doesn't want any trouble – he just wants me. Once he's got me, you'll get Gina back and that'll be the end of it. But if you start trying to "put things right", he's not going to like it one bit.'

'Nice try,' Mike said, shaking his head, 'but you're wasting your time. Iggy's not getting you. He's not getting Gina. He's not getting anyone. He's either leaving here with nothing, or he's not leaving here at all. That's all there is to it. Now, are you going to move that car or not?'

She stared at him and he stared back, and I could feel a troubled silence hanging in the air. I didn't like it. I didn't understand it. And I was sick of not understanding things.

Why the friction?

Why the conflict?

Why the complexity?

I'm scared to death ... I don't need any complexity.

They carried on staring at each other for a while, then Candy nodded her head, fetched her coat, and walked out of the cottage without so much as looking at me. I stepped into the doorway and watched her go. As she headed towards the car, with the gathering mist folding in her wake, I could sense something different about her. Something strange ... something distant ... almost secretive ...

I didn't know what it was.

As she got in the car and started the engine, Mike came up beside me.

'Is there a back way out?' he asked.

'What?'

'Another door ... is there a back door?'

I looked at him.

'Come *on*, Joe,' he said sharply. 'Snap out of it.' His eyes flicked up as Candy got the car moving. She drove slowly, with the headlights off, rolling the car across the clearing and around the back of the cottage. 'Don't worry about her,' Mike said to me. 'She'll be all right – she's tough enough. It's Gina we have to think about now.'

'I know,' I told him.

'She's everything.'

'I know.'

He looked at me for a moment, then turned away and stared off silently into the darkness. From behind the cottage, I heard Candy turning off the car's ignition ... then a few minutes' silence ... then the car door opening ... slamming shut ... another brief pause ... and then hurried footsteps as she moved back towards the cottage. When she came round the corner, she was walking briskly and clutching her coat to her chest. She seemed oddly surprised to see me. Her steps faltered for a moment, her mouth opened ... and then, without a word, she lowered her eyes and tightened her coat and hurried on into the cottage.

Lost in thought, perhaps ...

Or maybe just cold.

I turned to Mike for his opinion, but when I saw the look on his face, I decided not to ask. He was still just standing there, frozen like a monument, still staring out into the dark ... and the coldness in his eyes was terrifying.

'The back door's locked and double-bolted,' I told him. 'I've put the security chain on, too.'

'Good,' he said. 'What about these windows?'

We'd come inside and locked the front door, and now Mike was checking out the rest of the room while I kept watch at the front window. Candy was over at the kitchen sink, filling the kettle ... totally ignoring us. After Mike had finished in the front room, he went around all the other rooms – the bedrooms, the bathroom – meticulously checking that the windows were closed, locking all the doors behind him ... but leaving the lights on and the curtains open. When he came back into the front room, he told me to get the fire going. While I was doing that, he started moving the furniture around.

Candy asked him what he was doing.

'Making sure we're safe,' he said, sliding an armchair against the front door. 'If they can't get in, they'll have to talk, and that'll give us some time.'

'Time for what?' asked Candy.

'Thinking ... watching ...' He started shoving the settee across the room. 'Whatever's necessary.'

'Then what?'

He paused and stood up straight, looking at her. 'What's your problem?'

'What do you mean?'

'You *know* what I mean—'

'I don't—'

'What have you done since I got here?'

'I haven't done *anything*—'

'Exactly – apart from sulking and moaning and giving me a hard time, you haven't done anything.'

'I'm not sulking—'

'What *are* you doing, then?'

'Look,' she said, trying to stay calm, 'I'm sick, for God's sake. I'm sick and I'm scared and I feel like shit because it's my fault that Iggy's got Gina. And the only way to get her back is for me to go back to him. Why can't you understand that? Moving the furniture around isn't going to help. All you're doing is making things worse—'

'All right,' said Mike, 'what do *you* want us to do? You want us to give up?'

'No—'

'You want us dead?'

'No!' she yelled. 'Of *course* I don't—'

'You *want* to go back to your pimp?'

Silence filled the room for a moment. Candy's face tightened and her eyes filled with rage, and I thought for a second she was going to go crazy, but then her face seemed to die and her eyes went blank, and when she spoke, her voice was frail and empty.

'All right,' she said, staring coldly at Mike. 'You want to know what I want? Is that it? OK ... if you *really* want to know, I'll tell you ...' Her breath caught in her throat. 'I want to go home ... OK? I want to go home ...' Her eyes started glistening. 'I want to be what I used to be ... I want to say sorry ... I don't want to cry any more ... I just ... I just ...' Her voice broke down in tears. 'I just want to make everything better ...'

She was sobbing and trembling, out of control, burying her head in her hands. Mike was staring at her, unable to speak. And I was moving across the room, thinking of nothing but holding her ...

But I never got there.

A blaze of headlights burst through the window, freezing me in my tracks, and then we all heard the roar of a car outside – tyres screeching, engine racing, music thumping ...

It sounded like thunder.

And we all knew what it meant.

Mike reacted first, throwing himself to the floor and crawling behind the settee. 'Stay where you are,' he hissed loudly at me. 'Just do what I say, and don't look at me. I'm not here – d'you understand?'

I could only just hear him over the deafening music coming from the car. The heavy drums and booming bass were loud enough to shake the ground.

'Joe!' Mike hissed again.

'Yeah,' I said, 'I heard you. You're not here.'

'OK – how many cars are there?'

'Just one, I think ...'

'Can you see Gina?'

I shielded my eyes and squinted through the window. The car was parked about fifteen metres away, facing the cottage. The headlights were on full beam, blinding me.

'I can't see a thing,' I told Mike.

'OK,' he said. 'Just stay there and keep watching. If anything happens, let me know.' He called across the room. 'Candy! Get over here. You're supposed to be with Joe at the window.'

She didn't reply.

The music kept thumping.

'Candy!' Mike shouted again. 'Come *on*! What are you *doing*? They're waiting for you ... they won't do anything until they see you ... we've got to make them *do* something ... Candy?'

I didn't want to take my eyes off the car – I wanted to see Gina ... I wanted to *see* her – but Candy's silence was killing me. I had to know if she was all right. I had to see *her* ... I couldn't help it.

I turned my head and looked across the room. She was standing behind the kitchen counter, as dead as I'd ever seen her. Dull-eyed, staring, senseless, surrendered ...

'Candy,' I called out anxiously, 'Candy ... can you hear me?'

She didn't respond.

'Listen,' I told her, 'it's all right, everything's OK. Don't be frightened. Just come over here ...'

Her eyes never moved.

'Mike?' I said.

'I'll get her,' he said, crawling out from behind the settee and slithering across the floor. 'You watch the car.'

There was a lot of stuff building up in me now, stuff I hadn't felt before – fear and anger, cutting together like broken knives, grinding themselves into something I couldn't control – and as I turned away and stared into the headlights again, the blinding light burned madness into my eyes. The music pounded through my head, throbbing blood, like a bursting heart ... and I wanted to see faces. Darkness. Bodies. I wanted to crash through the window. I wanted to scream at the mist and run through the night and tear the trees down to the ground ...

I wanted Gina.

I wanted Candy.

I didn't want to die.

I wanted ...

Nothing.

Sudden silence.

The music had stopped. The engine was quiet. The headlights blazed mutely in the deadening hush. There was nothing to hear, just the hum of the aftersound echoing the night, and – from across the room – Mike's whispered pleading with Candy.

'Please ...' he was saying to her, 'for Gina's sake ... just show them you're here. All you have to do is stand at the window with Joe. I won't let Iggy do anything to you, I promise.'

I glanced over and saw them standing together at the counter. Candy hadn't moved. She was still dead to the world, still lost in what was left of herself. Mike was beside her, holding her lifeless hand, gazing desperately into her lifeless eyes.

'Hey!' called a voice from the car outside, snapping my

attention back to the window. 'Hey, kid – you listening?'

I shielded my eyes against the lights again, trying to see who was calling out. It didn't sound like Iggy.

'Open the window,' the voice said.

I hesitated.

'Do it,' Mike whispered from across the room. 'Do as he says.'

I fumbled with the catch and opened the window. The headlights brightened and my breath turned white.

'Where is she?' the voice called out from the car.

Now that the window was open I could hear a lot better, and I was fairly sure it wasn't Iggy.

'What?' I called back.

'You heard – where is she?'

'Where's Gina?' Mike whispered.

I didn't know what he meant. Was he asking me where she was? Or was he telling me to ask *them*? I wanted to ask him, but I couldn't. They were watching me. They'd see me talking. They mustn't see me talking ...

What should I do?

My mind started racing, panicking, trying to think ...

And then my mouth opened and I heard myself say, 'Who's asking?'

'What?' hissed Mike.

'What?' said the voice.

'You heard me,' I said. 'Who *are* you?'

'Christ ...' muttered Mike.

Inside the car, someone laughed – a cold hard laugh that shrank my heart – and I suddenly thought to myself – *shit, what are you* doing? *what are you* saying? *what the hell are you* thinking? *no questions, Iggy said ... no* questions ...

But then *his* voice called out, as deep and dark as the night, and the sound of it was weirdly comforting.

'We had a deal, boy,' he said calmly. 'You just blew it.'

'The deal was with *you,*' I called back, 'no one else. All I heard just now was a voice. It could have been anyone. I had to make sure it was you.'

'You sure *now*?'

'I don't know ... I can't see your face ...'

'I can see yours. I could drop you right now.'

I suddenly realised how vulnerable I was – framed in the window, lit up like a Christmas tree ... I was a sitting duck. If Iggy had a gun, he couldn't miss. *If* he had a gun? Of *course* he had a gun. Would he use it, though? That was the question. Would he shoot me? I didn't think so ... not until he was *sure* that Candy was here ...

No, I didn't *think* so ...

But that didn't make me feel any better. Every cell in my body was screaming at me to *move.* My heart was hammering, my senses primed. I could hear everything – Mike and Candy breathing hard, the cooling tick of the engine, the faint rustle of dead leaves – and I could see without seeing ... through the lights ... into the car ... I could see all the bodies, the heads, the hooded eyes ...

I could see Gina.

Watching me.

Waiting ...

'All right,' Iggy called out, 'that's it – get the bitch in the window *now*. You got ten seconds.'

'Gina first,' I said.

'What?'

'I'm not doing anything until I see my sister.'

'Another five seconds and you won't *have* a sister.'

Time was melting again ... everything was happening too fast, too slow ... but it didn't seem to matter. I was *in* time ... in control ... in touch with everything. I could hear

Mike getting hold of Candy, struggling with her, trying to pull her towards the window, and I could hear Candy resisting him ...

'Leave her, Mike,' I said.

'You *heard* him,' he hissed at me, 'he's going to hurt Gina—'

'No, he won't – let Candy go.'

The struggling stopped.

I stared through the window.

Not breathing, not feeling ...

No sound.

No heart.

Just white in the dark, like fire ... white in the dark of my heart ... a vision in white ... in me ... through me ...

White in the dark.

The headlights went out.

I closed my eyes and opened them again. Mist swirled in the darkness, shrouding the shape of the car – jet-black metal, frosted white ... silver catching the moon ... and I could see gold and white in the smoked-glass shadows ... I could see bodies and heads and chains and eyes ...

I could see them all now. Figures in the tinted glass. Two in the front of the car and three in the back; Iggy in the passenger seat ...

'Is she there?' Candy asked in a broken whisper. 'Is Gina there?'

'I think so ...'

I stared ...

I think ...

The car rocked slightly ... the rear door swung open ... and a man got out – lean, black, hollow-eyed. I'd never seen him before. He didn't look at me. He didn't look at anything. He just casually reached inside the car, got hold of something, and pulled it out.

It was Gina.

She could hardly stand. The man beside her was holding her up by her arm – not looking at her, just holding her up like an empty sack. She looked terrible – cold, dirty, dishevelled ... dazed. Drugged. Her eyes couldn't focus. Her head hung loosely on her neck. She was barefoot and pale ... shivering uncontrollably in a thin white T-shirt ...

But she was alive.

She was everything.

'She's there,' I said, as the man bundled her back into the car.

'Are you sure?' Candy asked.

'I just saw her,' I said, without taking my eyes off the car. 'She doesn't look too good, but—'

THUMP!

The sound came from across the room – a sudden dull impact ... a breathless groan – and I turned around to see Mike falling heavily to the floor. My heart stopped. The moment froze – Mike not moving, not making a sound, just lying there in a heap ...

Christ, I thought, *he's been shot ...*

But then I saw Candy ... standing over Mike, her face pale and tense, holding a length of metal in both hands. For a ridiculous moment, I thought it was a sword – a long, blunt, heavy-looking sword – but almost immediately an image flashed into my mind – an image of Candy coming back from Mike's car, looking surprised, clutching her coat to her chest – and everything became clear in an instant. It wasn't a sword, it was a steering lock. She'd taken Mike's steering lock from his car. She'd hidden it under her coat. She'd hit him over the head with it ... knocked him cold ... and now he was lying there ... not moving, not making a sound ...

I could see the blood on his head ...

Too pink to be real.

I could hear my heart.

And someone shouting outside ...

And Candy's shallow breaths.

'What are you *doing*?' I said to her. 'What have you done?'

'It's all right,' she said, dropping the steering lock to the floor. 'He'll be all right. He's not dead.'

Her eyes were pale and wild.

Another shout came from outside. I glanced through the window and saw Iggy getting out of the car ... and now I didn't know anything. I didn't know *how* to know. I looked over at Candy. She was opening a kitchen drawer ... taking something out ... moving without any feeling – walking calmly around the counter, across the room, looking into my eyes, coming towards me ... with a broad-bladed carving knife in her hand.

chapter twenty-two

I didn't do anything. I *couldn't* do anything. All I could do was stand there looking at her. Looking at everything. Her face, her lips, her cheeks, the almond death of her eyes. Her neck, her legs, the shape of her body. Her sweated skin. The gleam of the knife, her silvered hand ...

God ... the knife.

She was standing in front of me now, her eyes fixed on mine, her face devoid of all feeling.

What was I supposed to do?

Anything?

Nothing?

I tried to say something, but my mouth wouldn't open. I tried to reason, but my head was empty. All I could do was have faith.

It's up to you, Candy, I thought.

It's all up to you.

A loud metallic click came from outside. Candy cocked her head at the sound, then blinked slowly and looked back at me again.

'Stay here,' she said. 'Lock the door behind me, then call the police.'

'What?'

She reached up and placed a finger on my lips. 'Just do it, Joe ... please? Just do it.'

Silenced by the touch of her fingertip, I looked into her eyes, searching for an explanation ... or just some kind of truth. It was hard to find. There was *something* there, some kind of light in the darkness, but it was almost too faint to see. It was just something, a barely perceptible signal, like a flickering candle on a distant hill ...

It was there.

I knew it was there.

I nodded my head.

Candy said nothing. She removed her finger from my lips, leaned forward and kissed me, then turned around and headed for the door. I watched in silence as she slipped the knife inside her coat and pulled the armchair away from the door. I watched her pause for a moment, muttering quietly to herself, and then I watched in wonder as she unlocked the door, flung it open, and ran out into the clearing.

I really didn't know what she was doing then, and there was something of me that didn't care, either. She was doing what she was doing. It had nothing to do with me. I was out of it now.

I suppose I *wanted* to care, but the truth is, at that moment, I *was* out of it. Physically, emotionally, mentally ... I didn't have anything left. I didn't *know* what was happening. I didn't know who I was. I didn't know what Candy was. I didn't care about Mike ...

I couldn't reason.

I couldn't act.

I couldn't *connect* with anything.

I didn't lock the front door and I didn't call the police, I just stayed at the window and watched. Everything seemed unnaturally clear: the moon hanging high over the trees, its flattened light shining down on the clearing like a spotlight flooding the stage; the blanket of mist hugging the ground; the curtained backdrop of wooded darkness; and, in the midst of it all, Candy running towards Iggy ...

And the pistol in Iggy's hand.

And Gina.

And the rest of Iggy's crew.

They were all out of the car now. The two from the back had moved off to one side, taking Gina with them. One of them was holding her, while the other one – the one I'd seen earlier – held a gun to her head. I couldn't tell if the driver was armed as he was standing behind the open car door. Iggy was about five paces in front of him ... ten metres or so from the cottage. His arm was raised, his pistol pointing at Candy.

It didn't seem to bother her. She just carried on running towards him, calling out to him, calling his name ...

'Iggy!' she sobbed loudly. 'Thank God you're *here*. Help me, Iggy ... *please* ... you gotta *help* me ...'

She was crying ...

Why was she *crying*?

I watched her run up to him. I watched his eyes, watching her. They never blinked. His gun never wavered.

'Where've you *been*?' Candy gasped, stopping in front of him. 'What took you so long? Christ, I've been waiting—'

'What you doing?' Iggy growled.

'I missed you so *much*—'

'You ran out on me.'

'No, I didn't ... he *made* me ... I didn't want to—'

'You *shamed* me, bitch. You put me down and left me.'

'No,' she wept, moving towards him – cowering, begging, fawning. 'No ... please ... I didn't *mean* anything. Joe made me do it ... he *forced* me. I didn't want to hurt you. Why would I hurt you? I need you, Iggy ... please ... I *need* you ...'

He still had his pistol raised, but as Candy inched towards him, lowering herself like a wounded dog, he didn't do anything to stop her. He didn't hit her as she crept tearfully under his outstretched arm and buried her face in his chest. He didn't move as she put her arms around him. He didn't do anything. He didn't need to; he had what he wanted.

'I'm dying, Ig,' I heard her say, rubbing her hands all over him. 'I really need—'

'Shut up,' he told her, turning his eyes and the barrel of the gun towards me. 'Who's in the house?'

'I just need a little—'

His eyes didn't move as his free hand whipped down and cracked into the side of her head. She flinched, but didn't let go of him.

'Who's in the house?' he repeated.

'Just the kid,' she said dismissively. 'He's on his own.' She rubbed her head and looked up at him. 'Please, Iggy ... I *really* need a hit. Have you got any stuff?' Her hands started moving over his shirt. 'Please ...? I'm *dying* ...'

'Does it hurt?' he asked coldly.

'Yeah ...'

'Good. Now get in the car. I'll deal with you later.' He took his eyes off her and waved the gun at me. 'I got business to attend to – I got smiles to cut.'

'You like a smile?' Candy said quietly.

It was the voice I remembered from the station – sweet and clear, like a shining jewel in the gutter – only colder. A lot colder. She breathed ice, the words of a ghost, and – for a timeless moment – everything froze. Iggy's eyes, the mist, the night ...

Candy's devil ...

Iggy's heart ...

The two of them stilled in the moonlight.

And then her hand swung up in a silvered arc and she buried the knife in his throat.

Epilogue

I told the police afterwards that I didn't remember anything after Candy had left the cottage. From the moment she flung open the door and ran out into the clearing, to the moment the local police turned up – my mind was a blank. I couldn't remember a single thing. I'm not sure if they believed me or not – and I didn't really care. I told them everything else. I answered their questions – what, when, who, where, how, why – over and over again. It wasn't difficult. They asked me what happened; I told them what happened. They asked me again; I told them again ...

Why not?

There wasn't any point in lying. If they didn't get the truth from me, they'd get it from someone else. Gina would tell them. Mike would tell them. Forensics would tell them.

So I answered their questions. I co-operated with them. I gave them what they wanted: details, names, addresses, descriptions ... my mobile phone, my shoes, my fingerprints, my DNA ...

I gave them a statement.

Why not?

None of it meant anything.

Even if I *was* lying about how much I remembered ...

Which I wasn't.

Not entirely.

Even now, I'm not sure what happened to me when Candy stuck the knife in Iggy's throat. I know she did it ... the memory's *there*. I can see myself standing at the open window ... the moon hanging high over the trees ... I can feel the hush of violence, sucking the air from my lungs ... I can see the silent flash of the blade ... slicing through the dark ...

But then something happens inside my head. Something shuts down, some unknown part of me, and my senses aren't mine any more.

Time stops.

Iggy doesn't move a muscle. He doesn't fall, he doesn't flinch, he doesn't make a sound. He just stands there in the deadening silence, with the knife embedded deep in his throat ... and his vacant eyes fixed on mine ... and the gun still gripped in his hand ... and something inside me is thinking distantly of stone-black giants and deathless souls and nightmare beasts that refuse to die ...

But then it happens: Iggy breaks.

A crack appears in his death-mask face ... a faint look of surprise, the child in his eyes, a momentary shiver of fear ... and at last he's human. Ready to die. His eyes glaze over, his giant frame shudders, and he slumps to his knees in the mist.

Time starts again.

I have no feelings. I'm just hoping to God he's human enough to die.

I have no attachment to what I can see – Candy stooping down and ripping the gun from Iggy's dead hand. Movement at the car – the driver behind the open door. Candy straightening up and levelling the pistol at him. The driver's frozen face, the half-raised gun in his hand ... the flash of flame, the dull *crack*, the muffled *thud* ...

I know that Candy's shot him, but it doesn't mean a thing. I'm just watching him go down, bleeding from the chest ... and then I'm watching Candy as she lowers the gun and turns her attention to the other two men ... the two from the back of the car ... the two with Gina.

One of them still has a gun to her head.

Candy doesn't care.

'It's over,' she tells them, her voice a dream. 'There's nothing left.'

The two men look at each other.

Candy starts walking towards them, holding the gun at her side. 'The police are on their way,' she says. 'If you leave now, you might just make it. If you shoot the girl, you're dead. If you try taking her with you, you're dead.' She stops in front of them. 'What's it to be?'

Moments pass, silent and dark ... and then Gina is sitting alone on the ground and the two men are backing away towards the car. Candy is watching them all the way. I'm watching them, too. They're helping the wounded driver into the back of the car ... they're shutting the doors ... they're getting in the car and starting it up and reversing around the clearing ... and now I'm watching Candy again as she watches them driving away ... up the lane ... through the woods ... the glow of the tail-lights reddening the mist ... and she doesn't stop watching until the lane is dark and there's nothing left to see.

Another moment passes ... and now Candy is done. With a silent sigh, she sinks to the ground and sits in deadness beside Gina. They look at each other for a second, then they both close their eyes and bow their heads to the moon.

That's what I have inside me, and that's where it's staying. I suppose I could have tried explaining it all to the police, and maybe I should have, but I didn't know how.

How do you explain that what's in your mind isn't yours?

Or why you didn't do anything?

How do you explain that even when you *did* do something, the only memories you have are the second-hand memories of someone else ... of a slow-motion boy with tears in his eyes, helping two girls into a cottage. How do you explain that you can feel the coldness of their skin on his hands, that you can feel his eyes shutting out the corpse on the ground, seeing stone-black mountains in the mist? That you can feel his time passing ... his sensed little things ... hot drinks, blankets, movement, faces ... Mike on his feet, smiling at Gina through the blood ... Mike and Candy ... Mike and the boy ... Candy's ghost ... Mike outside ... Mike on the phone ...

Sirens and lights and squealing wheels ...

The midnight police, taking everybody away ...

How do you explain all that?

A lot happened in the next few months, most of which I don't want to talk about. It was nothing – just stuff: Dad stuff, me stuff, more police stuff ... there was even a bit of Mum stuff for a while, but that didn't last very long. Nothing lasted very long. The days just passed, as they do – days, weeks, endless months – and gradually things started settling down.

Gina slowly got better. The doctors kept her in hospital for a couple of days, but the drugs that Iggy had sedated her with hadn't done any lasting damage. Once they'd been flushed from her system, and she'd had time to rest, she was physically as good as new. Emotionally, though ... well, that was something else.

We talked a lot.

We held each other a lot.

We sat with each other and cried.

And when I wasn't there, she always had Mike. Out of all of us, I think he was the least affected by everything. Maybe I'm wrong, maybe he was just better at hiding his feelings, but it seemed to me that – apart from the stitches in his head – he was barely scarred at all. He just dusted himself down and got on with things.

I wish I could say the same about myself.

I did my best – or perhaps I didn't ... but I did what I could to accept things as they were. It was impossible, though. Without Candy, nothing seemed to have any meaning. I just wanted to *see* her, that's all ... or at least find out what was happening to her. But no one would tell me anything. All the police would say was that she'd been arrested and charged and released on bail, and that I wasn't allowed to see her as I'd probably be called as a witness at her trial.

Dad was even less forthcoming. Even if he *had* known where Candy was – which I'm not sure he did – he'd never have told me. He *hated* her. Despised her. He wouldn't so much as mention her name. As far as he was concerned, everything that happened was down to her. It was all her fault – she'd seduced me, she'd put Gina's life at risk, she'd messed up his family ... and he refused to listen when I tried to tell him otherwise.

I didn't really blame him.

He was wrong, of course ... and bigoted and blind and stupid – but I couldn't hold that against him. Not for long, anyway. Not after everything I'd put him though. He was my dad ...

And that was that.

So, in the end, I turned to Mike for help. I didn't *want* to go behind Dad's back, but by then I hadn't seen Candy for nearly four months ... and I knew I couldn't stand it any more. I was living in a void. Living and dying inside my head. Thinking about her, picturing her, trying to remember what she was like ...

That was all the world I had.

And it wasn't enough.

I needed to see her ... I *had* to see her.

I'm not sure how Mike managed it – and I'm not sure he wanted to – but a couple of weeks later I was sitting at a garden table, in the shade of a high brick wall, waiting anxiously for Candy to appear. It was a Sunday, the first week in July, about two o'clock in the afternoon. The sky was bright with the electric-blue haze of a perfect summer's day. Birds were singing. Small flies were swarming in the air, pulsing in the sunlight, and away at the end of the garden, through an open window in a tan brick building, I could hear the comforting sounds of someone at work in a kitchen – rattling pots and pans, hissing urns, low voices ...

The window was barred.

I looked around the garden. It was a small square of

lawned grass, surrounded by an old brick wall. There wasn't much to look at. A few more tables and chairs, some flowering shrubs, a couple of trees ...

No people.

Just me.

I looked over at the building again. It was exactly the same as all the other buildings in the complex – a single-storey structure with a grey slate roof and a dark blue door. There were six buildings in all – I'd seen the entire complex when I'd arrived: six brick bungalows, a couple of acres of mesh-fenced fields, a driveway, a courtyard, a car park at the front ...

Just outside the entrance, a discreet wooden sign with small gold lettering said: *The Melville-Dean Resident Adolescent Unit*.

'I'm not sure what kind of place it is,' Mike had told me. 'Gina would probably know, but I don't want her getting involved in this. As far as I can tell, Candy's been there since she was released on bail.'

And that was about all I knew. I didn't know what a Resident Adolescent Unit was. I didn't know why she was here. I didn't know what went on behind those walls ... behind those metal bars ...

I was looking at them now, recalling another time ... crouching in the bushes, watching the white house ... the black barred windows. I remembered again how I'd found myself curiously drawn to the bars ... how I couldn't stop staring at them ... studying them ... concentrating on their regularity ... the black lines, the width of the gaps, the background whiteness of the curtains ... and how, after a while, the lines had begun forming themselves into a perfectly focused grid, black on white, black on white, black on white ... and I'd started having really weird thoughts ...

imagining my chaos distilling itself into clearly defined elements, each embedded in its own neatly outlined rectangle ... one, two, three, four, five, six ... six perfect rectangles ... and how, inside the rectangles, there were symbols ... elements ... nameless shapes of things I didn't understand – shadows, shades, abstractions, forms – flickering colours on a pure white background ...

None of it meant anything to me.

Then or now.

It was just there.

But now the blue door was opening – and now *was* now – and a woman was leading Candy out of the building ...

And everything else was nothing.

The woman with Candy was carrying a slim black briefcase. She had short mousy hair and an angular face, and I think she was wearing some kind of trouser suit ... but I can't really remember. I barely looked at her.

I only had eyes for Candy.

It took me a while to see her at first. For a moment or two, all I could see was how plain she looked – plain blue jeans, plain black sweatshirt, no make-up, no jewellery ... no lipstick, no mascara, no bracelets, no leather. No life, no spark, no smile. She wasn't Candy any more. She was someone else, someone who *used* to be Candy ...

But then I looked closer, looking for the stuff that really matters, and instead of *not* seeing what I expected to see, I saw what was actually there. And that *was* Candy. It was Candy all over – her face, her lips, her cheeks, her eyes, the shape of her body ... her pale white skin ... the gleam of her chestnut hair ...

Nothing had changed.

She still looked stunning.

As the woman led her across the garden, I could feel all

the familiar stirrings inside me – the beat of my heart, the race of my blood, the rush of adrenalin tingling my skin ...

Nothing had changed.

I watched them getting closer. I could hear their footsteps on the sun-baked grass. Candy was walking with her head bowed down and her eyes fixed firmly to the ground. The woman was staying close to her, guiding her along with a careful hand on her back.

The air was thick ...

They were a few steps away from the table ...

I couldn't breathe ...

They stopped in front of me.

I looked up at Candy. She didn't look back.

'Kevin Williams?' the woman said.

I didn't reply.

'Are you Kevin Williams?' she asked again.

'Uh ... yeah,' I mumbled, still looking at Candy.

'Are you all right?' the woman asked me.

'Sorry,' I said, turning to her. 'Yes ... yes, Kevin Williams ... I'm fine.'

She held out her hand. 'Louise Hammett,' she said. 'I'm the Senior House Officer.' I stood up and shook her hand. She said, 'Doctor Davies has already had a word with you, I believe?'

'Yeah, I saw him on the way in.'

'Good.' She glanced at Candy, got no response, then looked back at me. 'Well, I'll leave you to it, then. I'll be just over there if you need anything.' She indicated a table on the other side of the garden. 'OK?'

'Yeah,' I said, 'thanks.'

She touched Candy's shoulder, then walked off briskly across the garden. I watched her sit down at the table. I watched as she opened her briefcase, took out some papers, crossed her legs, and started to read. I carried on watching ... not knowing why ...

I didn't *want* to look at her.

I wanted to look at Candy ...

But I couldn't seem to do it. I couldn't move my head. I wanted to look, but I was too scared of what I might see.

'Kevin Williams?' I heard her say.

When I turned to her, she'd raised her eyes from the ground and was gazing steadily into my eyes.

'It was Mike's idea,' I said. 'They wouldn't let me see you ...'

'I know.'

'I didn't know where you were.'

'I know.'

We looked at each other. I was lost for words.

'Do you want to sit down?' Candy asked.

'Yeah ... OK.'

We sat down opposite each other. Candy had a packet of cigarettes in her hand. She took one out, put it in her mouth, put the packet on the table, and clicked her lighter. I watched the cigarette smoke curl from her mouth and drift away over the garden.

'So,' she said, 'how are you?'

'Not too bad, I suppose ... how about you?'

'I've been worse.' She looked down at the tip of her cigarette for a moment, then her eyes came back to me. 'It's been a long time ...'

'Yeah ...'

'Four months.'

'I know.'

She lowered her eyes again. I watched her fiddling nervously with her cigarette – rolling it, tapping it, flicking ash to the ground – and I didn't know what to do. It was really strange. I'd spent so long thinking about this moment, thinking of all the things I wanted to say, but now I was here ... none of it seemed to matter. It was all just words. Noise. Nothing. I wished I could be inside Candy's head – just *be* there ... feeling what she felt ... knowing what she thought ... being together without any words ...

'How's Gina?' she asked quietly.

'She's OK ... she still gets a bit shaky sometimes, but I think she's going to be all right. She's getting married to Mike next year.'

'Really? That's great.'

'My dad doesn't think so.'

'Why not?'

'I don't know ... he's just a bit ... I don't know. He gets a bit funny about things sometimes—'

'Is he here? Did he come with you?'

'No, he was busy ... I came on the train. How about *your* parents? Have you seen them?'

'Yeah, they visit me every other week.'

'How's it going?'

'I don't know ...' She put out her cigarette and immediately lit another one. 'They want me to go back and live with them ... maybe go to college or something ...'

'Can you do that?'

'What – go to college?'

'No ... I mean, can you leave here?'

'Not at the moment. I'm still being assessed. It's part of the bail conditions.'

'Assessed?'

'Yeah ...' She looked at me. 'Psychiatric assessment ... it doesn't really mean anything. It's just stuff I have to do, you know ... it'll probably help at the trial ... counselling, rehab – that kind of thing.' She paused for a moment, staring blankly at the table, and that's when I noticed her fingernails. They were all chewed up, bitten down to the quick, red and ugly and raw. They never used to be like that. 'It's *supposed* to help, anyway,' she said suddenly.

'What is?'

'What?'

'What's supposed to help?'

'I just *told* you,' she said impatiently, 'the assessment, the counselling ... all the *shit* I have to go through every day.' She darted a glance across the garden, then leaned across the table and lowered her voice. 'They'll acquit me, anyway – self-defence ... and even if they don't, the most I'll get done for is manslaughter. I'll probably be out in a couple of months.' She stared at me. 'Did you tell the cops about Mason?'

'Who?'

'Mason – the driver ... the guy I shot ...'

'I said I didn't see anything.'

'Good ...' She frowned. 'What was I saying?'

'Uh ...?'

'Yeah, I don't *need* to be here ... it's no good for me. Did they tell you what happened?'

'Uh ... no,' I said.

'It wasn't my fault. I wasn't feeling right ... I got some stuff ... I couldn't help it ... the guy down the corridor brought some back at the weekend ...'

I really didn't understand what was happening now. Her eyes were darting all over the place and she was giving me really weird looks. She seemed angry. Disturbed. Upset about something. And I didn't have a clue what she was talking about – what *stuff*? what *guy*? what *corridor*?

'It was the song,' she said. 'They played it on the radio.'

'What song?'

'*My* song ... your song ...' Her face had stilled. 'You should have *told* me.'

Now I knew what she was talking about – my song, her song ... *Candy* – The Katies' first single. Jason had told me about it a couple of months ago. They'd recorded the demo without me, and the record company had liked it so much they'd signed the band – new bass player and all – and rushed out the song as a single. It wasn't a stunning success or anything, but it had been dribbling around the bottom of the charts for a while, and a couple of local radio stations had picked up on it, and The Katies had been featured in the national music press ...

I ought to have been really pissed off, I suppose – they'd stolen my song, my words, my music ... how *dare* they? – but I just couldn't be bothered. I'd tried to get angry when Jason first told me, but my heart wasn't in it. I couldn't see the point, anyway. I couldn't *prove* it was my song, could I? And even if I could – well, so what? It was only a song ...

'I'm sorry,' I told Candy, 'I didn't know anything about it ... I would have told you if I could—'

'It's not fair,' she said.

'I know—'

'It's about *me*.'

'Well, I know, but—'

'You said it was about me ... that's what you *said*. It's *my* song ... it's only for me ... you can't sing it to anyone else ...'

'I'm not ... it's nothing to *do* with me. I'm not singing anything—'

'I heard it on the radio ...'

She was starting to cry.

'I *heard* it ...'

I reached across the table and held her hand. It felt cold

and stiff and unfamiliar. 'It's all right,' I said, 'you don't have to cry—'

'No,' she sobbed, 'it's *not* all right. It's not ... I'm not ... I can't *do* it ...'

'You can't do what?' I asked quietly.

'Anything ... anything ... I can't *do* anything ...'

Her tears were falling on the back of my hand, as cold as a winter rain ... and I was there. I was *there*. Where I'd always wanted to be. But now it was somewhere else. It wasn't the same.

Nothing can be the same.

Nothing *is*.

The woman had rushed over from the other side of the garden, and now she was crouching down beside Candy, comforting her, muttering all the right words.

'It's all right ... come on, now ... it's all right ...' She turned to me, not unkindly, and said, 'I think you'd better go now. She needs some rest.'

I nodded and stood up, steadying myself against the back of the chair. My legs were shaking. My throat was tight.

The sun was still blazing down.

I looked at Candy. She was trembling and pale, her eyes swollen with tears.

'I'm sorry, Joe,' she whispered. 'I'm really sorry ...'

'It's OK,' I told her. 'It's all right.'

We looked at each other for a moment longer, then she lowered her eyes, and I walked away.

It's been almost six months now since that dull February day when I first met Candy, and I still find it hard to believe. When I'm sitting here at my window, just staring into the past, or when I'm lying on the floor, imagining all my skies, I often find myself drifting back to the beginning again, to those last few moments of my pre-Candy existence, when I was still just a boy ... just a boy on a train, a boy with a lump, a boy in a starry black hat.

I was innocent then.

I didn't know anything.

And, in a way, nothing much has changed – I still don't know anything now.

I don't know what's happened with Candy.

I don't know if she's lost her mind.

I don't know when I'll be seeing her again.

The only difference now, for what it's worth, is that I know that these things don't matter. I know that I don't *have* to know anything, and I know that I don't have to feel frightened of not knowing – I just have to be here.

In love and faith.

I just have to believe.

It's not easy – living in a void, living and dying inside your head ... wanting what you want so much that you'd give up everything else to get it – but the time still passes, the days go on ... and as long as there's still a tomorrow, there's always a chance.

I found out recently that Candy's been moved from the Resident Adolescent Unit, but no one will tell me where she's gone. I managed to track down her parents, and I've been watching their house for a while, but she doesn't seem to be there. Her mum and dad probably know where she is, but I'm not sure about asking them, and Mike seems fairly reluctant to help me any more ... which is fair enough, I suppose. So it looks like I'll have to wait for the trial before I see her again. I don't know when that's going to be, and I don't know if we'll be allowed to talk to each other anyway, but at least I'll get to see her.

And then, afterwards, when it's all over ... and if everything turns out OK ... or even if it *doesn't* turn out OK ...

Well – who knows?

I guess we'll just have to wait and see.

A note from Kevin Brooks

CANDY

One of life's many unwritten laws is that boys aren't allowed to talk about falling in love. We can talk about anything else – sex, drugs, rock 'n' roll – but we can *never* admit to falling in love. Which makes it really hard for us when we *do* fall in love – and, believe me, we do – because it means we have to deal with it all on our own. The unknown feelings, the fears, the wonders, the agonies, the ecstasies ... we have to keep them all bottled up inside us, whirling around in our heads and our hearts like a thousand crazy demons.

It's different for girls. Girls can let the demons out. But boys just have to live with them.

And I think, in a way, that's what *Candy* is all about: being a boy, falling in love, finding yourself in places you've never been before. I've been to those places myself, and I wanted to write about how it all feels, and what it does to you, and how the things that you want aren't always good for you, and you *know* they're not good for you ... but you still keep wanting them, don't you?

Kevin Brooks

Also from Kevin Brooks

KEVIN BROOKS

Caitlin's life changes from the moment she sees Lucas walking across the causeway one hot summer's day. He is the strangest, most beautiful boy she has ever seen – and when she meets him, her world comes alive. But to others, he quickly becomes an object of jealousy, prejudice and hatred. Caitlin tries to make sense of the injustice that lurks at every unexpected twist and turn, until she realises she must do what she knows is right in her heart.

From LUCAS

Over a surprisingly tasty meal of crab, boiled potatoes, stale crackers and black tea, we finally got round to discussing what happened at the raft race.

'I was on the cliff with Dad and Deefer,' I told him. 'We saw the whole thing. It was incredible.'

Lucas didn't say anything, just nodded slowly and concentrated on his food. There was only one plate, a battered old tin thing that Lucas had insisted on giving to me, so he was eating straight from the pan. He picked out a chunk of meat and gave it to Deefer, who took it with uncharacteristic grace.

'It was a good job you were there,' I said. 'If it hadn't been for you, that little girl would have drowned. No one else was going to do anything. I couldn't believe it. I don't know what was the matter with them.'

'It's just one of those days.'

'What?'

'Sometimes you get a day when all the lights go out, and everyone you meet is cold and bitter. They don't care about anything. Today's been one of those days. Didn't you feel it?'

I thought of Tait and Sara Toms and Lee Brendell at the sea wall ... the dirty looks, the mocking laughter ... but then, I thought, they're *always* cold and bitter. I knew what he meant, though. There'd been a sour taste to the air all day.

'What about you?' I asked. 'How come *your* lights weren't out?'

'They were – that's why the lady thought I was harming her daughter.'

'But you *weren't.*'

He shrugged. 'She was only doing what she thought right.'

'Well, anyway, Dad's going to have a word with her. That's why I came after you, to let you know it's going to be all right. He's going to explain what happened – in fact, he'll have already done it by now. So there's nothing to worry about. She won't be calling the police or anything.'

'Thanks, that's kind of you. Tell your dad I appreciate it.' He sipped tea from a tin mug and gazed out at the glade. The sun was out now. Pale light was filtering through the trees casting rippled shadows across the grass, and small birds were twittering in the sunlit bushes. The darkness of the day seemed to be lifting. But not for Lucas. From the look on his face, he didn't seem to share my opinion that everything was going to be all right.

'I'm sure it'll be fine,' I said, trying to reassure him.

'I'm sorry,' he said, turning to face me. 'Please don't think I'm being ungrateful, it's just that these things have a tendency to stick, whatever happens.' He wiped his mouth with his hand. 'No matter what your dad says, the police are still going to want to talk to me. They've already been sniffing around.'

'Why? You haven't done anything.'

He smiled knowingly. 'People don't like it when they don't know what you are. They don't like things that don't fit. It frightens them. They'd rather have a monster they know than a mystery they don't. In a place like this, the fear takes hold and spreads. It feeds on itself. Pretty soon the police are going to start asking me lots of questions, and then the rumours will start—'

'But Dad and I can tell everyone what happened—'

'It won't make any difference. I've been here before. I know how it works.' He started clearing away the pans. 'That's why it's always best to keep moving.'

'What do you mean? Are you leaving?'

'Not immediately. But it's going to start getting uncomfortable in a few days—'

'It might not.'

'It will, believe me.'

'But what about Dominic? You said you'd keep an eye on him—'

'I will.'

'For how long?'

'As long as it takes – a day or two, maybe a bit longer. Look, I'll make sure he's all right – don't worry about it.'

I wasn't worried about it – not just then, anyway. For all I cared, Dominic could go to hell. I just didn't want Lucas to go. But what could I say? I couldn't tell him how I felt. I couldn't *beg* him to stay, could I? He'd think I was an idiot.

'Why don't you stay until next Saturday?' I suggested.

'What's next Saturday?'

'The Summer Festival ... it's really good. Stalls, bric-à-brac, music ...' I paused, looking at the smile on his face. 'What?'

'It sounds quite similar to the regatta.'

'No, no, it's a lot better than the regatta. Honestly, you'd enjoy it.'

'Is there a raft race?'

'No, definitely not. No races. I'm running the RSPCA stall – well, I'm not actually *running* it, but I'll be there. You could come and say hello ...' I hesitated. 'I mean, if you're still here ... I could show you around, if you wanted ...'

He smiled again. 'Will you buy me an ice cream?'

'I might.'

'It's tempting ...'

'I think it'd be nice. You could meet my dad.'

'I'd like that.'

'So, you'll think about it?'

'I'll think about it.'

He got up and piled the pans and things outside the shelter, then he wiped his hands in the moist grass and dried them on his trousers. I went outside and joined him. Although I felt embarrassed by my behaviour, I was glad that I'd made the effort to persuade him to stay until Saturday. I would have felt worse than embarrassed if I hadn't. Lucas seemed happier, too. The troubled look had faded from his eyes.

As we stood in the warming sunlight watching Deefer jumping around in the stream, with the birds singing in the background and the smell of wood smoke drifting in a light breeze, I would have done almost anything to freeze the moment for ever. It was so quiet and peaceful, so simple, so serene.

I turned to see Lucas looking at me. His eyes shone with a savage sweet clarity that took my breath away.

'Where will you go?' I asked him.

'I don't know ... along the south coast, probably. There's some nice places in Dorset and Devon. I've always wanted to take a look at the moors.' He smiled. 'I'll send you a postcard.'

We stood there for a while longer, neither of us knowing what to say. Part of me wished I knew what he was thinking, but another part – the more astute part – was glad that I didn't. Sometimes it's best to rely on your imagination. Facts can let you down, but your mind will always look after you.

'I'd better get going,' I said eventually. 'Dad'll be waiting for me.'

'What are you going to tell him?' Lucas asked.

'About what?'

'Me.'

His honesty shocked me for a moment. It was the kind of question people *want* to ask but rarely do.

'I'll just tell him the truth,' I said.

Lucas looked at me and nodded. 'One day you will.'

I wasn't quite sure what he meant, if he meant anything at all ... but I didn't dwell on it.

I went back into the shelter to get my hat and coat. On the way out I noticed a row of small wooden figures lodged in the reeds of the wall above Lucas's bed. I knelt down for a closer look. They were crude, but remarkably beautiful, carvings of animals. No bigger than a finger, and carved out of driftwood, there were about a dozen of them. Dogs, fish, birds, a seal, cows, a horse ... there was only minimal detail in the carving, but each little animal had a character that stood out a mile. Beside the figures, hanging by a leather strap on the wall, was a bone-handled knife with a seven-inch blade. The blade was heavy and broad at the base, tapering to a razor-sharp point. It was hard to believe those wonderful little figures could be fashioned with such a deadly-looking tool.

Without thinking I reached across and picked out one of the figures, a familiar-looking dog.

'What do you think?'

The sound of Lucas's voice startled me and I jerked round, fumbling the little figure in my fingers. 'Oh ... I'm sorry – I was just looking—'

'It's all right,' he said, smiling. 'What do you think? Have I captured his soul?'

I looked at the carving in my hand. Of course – it was Deefer. It *was* Deefer. The look on his face, his head, the way he held his tail, everything. A miniature wooden Deefer.

I laughed. 'It's perfect ... it's *just* like him. How did you do it?'

'I just found a bit of wood and cut away all the bits that weren't Deefer.'

I nodded vaguely, not sure if he was joking or not.

'You can keep it, if you like,' he said.

'Are you sure?'

'He's your dog.'

'Thank you,' I said, rubbing my thumb over the carving. It felt smooth and warm, almost alive. I stood there for a moment, trying to think of something else to say, but I couldn't find the words to express myself. So I just thanked him again and slipped the carving in my pocket. 'I really do have to go, now. Dad's going to start worrying if I don't get back soon.'

'I'm ready when you are,' Lucas said.

With a final glance around, I put my hat on, slung my cape over my shoulder, and followed him out of the woods.